Also by Chloe Neill

Chicagoland Vampires series

Some Girls Bite

Friday Night Bites

Twice Bitten

Hard Bitten

Drink Deep

Biting Cold

House Rules

Biting Bad

Wild Things

Howling for You (eBook only novella)

Dark Elite series

Firespell

Hexbound

Charmfall

A Chicagoland Vampires Novel

BLOOD GAMES

CHLOE NEILL

The right of Chloe Neill to be identified as the author of this work
has been asserted by her in accordance with the
Copyright, Designs and Patents Act 1988.

First published in Great Britain in 2014 by
Gollancz
An imprint of the Orion Publishing Group
Orion House, 5 Upper St Martin's Lane, London WC2H 9EA
An Hachette UK Company

1 3 5 7 9 10 8 6 4 2

A CIP catalogue record for this book is available
from the British Library

ISBN 978 0 575 10824 0

Printed in Great Britain by Clays Ltd, plc

The Orion Publishing Group's policy is to use papers that are
natural, renewable and recyclable products and made from wood
grown in sustainable forests. The logging and manufacturing
processes are expected to conform to the environmental regulations
of the country of origin.

www.chloeneill.com
www.orionbooks.co.uk
www.gollancz.co.uk

This tome is dedicated to Lady Katherine Guinevere Pendrake Stacey, who acted with bravery and honor in a time of great need.

Special thanks to the attendees of WillyCon 2014, who provided valuable advice regarding swords and steel.

Make no little plans; they have no magic to stir men's blood.

—*Daniel Burnham*

CHAPTER ONE

EVERYDAY MAGIC

Early March
Chicago, Illinois

He stood beside me as cameras flashed, a man with a long and lean body, deeply green eyes, and golden hair. He wore shorts, sneakers, and a long-sleeved shirt that snugged against the tight muscles of his torso. His hair, which normally brushed his shoulders, was pulled back in a queue, and around his neck glinted the silver pendant that marked him as a Cadogan vampire.

But he wasn't just a vampire. Ethan Sullivan was Master of Cadogan House.

Even in running shoes, hands on his hips as he stood beneath the yellow arch that marked the starting line, a clock counting down to zero a few feet away, his Masterdom was undeniable. He looked nothing less than a leader of his people.

He glanced at me, an eyebrow arched in his usual imperious

expression. "Sentinel. You appear to be enjoying this a little too much."

I pulled my long dark hair into a ponytail using the elastic on my wrist, my long bangs across my forehead. I was also dressed in running attire—a Cadogan House Track shirt, midcalf running tights, and shoes in eye-searing neon orange that made me smile when I looked at them. But the apparel wasn't just fun; it was functional. It had to be if I was going to achieve my goal: beating Ethan Sullivan to the finish line.

"It's not every day I get the chance to best you in front of an audience."

Ethan snorted, a glint of amusement in his eyes. "I don't plan to let you best me, Sentinel. But I'm prepared to make it interesting."

There was heat in his eyes that nearly made me blush. But since we had an audience, I held it in. "How interesting?"

"Dinner. Of the winner's choosing."

As a lover of food, I didn't hesitate. "Done."

"I wasn't finished," he said with a sly smile. "Dinner of the winner's choosing—in the apparel of the winner's choosing."

"I do enjoy seeing you in jeans," I countered. He generally preferred fancy to casual, but even he couldn't run in a refined French suit and Italian loafers. But if the look in his eyes was any indication, he hadn't intended denim, leather, or wool.

He only snorted in response.

It was March in Chicago, and the air still carried the chill of winter. But spring had nearly broken winter's hold, and a thousand people stood on the sidelines to watch the Cadogan Dash, a race we'd organized to raise money for Chicago's food bank.

I was the House's social chair, and I'd been reminded recently about the importance of giving back. So I decided a charity event was just the thing, which was why we were standing in Grant Park on a brisk spring night, preparing to run three miles with a few hundred friends. While Malik, the second-in-command of the House, stayed behind (and separate from Ethan for succession purposes), others gathered in their running gear for a little friendly competition. Luc, the Cadogan guard captain, with his dark blond locks. Connor, a young vampire of my class with the easygoing personality of casual wealth. Brody, a new Cadogan guard with mile-long legs that were probably going to come in handy tonight.

But that didn't mean the race was just fun and games.

Times had been tough for Chicago's supernaturals, but humans' attitudes had seemed to improve over the last few weeks. Ethan had been cleared of charges he'd killed a vampire in cold blood; it had been obvious self-defense, since we'd been attacked at Cadogan House. My grandfather, Chuck Merit, was once again the city's official Supernatural Ombudsman, helping vampires, shifters, River nymphs, and the like with their various problems. And once again, the fickle pendulum of human emotion had swung to love. Sure, there were vampire detractors. Vampire haters. Vampire conspiracy theorists. But there were also members of the Ethan Sullivan fan club.

Most of the human spectators who'd crowded behind the barrier wore T-shirts bearing Ethan's image and I HEART ETHAN buttons. But much to my surprise, Ethan wasn't the only Cadogan vamp with fans in the audience. There were a few fans carrying hand-painted I HEART MERIT signs and wearing #1 SENTINEL T-shirts, which was cool, if a little unnerving.

A woman on the other side of the barricade held out a glossy eight-by-ten photograph and a permanent marker. "Ethan! Ethan! Can I have your autograph?" Her face was flushed with excitement, her eyes wide with promise.

"Your fans await," I said with a smile.

"You're my favorite fan," he said, and in full view of the cameras, spectators, and news vans, he kissed me.

By the time he straightened again, my cheeks were pink and Ethan's admirers were screaming with gusto. Apparently it didn't matter whom the golden god kissed—the sight of him kissing was enough to send them into a frenzy.

Given the look of intensity in their eyes, I doubted they'd have felt any compunction about kicking me out of the way to get a little closer to him.

"Go ahead," I told him. "Go see your admirers. Sign some autographs. It's good PR for the House."

He slid me a glance, smiled. "Not concerned one of the fans will try to sweep me away with words of love?"

"Oh, they'll try to sweep," I said. "But I have no worries you'll come back to me."

His smile was meltingly handsome. "Because I love you without measure?"

"Of course," I said.

Also, I had the car keys.

We needed the good PR while we could get it. I had a sinking suspicion the tide would turn again; humans always looked for scapegoats. Supernaturals made easy targets.

Humans weren't our only problem. Cadogan House had recently left the Greenwich Presidium, the European council of vampires that ruled European and North American vampires—but we hadn't left behind the drama. The GP was a hot mess. Some council members hated our House; others hated humans. It was an organization generally out of touch with the modern world.

And Ethan, who'd moved forward to commune with the crowd, was petitioning to take charge of it. He'd filed the paperwork a week ago. Which was awkward, since the GP already had a leader—Darius West, a powerful vampire whose unfortunate involvement with an American serial killer had stunted him emotionally, an impressive feat for an immortal. After ensuring the House and its finances were in order, Ethan announced his candidacy, and we'd heard nothing in the interim.

Darius had options. Vampires loved rules, and the *Canon*, the volumes of vampire law, laid out three official responses to Ethan's "Honorable Challenge." (Vampires also liked capitalizing things.) According to the *Canon*, Darius could give back snarky words, a response "by Wit," which I imagined would have been something like "Bring it" or "You just got served." Darius could challenge Ethan to a duel, presumably by katana, since that was the favored vampire weapon, or by "account of All Houses," which basically meant that Darius could call out all the other vampire Houses to gang up on ours.

He hadn't done any of those things yet, and the silence was more unnerving than an outright attack would have been. In the interim, Ethan called the Masters of the Houses that allied with Cadogan—whose insignia were mounted above the Cadogan House door—shoring up his support.

We'd decided to move forward with the race, but we were certainly, obviously keeping a close eye on Ethan. Because I was Sentinel of the House, his safety was one of my priorities. And I had allies in the crowd: my grandfather's employees—Catcher Bell, a sorcerer, and Jeff Christopher, a shifter—as well as the undercover members of the Red Guard, an organization of vampires created to keep watch on the GP and the twelve American vampire Masters.

Catcher's girlfriend and my non-vampire best pal, Mallory Carmichael—a sorceress in her own right—stood with Jeff and

Catcher, her blue ombré hair in a high topknot, a small Cadogan pennant in her hand. She waved the pennant at me, her blue eyes smiling, and gave me a very enthusiastic thumbs-up.

The RG members wore Midnight High School T-shirts to indicate their affiliation. They included my tall, handsome, and auburn-haired RG partner, Jonah, who stood near a woman vigorously shaking her décolletage at Ethan as he signed autographs. I gave the woman the stink eye, but her gaze skimmed right over me. I wasn't the object of her affection.

"They just pretend we aren't here."

I chuckled at the vampire beside me, a woman with a blond ponytail, hot pink shirt, and black running tights that skimmed her long legs. She was Lindsey, one of Cadogan's guards and Luc's sweetheart. And Luc had plenty of fans of his own, men and women who giggled each time he flipped his tousled curls out of his eyes. From the cheeky grin on his face, he didn't seem to mind the attention.

"The humans or the vampires?" I said.

Lindsey snorted. "Good question. I'm not sure Luc could pick me out of a lineup right now. Especially not when she's showing off the kids." She nodded toward a woman with pendulous cleavage and *Luclicious* tattooed in black script across her chest.

"He's never going to stop talking about that," I agreed.

"At least you have your own fans. There's one very delectable man who hasn't taken his eyes off you. Your two o'clock," she said, and I glanced casually over.

He had dark skin and a shaved head, a sprinkling of goatee beneath his generous mouth. His eyes were wide set and deeply brown. There was a small crescent-shaped tattoo near the corner of his left eye.

His gaze was direct, curious, and focused on me.

I looked back at Lindsey, mouth open. "He is stunning."

She nodded. "See? Fans of your own. As long as Ethan doesn't see him and beat him to a bloody pulp for staring at you, we're good. And even if he does," Lindsey said with a grin, stretching out one calf, then the other, "your backup fan club is right over there." She gestured to the Ombuddies, as we called Jeff and Catcher.

"They aren't fans; they're family." Maybe not genetically, but certainly in spirit. And, considering Catcher's YES, I HATE EVERY-BODY T-shirt, despite their personality quirks.

"Besides. They're on the job."

"Speaking of, any twinges?"

Vampires preferred to fight with katanas, and my own weapon had been tempered with my blood, giving me the ability to sense other weapons nearby. I'd mentally calibrated my senses to ignore the hidden blades carried by the RG members, and thus far, the crowd was clean.

"Nope," I said, scanning the bystanders, who smiled and snapped pictures. "All's well so far. Hopefully it will stay that way."

Lindsey snorted. "Darling, we're vampires. It will definitely not stay that way."

An unfortunate but valid point.

"All right, runners," said the race director through his bullhorn. "We're less than a minute away from the start. Please get ready."

"Good luck," Lindsey said, squeezing my arm. "We'll be right behind you."

I nodded. "You, too. Keep a sharp eye."

She winked. "The sharpest."

Ethan joined us, retying his hair with a bit of leather cord, and we moved to the front of the pack of runners, who were stretching their hamstrings and turning at the waist to loosen up.

He smiled at me, and I pushed down a bolt of lust that speared through me—and kicked up my heart rate better than any warm-up session.

Ethan leaned forward, elbows and knees bent. "Ready, Sentinel?"

"Always," I said with my own cocky grin. I rolled my shoulders, mirrored his stance, and prepared to move.

"Get set!"

"Dinner will be *poulet à la bretonne*," Ethan said, an obvious threat that I think involved French chicken.

"Hot wings," I countered, and Ethan shuddered.

"Go!" said the race director, and the shrill blare of an air horn filled the air.

I pulled up every ounce of strength I could manage and jumped off the line, inching out steps ahead of Ethan and trucking it down the street. Vampire strength varied. Some vamps were superstrong and superfast; others were barely stronger than humans. Fortunately, I was both. And so was Ethan.

I'd decided to make an aggressive start, to push out and try to get an early lead on him. I had to hope I could keep up the pace and wouldn't run out of steam before the finish line.

Two blocks down the road, I realized that might have been wishful thinking. He was taller than me, with longer legs, and as strong and fast as they came. He matched my pace, sidling alongside me with determined eyes and an easy smile.

Boeuf bourguignon, Ethan silently said, activating the mental link between us.

Tater Tot casserole, I challenged. He wouldn't beat me at that game. I was tall and trim from years of ballet and my vampire metabolism, but I knew food the way Ethan knew investments and European shoes. I could match him threat for threat without breaking a sweat.

A good thing, as the run was accomplishing that pretty well. We moved like machines, each joint and muscle moving precisely and so quickly our bodies blurred.

I couldn't see the rest of the pack, but I could hear them behind me—the front-runners bunched a few yards behind us, apparently content to let Ethan and me battle for the lead.

And battle we did. He wasn't going to give me this win, or submit to a dinner of chip-laden casseroles or meats on sticks. But he hadn't made a weak vampire; I wasn't one to give up, either. I glanced at him, saw the sweat that beaded on his forehead, tightened my core, and moved. Even as I scanned the dark street for threats, I pushed forward.

As a pseudo member of the House's guard corps, I trained every day, and I was pushing to inch ahead. Centimeter by centimeter, I took the lead, my blood pumping and heart pounding. Two feet, then three.

Members of the CPD perched on motorcycles blocked intersections, waving and whistling as we passed. The blocks sped by, the concrete and glass of downtown Chicago, the cafes and tourist shops. Humans lined the streets, some curious to get a look at us, and some with nastier signs that claimed our appearance signaled the end of the world. Since vampires had lived among humans since the dawn of time, the logic was disappointingly faulty.

We turned onto State, sped toward the Chicago River and then across the bascule bridge that crossed the road. Ethan was only a step behind me, probably on purpose, drifting in my wake to make his effort easier.

But I wasn't interested in making it easier for him.

One mile passed, then two, in much the same way. My legs began to heavy and tire, but I ignored it, pressed on, pushed harder. Maybe it was wrong or childish, but I wanted to win. I loved and respected Ethan, but tonight I wanted to beat him. I wanted to blow past him at the finish, triumph in my victory, and celebrate with food so fried, battered, and processed that it was hardly recognizable.

We made our final turn onto the straightaway that led to the finish.

Eyes trained on the arch, I narrowed my gaze, using every muscle in my body to propel my feet along, faster, faster, *faster*.

But then I heard them, the fans screaming at the finish line. "Ethan! Ethan! Ethan!" They were cheering for him, hoping for him to win. *Waiting* for him to win. He was their superstar.

I wanted to beat him . . . but not nearly as much as they wanted him to win. My winning would be fun for me. His winning would be fun for all of them.

I gave myself a moment to grumble, to accept that what I wanted—to beat him well and thoroughly and make him eat midwestern casseroles until ranch dressing oozed from his pores—wasn't anything I had to have.

I could give him this win, a victory for him and his admirers. A boost for his ego and a solidification of their fandom. Human fans weren't something to take for granted. Although I could live without the fan fiction.

But, I thought with a grin, while I could give him the victory, I was sure as hell going to make him work for it.

And work he did. I pushed faster, increasing the pace, my feet pounding so quickly my toes went nearly numb. I heard his footsteps behind me, his fierce and labored breathing, the scent of his cologne rising from his warm and nimble body.

I waited until we were five feet away . . . then dropped back a step. That was enough.

Ethan snapped through the royal blue ribbon at the finish with me only steps behind him. The crowd erupted, cheering like the Cubs had won the pennant.

Chest heaving, Ethan glanced back at me, eyebrow arched, a grin pulling up one corner of his mouth. His body gleaming with sweat, he was quite a sight.

"I believe I won," he said, all but beaming as he moved toward me, frantic women screaming his name. They might have been screaming—and offering to give him children and undergarments—but he kept walking toward me. In the bigger scheme of things, I had won.

He pressed a kiss to my forehead. "Well done, Sentinel. It was a good effort."

"I did my best," I said, hoping my humility seemed genuine. Because inside I was reveling in the fact that I probably could have beaten him. And that was an accomplishment all its own.

"And now I get to eat fancy French food I can't pronounce."

"It's never as bad as all that," he said. "I'll ask Margot for suggestions."

Margot was the House's chef. "No snails," I said. "Or anything with more than four legs. And nothing that resembles a spider."

"Your list is as curious as your palate," he said, "but I'm sure she can come up with something interesting."

"Congratulations!" said the race director, pumping our hands energetically before offering the race medals. The silver medals were shaped like the outline of Cadogan House, the ribbons wide navy blue grosgrain. I dropped my head while he placed the medal around my neck, then watched as he did the same to Ethan.

"Amazing show," he said, but looked chagrined. "Do vampires keep records? I'd have done an official tabulation if I'd known—that was just so fast."

"No worries," Ethan said, glancing at the board that marked our final time. "We were fast. But there are faster vampires."

"Well, in any event, damned impressive." He pumped Ethan's hand with enthusiasm. "If you decide you'd like to train, make a run at them, I'd be happy to work with you."

"I appreciate that," Ethan said, and the director disappeared to greet the others who'd crossed the finish line.

That was when I felt it: the telltale tingle of metal—of a gun—moving near us.

CHAPTER TWO

My adrenaline began to race, and time seemed to slow to a syrupy crawl—every movement exaggerated, every scent stronger, every sound louder. I scanned the crowd, looking for a flash of metal, a suggestion of danger. For something that explained the cold chill that was now slinking its way up my spine.

Ethan, I silently warned, moving in front of him. I felt his magic lift as he transformed from athlete to Master vampire and scanned the area. I also felt the irritated twinge of it. He was just alpha enough to be bothered that I'd shielded him.

A threat? he asked.

I'm not sure.

I sensed Luc and Lindsey move behind us. The weapon, whatever it was, kept moving, weaving through the crowd like a snake and sending goose bumps up and down my arms.

"Merit?" Luc asked.

The scene was perfectly innocent but for the lust that perfumed the air. For a moment I thought I'd imagined it, that I'd just misinterpreted the excitement for something more sinister.

But the feeling thrummed harder and louder, like the string on a bass had been plucked, sending uncomfortable vibrations through my chest. I caught movement, quick and malicious, in my peripheral vision and, when I looked back, caught eyes trained in Ethan's direction.

"A weapon," I said to Luc, gesturing toward the crowd where the magic lurked. "Get him into your car."

They'd keep him safe, I told myself. That was the plan we'd worked out. But a plan was one thing, and real life was something else. Fear and anticipation mixed with the adrenaline that rose at the thought of a possible battle, and there was little doubt my eyes had silvered, a sign of vampire emotion.

Luc took Ethan's arm, began to pull him away . . . and that was when the sound of gunfire filled the air.

"Go!" I screamed, shoving Luc and Ethan back and crouching low as a dark and shiny muscle car squealed forward through the darkness, scenting rubber into the air. The car hopped the curb, moved without hesitation toward the arch that marked the finish line.

Shots were fired from the car—two, then three. Humans screamed and dropped out of the way and toward cover; Luc and Lindsey moved Ethan back to Lindsey's SUV.

I stepped directly between them and the vehicle. If the driver was aiming for Ethan, he'd have to go through me first. Literally and figuratively.

I let my fangs descend, locked my knees to keep them from shaking, and stared back at the car with all the ruthlessness I could muster. That's not to say I wasn't afraid—I was staring down a lot of horsepower and a driver with an agenda. But fear, I'd learned long ago, wasn't an excuse.

Just like my existence wasn't an excuse for the driver to stop the car. He raced forward, and I forced myself to stay where I was, even as my heart raced, even as I imagined the blow and waited for impact.

But I would be damned if he'd get through me.

He was close enough that I saw the whites of his eyes—then he wrenched the wheel to the side, skidding the car to a grinding halt, sending gravel into the air and waves of magic toward me.

The side of the car stopped inches away, blowing the bangs from my face and giving me a look at the driver through the open window. The eyes, the goatee, the ink.

It was the man who'd watched me in the crowd, the one Lindsey and I had thought was a fan. But his interest, apparently, wasn't for me.

"If he knows what's good for him," the man said, his voice deep and lush, "he'll stay in Chicago, and out of London."

I'd expected vitriol about vampires being *in* Chicago, about our gall in holding an event on a public street, not the opposite threat. Since the GP was in London, the threat was obvious. The source wasn't.

"Who are you? And why do you care what he does?"

"I'm the messenger, and he should heed the warning. If he doesn't back off, he'll regret it."

He lifted the gun, the barrel trained on me, as if punctuating the threat. Just like his gaze, his hand was utterly steady. We stared at each other for a moment that stretched and lengthened like pulled taffy.

In that drawn moment, that slow interlude, I saw his finger move and felt the sudden heat, the concussion of air from the primer's ignition. I spun to the ground, my hair whirling around me, fingertips grazing across cold, wet asphalt.

The bullet *whizzed* over my shoulder, high and to the left. It would have missed, even if I'd been standing.

The steady hand, the steady gaze, the ability to park that car on a dime, and he'd missed the shot?

I whipped my head around to look back at him again.

"*Bang*," he mouthed, fangs glinting at the corners of his mouth.

With the ear-piercing shriek of rubber on asphalt, he peeled away and onto the road again.

Sirens exploded through the darkness as police cruisers stormed up the drive and after the car. And just like that, the chase was on.

A sorceress and her retinue of vampires—which included Jonah and the runners from Cadogan House—rushed toward me.

"Jesus, Merit!" Mallory put her hands on my arms, squeezed, looked me over. "Are you okay?"

"I'm fine," I assured her, giving Jonah a nod, although my hands and knees shook with built-up adrenaline and fear. But I made myself keep standing. "I'm okay. What about Ethan? Where's Ethan?"

"He's fine," Brody said. "They're on their way back to the House. Luc took the long way home. Didn't want to get stuck on the freeway."

Where they'd have been sitting ducks. Good plan.

"And Malik?" I asked.

"At the House, and he's fine, too. Kelley and Juliet are with him—and they aren't letting him out of their sight." They were the two remaining Cadogan guards, good and experienced. "Kelley said there's been nothing unusual there. Maybe this was someone showing off?"

I made a noncommittal noise. This wasn't a vampire showing

off; this was a vampire trying to make a very specific point. "We'll see," I said.

Christine, a lithe and pretty vampire, stepped forward. She wore workout gear in vibrant shades of purple, and her sable hair was pulled into a perfect ponytail. Her makeup was also perfect despite the three-mile run; she looked like she'd just stepped out of an ad for VitaBite, Blood4You's new line of vitamin-enhanced drinks.

"What should we do?" she asked me.

I glanced around. A few of the human spectators had been injured in the chaos, and Catcher and Jeff helped the CPD calm and stabilize them while waiting for the EMTs. And with Luc and Ethan gone, I figured that made me the Cadogan vampire in charge.

I gestured toward the human crowd. "Mallory, Brody, why don't you give Catcher and Jeff a hand with the humans?"

Mallory nodded, squeezed my arm, and set off at a jog. Brody followed.

I looked back at the rest of the Cadogan vampires. They weren't guards or staff, but House civilians. They needed to get to safety.

"For now," I said, "until we figure out what's going on, get back to the House. That's the best option until Ethan gives us orders."

At least I hoped it was the best option. But they agreed without argument, nodding and pulling off racing bibs as they headed for vehicles or the El.

That left Jonah and me alone together.

"Merit, what the fuck was that?"

"It was about the GP," I said, looking up into his worried blue eyes. "The driver said Ethan had to stay in Chicago and out of London."

"Jesus," Jonah said, eyes wide. "Did you recognize the driver?"

"He was in the crowd—I saw him before the race. Vampire, no obvious accent, presumably someone who doesn't want Ethan to challenge Darius. But he said he was just the messenger."

"Because he works for Darius?"

"Maybe. Or for someone who has a vested interest in control of the GP—and doesn't think Ethan would be sympathetic." I scanned my mental list of the other eleven Houses' Masters; the driver didn't match any of them. But he did have one noticeable feature.

"The driver had a crescent-shaped tattoo near his left eye. That mean anything to you? Symbolize something vampirey?"

"Is 'vampirey' a word?"

I just looked at him.

"Sorry," he said, stuffing his hands into his pockets. "You're not the only one who uses sarcasm to cope. Unfortunate tendency."

"My tendency isn't unfortunate. And I'll take that as a no."

Jonah nodded. "That's not a marker that's familiar to me. There are some Rogue subgroups on the West Coast who use ink to mark their lack of affiliation."

"Ironic."

"Very. But they're the only ones I know of. Anyway, I can check the RG archives. That'd be the way to go."

"The RG has an archive?"

He rolled his eyes. "As partners go, you're not terribly impressive."

"Thanks, darling. I appreciate you, too." But the comment hit home. Most RG partnerships were intimately close—physically and emotionally. I couldn't offer that kind of relationship to Jonah, but I hadn't been great with the business end of things, either. I always seemed to be dealing with some vampire drama or other.

"Don't take it personally," he said, knocking me playfully on the shoulder, a grin in his almond-shaped blue eyes. "We knew when you came on board that you'd be a different kind of guard."

I blinked at him. "I really want to discuss that at length, but maybe at a more appropriate time."

"You need to go back to the lighthouse," Jonah said. "It's past time."

I couldn't argue with that. The RG was headquartered in the lighthouse that stood sentinel at the harbor in Lake Michigan. In the several months I'd been an RG member, I'd visited only once.

"You have my word. Although it might be hard to get away right now, all things considered."

Jonah's phone rang. He pulled it out, checked the screen. "That's Scott. I need to get back to the House. I'll message you tomorrow."

I nodded, watched him walk away.

"They lost the driver."

I glanced behind me, found Catcher moving toward me from the group of bystanders. I didn't mistake the grimness in his voice. "You're kidding me."

"Unfortunately not. He ditched the vehicle, and the CPD lost him on foot in Little Italy. They're canvassing the neighborhood. Maybe they'll get lucky."

"Maybe," I agreed, but I didn't think so. He was a vampire, and probably stronger and faster than the uniforms.

"The forensic unit's on the way," he said. "They'll check the car, grab the bullet casings, see if they can get fingerprints. Maybe they can match the weapon to another crime, get us an ID."

I nodded. "Maybe. The driver was a vampire. He was here for Ethan. Had a warning to pass along," I said, and told him what the driver had said.

Catcher's brow knitted with concern. "Is Ethan safe?"

"Last I heard," I said, but I pulled out my phone to check for an update and found the waiting text: EAGLE HAS LANDED.

"He's home," I confirmed, the band of tension across my shoulders easing just a bit.

"Well, that's something. Good thing he was out of here before he could see you play chicken with a few thousand pounds of American-made steel."

I grimaced. I wasn't sure Ethan had missed my stand against oncoming traffic, but I was pretty sure I'd know the second I put a toe in the House again. He'd be furious if he'd seen.

On the other hand . . . "When your body is your only weapon, you use it."

Catcher smiled, and there was a tiny gleam of pride in his eyes. He'd been my trainer before Ethan, the first man who'd taught me to stand, to fall, and to bluff.

"I couldn't agree more. You did good."

"I tried. But I'd rather have stopped him here than know he's still out there, whoever he is, waiting to cause trouble."

"You know how these things go, Merit. He'll probably cause trouble again, and you'll get your chance to square off again."

That was exactly what I was afraid of.

Catcher, Jeff, and I stayed until the vampires had gone back to their Houses and the humans who'd been injured—six of them—had been taken care of. And then we answered the CPD's questions. The detectives who interviewed us were polite but wary;

they knew my grandfather, respected him and his long career in the CPD, but weren't thrilled about supernatural violence spilling onto their streets.

Not that I could blame them. I was relieved to be back in my car and on my way back to the House.

Cadogan House was three stories of white stone, plus a basement of offices and training rooms. It sat in the midst of lush grounds in Chicago's Hyde Park neighborhood, and the décor was as fancy as the vampires who filled it. Subtle colors, fine fabrics, gorgeous wood.

I parked in the basement—a gift I'd earned for driving a silver confection of a car—then headed upstairs to Ethan's office. I found him waiting with Luc and Malik, the House's three senior staff. Ethan and Luc still wore their running clothes and race medals. Malik, tall with pale green eyes that offset his dark skin and closely cropped hair, was the only one dressed in the Cadogan House uniform: a slim-fitting black suit, crisp button-down, no tie.

Luc and Malik were seated in the office's sitting area. Arms crossed, Ethan was in the middle of the room, pacing its length. His gaze flashed back to mine, body stiffening as he looked me over, checked me for injuries. He exhaled when he realized I was whole, but that didn't stop the imperious arch of his eyebrow or the burst of magic that lit through the room.

I guessed he'd seen my standoff.

"I'm fine," I assured him, stepping inside the office and closing the door. "He drove off, led the CPD on a chase. Abandoned the car and got away on foot."

He walked toward me, clamped his hands on my arms. I saw the battle in his eyes—fear warring with fury, pride with concern.

I'm fine, I silently assured him. *I'm worried about you.*

Christ, Merit. He moved his hands to the nape of my neck, pulling our bodies together, touching his lips to my forehead. *We'll discuss this at length when we don't have an audience.*

So I had that to look forward to.

He kissed me again, released me. When I realized my sudden dizziness wasn't just the result of adrenaline and magic, I walked to the bar inset in the long wall of bookshelves and grabbed a bottle of Blood4You. I'd earned it.

I popped the cap, drank the blood in seconds. It wasn't until I'd finished it that I realized the blood had a strange, piney aftertaste.

I glanced at the bottle, brows lifted when I saw that I'd just imbibed a bottle of Cantina Lime blood. Who was coming up with these flavors? Not a vampire with good taste, certainly.

I put the bottle in the recycling bin and glanced back at the group, which watched me with anticipation.

"Big night, Sentinel?" Luc asked with a smile.

"Long night," I agreed, and sat in one of the empty chairs. I glanced at Ethan, who still watched me warily. "Six humans injured, half of those when people rushed to avoid the gunshots. Most of the injuries were minor. And as it turns out, the driver was a vampire with words to say—and a message to pass along to you."

Ethan's eyes widened, and he moved closer. "Oh?"

"You should stay in Chicago. Give up your plans for London. Otherwise, you'll regret it."

Fury flashed in Ethan's eyes again. He wouldn't have appreciated the message or the delivery.

"Someone doesn't want you to challenge Darius," Malik said.

"That list is undoubtedly long and distinguished," Ethan said, but his voice was tight.

"Darius himself?" Malik asked, and Ethan shook his head.

"Darius is many things, but cowardly is not one of them. And only a coward would attack unarmed civilians in order to get to me."

"In fairness," I said, "I think he tried to get to you."

Ethan's look was bland. He wasn't pleased by the reminder—or the fact that I'd been the one to step between them. "You're likely correct," he said. "And strategy or not, a phone call would have sufficed."

"Any idea of the source?" Malik asked, leaning forward, elbows on his knees, hands linked in front of him.

Ethan made a vague sound. "Beyond the long and distinguished list? No." He glanced at me. "No mention of specifics? Of who was sending the message?"

"None. Someone in Chicago, maybe, since they had someone on the ground, knew about the race?"

Ethan frowned. "Scott wouldn't care. Morgan might, but this isn't his style."

Morgan Greer was the newish Master of Navarre House. Scott Grey was the Master of Grey House, and Jonah's boss.

"I'd tend to agree," Luc said, then glanced at me. "The driver look familiar?"

"No. He's not a Master, or anybody I recognized." I gave them the basic physical description, and he wasn't familiar to them, either. "He did have a tattoo—small crescent moon near one eye. Does that ring a bell?"

Ethan and Malik shook their heads, looked to Luc. "No, but we can search for it. Maybe it signifies something. Group symbol, maybe."

"Do that," Ethan said. "And check the tapes. See if the car—or the driver—has been near the House."

Luc nodded, and a heavy silence fell. "Do you want to make a response to the threat?"

The unspoken question was easy enough to catch: Are you sure you want to go through with this? Stay on this path, which is clearly fraught with danger?

"No response," Ethan said. "We do not, as they say, negotiate with terrorists."

Luc stood, resignation in his features, and scrubbed his hands through his curly locks. He'd been supportive of his Master's candidacy, but less thrilled that his colleague, his friend, was putting himself in danger to lead an organization no one respected. But that, I guessed, was part of the reason Ethan was doing it: to make it the organization it could be.

"You'll need a guard when you leave the House."

Ethan didn't turn around. "No." His tone brooked no argument. "We knew there was a possibility someone would make an attempt."

"And now they have," Luc said. "So we step up our game."

"This won't be the first or the last threat against me."

"No," Luc said, "but most of those threats don't involve gunshots in public places and playing chicken with our Sentinel."

Magic rose in the room, peppery with anger. Ethan turned back, his eyes as cold as emerald ice. He got testy when faced with fears he couldn't manage, couldn't handle with strength, intelligence, political savvy. "You think I'm not cognizant of her welfare?"

Luc fixed his gaze on Ethan. "I know you're cognizant of her welfare. And I trust that she could handle herself because of the above-referenced chicken playing. We weren't sure if the GP was paying attention. It looks like they are. We have to be more careful. *You* have to be more careful."

"I'm still in the room," I pointed out. "Let's not discuss me in the third person." But they were too absorbed in their own struggles to notice.

"Merit is usually with me when I leave the House," Ethan said.

"Then you'll *usually* have nothing to complain about." Luc's voice, usually full of humor, was tight with concern.

"I am Master of this House."

"I don't think we're confused about your position, *Liege*."

"Hey," I said, stepping between them, arms extended in case either of them tried to do something stupid. "We have enemies enough outside the House. Yeah, this situation sucks. But let's not make it worse with infighting."

"Yes," Ethan said. "Let's not."

Luc strode to the door. "I'm going to take a shower."

"Do that," Ethan said, granting permission, but Luc was already in the hallway.

"He feels he's to blame," Malik said.

"That's idiotic."

Malik's brows lifted. "Perhaps. But it is his responsibility to keep you safe. You aren't being especially cooperative."

Ethan just looked at him.

Malik gave me a long-suffering look that I appreciated more than I should have. "Talk to him," he said, then followed Luc out the door and closed it behind him.

I glanced back at Ethan, expecting him to be staring daggers at the door Malik had shut with a surprising amount of force and irritation.

His eyes were flaming shards of emerald . . . but they were directed at me.

"What did I do?"

He gave me a pointed look, walked to the bar, and poured amber liquid from a crystal decanter into a short glass. He sipped it wordlessly, his eyes still on mine, and still fierce.

It wasn't often that Ethan needed time to compose himself. The fact that he needed it now nearly had me sitting down. He loved me, I'd no doubt. But no one liked to face down an angry vampire.

And when he did speak, his words were cold and short. "You stepped in front of me. Correction: You stepped in front of a racing car."

I paused, choosing my response carefully. "It's my job to protect this House, even if that means putting myself between you and danger. I stand Sentinel."

"I am well aware, Merit, of your position in this House. I won't have you take blows intended for me."

"You took a stake that was meant for me," I pointed out, and I'd grieved for months when he'd been gone. "I'm not going to stand by and let someone take a shot at you."

He cursed gutturally in what I thought was Swedish.

"If you're going to yell at me, do it in English, please. I'd like to understand the insult so I can frame an appropriately pithy response."

He looked back at me, eyebrow arched, but one corner of his mouth twitched. It was a good thing he appreciated sarcasm, since it was usually my first response.

"I am Master of this House," Ethan said. "It's my job to protect my vampires."

"Respectfully, Ethan, stop reminding us of your job. We know you're Master. We don't doubt it. We do exactly what we're supposed to do—protect you."

"You're my world," he said, putting down the glass. "You're mine to protect."

"And I'd say the same thing about you."

His eyes went hot again, and he stared back at me from across the room, magic roiling off him in hot waves. "Will you stop being so goddamned stubborn?"

I kept my eyes on his, my tone even. "No. Will you?"

"I want to keep you safe."

"And I want to keep you safe. I *did* keep you safe," I pointed out. "And still no thank-you for that."

Ethan pushed his hands through his hair and walked to the other end of the room, where he stared out the giant picture window, shoulders stiff. Before dawn, automatic shutters would come down, leaving the office in vampire-friendly darkness. But for now, they offered him a view of the House's grounds.

He stood silently for a moment before glancing back at me. "I'm afraid you'll be hurt. Afraid you'll be targeted."

"Why would they target me?"

"Because I love you. Because love, to some, is a weakness. A pressure point. Because I would give up anything for you, including the GP. And because I don't mean to give up either."

I went to him without hesitation, stepped into the arms he extended.

"I love you," he said, wrapping his arms around me.

"I love you, too. But love or not, my job is to protect you."

"Then maybe I should reassign you to the library."

I laughed. "Sullivan, we crossed that bridge a long time ago. You've made me—trained me—and there's no going back."

He humphed.

"Still waiting on that thank-you," I cheekily said, since we'd broken the ice.

He smiled, rubbed a thumb along my jaw. "Did you know your eyes darken when you're serious? From cloudy sky to deep, dark ocean." His gaze went absent as he scanned them, his green eyes tracking across my gray-blues. "So much there. Dedication. Honor. Love."

He was skilled enough to flatter, but the depth of emotion in his eyes told me he was being sincere. My blood began to hum at the passion in his eyes, from the soft kiss he pressed to my lips.

"That'll do for thanks," I quietly said, pulling the reins on my hormones.

"Oh, Sentinel." He put his arms around me again, enveloping me in comfort and his crisp-cotton cologne, then rested his head atop mine. "What am I going to do with you?"

"For starters, a shower."

"I didn't mean that exactly."

I leaned back, gave him my sultriest expression. "Oh," I said. "But I believe you did."

—◆≡◆—

CHAPTER THREE

EVERYDAY MAGIC

We shared the Master's apartments on the House's third floor. A sitting room, bedroom, bathroom, and gigantic closet large enough to be a room itself. It was like a permanent spa retreat: beautiful, luxurious, scented faintly like cologne and hothouse flowers.

I walked into the bathroom and wasted no time peeling off my clothes and dropping them on the floor, leaving me naked but for the Cadogan pendant around my neck.

The bathroom was colossal, with a lot of warm stone and a giant soaking tub. But it was the shower that I wanted, with ample steam and water. I set the temperature of the various sprays, waited until the water was near boiling, and stepped inside.

The sensation was delectable. Every muscle relaxed, goose bumps of pleasure racing along my skin. And when Ethan stepped behind me, naked and tall and impressively aroused, things only improved from there.

But that didn't staunch my humor.

"Oh, François," I breathily said. "You'll have to hurry. My boyfriend will be back soon."

Ethan grunted and slipped his arms around mine, pulling him tight against my body. "My desire is impatient," he said in a French accent that was surprisingly believable. "It will not wait, and damn your boyfriend."

I turned to face him, wrapped my arms around his neck, and caught his bottom lip gently between my teeth. "Then by all means, François, let's get to it."

Wrapped in a thick, white robe, I emerged from the bathroom twenty minutes later decidedly more relaxed than I'd gone in.

But I stopped in the doorway, scenting the air.

"Something wrong?" Ethan asked, stepping behind me, his voice low. I felt the rise of his magic as he awaited my response.

"Hardly." I followed my nose into the sitting room, found on a side table a tray bearing silver-domed plates, bottles of Blood4You, cups of fruit, and gold-wrapped chocolates. I lifted one of the domes, found a set of folded tortillas spilling with fragrant, spicy pork.

Suddenly starving, I glanced back at Ethan, who watched me with amusement.

"You ordered dinner."

"I expected you'd be starving," Ethan said. "So I asked Margot to bring this up."

"Why do people always think I'm hungry?"

"Because you're always hungry."

"Well, I did run three miles today."

"Hardly a formidable exertion for a vampire."

"Exertion enough." I plucked up a plate, bottle, and silverware and carried them to the sitting area, where I took a seat and began to nosh.

The tortilla was delicate; the pork, as expected, was delicious. Margot was an amazing cook.

But then my smile faded, and mortification colored my cheeks. "Margot brought this in while we were having sex."

Ethan smirked. "Probably."

I closed my eyes. I was not an exhibitionist and had no interest in other Novitiates hearing anything of my intimate moments with Ethan.

"Sentinel, the vampires of this House are not naive. I strongly suspect they know what goes on behind these doors."

Since we'd shaken the House's foundation with sex and magic, that was undoubtedly true. "*Still*," I said, but managed another bite of dinner, my appetite unburdened by embarrassment.

Ethan sat down beside me, plate and bottle in hand, then flicked something beneath the coffee table. With a low hum, a portion of the table lifted smoothly up on hinges to meet the plate he held out. He sat it down, then whipped the napkin into his lap.

I stared in amazement. "How long has it done that?"

"For the entirety of its existence."

I gave him a dry look that he ignored, but he flipped the notch on my side of the coffee table. Like magic, the table on my side lifted as well.

"Magic," I said, inordinately happy that the fancy piece of European furniture turned into a TV tray.

"I am a man of many talents."

I grinned, arranged my plate on the raised surface. "And apparently some of them don't require nudity."

"Har-har."

A peaceful silence fell, and we ate quietly for a few minutes. But there was still a thread of tension in the air.

"You'll have to talk to Luc," I said.

"He'll be sullen."

I smiled, speared a chunk of pineapple. "He's already sullen. It will only get worse if you treat him like he's not equipped to handle this. He's captain of your guards, after all. Just go down there and talk to him."

He looked up, staring blankly into the room, and sighed.

I pierced a grape, held it up for him. "Fruit?"

"Somehow that makes me uncomfortable."

I bit it toothily.

"As does that," he said. "Perhaps we should change the subject."

"All right," I said. "What's new in Masterdom?"

"Masterdom?"

"You know," I said, gesturing with a fork. "All of this."

He smiled lightly. "Well, our portfolio is underperforming. I'd prefer a return much higher than we're getting right now. But I can move things around a bit, remedy that."

"The House will appreciate it."

"Not the House's portfolio," he said. "Ours."

I stiffened.

Ethan chuckled. "It hasn't escaped my attention, Sentinel, that you cringe every time I mention our future."

"I don't cringe. I only cringe when you pretend-propose." He had a penchant for going down on bended knee—and straightening a hem or helping me with a shoe. "Nobody finds that amusing."

"I find it excessively amusing. You do realize, don't you, that the proposal won't always be fake?"

I looked up at him, found there was no mistaking the earnestness in his eyes. We'd been Master and Sentinel for nearly a year, but we'd been a couple for only a handful of months. It didn't seem to matter to Ethan; he was utterly sure of me even after so little time.

Ethan sipped from his Blood4You. "I love you, Merit. You are my future, and I intend to make certain you—and the rest of the world—know that, when the time is right. Why does it surprise you so much?"

I struggled to put the emotion into words. "It's not surprise at you. It's not doubt. It's just—it's just blossomed so fast. Four hundred years of dating, and you've made up your mind about me so quickly." That didn't even touch on the fact we'd been prophesied to have a child together—the first vampire child in history.

Something in Ethan's eyes darkened, shifted. Not for very long—but for a split second, there was a cloud across his eyes. Because I'd mentioned his past? I knew there'd been women before, just as he'd known I'd dated. Once upon a time, I'd walked in on him with one of them, his former Consort, which had once been an official position in the House . . . a position he'd offered to me.

As if a breeze had blown it away, the shadow passed, and his eyes flamed green again.

"I made up my mind because we fit," he said, reaching out to take my hand, to squeeze it. "You make me better, and I like to think I do the same for you."

I thought of the awkward human, then vampire, I'd been, and the slightly less awkward vampire I was becoming. "It's just—you were very unexpected."

"That's because you'd only explored one half of yourself, Sentinel. I merely gave you the chance to blossom. To be the person you were always meant to become."

Tears rushed into my eyes, and I knuckled them away. "Damn it, Ethan. How do you come up with things like that?"

"I keep a notebook. I intend to make you mine, Sentinel. Not just for tonight, or for tomorrow, or for the decade. For eternity.

And I'll have my ring on your finger. I'll have the world know that you're mine. I suggest you get used to the idea."

With a frisson of excitement speeding my heart, I decided I'd find a way to adapt.

We'd just finished the meal when my phone began to ring. I pulled it out, found my grandfather's name on the screen.

"You made it home okay," he said with obvious relief.

"We did. Anything new on the attack?"

"Not yet. They've gone through the car, sent what they found to the lab, but we don't have the results yet. Although that's not why I'm calling. I'm afraid I'll have to interrupt your night again. We could use your help."

"With what?"

"There's been a murder."

My heart nearly stuttered, as if unsure whether to stop or start wildly racing. I put a hand on my chest. "A murder?"

Ethan's gaze flashed toward me.

My grandfather cleared his throat. "The victim was Arthur's son."

I closed my eyes. Detective Arthur Jacobs was a stand-up member of the CPD—both a good friend to my grandfather and an ally of ours. I wouldn't have wished death on anyone, and certainly not the loss of a child.

"I'm so sorry," I said. "So very sorry."

"He's not here—too close to it, of course. He's with his family. But obviously this is important to him, which makes it important to me. And that's why I'm calling. It's the manner of his death. I'm here with Catcher and Jeff, but we'd appreciate your thoughts— and Ethan's, if he's available."

This time, my stomach fell. The last thing we needed was another vampire accused of murder. It would be a quick end to our temporary peace. "You think a vampire was involved?"

"We aren't sure. The victim was found at Fourth Presbyterian Church," my grandfather said. "On Michigan Avenue. He's in the courtyard."

That church—and the courtyard—was beautiful. It was a refreshing patch of green along the bustle of Michigan Avenue. I wasn't sure if it was better or worse for the victim to have died in such a lovely place.

"It looks like someone may have tried to tie vampires to it. That's part of what we'd like your thoughts about."

"We'll do whatever we can to help. And we'll be there as soon as we can."

I said my good-byes, hung up the phone, and met Ethan's gaze again. His expression was blank; he knew something was wrong, and he'd already moved into Master mode.

"What's happened?"

"Detective Jacobs's son was killed," I said, and caught his sympathetic wince. "They found his body at a church on Michigan Avenue, and my grandfather would like us to consult."

Sympathy turned to concern—probably fear that vampires had been involved in such a heinous crime. "Vampires had something to do with it?"

"He's not sure; that's why he wants us there. I don't want you to go," I said. "Not after what happened earlier."

"I can't—I won't—stay interred in this House in the meantime. And I won't let you go alone."

I could have argued with him, but he'd insist on going, as much for my protection as for his.

"I know," I said. "I'm going to message Jonah and ask him to meet us there." When Ethan's eyes flashed, I gave him a warning look of my own. "I can't help with a murder and keep you safe. Jonah can. One more sword. One more pair of eyes."

I saw the fight in Ethan's eyes, the battle between pride and logic. But he finally relented.

"Contact him," he said, moving the table back and rising to his feet. "I'll tell Luc and Malik."

"You should apologize while you're at it. You're grouchy when you're attacked."

"Don't push your luck, Sentinel," he said, even as I was stealing a cube of pineapple from his plate. Because I lived in the danger zone.

I texted Jonah, got his agreement to meet us at the church, and then headed to the closet to dress. I generally opted for leather pants and jacket when facing potential calamity, but the ensemble seemed too flashy for the circumstances. I opted for my own fitted, black Cadogan suit and a black tank. I finished with black heeled boots, decided to leave my hair down. A ponytail seemed too perky.

I finished dressing before Ethan. While he fixed cuff links and pulled on a watch, I checked my pride and joy, my ancient katana.

She was housed in a deeply red lacquered scabbard, stored horizontally on a rack Ethan had placed above a console table in the sitting room. His own katana lay below it in its glossy scabbard.

I lifted my sword carefully from its rack, unsheathed it with a delicate *whoosh*. The steel, tempered with my own blood and carefully cleaned, gleamed in the light, which flowed down the blade's gentle curve like water. Assured she was ready, I tipped the end back into the scabbard and slid her home again.

"You think we'll need those?"

I turned, found Ethan behind me in his well-fitted suit, hands in his pockets, hair pulled back. He looked more like a captain of industry—and possibly an illegal one—than a Master vampire. Captain or not, he could handle himself.

"I hope not," I said. "But better safe than sorry."

And speaking of safety, Moneypenny, my silver Mercedes coupe, was beautiful, but she was also recognizable and predictable. Moneypenny had the curves of a 1957 300SL Mercedes roadster but the speed of a Formula One prototype. She was a bombshell. Absolutely beautiful, and absolutely mine.

Lindsey, on the other hand, drove an SUV. It was large, black, and ubiquitous in Chicago. Midwesterners preferred heavy vehicles for treacherous winters.

Well, most midwesterners. Ethan drove a Ferrari. Of course.

"I'm ready if you are," I told him. "Although I'd like to stop by the Ops Room. I need to make a request."

Although much of Cadogan House was built to impress, the Operations Room was built for work. It was located in the House's basement beside a well-stocked training room and an arsenal of weapons.

The Ops Room was also the headquarters of the Cadogan guards, which was why Luc sat at the central conference table, ankles kicked up on the tabletop, eating potato chips from an open bag beside him as he stared at the giant screen on the opposite wall.

He looked up when we walked in, gave Ethan a flat look before glancing at the screen again.

"Liege," he sniped.

Ethan's lip curled, but he managed not to verbally respond. Still, the hot wash of magic that filled the room made it clear how he felt.

"Lucas," he said, and Lindsey, who'd turned to watch, cringed at one of the computer stations that lined the room.

"Any luck with video of the Mustang?" I asked.

"We haven't found any footage of him so far. Nor any hint online the crescent tattoo signifies anything vampiric." His gaze caught my belted sword, and he looked up at me. "Going somewhere?"

"There's been a murder downtown—Detective Jacobs's son. My grandfather asked us to consult."

Luc's expression fell. "That is rough. He's a good man. Always been good to us. I presume he's human, so why us?"

"That, we aren't sure about. Only that the death has some tie to vampires. Considering what Jacobs has done for us, I didn't argue."

Luc glanced at Ethan. "You're going with her?"

"I am," Ethan said, his tone a challenge. "I certainly wouldn't have her go alone."

"I didn't suggest you have her go alone," Luc said, bristling at the insult.

"Jonah's going, too," I said. "He'll give us another pair of eyes, another sword in case anything goes wonky. Which I wouldn't expect it to, considering the fact that we're visiting someone else's crime scene and a cadre of CPD uniforms and detectives."

Luc grunted, which I took for agreement. Having advised him of our next steps, we were technically ready to leave, but I wasn't leaving the House with the two of them in a snit.

I walked to the Ops Room door, gestured to the hallway. "Luc,

Ethan, could I please speak to you for a moment? Perhaps in the training room?"

They both looked suspicious, but I ignored the questions in their eyes and kept my own expression neutral. Ethan moved first, and when Luc saw that he'd relented, he kicked his boots off the table and rose.

I stood in the doorway until I was assured they'd moved, then walked past them to the training room, where I pointed inside.

"In. Both of you."

They gave me equally dubious looks.

"You're giving us orders?" Ethan asked.

I gave back the haughtiest expression I could manage, which was equal parts Ethan Sullivan (my Master) and Joshua Merit (my father).

"I am," I confirmed. "It's been a dramatic night, and we're about to head into a pretty crappy situation. We don't have time for attitude." Both of them opened their mouths to protest, but I held up a hand to stop them.

"You're colleagues and friends, and you both feel crappy that something dangerous happened tonight which made you question your control, your respective abilities to protect the ones you love."

I looked at them for a moment, waiting for them to argue. To my great satisfaction, both of them shut their mouths tight. I gestured them forward into the training room. "Talk it out, punch it out, kick it out, whatever it takes. Just get it out there, and let's move on. You have five minutes."

I waited until they walked inside, grumbling the entire time, and closed the door behind them.

I found Lindsey in the Ops Room doorway, arms crossed and grinning. "Boy trouble?"

"When *aren't* they trouble? While they battle it out in there, I need a favor."

"Anything."

"I need to borrow your car."

When they emerged three minutes later, I had Lindsey's keys in hand. Her dark SUV was considerably less conspicuous than Moneypenny, which would, I hoped, make the trip safer.

My excellent plan notwithstanding, both Luc and Ethan wore dirty looks.

"Love you guys!" I said with sickly sweetness. "You get everything worked out?"

"We've decided you're the biggest pain in our ass," Luc said.

"Oh, good!" I glanced at Ethan. "Now, if you're done fighting and making up, can we please get to work?"

Ethan glanced at Luc, shared a long-suffering look. Which was fine by me, as long as they weren't sniping at each other. The world outside the doors of Cadogan House was chaos enough; we didn't need chaos inside.

"Phones on, and stay alert," Luc said. "And tell Jonah we said hello."

"Lucas," Ethan politely said, "kiss my ass."

And they were back.

We drove Lindsey's SUV to north Michigan Avenue—Chicago's Magnificent Mile. Parking, as usual, was ridiculously limited, but we found a spot a few blocks west of Michigan and hiked back to the church.

I was no country mouse, and I normally thrived on the energy of downtown Chicago. But this time my senses were on high alert: Every shadow got a second glance, every bystander a double look.

Ethan was under my protection, and I wasn't about to lose him on my watch.

Jonah stood on the corner of Michigan and Chestnut, his auburn hair blowing in the light breeze. With his tall, rangy build and chiseled features, he was movie-star handsome. Considering his great personality and sense of humor, he had no business being single. Unfortunately, he hadn't had much luck in the dating arena.

"Merit, Ethan," he said with a nod.

"Jonah," Ethan said. His tone was unerringly polite, but he still wasn't one hundred percent certain of the handsome guard captain—particularly since Jonah and I, as RG partners, were tied together in a way that Ethan and I weren't. And Ethan was alpha enough to find those ties a little too binding.

"You haven't seen anything yet?" I asked.

"Not yet. I waited for you since you sent the invite. Too many vampires spoil a party." He gestured to the church, which was surrounded by official vehicles and ambulances. "Lot of cops around. I think the chance of a replay of the Cadogan Dash drama is slim. You drive Moneypenny?"

"Lindsey's SUV," I said.

"Good. Decreases the odds he'd follow you here—assuming he was looking."

"No evidence of that so far," I said as we walked together up Michigan. "But we're still looking."

"Show like that, you expect a second round."

"We're expecting it," Ethan agreed. "We'll be prepared."

I hoped he was right but didn't discount the risk. The cost was simply too great.

The Fourth Presbyterian Church property was nestled between shops and high-rises in Chicago's bustling tourist sector.

There was a sanctuary and separate parish buildings, and the space between them created a courtyard separated from Michigan Avenue by an arched, covered walkway.

Tonight, that courtyard was bounded by yellow police tape, that immediate indicator that something bad had gone down. Gawkers were gathered along the tape, cell phones extended to photograph the scene.

My grandfather moved toward us in brown shoes with thick soles, a plaid shirt tucked into brown slacks. There wasn't much hair left on his head, and his face was comfortably lived-in. I loved him ridiculously.

He walked with a cane these days, his body still healing from an unfortunate run-in with the man who'd formerly held his position. But he moved quickly and, although his expression was dour, offered me a hug.

I tried to thread the needle between showing affection for my grandfather (with an affectionate hug) and keeping him safe (with an affectionate hug that didn't rebreak his ribs, which were only just healing). He didn't grunt in pain, so I considered that a victory. He smelled like the mentholated rubs he preferred for sore muscles, a scent I'd forever associate with weekend sleepovers at my grandparents' house.

"I'm sorry to bring you out again after the evening you've had already," he said, releasing me and offering Ethan a hand. "Ethan."

"Chuck," Ethan said. "No apologies necessary." He motioned toward the cane. "It appears you're getting around."

"Not as well as I used to," he said, "but better than I was, certainly."

"And you remember Jonah, Grandpa. Guard captain at Grey House."

"Of course," my grandfather said, and they shook on it. "Nice to see you again."

I took a look at his face, saw lines of grief etched around his eyes. He stood Ombudsman now instead of homicide detective, but there was no mistaking the cop in his eyes.

"We're so sorry to hear of Detective Jacobs's loss," I said. "Did you know his son very well?"

"Not very," my grandfather admitted. "Brett was twenty-five, already out on his own, but I'd met him a time or two at Arthur's house for dinner. Good kid, by all accounts. No reason to believe he'd done anything that would make him anyone's target."

"I suppose they'll wait until after an autopsy for funeral arrangements?"

"I expect so. Could be several days before they're ready to release his body. He's taking some time off in the meantime, keeping his family close."

"Please offer our condolences," Ethan said.

"I will," my grandfather said. "Let's do our part for Brett and take a look."

CHAPTER FOUR

━━◆◆◆━━

REQUIEM

We dipped under the tape and moved through the passageway and into the courtyard, a large grassy rectangle bordered by buildings and hedges. A fountain stood in the middle. The area bustled with cops and investigators—and no one I'd recently seen aiming a handgun at my person. A forensic unit surveyed the grass, sweeping flashlights back and forth across the ground.

Between the fountain and one of the buildings was a tall, square enclosure of yellow plastic. A bit of privacy for Brett, I presumed. A stand of temporary lights had been placed inside, the bulbs visible above the plastic, which crackled stiffly in the breeze. The smell of blood—and much, much worse—stained the air.

Steady? Ethan asked.

Vampires were innately attracted to the scent of blood, but there was nothing attractive about this scent, mixed as it was with the unmistakable odor of death.

Fine, I promised. And hoping to keep my dinner down.

We followed my grandfather toward the barrier. He stopped a

few feet away, gestured to a brunette in a classic black suit. She was handsomely pretty, with strong features and a wide mouth, her hair waving over her shoulders. Midthirties, I'd have guessed, with hard eyes unmistakably belonging to a cop.

"Detective Bernadette Stowe," my grandfather said. "Ethan Sullivan, Merit, Jonah."

She nodded, held up gloved hands. "I'd shake, but I'm already prepped. You're our vampire experts?"

"No one better," my grandfather said. I wasn't sure about that, but we certainly had the practical expertise.

We reached the barrier and Stowe pushed it aside, allowing us to enter. I went in last, taking a final glance around the courtyard, making sure I didn't recognize the driver among the men and women who surveyed the scene.

Catcher already stood inside the plastic, looking down at Brett Jacobs, who lay on the new spring grass. He nodded at us, moved aside to let us enter.

Brett's hair was short and dark, and his eyes were deeply brown and stared up, empty. He wore jeans and a navy T-shirt, but his feet were bare, and there was a blue mark on the back of one hand, a small, square cross. Beneath it, his dark skin had a gray cast: the pallor of death.

His body was posed as if he'd been crucified: arms outstretched, his palms flat on the grass, legs straight. His careful positioning was strange, but that's not why they'd called us.

Blood made a dark stain on his shirt and stained the ground beneath him. Two gently curved and gleaming katanas had been plunged into his abdomen like horrible skewers, crossing each other below his breastbone like an "X."

That was why they'd called us. Because they were katanas, and we were vampires, the only supernaturals that used them.

I'd seen death before, but that didn't make the sight of it any easier to stomach. I glanced away, closing my eyes for a moment until the world stopped spinning.

"Brett was twenty-five," Stowe quietly said. "Graduated from Columbia College three years ago, has a bachelor's in music. Plays violin for a string quartet that does weddings, events, and works at a restaurant in the Loop. Shares an apartment with a friend in Wrigleyville. No girlfriend. No sheet. By all accounts, lived a clean life."

"This should not be the reward for someone who lived clean," my grandfather said.

"No," Stowe quietly said. "It is not. And I'm sorry for it. And for Arthur."

"When did he die?" I quietly asked.

Stowe checked a delicate silver watch. "We're waiting for the coroner yet, but our preliminary estimate is about four hours ago. Custodian found him."

"Witnesses?" Ethan asked.

"None that have come forward," she said. "The fountain shields the body from the passageway and the street, and you'd have to walk over here to see it. Not many tourists doing that at night in early March."

Ethan turned his gaze to Stowe. "You've asked us here because of the swords."

She nodded. "Vampires use swords, fight with them. It's well-known Detective Jacobs has worked with you before."

"We're not suggesting you were involved in this," my grandfather said, stepping forward and drawing Ethan's ice-cold gaze to him. "But we don't have much else to go on."

Since Catcher's magical expertise was in weaponry, he must have been stumped.

Ethan looked at him. "Your impression?"

Catcher crouched, gestured to the swords. "They're replicas. Good replicas, but replicas all the same. The arc of the blade looks correct. The *tsuba*'s circular, engraved. Leather cord braided around the handle. All that's right . . . but the steel's wrong."

I tilted my head to glance at it, noted how shiny the metal was. "It's not folded," I said, and Catcher nodded, obviously pleased.

Catcher looked up at Stowe and my grandfather. "Vampires fight with traditional katanas—high-carbon steel weapons, usually *tamahagane*, steel that's folded repeatedly. The folding creates a pattern in the steel that looks like wood grain. This isn't carbon steel." He pointed at the blade, to a mark stamped into the metal.

"Looks like '440,'" Stowe said.

Catcher inclined his head. "That's a grade of stainless steel—which they might use in replicas."

Jonah nodded. "A midgrade replica, at that." He pulled a mini flashlight from his pocket, pointed it at the *tsuba*. There were minuscule daubs of a clear substance in the hairsbreadth space between guard and blade.

"Probably silicone," Jonah said. "Not a horribly sloppy job, but not an authentic construction method. And nothing a vampire would use."

"Damn," Stowe quietly said, crouching beside Jonah, careful not to touch the blood or disturb the body. "Good eye."

"That's why we called them," Chuck said with an approving nod. Even Ethan looked impressed.

Stowe looked at Jonah, then Catcher. "You think vampires wouldn't use replicas?"

"No," Catcher said without hesitation.

"In case you aren't familiar," I said, "vampires are particular."

Stowe glanced back at Brett Jacobs. "Surely it's possible some vampire who didn't have an authentic katana or access to one grabbed a replica, used it."

"Not all vampires fight," Ethan said. "Those who do fight—and who consciously choose to use katanas instead of guns, knives, Tasers, or any number of other weapons which are easier to hide, carry, and use—use authentic katanas. It's our way."

"That's where I get stuck," Catcher said. "The use of the weapons has a vampire ring to it. It hints that a vampire committed the crime. But anybody who knew anything about vampires would know that a vampire isn't going to use a replica like that."

"Chuck?" Stowe asked, immediately rising in my estimation in that she'd look to my grandfather for his thoughts, his take.

"I'd tend to agree. You can't rule out the possibility a vampire was the perpetrator. But vampires, finicky as they are—no offense—"

"None taken," the three of us put in.

"—are not likely to do something like this. If they want the world to know that they've killed a human, and the son of a cop, using their own preferred weapon, they're going to do it full out, as the kids say."

"I don't know that the kids say that," Stowe said lightly, "but I appreciate your candor. Vampires or not, someone had to buy these replicas. What about a source?"

"You can buy pretty much anything on the Internet these days," Jonah said, still crouched as he surveyed the swords up close. "But even if the construction's not fantastic, they're still pretty solid. See the designs here on the *tsubas*?" he asked, pointing.

Stowe leaned in. "Looks like fish around a pond, with some symbols. They're very detailed for something so small."

"They are," Jonah agreed, gesturing with his pinkie. "There's some colored enameling, even. *Tsuba* designs are specific to the maker. I don't know the artist of these motifs, specifically, but that's how we identify him or her. If I can take pictures, that would probably help."

Stowe looked at Chuck, who nodded. "They won't go any farther than they need to," he assured her.

"Then go ahead," Stowe said, rising again while Jonah pulled out his phone and snapped shots. She peeled the gloves from her carefully manicured fingers and stuffed them into a ball, then walked around Brett's body, surveying it, eyes tracking from one body part to another, then following the curve of the katana blades.

"What about the placement of the swords?" she asked, without lifting her gaze to us. "Their location in the body, the fact that they're crossed, form an 'X'?"

"I don't recognize it from swordcraft canon," Catcher said, glancing at Ethan and Jonah.

"Using two katanas is a high-level skill for vampires," Ethan said. "It's more often found among guards, those who soldier, than the average Novitiates. But as to the crossed swords, the placement in the chest . . ." He stood up and took a step back, head canted as he surveyed the scene. "It's not familiar to me. Jonah?"

Jonah shook his head. "It's unfamiliar because it's not a thing. Not to vampires, anyway. There's no specific ritual or *kata* associated with plunging two katanas in the chest, much less leaving two katanas in the body. A swordsman or woman, someone who trained with his or her katana, isn't going to leave one, much less two of them, and just walk away. It'd be like leaving a friend behind in battle."

"Another fact that leans against a vampire perp," my grandfather said.

"Could this"—Stowe waved her hand in a circle around the upthrust handles—"be done in a fight? Just a lucky strike of some kind? A final blow?"

Jonah moved closer. "Could have been," Jonah said. "But it probably wasn't here."

I caught the buzz of interest in her expression. "Why not?"

"Each type of bladed weapon has a purpose. Foils are for probing—for direct thrusts. Broadswords, big ancient weapons, were for hacking. Katanas, generally, are for slicing. But the body doesn't show any signs of slicing. Or anything else."

I walked incrementally closer. "He's right. There aren't any cuts on Brett's body. No bruises. If this had been an honest-to-God fight, he'd have been scraped up. There would be injuries other than the obvious one. But I don't see anything at all. It looks like the perp just walked up and plunged them in."

"A vampire certainly would have had the strength to do that," Jonah said. "But why wouldn't anyone angry enough to do this get in a few shots first? And why didn't Brett fight back?"

Before Stowe could ask her next question, a new voice intruded.

"There are a lot of people around my body."

We glanced back. A man had moved into the plastic enclosure and stood behind us in a black jumpsuit with CORONER across the front in white block letters. His hair was short and dark, his eyes slightly tilted, his body compact but obviously muscled. He carried a black plastic box, probably a field kit, in his right hand.

"Grant Lin," Stowe said. "He's with the medical examiner's office. And tonight, he's late."

"Good to see you, too, Detective. Unfortunately, Mr. Jacobs isn't the first gentleman on my agenda tonight." He glanced at the body, then at us. "Friends of the dearly departed?"

"Weapons consultants," Stowe said.

"Never thought I'd see the day when vampires were consulting for the CPD."

"That's because immortality would put you out of a job, Grant. We take our experts as we find them. We'll get out of your way. We'd appreciate knowing TOD and cause as soon as you've got it."

Lin grunted and moved toward the body as we stepped back. He inspected the wounds, and with the help of an assistant gently tilted Brett's body, surveying the ground beneath him.

"Volume of blood loss suggests the insult occurred before death," Lin said. "That blood loss could have been the cause, but the body will tell us that."

"We'd appreciate knowing your findings as soon as possible," my grandfather said.

"Jacobs is a good man," Lin said. "You'll get them."

"He's very good at his work," Stowe quietly said when we'd followed her out of the barrier and into the courtyard again. "Kind of an ass, but good at his work." She glanced at me. "You were saying you didn't think this looked like a fight."

I nodded. "But I doubt Brett just let himself be used to make a statement—or let the perp just plunge the swords into him. Who just stands there and lets it happen?"

"Maybe he wasn't just standing here," Ethan said, hands on his hips. "He could have been drugged, intoxicated. Magicked, although that seems unlikely."

"Why?" Stowe asked.

"Because there's no magic here," Catcher said. "Magic would have left a trace."

Her eyes widened incrementally. She must not have dealt with many supernaturals. "Which you could feel?"

We all nodded.

"So there's no magic, and there's no evidence of a fight," Stowe said, brows knitted as she surveyed the scene. "No evidence Brett was injured other than the obvious insult. But that insult is grandiose. Not just one sword, but two. And not just left for dead, but displayed in the middle of a church courtyard."

"It's a message," Jonah said, tucking his phone away again.

"Then who's the audience?" my grandfather asked.

"Vampires are the obvious target," I said. "We're the supernaturals who use katanas."

"That was our concern," my grandfather said, caterpillar eyebrows bunched in as he looked at me.

"So the perp is trying to send a message to us, or he's trying to put the blame on us?" I asked.

"Hard to say without more information," Ethan said.

"We'll handle the forensics, canvass the neighborhood, speak to his friends," Stowe said. "But if you can get any additional information about the origin of the swords, we'd appreciate it."

Jonah glanced at his watch. "We don't have much time before sunrise, but we'll check our connections, be in touch with you tomorrow."

"I'd appreciate it," Stowe said. "We'll let you know if we obtain any further information that would help."

When one of the forensic techs approached her to discuss the case, my grandfather gestured toward the small parking lot on the other side of the courtyard.

"Let's get out of their way."

"Where's Jeff tonight?" I asked.

"Actually, he's waiting to show you his new office."

We walked across the courtyard. Ethan and Catcher walked behind me, and Jonah stuck close to Ethan, gaze on the courtyard and any potential threats that might emerge.

On the edge of the lot was a gleaming white panel van, OM-BUDSMAN stenciled across the side in black block letters. Jeff was just climbing out the open back. When he saw us approaching, he offered a muted smile—the circumstances weren't exactly cheery—and a wave.

"Hey, Merit," he said. We exchanged hugs, and then he offered manly grunts and nods to the rest of the guys in the way that guys do.

"Crappy night," Jeff said, putting his hands on his hips. He'd swagged out his wardrobe, exchanging his usual button-down shirt for a pullover with OMBUDSMAN embroidered on the chest.

"The crappiest. Did you know Brett?"

"Not really. Seemed like a good guy, superquiet. I hear he played a mean violin. Has a degree in it."

"That's what Stowe said. Horrible way to lose a child."

"I'm not sure there's any non-horrible way," Ethan put in.

"Fair point," Jeff said, then rapped his knuckles on the side of the van. "And that's where I come in." We followed him to the back of the van, where the double doors were already opened. "Step inside my lair."

And it was a lair—and a tech whiz's dream. The van was outfitted with walls of built-in computers and monitors and equipment I couldn't name, but which I didn't doubt cost a lot of money.

The fact that they'd gotten an official van—and that it was filled with Jeff's favorite variety of toys—was a very good sign. Chicago's mayor, Diane Kowalcyzk, had fired my grandfather and hired a maniacal ex-military type to replace him. We'd managed to take down the crazy replacement and, supplemented with a little blackmail, get my grandfather hired again.

I guess she knew a good deal when she saw it.

Jeff offered a hand, helped me up into the vehicle. I sat down at a stool, glanced at the screens, which currently showed aerial photographs of the church and surrounding streets.

"This is impressive," I said, turning around on the stool to glance back at Jeff.

Catcher, Ethan, Jonah, and my grandfather gathered outside the doors and looked in. My grandfather nodded, a supportive arm on the doorframe. "We'll be able to do a lot more out there. Quick response. On-site research. And a hell of a lot more credibility with an official vehicle."

"Can you do all your officing here?" I asked.

"Just about," Catcher said. "Certainly anything you'd need on a mobile basis."

Ethan glanced at my grandfather. "And a permanent office?"

"The mayor has graciously set aside office space at a community service center on the south side. We move in next week."

"Successful blackmail is the best blackmail," Jonah murmured.

"No kidding," I said, then looked at my grandfather. "This is great. I know you'll be glad to be settled." Before he'd been fired, my grandfather had rented a small office on the south side. After he'd been fired, the team worked out of my grandfather's basement. And then McKetrick, my grandfather's replacement, had it firebombed.

It had really been a tough year for the Ombuddies.

"It will be nice to put down some roots," he agreed.

"And how is life at home?" While my grandfather recuperated, he was staying with my parents. They were very nearly his opposites: rich, fusty, and very, very fancy.

"Your father has been nothing but gracious," he said with a smile that looked a little bit tight at the corners.

I smiled knowingly back. "You're very kind. I'm sure he's driving you batty."

"Nothing but gracious," he repeated. "He's hired a physical therapist, nurse, and dietician to oversee my recovery."

"Your Oreo stash?"

"Depleted."

"We'll restock you," I assured him. "How is Dad?"

"Busy. He's got a new project in the works—a high-rise in Streeterville. Towerline, it's called. He's very focused on getting it up."

Real estate was Joshua Merit's particular wheelhouse—and not houses in the suburbs. *Entire* suburbs. Skyscrapers. Condos along the lake. If it was big, splashy, and expensive—and mentioned in the architectural river or lake tours—he probably had a hand (or a dollar) in it.

"I hope it works well for him. I haven't seen Charlotte and Robert in way too long." They were my elder brother and sister, whom I hadn't seen since I'd taken Ethan home to meet them. We weren't especially close, but I knew I was lucky to have a family.

"Or Robert's new baby," my grandfather said. "Frankly, you could stand to visit the entire family." It wasn't often he pushed where the family was concerned—our long-running differences were well-known to him—so I knew he meant it this time. And since he was right, I gave him the victory.

"I should," I agreed. "We should plan a dinner."

"We could have them to the House," Ethan said, but cast a glance at the eastern sky. The pink fingers of dawn were beginning to reach above the horizon, which was our cue to leave.

"We can discuss that later," my grandfather said, offering me a hand to help me out of the van. I took it, jumped down, straightened the hem of my jacket.

"I've got some ideas on the swords," Jonah said, with a glint of amusement in his eyes. He definitely had something planned.

"I'll check in with Merit at dusk, and we'll check it out and report back."

Ethan managed not to stiffen or swear at Jonah's planning my schedule for the evening, but I felt the brush of irritated magic against my skin. It had all the subtlety of stampeding wasps. Assuming wasps stampeded.

"Appreciate it," my grandfather said. "We'll dig in a bit more here, see what we can see. Hopefully, we'll make some headway and find some justice for Arthur and his family."

Justice would be good. But I knew it wouldn't be good enough.

Jonah walked us back to the SUV, just in case, and we scanned the tourists and alleyways for possible threats against Ethan. When we reached Lindsey's SUV, I unlocked the car and opened the driver's-side door.

"I'll be in touch tomorrow," Jonah said. "Don't forget about our date."

He offered Ethan a wave, then mixed back into the pedestrian traffic and headed down the street, drawing a handful of interested glances from the men and women he passed.

I glanced back at Ethan, found his gaze on me, his expression flat and a twinge of jealousy darkening his eyes. It would be a lie to say that twinge didn't thrill me a teensy bit, but since I had to live with Ethan, it wasn't in my best interest to let him stew all the way back to Cadogan House.

"Business date," I reminded him. "Investigatory date. You're the only vampire on my mind."

"Oh, I know," he said, opening the door. "If I thought for a moment he was making a serious move, I'd have beaten him senseless."

I didn't think he was joking.

Ethan was halfway inside the car when he stilled and reached outside, plucking something from beneath the windshield wiper.

In his hand was a piece of white paper, slightly larger than a business card. It was thin enough to see that there was print on one side—words that had his eyes instantaneously widening—before he stuffed it into his pocket.

"What's that?"

"Nothing, Merit." He climbed inside, closed the car door. "Let's get home before the sun rises."

"Is it from the driver?"

"It's nothing, Merit."

"Ethan—," I began, but he shook his head.

"It's just . . . a flyer. For a restaurant down the street." He looked at me, smiled lightly, and pulled the door shut. "Let's be on our way, Sentinel."

He was lying. There wasn't a doubt in my mind. He'd seen something on that paper, and he'd lied to me about it.

That scared me more than whatever might have been written there. But dawn was approaching. Seeking shelter from the rising sun was paramount, so I pulled the car into traffic and drove us both home.

He made conversation on the way back to the House, as casual as ever. By the time we'd pulled up to the House, I was nearly convinced.

Nearly.

We reported to Luc, briefly told him about the murder, the swords, the evidence so far.

Luc confirmed they'd seen no more of the driver, and the guards were preparing to turn the safety of the House to the human patrol at the gates.

We'd had a bad run of luck staffing the guards who watched the gate, a necessity when we were unconscious during the daylight hours. We'd previously hired mercenary fairies, strong supernaturals with serious fighting skills, but they'd betrayed us for an ancient artifact they were convinced we'd stolen. (We hadn't.) We'd then hired humans, but two had been killed in the line of duty by Harold Monmouth, a former member of the GP, who'd himself been killed. (We were responsible for that one.) We'd stuck with humans but turned to off-duty officers, who we hoped stood a greater chance of survival.

It was an unfortunate irony that the monsters they guarded were the least of their worries.

Our report given, we took the stairs to our apartments on the third floor. The lights had already been dimmed to a soft glow, and classical music played quietly in the background. And because Margot was the coolest chick ever, there was a tray of snacks and water. Turndown service was one of the better perks of dating the Master.

The other was the Master himself, who stood on the other side of the room, one hand on his hip, perusing a stack of papers as he removed his cuff links and placed them on a bureau.

I watched him, looking for a hint of worry or deceit, for the truth of what he'd seen on that small piece of paper.

Perhaps sensing my gaze, he looked up at me. "Sentinel?"

I had no idea what to say, but we'd been through many trials together, and this wasn't the time to bury fear.

"The paper you found—it wasn't a flyer for a restaurant."

Ethan didn't answer. He finished with his cuff links, began

unbuttoning his shirt, revealing the flat, muscled plane of his abdomen.

"What would you like me to say?"

"Obviously, I'd like you to tell me the truth. What was in the note? Was it a message from the driver? Another threat?"

He watched me, his eyes colder than I'd seen them in a very long time. "Don't you trust me, Sentinel?"

I felt like we were having two different conversations. "I want to know if someone is out there gunning for you."

"It's something I need to handle."

"That wasn't an answer."

"It's the answer I'm prepared to give right now." His features had tightened into Master vampire haughtiness, which drove me crazy. He looked at me, green eyes alight. "Do you think I'm not capable of handling my own problems? I managed to run this House before you were named Sentinel, and I can run it now."

He wasn't angry at me. But in true Sullivan style, he was pushing my buttons because he was angry at something else, and I was here.

That only irritated me more. I was here because I cared about him. Because I worried for him. My own anger rose swiftly.

"I don't doubt it, or that you'll push me away because you're angry or afraid. But that's not how this works. That's not how you and I work, and it's not how the House works."

His expression went stony. "That's how *this* will work."

I took a step forward. "Ethan, you're in danger. And if it's a threat, I need to know about it. This isn't something you pretend not to see."

"No, it's something I see very clearly, and something I'll handle on my own."

He turned, walked into the closet, where I heard the shuffling of fabric.

My eyelids felt suddenly heavier, both because of the rising of the sun and because this conversation was exhausting.

I walked to the closet, ignoring Ethan, kicked off my boots and pulled off my jacket. I left the rest of my clothes in a pile on the floor, pulled on a tank and shorts, and headed back to the bed. Ethan walked in and sat on the edge, wearing his Cadogan medal and emerald silk pajama bottoms, phone in his hand.

I stood there for a moment, waited until he put the phone down and looked up at me again.

"Come here, Sentinel," he drowsily said, and I stepped between his thighs, threaded my fingers into his golden hair. Ethan wrapped his arms around me, rested his head against my chest.

"Be still," he said. "For tonight, let's both be still."

The automatic shades closed over the windows with a mechanical *buzz*. I fell into bed beside Ethan, and he turned off the lamp, leaving us in darkness.

✦ ✦ ✦

CHAPTER FIVE

BED-AND-BREAKFAST

I woke alone, Ethan's side of the bed already cool.

That wasn't necessarily a problem. Although vampires theoretically woke when the sun set, in reality there was some variation. Ethan always woke earlier than me, so it wasn't unusual for him to begin work before I'd been dragged back into consciousness.

Still. I felt like there was something between us, and I didn't look forward to dragging it out of him.

Maybe, like Ethan, I could avoid it for just a little while.

I grabbed my phone from the nightstand, typed out a message for Jonah: AWAKE. YOU READY TO INVESTIGATE?

While I waited for an answer, I scanned the dailies, the schedule, alerts, and other info Luc provided to guards every evening. "Fret over GP" wasn't listed, but I'd put good money on the possibility it would fit into the schedule somehow.

My phone beeped when Jonah responded. I HAVE SOURCE IN MIND, BUT PARKING'S IFFY. PICK YOU UP IN AN HOUR?

DONE, I told him, and climbed off the bed to get dressed.

Since I'd be out and investigating, I skipped the Cadogan black suit for jeans, a long, dark tank, and my leather jacket against the spring chill. When my hair was brushed and gleaming, my medal was in place, and my katana was in hand, I headed downstairs to the House's first floor.

I paused at the first-floor landing, eyes closed and a hand on the banister, reveling in the scent of freshly cooked bacon. The back of the House's first floor was filled by a school-style cafeteria that served more shade-grown, free-range, organic nonsense than a processed-food lover like me usually preferred to eat. Thankfully, though, Margot rarely skipped the bacon. If that's because we were friends, it was fine by me.

My stomach growled with hunger, undiminished by the small thread of worry woven in my thoughts. There'd been at least one threat against Ethan, and I suspected the note was a second. But he wouldn't give me the details, and I wasn't confident he'd tell anyone else.

Well, screw that. He had to either tell me or tell Luc. I could live with either. The latter would sting, but I could live with it.

What kind of threat couldn't he tell me about? If it was about me, he'd have locked me away in the apartments; there'd be no avoiding it. If it was against the House, he'd have told me and Luc, probably in a meeting.

Perhaps, I thought, as I walked to his office, the issue wasn't the nature of the threat, but its source. Someone he didn't want me to know about? A former enemy? I didn't doubt that Ethan had them, but the only ones I was aware of were deceased, or he'd already challenged them. Celina Desaulniers, the former Master of Navarre House, was dead by my hand. He'd outright challenged Darius. The vampire who made him, whom I knew only as Balthasar, had been a monster, but he was dead.

I peeked in the open doorway, found the office empty. Since my stomach growled insistently, I walked to the cafeteria at the end of the hallway. It was arranged in college fashion—a buffet line of food on one side, wooden chairs and tables on the other. The back wall was glass, picture windows that looked out on the Cadogan grounds. The world outside was dark, but landscape lights and torches lit the spring grounds like a fancy resort.

I grabbed a tray, moved into line, and selected orange juice, blood, bacon and eggs, and a chocolate croissant as big as a softball. Not that I had any problem with that.

My tray full, I scanned the tables, looking for friendly faces, found Lindsey and Margot at a table together.

Lindsey wore her Cadogan black suit, her blond hair pulled into a high knot. Margot wore her chef's whites, her sleek dark bob perfectly edged, with bangs that dipped to a point in the middle of her forehead, framing her eyes. Apparently taking a break from her cooking duties, she scooped oatmeal and fruit from a pretty flowered dish.

I walked over, only barely managing not to attempt a hands-free bite of the croissant, but I did have some pride.

"Good evening, sleepyhead." Lindsey patted the seat of the chair beside her. "How was your double date?"

I smiled, slid out the chair, and took a seat. "It wasn't a date."

"Ethan plus Jonah equals date," she said.

"Ethan plus Jonah equals snarky comments. And in this case, murder."

Margot frowned. "Yikes. That's unfortunate. Anyone we know?"

"Detective Jacobs's son, unfortunately."

Margot put a hand on her chest. "Oh, that's awful. Jacobs is the one who helps us out, right? Your grandfather's friend?"

I nodded. "Jonah and I are going to do some follow-up today

about the murder weapons. Hopefully we can use that to find some information about the killer."

"You had a big night," Margot said. "Barely avoid a drive-by, then drive right into a crime scene."

I took a bite of eggs. "The life of a Sentinel is often less than glamorous."

"You got an Ethan Sullivan out of the bargain," Margot said with a wink. "Suck it up."

I managed not to mention the downsides of that particular arrangement.

"So the drive-by thing," Margot said. "That's got to be GP related, right?"

"It's GP related," I agreed, opting not to offer up the specifics. I didn't think there was anything to be gained by frightening the rest of the House with the details of the threat.

"Ethan's a challenge to the status quo," Lindsey said. "Some aren't comfortable with that."

Margot nodded. "You are preaching to the choir. Blood notwithstanding, vampires aren't the most culinarily adventurous group."

"That reminds me—Ethan will be coming to you about a bet that I lost."

Her brows lifted with amusement. "I am intrigued."

"Cool your jets. It was about the 5K. We bet a meal, and he won. If he requests you make something like duck fingers in aspic, try to steer him away, will you?"

"A novel idea," Margot said. "I don't think ducks have fingers, but I get the point."

"Speaking of novel ideas, which I'd swear to God are the sole property of the women in this House, nice job getting Luc and Ethan together yesterday. Luc was feeling much, much better at sunset." Lindsey smiled wickedly over the rim of her juice.

I bit into bacon, shook my head. "I don't need to know that. And I'd bet Margot didn't either."

"Oh, I'm fine with it," she said, popping a blueberry. "I've been single lo these many months."

Lindsey gave Margot an appraising glance. "You know, Jonah's also single."

Margot waved her spoon. "I wasn't complaining; I'm on a hiatus. Long-term relationship gone bad," she added, with a glance at me. "I'm not in a place to date anyone else, and perfectly happy on my own."

"Brown butter and foie gras can't keep you happy forever," Lindsey said.

"Says you. Throw in a decent lemon tart now and again, and I'm perfectly fine." She glanced at her watch. "And speaking of which, I've got meals to prepare and vampires to feed." Margot rose, pushed in her chair. "I'll see you ladies later."

"Later, gator," Lindsey said.

"Ladies," Brody said, pulling a chair around and sitting down backward, his long and lanky legs straddling the chair, his blue eyes shining. "What's the story?"

"Sun's shining on the other half of the world," Lindsey said. "That's all I need to know." She gave him a flat stare. "Aren't you on duty right now?"

"Yeah. I mean, in a few minutes." He smiled guilelessly. "Just came down to grab a bite. I am starving tonight."

I could practically see the glint of wickedness in Lindsey's eyes, and I pushed back my chair just slightly to get out of her verbal path.

"So, to be clear, the fate of this House is in your hands, but you decided that instead of getting to the business of security a few minutes early, you'd cowboy into the cafeteria and 'grab a bite'?"

Brody's cheeks pinkened. "Um, so, I just thought—"

"You thought?" Lindsey prompted.

He got up so fast the chair toppled over, hitting the floor with a *clatter* that had the rest of the vampires in the room turning to look.

"Sorry," he said, waving sheepishly as he righted the chair. "I'll just grab something to go and get to work." Without waiting for her approval, he scurried toward the food line, grabbed two bottles of blood, and hustled out of the room.

I glanced back at her, found her eyes narrowed, her lips pressed together.

"You enjoyed that a little too much."

She shook her head. "Nope. There's no such thing."

"This isn't a military school. You don't have to haze him."

"I don't *have* to," Lindsey said with a wink. "But if I can't haze the newbies, what's a vampire to live for?"

Bacon seemed the obvious and eternal answer.

My hour before Jonah's pickup was nearly up, so I tried one more time to check in with Ethan before leaving the House. I knocked gingerly on the office door and, at Ethan's terse "Come in," opened it.

Ethan and Malik were in the sitting area on opposite sides of the coffee table, papers spread between them.

Ethan glanced up, nodded. "Sentinel."

"Sullivan." I walked closer, took in spreadsheets and dollar signs. "This looks unfortunately numeric."

"The welfare of the House is never unfortunate," Ethan said, and a glance at Malik's bland expression told me he trotted that one out regularly.

"Mmm-hmm. So, as we discussed yesterday, Jonah texted.

He's got an idea about sourcing the sword. He's going to pick me up in a few minutes."

"I believe I'll let you handle that particular assignment. But I'll walk you to the door."

"Be careful out there, Merit," Malik said.

"I'm going to try my best. Good job with those numbers."

Malik winked in response.

The hallway was busy, well-suited Cadogan Novitiates hustling to the cafeteria or the front door and the jobs that awaited them outside the House. They smiled at Ethan, called him "Liege" as they passed, making note of their equally well-suited Master.

We stopped in the foyer, and I waited a moment, expecting Ethan to kiss me good-bye. Instead, he launched into instructions.

"Find out if they have any information about Darius. I still don't think he sent the driver, and if he didn't, then he's not responded to my challenge. Perhaps they've heard more than we have—a plan. A response. When we might expect the bomb to be dropped."

"And here I thought you were going to kiss me good-bye. Can I remind you that you objected to my membership in the RG?"

"I use the tools in my arsenal," he said. "And the RG, as we know, is a valuable source of information. Be safe," he said, pressing his mouth to mine. The kiss was hot and insistent. Brief as it was, by the time he released me, I thought my body might burn from the inside out.

"I will," I said, when I could manage words, and tapped my katana. "I'm armed. I'm sure Jonah will be, too. Don't leave the House without a guard."

"I won't," he said, but I wasn't sure if I believed him. Ethan

Sullivan would do whatever he damn well pleased, because he was Master of his House and wanted to be the Master of all of them.

But I'd known that from the beginning and signed up anyway.

We said our final good-byes, and I walked outside and trotted down the front stairs. Jonah's car sat in front of the gate, where two humans, a man and a woman, stood guard.

I had a twinge of regret and guilt as I passed through them, thinking of Angelo and Louie, the human guards who'd been struck down to keep us safe.

"Ma'am," said the woman, standing at attention as I walked past.

"Have a good night," I told them. "And a safe one."

"That's our job," she said with unerring confidence.

I appreciated the enthusiasm and hoped their luck held out.

Jonah, who knew me much too well, had a bottle of blood and a candy bar ready when I climbed into the sedan.

"I ate breakfast. And even if I hadn't, I don't need to be fed."

He checked the mirrors, pulled into traffic. "Since you've already opened that candy bar, I presume said breakfast didn't do much for you."

I considered offering him a bite but decided he didn't deserve it.

"Where are we going, exactly?"

"To a place with abundant weapons and folks interested in them. We're going to use the *tsubas* as fingerprints and track down the fingers from whence they came."

"That is a very weird metaphor."

"I buy you a candy bar, and you insult me. Well, the joke's on you. It was loaded with protein and vitamins."

"Spoilsport."

"I'm your partner, not your boyfriend."

Since Ethan usually tried to ply me with protein and vegetables, rather than foods of the overprocessed, candy-coated, and deep-fried varieties, I didn't think the distinction held much water. But Jonah had fed me, so I didn't argue the point.

"Just drive the car," I grumbled.

The drive took thirty minutes through stop-and-go traffic, and that only got us to the exit. Cars were lined up on the off-ramp, a circle that dumped nearly into the main entrance of the Chicago Mid-City Convention Hall.

A purple-and-gold SpringCon banner hung across the road, and men, women, and children in superhero T-shirts and costumes walked toward the convention center beneath the glowing streetlights.

"Preview night," Jonah said, as we parked the car in a lot a couple of blocks away. "Have you ever been to a big con?"

"I have not. I've been conned. But I don't think that's what you meant."

He clucked his tongue. "You're going to need better lines than that if you want to survive this gauntlet."

I began to unbelt my katana, but Jonah shook his head. "No need," he said, belting on his own weapon. "They'll think it's part of your costume."

I looked up at him. "What costume?"

He grinned knowingly. "This is going to be even more fun than I thought."

Belted and ready, we slipped into the throng of orcs, browncoats, robots, superheroes, and elves heading toward the front doors.

I didn't think we'd make much headway; the line to get into the convention center extended nearly the entire sidewalk to the parking area. But when we reached the end of the line, Jonah kept walking.

Nerves and excitement spilled off the line of humans—and the occasional pop of magic sprang from a supernatural. They spanned all shapes, sizes, colors, genres. From anime baby dolls to hairy cryptomonsters, the line had it all.

I followed Jonah into the ticket area of the convention center, weaving through and toward a small booth with a VIP sign. I straightened my shoulders, excitement building, and leaned toward him.

"Are we VIPs?"

"Not yet. Friend owes me a favor."

The friend had bulging triceps, a gleaming dome, and dark sideburns cut into neat lightning bolts. His eyes were brown, and he wore a well-loved Hulk T-shirt.

"Jonah," he said, half rising from his perch on a stool for a complicated hand-to-wrist-to-biceps handshake.

"Tyler," Jonah said. "My friend Merit."

I offered a wave.

"Good costume," he said, and when I opened my mouth to object, I caught Jonah's warning glance and shut it again.

"Thanks, I think."

"Tyler's a comics artist," Jonah said, as Tyler flipped through a small metal cash box on the counter of his booth.

I nodded encouragingly and smiled as Tyler pulled out two laminated cards attached to woven lanyards. "Your passes, my friend."

"Appreciate it," Jonah said, taking one, draping it around his neck, and handing the other to me. It was an eye-searing shade of yellow and featured the SpringCon logo—flowers entwined in a hazardous-materials logo.

"You got some time next week?" Tyler asked.

When a faint blush appeared on Jonah's cheeks, my curiosity grew. "Sure, man. Get in touch."

"Five by five," Tyler said, and turned to the next person in line.

"Five by five?" I wondered aloud, as I pulled on my pass and walked to the doors that led into the convention center.

"It means he understands. Military term."

I added that to my mental list of phrases to use with Luc. "And what does he want your time for?"

He diverted to a poster that bore a map of the convention center floor. "Oh, I just consult," he said offhandedly.

"Consult? With a comics artist?"

He looked back at me, sheer embarrassment on his face, and realization struck.

"You don't consult with him," I said with a dawning grin. "You *pose* for him."

Jonah rolled his eyes dramatically. "He wants to get the body right. The anatomy. He's a perfectionist."

The options for teasing him were legion. Truly numerous. But Jonah—tall and gorgeous and auburn haired in the way of an Irish prince—looked absolutely mortified. And besides, he'd been doing a favor for a friend.

"Good," I said with a smile. "Good. You've got a good build for that."

He looked back at me with obvious suspicion as folks in Spring-Con T-shirts flowed onto the floor. "Okay," he cautiously said. "That's all you're going to say?"

"You got us in here to help my grandfather. I'm giving you a pass."

He looked utterly relieved and led the way onto the main convention floor.

Yes, I was in love and committed. But I still snuck a peek at the guard-slash-model's assets . . . and made a mental note to find out which comics Tyler worked on.

CHAPTER SIX

SENTINEL SQUARED

The line outside, as eclectic as it had been, was nothing compared to the convention center's main hall.

Artists, writers, and stars of sci-fi movies and television shows sat at dozens of rows of tables, and men, women, and children moved through the rows with excited expressions. Animated screens, movie posters, and spinning video-game signs reached fifteen feet into the air. Fans funneled in and out of giant rooms that seemed to be built entirely of rolled-up T-shirts, and inflatable characters roamed the narrow pathways like video-game monsters. Scantily clad women and men in loincloths posed for photographs. Music blared from all directions, and fans chatted over the cacophony, excitedly showing their treasures from the corners of the floor. Posters. Bags. Plushies.

It was an assault on all five senses, and probably a couple I hadn't even known I had.

Jonah and I strolled across the floor dodging zombies, caped superheroes, anime princesses, and an awful lot of Wookies.

"This is a lot to take in," I said, dodging a child in a small, pink

Darth Vader costume who ran to her father with an autographed picture in hand. Actors from various sci-fi shows sat at long tables behind her, signing photographs and posing for pictures, pressing cheeks with fans willing to shell out the cash.

"I love a con," he said over the din. "The energy. The love. The geekery. Where else do you get so many people passionate about so many different things in one place?"

"There is definitely a lot of energy here," I said, as we passed a bevy of fans at the "Vampire Arts" table. I only barely glanced at it, expecting to see photos of Buffy, prints of Dracula and Edward, posters of Selena and Blade in battle mode.

I did not expect to catch sight of a plastic-wrapped print of a watercolor featuring a woman with dark hair, fangs, and familiar blue eyes.

I pulled Jonah to a stop, then yanked him toward it. Goggling, I picked it up, stared at the drawing of me.

I recognized the image—it was modeled after a photograph that had appeared in the paper above the headline "Ponytailed Avenger." And that, by the look of it, was the title of the artwork, scrawled in thin, scratching strokes across the bottom right of the picture.

"It's nicely done," Jonah said.

"Archival paper," said the young guy manning the table. He hadn't yet looked up and was busily penning another drawing, this time of Lindsey with sunglasses and tight jeans. "Suitable for framing."

And according to the tiny sticker in the bottom corner, very affordable. For thirty-five dollars you could take home your own Sentinel.

The artist, whose index and middle fingers were smeared with ink, looked up. "Nice costume."

"I think you're going to want to see this."

I heard Jonah speak but was so flabbergasted and creeped out—and, yeah, a little flattered—by the assortment of drawings that I didn't really hear it. Not until he said my name again, then took me by the shoulders, turned me around to face a table dotted entirely with photographs and swag featuring "Chicago's Hunkiest Vampires."

Photographs, prints, T-shirts, mugs, sweatshirts, blankets, and underwear, all featuring the smiling face of Ethan Sullivan.

"Dear God," I said, dodging a pair of zombie cheerleaders to cross the busy pathway to the "Hunkiest" table, staring down at the assortment of pink, white, and pale blue panties, Ethan's green eyes staring out from the front triangle.

I had no argument with their appreciation of Ethan; he was a miraculous specimen of vampire. A blond genetic gift. And I understood the women who'd cheered him on at the Cadogan Dash. Hot guy running? Sure, I'll show up for that. I *did* show up for that. I knew there were Web sites devoted to Ethan. I might, in a moment of curious weakness, have visited Ethan SullivanIsMyMaster.net and smiled at the bloggers' obvious adoration.

But underwear? *Underwear!*

"Pretty hot, isn't he?" asked the clerk.

I was bewildered. Of course he was hot. But he was *my* hot. "Yes?"

"Handsome? He is utterly and completely *en fuego*. But I hear he's taken. My loss, right?"

"Probably dating some skanky vampire," said one of two girls who clutched "Master of My House" nightshirt and panty sets.

It seemed this entire episode was designed to test my grace under pressure.

"He's dating me, actually." The words slipped out before I thought better of it.

But they didn't faze the shopper. She looked at me, cocked her head. "Oh, I get it. You're doing the girlfriend—what's her name? Megan?"

"Merit," answered the girl at the table. "And it's a pretty good costume."

I opened my mouth to object, to proclaim that I wasn't *doing* Ethan's girlfriend, I *was* Ethan's girlfriend, and I was *doing* Ethan. But I got a pinch on the arm from Jonah for my trouble. I glanced back at him, could feel my eyes silvering in irritation, caught the warning look in his expression.

"Investigation," he quietly said. "We're keeping it low-key."

Oh, I'd keep it low-key, I thought, imagining for a moment the pummeling I could give these mere mortals. I'd keep it real low-key.

But that was not what Jonah had meant, so I sucked it up.

"Yeah, I'm wearing a Merit costume," I said, with a forced smile, and strode away.

"You knew he had fans," Jonah said when he caught up with me.

"There are fans, and there are *fans*. Fans buying underwear with my boyfriend's face on them."

"You're awfully young to be a prude."

"I'm not a prude. I'm just—it's underwear." I glanced at him. "Would you want your face on underwear?"

"No. But then again, I'm not Master of the House, dating one of Chicago's most eligible bachelorettes, and constantly in the news."

My expression and tone were bland. "So he asked for it?"

"I'm just saying. He's pretty famous, and he doesn't seem to mind it. But he obviously only has eyes for you, if that's what you're worried about."

"I'm not worried about anything. It's just . . . weird. They don't know him."

"They'll know him intimately pretty soon."

"You can stop now."

"I'm not sure that I can," Jonah said, with a cheeky grin. "I'm having entirely too much fun. I may not ever stop. I wonder if they make blow-up Ethan Sullivan dolls."

"I am not having this conversation with you. But I am going to find those comic books you pose for. I'm going to find them, and I'm going to display them on easels in the foyer of Grey House."

He stopped short near a fourteen-foot-tall plastic Godzilla with waggling, inflatable arms.

"I won't mention your 'costume'; you don't mention the comics gig."

"We get to work, and we never mention this again."

"Agreed," he said, and, both of us mortified, we looked around the floor to get our bearings.

"Who are we seeing today?" I asked.

"Them, actually," Jonah said, nodding to a nearby vendor stocked with weapons.

The scrolled wooden sign read FaireMakers and listed an address in Schaumburg. A man and a woman worked the booth. The man, who sat at the table, had short hair and a precisely trimmed goatee, and he wore a tunic, brown pants, and soft brown boots. The woman, who stood behind him, flipping through an old-fashioned ledger, had a mass of wavy strawberry blond hair that reached halfway down her back and wore a wide circle skirt and linen peasant's blouse. Her breasts were ample, and a round pendant lay nestled between them.

As we walked to the table, the man moved toward us with a wide grin. "Good evening. How can I help you on this lovely spring night? We have all variety of weaponry," he said, gesturing toward the wall. There were maces, daggers, a couple of replica katanas, and several two-handled swords. Some of them looked like good replicas; some looked like well-worn antiques.

"Actually," Jonah said, pointing at the woman behind him, "we need to talk to her."

"Nan," the clerk said, touching her shoulder to get her attention.

Nan turned back to us, her round face brightening at the sight of my RG partner. "Jonah! Such a pleasure. I haven't seen you in forever."

"It's been a while," he agreed, then put a hand at my back. "Nan, this is Merit, Sentinel of Cadogan House."

"Namaste," Nan said, pressing her hands together and bowing just a little.

"Hi." I offered a little wave.

"Nan helps source our katanas and practice weapons," Jonah said. And since he was captain of Grey's guards, I bet he was responsible for purchasing and arranging all those weapons.

"Nice to meet you," I said.

She looked between us. "Are you looking to buy something? We only have replicas today, but perhaps there's something . . ." She gestured to three katanas that hung behind her, their blades shining like chrome.

"We're just looking for information, actually. We're trying to identify swords that were recently used in a crime."

Nan put a hand on her chest, leaned in. "Oh my God, are you

here about the murder at that church? We saw it on television last night. Horrible thing. I certainly hope you find out who did it."

"So do we," Jonah said. He pulled out his phone, offered her photographs of the *tsubas*. "Do these look familiar at all?"

Nan squinted down at the phone, then glanced surreptitiously around and pulled a pair of funky leopard reading glasses from a beaded chain hidden beneath her shirt. She fitted them on, stared down at the phone.

"These are nice. Nice pictures, and very well rendered. Good three-dimensional qualities, good detail. We tend to stay away from fish images. We prefer dragons and bamboo."

"Any idea who does prefer fish?" Jonah asked.

"Actually, yes." She pointed at the phone's display. "The colored enameling's the giveaway—it's called cloisonné. Gained traction in Japan in the seventeen hundreds. You don't see it very often, and when you do, it's usually an older piece. Not many craftsmen making it these days. Did you get any photos of the edge?"

"Let me see," Jonah said, taking the phone back and moving through pictures. "I got one—there were markings there, and I thought maybe it was an artist's mark."

He handed the phone back, and she peered at it, tilted her head, leaned closer.

"Mmm-hmm," she said. "Not an artist's mark per se, but similar. And you got very, very lucky."

"Oh?" Jonah asked.

She held the phone out, the photograph zoomed in on a couple of small, raised squiggles on the edge of the *tsuba*. "See those?"

"Looks like an 'M' and an 'S,'" I said.

"Precisely. Stands for the Magic Shoppe. Located right here in Chicago. Hipsters, if you ask me." By her flat expression and tone, she was not impressed with the Magic Shoppe. "They sell replicas, but they customize. Pick your blade length, your cording, your *tsuba* design. They have *tsubas* made at a small workshop in Kyoto, have the store's initials added to the side.

"They also do the con circuit, but they aren't here. No loss, in my opinion. Yes, they have good merch. Some nice pieces. But they're disorganized. Snooty. Expensive. And despite all that, they're convinced they're the best vendor at any con."

She shook her head, but smiled. "Different con, same drama. I certainly hope the store isn't directly involved. We get enough of a bad rap as geeks and nerds. We certainly don't need to add murder to the equation."

"No, we don't," Jonah said, taking the phone from her and tucking it away again. "As always, Nan, you've been invaluable."

She blushed, swished her hand in front of her face to downplay the compliment. "You stop it."

"I'll call you in a week or two about those *bokken* we were talking about."

"I'll be ready and waiting," she assured him, smoothing her skirts. "Oh, and here." She offered up two pens featuring the images of lusty wenches holding very large bastard swords.

"A little souvenir," she said with a wink. "We look forward to serving your future melee needs."

With the Magic Shoppe as a promising lead, we turned toward the exit and began maneuvering through the crowd. We'd nearly reached the door when I stopped short, grinned.

It seemed kismet that the last booth I'd see was an homage to Jakob's Quest, Jeff's favorite online role-playing game. Fifteen-foot-tall shelves were filled with green T-shirts featuring the Jakob's Quest logo, images of the characters in battle, and quotes I assumed were from the game. There were plastic figurines, plush dolls, hats, and even bags of Jakob's Munch trail mix, perfect for the gamer on the go.

I spied a bobblehead doll of Roland, the brown-haired warrior that Jeff preferred to play. I flicked the head, which, appropriately enough, bobbled wildly.

This had to go home with me. It was possible Jeff already had one; hell, there was a good chance he had one for each character in the game. But since his last office—my grandfather's basement—had been torched, he probably wouldn't argue overmuch with a new one.

"Tap the button."

I turned to find a curvy girl with a crop of bright red hair behind me. Along with her staff credentials, she wore a JQ-appropriate costume: green tunic and tights, soft brown leather boots.

"Okay," I said, and tapped the square button on the doll's square plastic base.

"Bravely into battle!" said a digitized male voice. "And victory for all."

"Oh my God, just take my money," I said, grinning as I imagined how much Jeff would love it and shoving a wad of bills from my pocket into her hand.

"I'll grab one that's boxed," the clerk said, moving back to the register.

"There you are." I turned, found Jonah grinning at me. "Have you suddenly become a gamer?"

I answered with another tap of the bobblehead's button. "Bravely into battle! And victory for all."

"That's my counter to that question."

"Nerd," he said with a grin.

"It's for Jeff. I couldn't pass it up."

The clerk returned with a plastic bag and change. I tucked the bag under my arm, stuffed the change into my pocket.

"If you're ready," Jonah said with a half bow, extending an arm toward the exit.

With an offer like that . . .

We reached the doors, were about to walk through, when a hand gripped my arm. I instantly reached for my katana, and then I looked at the grabber.

She wore black leather pants and a burgundy tank that showed a lot of cleavage. Her hair was dark and straight, with a fringe of bangs and a long ponytail. Her features were voluptuous: apple cheekbones, pert nose, lush lips. In her hand was a plastic katana.

"Dear God," I murmured, looking over the woman who apparently had tried to look like me.

"It's not a bad costume."

I made my way back to her face, found her expression appraising. Her lips were pursed as she looked me over.

"What?" I asked.

"The sword's a really nice touch—did you get it at Faire Makers?—but I'm not buying the attitude. It's not really Merit. You should be channeling your inner vampire sex warrior. Like this," she said, then put her hands on her hips, canted out one leg, and smiled sensually.

"What?" was all I could think to say.

"Maybe a little more cleavage, too."

"Cleavage."

She nodded, winked. "A vampire sex warrior can never show too much cleavage." She waved at a man who gestured to her a few feet away. "Good luck," she said, before sauntering to greet him.

Jonah joined me, and we watched silently as she stopped to

pose with a couple of teenagers in white T-shirts. They took pictures, and she signed their T-shirts and pressed lipsticky kisses to their cheeks while they stared down at her double-Ds.

"You have a doppelgänger," he said.

"That woman had the balls to tell me I didn't look like Merit."

"I doubt she had balls," Jonah said, smile wide as he took in her enviable curves. "And I told you people would think you're in costume."

I humphed. "I'm not in a Merit costume. I'm *Merit*—the actual Merit. I know how I dress."

"But you aren't Merit right now. Not really. Not stalwart, ass-kicking Cadogan Sentinel. You're in Diana Prince mode."

"Who's Diana Prince?"

"Wonder Woman," he said with a smile. "You're in an investigation frame of mind, and that shows in your face, your body language. Lose the jacket, unsheathe that sword, and give her the same ragey expression you're giving me right now, and she'll see exactly what you're made of."

I considered that. "She did say I had a vampire-sex-warrior quality."

"Since I like my very pretty face just the way it is, I'm going to leave that one alone."

"Wise choice," I said, and we left Merit 2.0 behind and headed for the escalator. "There could be Jonah doppelgängers walking around here, too, you know," I said, when he fell into step beside me.

"There could be." He smiled cheekily. "And they would undoubtedly be vampire sex warriors."

I decided it was best not to comment. "I think I need a drink," I said instead.

———

Ten minutes later, I was drinking the smallest bottle of water I'd ever seen, which Jonah had pulled from his glove box. Two good sips and I'd finished it off, but at least we'd made it back to his car, where I very much looked like Merit.

The most like Merit of anyone, as a matter of fact.

While he looked for directions to the Magic Shoppe, I checked in with the House, found the crew safe and Ethan ensconced in his office, which was fine by me. A slightly overworked vampire was a safe vampire in my book.

We were en route when my phone rang. It was Ethan, which made my heart stutter with nerves. I answered it immediately.

"Are you all right?"

"I'm fine," he said. "But I need you back at the House."

I felt Jonah's gaze snap to mine, probably because of the spike of magic I'd shoved through the car. "What's wrong?"

"Nothing yet," Ethan said. "But I expect that may change. Darius is in Chicago."

Jonah drove me back to the House. In addition to the patience-melting stop-and-go of Chicago's traffic, we debated the possibilities that awaited us at the House—and I interrogated Jonah just as Ethan had requested.

"By coming back to Chicago, you think he means to challenge Ethan?"

"That would be the obvious reason," I said. "Have you heard anything about his intentions? Any rumors about GP activity against the House?"

"Not a peep," Jonah said. "And I hope you know that I'd tell you."

He had a point. He'd tell me—but that didn't mean he wouldn't kill me in transit. I gripped the armrest as Jonah stopped short to avoid hitting the minivan in front of us. The cabbie behind us honked furiously.

"Sometimes," Jonah said, glancing into the rearview mirror and staring down the cabbie, "I wish I had a message board on my car—like the scrolling ones they use for stock reports. I'd tell this asshole I'll eat him for lunch if he doesn't lay off the horn. I have got to start taking the El."

"According to the *Canon*, Darius could challenge Ethan to a duel," I said. "Or a battle of wits."

"Like, they play bar trivia for the throne?"

"I guess," I said, wishing it would be that simple. I hadn't been to Temple Bar, the official Cadogan House watering hole, in much too long. I'd much rather squeeze into a booth with Ethan, Darius, and a gin and tonic than watch them square off with weapons, winner take all.

The thought of it made my stomach ache. *It was the note*, I thought. That goddamned note that Ethan wouldn't tell me about.

Jonah pulled in front of the House. "I've always liked the look of Cadogan," he said, gaze on the building. "Always thought it had good bones."

"It does. And good vampires. And hopefully they'll still be safe and sound at the end of the night."

"You want me to come in?"

I appreciated the gesture, but if Darius and the GP had turned their wrath on Cadogan House, I didn't want that spilling onto Jonah and his friends.

"Better not," I said, climbing out of the car. "But I'll keep you posted."

"Do," he said. "I'll call your grandfather, tell him about the Magic Shoppe. The more I think about it, the more I suspect they'll want to do that part of the investigation themselves. Warrants and legalities, and all that."

"Good thought. And thanks for that."

"That's what partners are for. Take care, Merit."

I nodded and closed the door, and Jonah drove off into the night.

CHAPTER SEVEN

DATE NIGHT!

Fear sitting over me like an ominous storm, I didn't take the time to make nice with the guards, but ran through the gate, into the House, and to Ethan's office.

The door was open. Luc, Malik, and Ethan were in the sitting area, tense magic in the air between them. Ethan had removed his tie and his jacket, and the first button of his shirt was undone. His hair was down but tucked behind his ears, and worry had tightened his forehead.

"Sentinel," Ethan said. "Come in and close the door."

It was times like this that could drive a vampire to drink, I thought, which explained why all three of them had glasses in hand.

"Scotch?" Luc asked, holding up his glass. Scotch floated over cubes of ice and a curlicue of lemon zest.

"No, thanks," I said, taking a seat beside Ethan on the tailored leather couch.

"Your trip?" he asked.

"Successful. Swords came from a place called the Magic Shoppe. Jonah's going to tell my grandfather."

Ethan cocked his head. "How can you tell?"

"The *tsubas*. Colored enameling, which is rare, and they're stamped 'MS' on the edge. The store orders them that way." I didn't bother with a segue. "Why is Darius coming to Chicago?"

"We aren't entirely sure," Ethan said, and began to lay it out. "Victor Cabot called a short while ago." Victor was the Master of New York City's Cabot House, one of the nation's oldest, situated in a grand dame of a building on the Upper East Side.

"Darius was in New York but didn't advise Victor. He was at dinner, happened to look out the window and see Darius across the street."

"Well," Malik said, crossing his arms. "I bet that's not something Victor sees every night."

"No, it isn't," Ethan agreed. "And he and Victor are friends, I'd say, which makes it even more curious. Victor followed him a bit, feigned a random meeting."

"On turf he'd probably already scoped out," Luc said, then glanced at me. "Victor has a history in, let's say, international espionage."

Vampirism took all kinds. I nodded, looked back at Ethan. "And what did Darius say?"

"Apparently very little. Their interaction was very brief, but Victor said he was acting oddly. Seemed, he said, dazed."

"Dazed?" Luc said. "What does that mean?"

Ethan lifted his hands. "I've no idea."

"Were any other GP members with him?" Malik asked.

In addition to Darius, there were five remaining members of the GP: Dierks, Danica, Edmund, Lakshmi, and Diego. Ethan counted Lakshmi and Diego as allies. Edmund had helped Harold Monmonth attack the House, so he was clearly an enemy. I didn't know Danica and Dierks to be enemies per se, other than because they were members of the GP. Which was probably enough.

"None, Victor said." Ethan crossed one leg over the other. "Nor was Charlie with him." Charlie was Darius's majordomo, and usually his travel companion. "But he had muscle. Three solid men."

Luc leaned forward, a glimmer of interest in his eyes. "Because of the challenge? Or because of the response?"

"Victor didn't know. He didn't tell Victor either way."

"If he's here to take you on, to respond to the challenge, why would he make a pit stop in New York?"

"That, Sentinel, is part of the question. Darius only told Victor he had business in the city. That same business, reportedly, is what's bringing him to Chicago."

"When is he scheduled to arrive?" I asked.

"He's already here."

I blinked. "He's here? And Victor just got around to telling you?"

"Like I said, they're friends. I think he didn't necessarily want to spill any pertinent details to Cadogan House, Darius's self-professed enemy. But he also knows we get things done. Victor used his own channels to investigate, whatever those might be, and wasn't satisfied by what he found. The only specific information was his plan to visit Chicago, and he only learned that because a member of the hotel staff overheard the muscle mentioning it."

"Espionage," Luc said, pointing at me, an I-told-you-so gesture.

"So Darius is in New York for reasons unknown," I summarized. "He didn't tell Victor Cabot, the resident Master and his buddy, that he was coming to town, barely spoke when Victor saw him on the street, didn't mention the challenge at all, and then hightailed it to Chicago."

Ethan nodded. "That appears to be the warp and weft of it."

"It's not necessarily surprising Darius didn't detail how he intends to respond to Ethan's challenge," Malik put in. "Loose lips sink ships, and all that. But it is odd he didn't mention the challenge at all. The GP is in a time of chaos—Darius's reign is in a time of chaos. He's facing a coup d'état, and in the home of an ally. You'd think he'd have at least broached the issue, griped about the challenge, leaned on Victor's shoulder."

"It is odd," Ethan agreed.

I blew out a breath. "So what do we do? Batten down the hatches? Get the House ready for a fight?"

Ethan rose, paced to the window across the room, used a fingertip to push aside the silk curtain. I wondered what he thought as he looked outside, if he weighed the future as he surveyed his domain.

"If I'm to be head of this organization—and I aim to be head of this organization—I cannot lurk in shadows waiting for others to make their moves. We strategize, we act, we move forward."

"Meaning?"

"Meaning, Sentinel, that if Darius will not respond to our challenge, we'll take our challenge to him."

We didn't know how long Darius would be in town, so we took a chance, climbed into Lindsey's SUV, and headed downtown. Luc drove, because he'd decided he was the only one who could "handle" the car in the event of "exigent circumstances."

That explained the aviator glasses, considering it was full dark.

In reality, I think Luc was hoping for a car chase that would have him spinning and drifting the vehicle like he was a stuntman in an action movie.

Fortunately for my nerves and my stomach, that did not happen.

According to Victor, Darius intended to say at the Portman Grand, a hotel on Michigan Avenue across from Millennium Park that practically reeked of old money. It had been built in Chicago's gilded age, a time when cattle and steel barons ruled the city. Lots of marble, gold accents, and dark fabrics.

We circled the block twice looking for a spot, lucked out the third time around, and grabbed a spot in front of a Chinese restaurant wedged between a Starbucks and a jewelry store.

"I presume no swords?" I said, thinking of the chichi hotel and the fact we'd be utterly conspicuous wearing them. We'd also present ourselves as an immediate threat to Darius.

"No swords," Luc agreed, then popped open Lindsey's glove box. Half a dozen holstered blades had been stuffed inside, a mini-armory in the comfort of an SUV. Vampires didn't generally care for small blades, but these were exigent circumstances. Since I hadn't noticed those the night before, he must have just loaded them.

"Do you have enough knives there, hon?" Lindsey asked, picking through the stack for a specimen she liked.

"Better safe than sorry." He reached over, pulled out a pink camouflage holster. "You like?"

"I do not." She patted one of the knee-high black boots she'd pulled over jeans. "Not my style, but I'm already prepped."

He nodded, glanced into the backseat at me and Ethan.

"I'm good," I said. Ethan had given me a sleek dagger that was, like Lindsey's, tucked into my boot.

But Ethan held out a hand. "Do you have anything slightly less pink?"

Luc pulled out a holster covered in rhinestones.

"I really feel like you've missed your target audience," Ethan said with amusement. "Or you've a feminine side we really haven't explored."

"I prefer you not explore my feminine side," Luc said, stuffing the rejected knives back into the box and pulling out a third. This one was much more Cadogan style: a glossy, curvy handle with nubby grips on the finger notches, and a sleek, double-sided blade honed to a gleaming and lethal point.

"Now, that will work," Ethan said, appreciation shining in his eyes. "And not a bit of glitter in sight."

"Not on that one," Luc said, closing the glove box again. "But I have others."

We climbed out of the car, checked phones and weapons. "You might want to go with him next time he stops for weapons," I whispered to Lindsey. "I understand Jonah uses FaireMakers."

"As opposed to Victoria's Scabbards?" Lindsey said, tugging the tops of her boots.

"My point exactly."

"All right, kids," Luc said. "We ready to undertake what will solely be an informational mission in which we go inside the hotel and gather information? Informationally."

"Wait," Lindsey said. "Wait. You're saying we *shouldn't* run in, arms waving, and yell that we're here to kidnap Darius?"

Yes. Vampires also used sarcasm to combat pre-op nerves.

"I think we play it more subtly," Luc said. "This is a public place, and a fancy one. Darius may have no love of humans, but he loathes bad press. He won't cause trouble in the hotel, so we aren't going to cause trouble in the hotel. We're going to keep an eye out for Darius, feign coincidence that we're in the same hotel, and make nice. Victor thinks something's odd about his manner. We'll give that theory a ride."

Lindsey raised her hand. "Shouldn't that be hypothesis?"

"I will give you the rhinestone knife."

The threat apparently was enough; she mimicked zipping her lips.

Luc developed the cover story, another feigned meeting with Darius: We were two couples out on the town, enjoying a night in Chicago, celebrating the approaching end of winter.

We walked inside the hotel, shoes clicking on the shiny stone floors. Giant vases of flowers sat inside the entrance on marble and gold tables, scenting the room with the fragrance of lilies and hyacinths. Men and women in impeccably tailored clothing sat in the lobby's conversation areas, or spilled out with the jazz from the bar across the room.

"Fancy," Luc said.

"Any sign of him?" Ethan asked, lifting my hand to his lips.

"Not that I can see." There were several humans and a possible River nymph, but not a vampire in sight.

Luc gestured toward the bar with his and Lindsey's linked hands. "Couples in love hit the bar, have a drink, and survey these lovely surroundings for the man who may or may not want to end us."

"Oh, I suspect he wants to end us," Ethan said, as we followed Luc and Lindsey. "But he may not want to do it here."

Lindsey ordered the drinks: gin and tonics for us, Scotch on the rocks for Luc and Ethan. And when she came back with a small bowl of steaming edamame dotted with flakes of sea salt, I decided not to complain that she'd assumed I'd be hungry.

We took seats beside men and women who looked like they'd spent the day cornering their respective financial markets. With our drinks and snacks, and a fabulous view of the Portman and its patrons, we awaited our former king.

It took seventeen minutes.

Darius emerged from the first elevator, tall and lean, with a narrow waist and broad shoulders. From a distance, he looked completely normal. His head was shaved, his features strong, his eyes bright blue. He wore a button-down shirt that matched his eyes, tucked into slim black slacks.

Two vampires walked closely behind him, the muscle Victor had referred to.

The one on Darius's left, the bigger of the two men, was an ugly son of a bitch. Bug-eyed, a nose squashed from one too many jabs, hard, square jaw. His was a face only a mother could love, but it was refreshing to have a bad guy whose soul matched his outward appearance. There'd been too many wolves in designer sheep's clothing lately.

While the main man was noticeably ugly, his associate on the right was remarkably plain. Light skin, brown hair, brown eyes. Medium height, medium build.

But their status as security was obvious—they scanned the room with flat eyes and suspicious expressions, and they vibrated from an abundance of weaponry.

"Guns," I said, sipping my drink. "Several of them."

"They look like the type," Luc said, his gaze on Lindsey, a hand on her shoulder, rubbing lightly as if they were two lovers anticipating a night of passion. "Shoulder harnesses, probably. And the classic tucked-into-the-back-waistband approach."

"Always turns me on when a man has a magnum in his pants," she said.

I barely bit back a laugh, so the sound came out as a strangled snort.

Ethan shook his head. "You two are no longer allowed on ops together."

"This is barely an op," Lindsey said. "It's more like an exploratory committee."

We watched as Darius took a seat in a low, square chair in the sitting area. His guards took up point beside him, each about six feet away.

"And I believe it's time to explore," Ethan said, sliding his glass forward and rising. "Merit, you're with me. Lucas—"

Luc nodded before Ethan could finish the order. "We're here, just in case. Do us all a favor, Liege, and try to keep yourself alive?"

"It's the second-highest thing on my list right now," Ethan grumbled. He straightened his jacket, his features transforming from operative to Master vampire. Haughtiness, arrogance, and utter confidence returned.

He strode toward Darius, and I fell into step behind him, the (ahem) meek Sentinel. The muscle watched us close in, lips curled in distaste. They let us approach to ten feet, then moved forward, hands outstretched like linebackers ready to stop Ethan's forward progress.

Ethan ignored them, kept his gaze on Darius, who hadn't yet seemed to realize that Ethan Sullivan, the Master vampire who'd challenged him for the throne, was standing only ten feet away.

That was, to say the least, odd.

"Darius," Ethan said. "It's good to see you again."

Darius looked up at him blandly. "Is it?"

This man clearly looked like Darius, from the dent in his chin to the perfect posture. But the Darius West I'd met would never have looked blandly at an enemy.

Ethan was momentarily taken aback, but he covered it up. "It is," he said, his tone unfailingly polite. "We're old friends, and old friends who don't get to speak as often as we might."

"I suppose . . . that's true enough. Where's your boon companion? Your Sentinel?"

"She's here," Ethan said. I walked forward, taking the hand that Ethan offered me.

His eyes, Ethan silently said. *Look at his eyes.*

Darius had been in the tall man's shadow, but as I moved forward, the man shifted, as did the light across Darius's face. His electric blue irises were narrow, dwarfed by wide and ink-black pupils. Whether by drugs or magic, something was affecting our former king. And deeply.

"Merit, it's good to see you again."

"It's good to see you, as well." A lie, and not. Whatever his issues with Ethan, this man was no threat to him right now. Not in this condition. Not with those eyes, that manner.

Darius nodded, but that was the end of his interest in me. His attention had flitted elsewhere. "If you'll excuse me, I have some business to attend to."

"Of course," Ethan said. "It was good to see you again."

Having been dismissed, we went back to the bar.

"He's not well," I murmured, taking a sip of my gin and tonic, relishing the cold, astringent punch. I needed it to wash away the weird encounter.

"He's not," Ethan said, rubbing his forehead. "I had no clue what I'd see tonight, but I don't think I expected that. That isn't Darius."

"How so?" Luc asked.

"He barely registered Ethan," I said. "And not in the arrogant, you're-beneath-me way. In the I'm-currently-drugged-out-of-my-gourd way."

"His eyes were dilated. His movements slow and stiff."

"Magic?" Lindsey asked.

"I don't know," Ethan said.

"If it's glamour," I asked, "wouldn't we have felt it?"

"That is another question to which I don't have an answer." Having drained his finger of Scotch, he turned to mine, took a sip, grimaced.

"It wasn't your drink," I reminded him, taking it back.

"Darius has more company," Luc said, and we casually glanced back. A silver-haired man approached Darius, a large leather envelope in hand, the type used to carry documents. He and Darius shook, and the muscle escorted the pair back to the elevators.

"I suppose that's the business," Lindsey said.

"We could tail him," Luc said, but Ethan shook his head.

"I don't like this, and I don't want us here, without preparation and backup, any longer than necessary."

Luc pulled bills from a long, narrow wallet, and placed them on the table. "That's fine by me. Let's get the hell back to the House."

Ethan glanced at me. *We need to know what was in that envelope,* he silently said.

Shall I contact the previously discussed tool in your arsenal? I asked.

He nodded, and I pulled out my phone, sent the necessary message: NEED YOUR EXPERTISE. PERHAPS A VISIT TO THE LIGHTHOUSE?

The Chicago Harbor Light, tall and white, stood sentinel at the edge of the breakwater that provided a harbor for boats on Lake Michigan. You could get in on foot—if you had the gumption to walk the quarter-mile stretch of rocks and riprap that tethered the lighthouse to the shore near Navy Pier.

The last time I'd tried it, the rocks had been slick and icy. Tonight, as Jonah and I stood in the darkness of the parking lot and stared them down, they were no longer icy. But they were still slick and dark.

"Might as well get this over with," I said, and stepped onto the first boulder.

Going was still slow as we hopped from stone to stone, pausing after each bit of progress to regain our balance.

"I'm surprised there's not a faster way out here," I said, arms outstretched at my sides as I worked to stay upright.

"There is. We could take the boat."

I stopped, stared back at him. "There's a boat?"

"Of course there's a boat."

"Then why are we doing this?"

He grinned back at me. "For the challenge." Jonah bobbled, momentarily losing his balance. Fortunately for him, he took a step, found purchase, managed not to fall into the drink. Which was good, because I wasn't going to help him.

"For the challenge," I mimicked, but I kept walking until we'd crossed the rocks and reached the concrete platform that held the lighthouse and the two small buildings that straddled it.

Jonah tapped a code on the keypad by the door, and we walked inside.

The lighthouse had been built in 1893 for the World's Columbian Exhibition but had been moved and renovated several times since then. The décor was sparse and hadn't been updated since at least the 1970s. But the décor wasn't the point—the three-hundred-and-sixty-degree windows and views of the city and lake were.

"You can all relax," Jonah said, hands lifted, to the handful of vampires who looked up as we entered. "I'm here. You're safe."

"You're here—and full of shit," said the vampire at the table across the room, whose muttonchop sideburns were immediately recognizable. Horace, an RG guard and Civil War veteran, wore a simple linen shirt and dark trousers. He turned, and his dark eyes widened. "And you've brought a guest."

"You're hilarious," Jonah said. "Merit, you remember Horace."

I nodded. "Hi."

There was suspicion in Horace's expression, maybe because he hadn't seen me here enough for his own comfort. Not enough to vet me, anyway.

"Is Matthew here?" Jonah asked.

"Basement." He cocked his head. "You need data?"

"This is your gig," Jonah said, prompting me.

"It's about Darius."

Horace nodded. "He's in Chicago. And you met with him today."

"It's about Darius. He's in Chicago. And we met with him today at the Portman Grand. He had a security team, and he met a man who appeared to be carrying some papers."

"You interact with him?" Horace asked.

"Ethan and I both. And he seemed completely off. Polite, but barely communicative. Dilated pupils."

"Glamour?" Horace asked.

Glamour was an odd side effect of the magic that spilled from us. We couldn't create magic—not like Mallory or Catcher—but we could manipulate the magic that escaped from us. It was, maybe not coincidentally, a manipulative magic. The ability to nudge, subtly or otherwise, people to do what we wanted. I had some immunity to it, but I also couldn't make the magic myself.

"It was a thought. But we didn't feel any magic. Nothing beyond the usual, anyway. Victor Cabot said Darius also acted strangely when he was in New York, although that interaction was brief. Darius apparently didn't mention the GP, the challenge, or anything else to Victor while he was there."

Horace sat back in his chair, linked his hands together on his chest, and rocked. The chair squeaked beneath him. "He and Victor were close."

"That's what I hear," I said with a nod. "You'd think you'd talk to your allies if you were about to rush Chicago and kick aside a would-be challenger for the throne."

"So you think he's not here to challenge Ethan?"

"I have no idea what he's going to do. That's precisely the problem. I've met Darius before. He runs hot. I'd have expected him to be pissed off by the challenge, insulted by it. Not to play nice with Ethan. Darius has many irritating qualities, but being coy isn't one of them.

"I don't like the GP under the best of circumstances," I added. "But I especially don't like it when the head of the GP is acting oddly, and my House—and my Master—are on the line."

Horace leaned back again; the chair squeaked. "You know being in a relationship with Ethan puts you in an awkward position regarding the Guards."

I kept my gaze steady. "It's only awkward if he's elected and becomes an asshole. The first one's possible. The second isn't."

"Absolute power corrupts absolutely."

"And Napoleon might have been better behaved if Josephine had been a member of the RG."

Jonah smiled at me. "You had that one in the chamber, ready to fire."

I shrugged. "Frankly, I'd ask the same question if I was you. It's a fair question. But my answer's the truth. I've been around money and power for most of my life. It doesn't control me."

"Touché," Horace said.

I nodded in acknowledgment. "I don't know how long Darius'll be here, or what he's planning to do. But he's in my territory, and I'd appreciate any information you can provide."

Horace rose, the chair rocking rhythmically in his absence, its *squeak* ringing across the room. "Then let's get to it," he agreed, and gestured to the metal spiral staircase that stood in the center of the room.

The staircase was narrow, barely wide enough to accommodate the guys' wide shoulders. I'd known it went up but hadn't noticed it also spiraled down into the floor—and presumably beneath the lakebed.

We spiraled down for several seconds and what felt like several stories, emerging into a concrete room that stretched at least the length of a football field. The floor was glossy, the walls scored in what looked like a really large, concrete version of soundproofing. And down the middle of the room was a series of black, glossy cabinets. The room was chilly, and it hummed with energy.

"Holy shit," I murmured, staring at the space.

"Welcome to the sparkplug's data center," Horace said.

"Sparkplug?"

"The lighthouse," Jonah said. "It's a nickname for this particular style."

"This is . . . impressive," I said, except that I wasn't sure what I was looking at. "What, exactly, am I looking at?"

"Two centuries of data," Horace said. "Correspondence, GP rulings, intelligence, financials. They're stored on drives with double tape backups."

"That's a lot of information."

"It is," Horace said. "And that's why we have Matthew."

He gestured to the lone desk in the room, a long glass table on which sat a single computer terminal. The chair was occupied by a vampire who looked like he'd been changed in his early twenties. He had golden brown skin, a wide mouth, and glasses with thick black frames. He wore a gray hoodie with the green Jakob's Quest logo across the front.

Dear God, I thought. The RG had a Jeff.

"Matthew Post, this is my partner, Merit," Jonah said. "Matthew's a rogue, so he gets both of his names, the lucky bastard."

"Hi," Matthew said, fingers flying over the keys.

"Hi," I said. "Jakob's Quest fan?"

"Bravely into battle," Matthew said, eyes on the screen.

I grinned. I knew this one. "And victory for all."

He paused, looked back at me, appraised, nodded. "Cool."

And with four simple words, I'd passed Matthew Post's Test of Acceptability. I counted that as an achievement.

"We run a pretty lean shop. Matthew's our analyst and IT expert. He responds to requests for information—like yours— and analyzes data for anomalies if they arise. We rely primarily on human intelligence," Horace said. "But Matthew and the data center are crucial to our operation. Matthew, Darius is apparently in Chicago, after a trip to NYC. What's the GP's latest traffic?"

Matthew's long fingers worked the buttons like a pianist, each movement smooth, dancerly, and precise.

"Nothing unusual," he said, scanning the data he'd pulled up on the screen. "Rules and regulations have been issued. Payments have been made. House tithes have been collected. Operations appear normal."

"Go a level deeper," Horace suggested.

"Running anomaly check," Matthew said. This one was all business, and not nearly as keen on the witty small talk as Jeff. IT folks came in all flavors.

"Hey, anomalies," Matthew announced after a moment.

We all moved closer. "What anomalies?" Horace asked.

"Not on the surface," Matthew said. "The trust accounts are normal. Any deviation is standard. And so are the operating accounts."

I decided this wasn't the time to ask about the ethics of our sneaking into the GP's bank accounts.

"But?" Horace prompted.

"The American Houses' operating subaccounts are off. The GP keeps an account in each city with Houses. A portion of the Houses' tithes go into the subaccounts, which the GP distributes back to the Houses for renovations, special projects, what have you. There are withdrawals in some of them."

My blood began to hum. That was a definite bump. "How large? And which ones?"

"Boston, New York . . . and Chicago. Six point eight mil and change in total."

"Darius has been in at least two of those cities recently."

Jonah looked at me. "Did Victor say where he'd been before he got to New York?"

"He didn't. I don't know if he knew." But I could find that out easily enough. I pulled out my phone, showed it to Horace and Matthew. Candor seemed the best bet considering their doubts about me. "I'm going to check with Ethan. Any objections?"

"Do it," Horace said, and I sent a quick message, kept my phone in hand to await Ethan's response.

"Where's the money going?" Jonah asked, leaning on the desk beside Horace.

Matthew clicked keys. "Zurich. Two numbered Swiss accounts. Bulk of the money was moved into one account. The other one received"—he paused as he looked it up—"a forty-thousand-dollar transfer."

Jonah and Horace exchanged a glance. "Ten bucks says the smaller account is a payoff."

Horace paused, nodded. "I'll take those odds," he said, and they shook on it.

"So, to summarize," I said, "we think Darius is visiting U.S. cities, transferring money out of the GP's local accounts, and funneling the money back into Swiss bank accounts." I looked between Jonah and Horace. "For what purpose? Is he going to just take the money and run?"

"Why else would you open a Swiss bank account?" Horace asked.

It was a good point. "Still—why the travel? If he wanted to secret the money out, why not just have it wire transferred?"

"Because it's not allowed," Jonah said. "There are strict restrictions on taking money out of the GP subaccounts intended to protect the Houses."

When we all looked at him, he shrugged. "We had to learn the rules when they firebombed the House. We got money from the Chicago subaccount to get into the new building and start the renovations on the old one."

"So what are the restrictions?" I asked.

"Wire transfer is fine for any money going from the subaccounts to the Houses, because they consider it their money. But you can't transfer money to any other recipient electronically; they'll only issue it by cashier's check."

"Which means somebody has to be here to pick up the check," I said.

"Yep. The accounts are large enough, and Darius is wealthy enough, that he probably doesn't even have to go to the bank to do it."

I thought of the man with the leather portfolio. "So the banker comes to him, even after hours."

"Exactly."

"And where's the rest of the GP? How is no one else noticing this?"

"Because the primary accounts look fine on the surface," Matthew pointed out.

"The local accounts work like escrow—holding the Houses' tithes until they're periodically moved into other accounts."

Jonah stood up again. "Darius could have told them he was coming here to prepare a response to the challenge," he said. "He's head of the GP. He's allowed to visit the cities that hold his Houses."

True enough, but still odd. And completely out of character. Since when did Darius, who was essentially the king of North American and Western European vampires, sneak around with finances, or anything else? For that matter, since when did he show up in Chicago and make nice with Ethan?

My phone vibrated, and I looked down at it. "Boston," I said. "Darius was in Boston."

"Three cities, three transfers," Matthew said.

"The Swiss accounts," I said. "What can you tell us about them?"

"Pretty much nothing," Matthew said. "What little identifying information the bank collects is encrypted beyond even our capabilities—which is the point of having a Swiss account."

I nodded. And I didn't doubt Matthew's or the RG's capabilities, but I had a family member with lots of money and lots of financial connections.

"Can I get the account numbers? The transaction numbers?"

Matthew glanced back at me. "You got friends in Switzerland?"

"Not exactly. But I may have someone who knows someone in Switzerland."

"Worth a shot," Horace said, nodding as I took photographs of the numbers to send to my source later.

"Thank you."

Horace crossed his arms, looked at me. "What will Ethan do now?"

"When I tell him Darius has stolen nearly seven million dollars from the Houses? What do you think he'll do?"

Horace smiled, but there was no joy in it. "I imagine Ethan Sullivan will do what Ethan Sullivan does best: He'll go to war."

I couldn't decide whether I found that flattering or not.

+ ⊷≣⊷ +

CHAPTER EIGHT

THE SEVEN-MILLION-DOLLAR MAN

"Nearly seven million dollars," Ethan said. He sat at the end of the conference table in his office.

Although we'd normally plan an op in the aptly named Ops Room, this particular topic was sensitive enough that we'd convened in Ethan's office and gotten Victor Cabot on the phone.

"Your thoughts?" Victor asked.

"As you noted, we found his behavior abnormal. I've known Darius a long time. There's no love lost between us, not that you'd know it today, as he seems to have dissociated completely."

"He was shaken by Michael Donovan's attack," Luc said. "We've known that haunts him. Maybe it's vampiric post-traumatic stress disorder."

"That could be part of it," Victor said. "But I don't think that's enough."

"'Dazed' was the word you used," Ethan reminded him. "What are you thinking?"

"Drugged? Magicked? Frankly, I don't know." He sighed, audible even across the distance. "The theft suggests a motive, if indeed someone is directing his behavior. My fear, of course, is what happens when the thief is done with Darius, either because he's caught or because he has no further need for him."

"If the perpetrator has stolen millions of dollars he doesn't want anyone to know about, then Darius becomes a risk," I said.

"Precisely," Victor darkly said. "How did you learn about the transfers?"

"Our Sentinel has connections. She wishes to protect her source, but we have no doubt the information is reliable."

"None?" Victor asked.

"None," Ethan replied. "It also explains what we saw in the hotel: Darius was visited by a man in a suit who apparently had papers."

"And we don't know to whom the money is being transferred?"

"We do not," Ethan said. "Only that it's going to two Swiss accounts—a primary account and what appears to be a smaller, secondary account."

That reminded me that I hadn't yet done my due diligence. I grabbed my phone, sent the photographs of the accounts to my father, requested any information he could obtain about the individuals who'd opened them.

"Where is the rest of the GP while all this is going down?" Malik asked. "While the transfers are being made?"

"I understand the transfers would be difficult to see on the surface," I said. "The House accounts are subaccounts, so you'd have to go down a level to even look."

"And they could be in on it," Luc said. "The members of the GP have the most knowledge about the GP accounts. If they think Darius is on the way out, they may have seen this as their best opportunity for financial gain."

Luc frowned. "And none of them have noticed Darius is missing?"

"Technically, he's not missing," Malik put in. "He's visiting cities in which there are GP Houses. And he's in Chicago, where he's been challenged. Not unusual that he'd do any of those things."

Ethan nodded. "I suspect that's precisely what they'd think. They'd give him space to act as he feels appropriate for the GP, especially considering the current turmoil."

"What a mess," Malik said, rubbing his forehead.

"I may be able to assist," Victor said. "I have a team. Men who take care of . . . special problems that may crop up from time to time." He cleared his throat. "In anticipation of trouble, I sent them to Chicago at sunset."

Ethan's brows lifted with obvious interest. "Oh?"

"He was only in New York for thirty-six hours. In the event you had to act, I wanted to help you act quickly. I apologize for not advising you of their presence. I hoped they'd prove unnecessary, that I was worrying without cause. But I find myself glad that I arranged it.

"I'm not suggesting that I support your challenge, or the overthrow of my king." Victor's voice was careful, his words obviously measured. "But this cannot stand. Darius cannot take our funds for his own personal use, presuming that's what's happening here. And if these actions are not his own, a wrong is being done to him, and I cannot support that."

Ethan leaned toward the phone, as if he was speaking directly to Victor. "I have no doubt of your loyalty to the GP or to Darius, Victor. Nor would I feel the need to advise anyone of your participation, unless you wish it."

"I thank you," Victor said, with obvious relief. "They're standing by, and near the House in the event you need them. I'd hoped they'd prove unnecessary, but as it is . . ."

"We'd appreciate their expertise," Ethan said. "I presume they'll understand the need for covertness? And for keeping civilians safe?"

"Of course," Victor said. "But a reminder never hurts, and I'll do so. Be careful, Ethan. Your issues with the GP and Darius notwithstanding, take care not to make things worse than they already are."

"This is no longer about the challenge, Victor. This is about Darius. And as far as I'm concerned, it's now a rescue mission."

"We should tell the other GP members," Victor said. "I'm not particular about who—if you believe Darius has a particular ally. But a division between the American and European Houses has already opened, and I do not wish to exacerbate the situation."

I can handle that, I silently told Ethan. Jonah and Lakshmi were friends of a sort; she had a crush on him, and he wasn't interested. But they'd communicated, and she'd reached out to me before through that relationship. I could do so again now. So while Victor, Ethan, and the others discussed plans, I pulled out my phone, sent Lakshmi a message.

DARIUS IN CHICAGO. REMOVING MONEY FROM HOUSE ACCOUNTS, POSSIBLY IN DANGER. OP IMMINENT.

It took only seconds for her to respond. NO TRANSFERS AUTHORIZED. I'LL ARRANGE TRAVEL. PROCEED WITH CAUTION.

It was, for our purposes, as good as permission. I passed the phone to Ethan.

"Lakshmi has been apprised," Ethan said, glancing at the screen and handing the phone back to me. "And, more importantly, she has not objected."

Malik, Lindsey, and Luc stared at me, at the phone, undoubtedly surprised I could make that kind of contact.

"That will have to do for now," Victor said.

They said their good-byes, and Ethan pressed a button on the phone to end the call. Then he sat back in his chair, ran his fingers through his hair. "It appears we'll soon be storming the Portman Grand. Lucas, find out Darius's room, get plans. Get plans for the entire building, if you can find them. I'll go, with Merit, Lindsey, Luc, and the Cabot team. Malik, you'll have the House."

Malik nodded. "Do you have any concern about Victor's people? That this is part of some larger charade?"

"I wouldn't be Master if I didn't have doubts," Ethan grimly said. "But I believe Victor's solid. He supports the GP, but he's direct. If he had issues with me or the House, he'd let me know about them."

He looked at me. "You might call your grandfather. Considering we'll be in a public building, and the risk of trouble, it would be good to give him a heads-up."

I nodded, pulled out my phone, and stepped into the sitting area to have a little bit of privacy.

"Baby girl," he said. "I'm glad you called. I've got some news for you."

"Oh?"

"There's been a break in the Jacobs case. Jonah told us about the Magic Shoppe, and Detective Stowe stopped by. They recognized the *tsubas*. They were purchased by a Magic Shoppe employee named Mitzy Burrows. Arthur confirmed she and Brett dated briefly. Stowe went to interview her, but her house was empty. It looked like someone left in a hurry."

"She fled."

"That's what they believe. They talked to neighbors, who said they heard yelling. Possibly her breakup with Jacobs was unpleasant. The CPD's looking for her.

"Additionally, the ME found drugs in Jacobs's system. A pretty good dose of Rohypnol. More than enough to knock him out."

"That explains the lack of defensive wounds."

"It does," my grandfather agreed. "We'll keep looking on our end, let you know if we find anything else."

"I appreciate it. Unfortunately, I called about something else. Darius is in trouble, and we have to run an op. We'll be downtown at the Portman Grand. We wanted you to know just in case . . ."

My grandfather sighed. "I don't suppose there's any point in asking you to wait for CPD support? Or for a SWAT team?"

"I think not. This is a vampire matter, and the vampires want to handle it. And there may be magic involved; we don't know how that might affect humans. We'll do everything we can to stay inconspicuous and to keep the humans safe. We just wanted you to know."

"I appreciate it," he said, then paused. "How dangerous is this likely to get?"

"They have muscle," I said. "But I understand we're basically getting an advance team from a New York House. Ethan made it clear civilian injuries are not an option."

"Good," my grandfather said, murmuring the way he did when he considered and planned.

"I'm going to send the van," he said. "We'll stay a couple of blocks away, but I want to be nearby if anything goes wrong."

Relief surged through me. I didn't want my grandfather in the middle of this war, but I was glad to know he'd be close. "Thanks, Grandpa. We'll keep you posted."

"Do, Merit. And good luck to you."

I messaged Jonah about our plan, and advised the group about our backup Ombuddies. Half an hour later, Victor's team stood in our foyer: three muscled men in black thermal shirts and fatigue pants.

One stood in front of the others, his skin deeply tanned, his shoulders broad, his waist narrow. His nose was a hawkish wedge above a dark, full beard. Two other men stood beside him with nearly the same coloring. I'd have guessed they were brothers, and considering their physiques, they certainly had the look of special forces soldiers.

"Ethan Sullivan," he said, moving forward with an out-stretched hand.

"Ryan," said the man in front. He gestured toward his team. "Cord, Max. Victor indicated you'd spoken." Ryan's voice carried a faint accent that I would have pegged as Texan.

Ethan nodded, then gestured to us. "Malik, Second. Lindsey, guard, and Merit, Sentinel. Our captain, Luc, is pulling plans for the hotel."

"Excellent," Ryan said. "And it's nice to meet you. Is there a place we can talk?"

"My office," Ethan said, and led us back there. A tray of bottled water and blood had been brought in and now sat in the middle of the conference table.

"Help yourselves," Ethan said, pointing to it, "if you need to refresh."

Luc walked in with paper in hand. Recognizing that the team had been assembled, he closed the door behind him, spread the paper on the table.

Ryan extended a hand and introduced himself and his team.

Luc responded in kind, then looked at Ethan. "Darius is in

the Burnham suite on the twenty-seventh floor. It's the penthouse."

"How'd you confirm that?" Ethan asked.

"The elevator Darius used—it's private, only goes to one floor."

"Private elevator," Ryan said, looking over the plans. "Tricky to only have one exit, but handy in reducing collateral civilian damage."

"Yes, and my thoughts exactly. Civilian damage is not an option." Luc flipped around the paper and pointed to a layout of the hotel's first floor. "Private elevator's the first in the bank of elevators." He pointed to the back of the hotel, where a loading dock and staff entrances were situated. "There's a route from the back entrance—a staff hallway—that opens onto the main floor just behind the private elevator."

"Could be a guard on the elevator," Ryan said.

Luc nodded. "Wasn't one earlier tonight, but that doesn't mean the muscle hasn't wised up." He pointed at the vendor entrance. "We'll want bodies here to secure the exit, someone to handle the man on the elevator and guard it until we come down, and a team to go upstairs."

"And when we get there?" Ethan asked, moving around to stand behind Luc and get a better look at the floor plan.

"The suite has five rooms—living room with a kitchen area, two bedrooms, two bathrooms. We can divide up, check the rooms."

"In addition to securing Darius," Ethan said, "we'll want to look for the papers that might have been in that portfolio. We'll assume it was related to the monetary transfers, but let's be certain if we can."

Ryan nodded. "We make this as quick as possible, with minimal collateral damage. We find him, evaluate him, and get him out. Violence only if necessary. Darius West is still our king."

"Understood," Ethan said. "But you'll have heard from Victor, and we verified today that he's under the influence of someone, or something. He may not act like your king tonight, but your enemy."

"Yeah," Ryan said. "And that's really pissing me off." He looked at each of us. "I understand you've got politics to consider. I propose we go in first, your team behind. My man will take out the guard on the elevator; you assign people to secure the escape route."

Ethan looked to Luc, who nodded. "Lindsey and I will take the exit, keep it secure. You and Merit take the penthouse; you know Darius better."

"Max, you'll have the elevator," Ryan said. "Cord and I will go up with Merit and Ethan. We've got weapons, if you'd like to use them."

"We have an arsenal," Luc said, "but we're katana people. Especially in a public place where bullets won't be friendly—katanas are our comfort zone."

Ryan nodded. "We prefer handguns, but we're cognizant of the risks. We'll be careful around your humans."

The deal was sealed, earpieces were passed out, and nerves began to build.

Cord, Ryan, and Max were clearly men with experience, savvy, technical know-how.

They were also men who'd driven to Cadogan House in a white panel van with MINELLI'S CATERING stenciled along the side.

Luc looked at it, hands on his hips. "Minelli's Catering?"

Cord pulled open the side door, rolled it back so we could get in. "People are less suspicious—they poke around a lot less—when we've got vinyl on the van."

"Good plan," Luc said. "I guess food comforts people."

Lindsey slid me a sideways glance.

"No snark on an op," I reminded with a pointed finger, and climbed inside.

The ride was quiet, intense. Nervous magic filled the small space, as our seven-person team prepared to liberate a Master vampire—the master of them all—from his magical captivity in the penthouse of a Chicago hotel.

What could go wrong there? For starters, we could be injured or killed, we could hurt civilians, we could piss off the GP even further.

I glanced at Ethan. One arm was crossed over his chest; the other rubbed the bridge of his nose as he stared out the front window. What did he think about at times like this? Darius? His challenge? The House and its vampires? All of those things, probably, tempered by the secret he was holding and the adrenaline that was probably beginning to flow as the operation drew nearer.

I tucked my arm through his, leaned my head against his shoulder. We weren't yet balanced, but for now, we'd be unconditional allies.

Thirty minutes later, we pulled into the service area behind the Portman Grand. It was late—too late for parties—and not early enough for the next day's food deliveries. Another bit of luck for us.

The Cabot team, Luc, and Lindsey climbed out of the van.

"A minute," I said, putting a hand on Ethan's arm, keeping him inside until the vehicle was empty.

"Is there anything else I need to know before we go in there?"

Ethan's eyes flattened. "About?"

"That note."

This time, his eyes flashed. "No."

I watched him for a moment, gauged his honesty. That he wouldn't offer more—explain more—knifed at my gut, but I believed that it wasn't relevant to today.

"Okay," I said. "Be careful out there. Don't play the hero."

A corner of his mouth lifted just slightly. "Don't I usually give you that speech?"

"You do. But this is my turn." I put my hands on his face. We'd hardly talked today, hadn't had time or, considering our current issues, the inclination. But I wanted—needed—a moment to look at him, to see his face.

"You're mine as much as you are the House's. Whatever stands between us right now, I prefer you in one piece."

His eyes softened, and he leaned forward, pressed his lips to mine, offered a slow and lingering kiss. "Let's both be careful. And let's both get out of this car, because people are beginning to stare."

I looked up, found Luc peering, narrow eyed, into the tinted windows. He tapped on the glass. "Let's go, Romeo and Juliet."

"Let's get out before he starts quoting *Die Hard* again," Ethan said.

A solid choice.

I stepped outside into the cool air, belted on my katana, adjusted my ponytail. The Cabot House guys inserted daggers into their boots and pulled on shoulder harnesses for handguns.

When everyone was outfitted and weaponized, we circled together.

"We go in," Ryan said, "and we look like we belong."

"Cover?" Cord asked.

Luc smiled. "I've got this one. He's in the penthouse suite, so the staff know who he is. They'll have been briefed." He gestured at his clothes. "We're vampires, with swords. We're part of his security detail. Anyone questions you—question them back."

"Nice," Ryan said, and he and Luc exchanged manly nods of approval, already the best of friends.

"And now that we've honored the bromance," Cord said with a wide grin, "let's get this under way."

We formed a line, moved swiftly and silently to the vendor door. Ryan, Max, and Cord, then me and Ethan, Luc and Lindsey.

Adrenaline rushed through me, and fear evaporated. We were here now. There was no turning back, no running scared. Most important, there was no more waiting, only forward progress. It felt glorious to move, to act, to concentrate on the task at hand.

Your vampire is showing, Sentinel, Ethan said, with what I took to be awe in his voice.

Waiting is the hardest part, I responded. *I may not be a great fighter, not yet, but I'll be damned if the op's not better than the anticipation.*

Spoken like a soldier, he said.

After a year of training, I'd better sound like one.

The lock on the vendor door was busted; the door opened easily. Fist raised to keep us still, Ryan eased the door open, looked inside, then motioned us forward.

We slipped into the hallway behind him, left Luc at the exit to guard the van, ensure we had a way to get out if things went bad.

The staff hallway was unburdened by décor or color: drab gray walls, drab gray floor. Easy to clean, but nothing to look at. The hallway branched several times here and there, and I wished I'd brought flags—or bread crumbs—to mark the way.

We followed Ryan in silence, stopping at another raised fist. He pointed toward the door we'd reached, LOBBY stenciled in all caps across the gray steel.

Ryan pointed to Lindsey, then at the ground, signaling her to stay here, to protect this portion of our escape route. She nodded, her expression as steely eyed as that of the man in fatigues who was leading us. Lindsey might have been high maintenance, but she was a soldier to the bone.

I waited until our eyes met, mouthed, *"Good luck,"* to her.

She winked in response.

Ryan pulled open the door, peered into the lobby, then signaled with his index finger. One guard on the elevator.

He was Max's responsibility.

As Ryan held the door, Max slipped into the hallway. My heart thudded in my ears, thunderously loud, as we stood in the dim hallway, waited for our sign.

There was a soft thud, a soft shuffle, and Max's back appeared in the doorway again, pulling the man on the elevator into the hallway. His breathing was heavy but steady, his head rolling on his neck as Max dragged his deadweight into a service area. Ethan helped Max zip-tie his hands and feet, then pull him into a corner near gas and plumbing access pipes. If our luck held, he'd stay there, conked, until we were long gone.

And now that the man was down, it was our turn to act.

Ryan pulled open the door again, mere centimeters this time, watched the lobby as footsteps sounded, passed. And then, as fast as lightning, he signaled, and we moved. Single file, one after another, silently from the hallway door to the bank of elevators. Ryan pulled a black card from his pocket, flashed it over the access panel, and the doors to the private car slid open.

We funneled in behind him, and Max flashed a thumbs-up, watching the doors close just before the elevator whisked us up and away.

Pop music played cheerily in the elevator as the lights above the door flashed the floor numbers.

"So the Cubs," Ryan said, scratching absently at a spot on his shoulder. "Good team this year, or . . . ?"

Ethan nudged me gently. "Um, yeah, solid," I said. "We've got a pretty deep lineup right now. You a Yankees fan?"

"Go, Yanks," Ryan said.

"Yanks rule all," Cord said behind him, with the staccato tone of a military man.

I shook my head. "And just when I was beginning to like you two."

The floors ticked upward. Twenty-three, twenty-four, twenty-five . . .

"Ready," Ryan said, and the elevator dinged, the door sliding open, revealing a spacious foyer with a marble floor and a wall of windows that overlooked the lake.

A man in jeans and a sport coat, another unfamiliar guard, jumped up from a stool beside the elevator, pivoted to face us.

"Hey, Jack, did you remember the drinks? Fucking mini-bar's—"

He stopped short, realizing we weren't the other guards, who'd apparently gone on a food run.

"Shit," he said, reaching clumsily inside his jacket for a weapon, but Ryan was prepared—and Ryan was faster. He swept the man's legs, unbalanced him, and snagged him in a choke-hold.

He's really efficient, I silently told Ethan, as he flipped and zip-tied guard number two.

And remarkably quiet, Ethan said. I wasn't sure if that was a compliment—or a concern.

The guard addressed, Ryan looked back at us, motioned us to the right, where a wide doorway led to the living room. The bedrooms would be beyond it, again to the right, as the penthouse circled around half the building's top floor.

We formed our line like kindergartners at recess—Ryan, Cord, Ethan, me—and moved silently into the living room.

The room was dark, empty. Ambient light from the surrounding high-rises streamed in through another floor-to-ceiling window. Marble floors and warm, taupe walls were a canvas for pops of color from a crimson sectional sofa and accent rugs. There were no signs of life.

Without a sound but my pulse—which still pounded in my ears like ocean waves—we crept through the great room to the hallway beyond. Pin lights illuminated architectural prints and provided a bit of light in the otherwise dark space, which split off into the two bedrooms.

Ryan and Cord slipped into the first, and we slipped into the second.

Where the hell is Darius? I asked Ethan.

Possibly gone. He could have run or been told to.

I didn't want to think about gone, not when we were so close to putting closure on our issues with Darius West, so I did what a good investigator would do. I checked the trash can (empty), the drawers (empty), the closet (empty) for any sign of the documents Darius had executed, or any other hint about who'd been manipulating him. Ethan checked the mattress and between the towels in the bathroom for any sign, then walked back into the living room and checked that room as well.

A creak behind me had me spinning around, katana in hand and at the ready.

The curtain on the left side of the wall billowed, its hem rising like the swirling skirt on a dancer, and a breeze blew in.

I blew out a breath, chastised myself for making monsters in the dark, and took a step forward.

I pushed aside the curtain, revealed an open doorway. A cool spring wind blew from the terrace beyond it.

There's a terrace, I told Ethan. *The door's open. I'm going outside.*

There hadn't been a terrace on the plans Luc had found. Maybe it had been a later addition, an afterthought to make the enormous, marble-floored penthouse even more desirable to the people who preferred their marble-floored penthouses with terraces.

Adjusting the grip on my katana, I walked outside. Moonlight glinted off the surrounding high-rises, casting a glow across the stone floor, the giant urns that lined the stone rail . . . and the lone, lean figure that stood on the other end of the balcony.

I felt Ethan move behind me, held up a fist to stop him, and pointed out the tall, lean vampire who stood in the wedge of moonlight.

Let's say hello, shall we, Sentinel?

Ethan walked forward, one hand on his katana handle, then passed me as he moved closer to Darius.

If he knew we were there, he didn't acknowledge it. His hands were braced on the thick stone parapet that sat on turned-stone balusters.

"Darius," Ethan said, quietly stepping forward.

He looked back at Ethan, eyes widening with an increment of surprise. "Ethan. It's good to see you again."

There was no obvious untruth, no apparent duplicity. Darius seemed completely earnest and by all accounts was happy to see Ethan again. That was the part that rang false. But we already knew something was wrong. The issue now was fixing it—and isolating the rest of the issue.

"You as well."

I felt the team moving quietly behind me, creating gentle ripples in the magic that enveloped us all as they surrounded us.

"Perhaps we should go inside?" Ethan politely asked.

Darius frowned. "We might as well. A chill wind is blowing."

That was hardly his only problem.

CHAPTER NINE

WORTH HIS SALT

Darius sat in an armchair, feet on the floor, hands together in his lap. His posture was as meek as his attitude.

"I don't want to take him out of here until we're sure it's safe," Ryan said. "This looks like magic to me, and there could be a fail-safe."

"Agreed," Ethan said. "But let's be fast about it. Whoever's done this could be on his way."

"And we still haven't seen the two guards we saw in the lobby earlier today."

"Agreed," Ryan said, glancing between Ethan and Cord. "Since he's still my Sire, I'll take the first stab, if you don't mind."

Ethan nodded, and Ryan pulled up a chair in front of Darius.

"Sire. I'm Ryan, New York's Cabot House, NAVR Number Three."

Darius nodded. "Ryan."

"Could you tell us how you came to be here?"

Darius frowned. "Here? I came here from London."

"Why?"

"Business," Darius said, crossing one leg over the other, smoothing the fabric over his knee.

That Darius was here on unspecified "business" was becoming a common refrain; he'd told Ethan and Victor the same thing.

"Business?" Ryan asked.

"Transactions that required my attention."

"I see," Ryan said. "And what was the nature of those transactions?"

"Financial," Darius said. "For the good of the Presidium and its Houses."

"Oh?" Ryan asked. "For new projects?"

"For the good of the Houses," Darius said again, parroting the phrase like he'd read it from a script. And if someone was working him magically, suggesting his thoughts and emotions, that might just be true.

"Thank you, Sire," Ryan said, rising. "If you'll excuse me for just a moment?"

Darius gave him a regal nod, picked another mote of dust from his knee, linked his long fingers together.

Ryan rose, pointed toward Cord, then Darius, assigning him to guard the king. Then he gestured the rest of us into the hallway between the bedrooms.

"Magic," Ryan said when we were assembled.

I didn't feel any glamour around us now, but that didn't mean it wasn't here. It might have been low-grade but still insidious.

"There's no one else here but us," Ethan said.

"Yeah," Ryan said, "but there aren't any other options. If no one's here, they've figured out a way to transmit glamour to another location."

"Like an antenna?" I asked. "Is that even possible?"

"Consider the context and the circumstances," Ethan said.

"Does anything seem impossible at this point?" He scanned the floor, walls, ceiling.

"Assuming such a thing is possible," I said, "why isn't it affecting us?"

"It could have been calibrated for Darius."

"So if it's not working on us, and we can't feel it, how do we find it?"

"It's still magic," Ryan said. "We can all feel magic, so we look for it that way." Ryan glanced at his watch. "If we're going to do it, we need to do it quickly. Cord and I will take the bedrooms. You look in here."

My senses were acute, sometimes distractingly so. I usually kept mental barriers in place so I could function. Dropping my mental shields, I closed my eyes, blew out a breath, and imagined my awareness of the world was a bubble around me, that I was in the center of it. I took a breath, and then another, and with each inhalation imagined the bubble expanding, enclosing more and more of the rooms.

Odors, sounds, and tastes filled my consciousness until I felt like a child in a tempest of sensation.

I walked to the back corner of a room, to the kitchenette, and felt the faintest brush of magic. It was soft, the magic lapping in light and gentle waves, almost comforting to the touch.

I opened my eyes, stared at a closed cabinet door that seemed, now that my barriers were down and I was staring right at it, to faintly pulse with magic, like the wood grain had a heartbeat, pulsing in and out.

I reached out, pulled open the cabinet door.

It was six inches tall, shaped like an obelisk, and looked like stone, matte shades of white and ivory that seemed to glow from within.

"Ethan."

He walked toward me, brow unfurrowing as he saw it.

"It pulses," he said, and I was relieved it wasn't just me.

He called Ryan's name, and footsteps echoed quickly behind us.

"What did you find?"

Ethan moved aside so he could get a look at it. "Alabaster, I believe. Perhaps a receiver, or an antenna designed to receive and enhance magic."

"In Darius's direction," I said, and Ethan nodded.

Ryan looked at the object, then Ethan. "A vampire could provide the glamour. But not the object."

Ethan nodded. "He or she would need a sorcerer. Someone with the skill to create this magical—I suppose 'appliance' is the most appropriate word, considering."

"We have friends who are sorcerers," I said. "We can get it to them, ask them to take a look. Maybe they can ferret out who did it. Reverse engineer it."

"We should have brought Catcher," Ethan agreed, and I made a mental note to pass that nugget along. It would make his month.

"Do that," Ryan said. "But for now, we need to neutralize it. Get it onto the countertop."

Ethan rubbed his fingertips together, then reached out and touched the object. It glowed with his touch, light shifting within the stone.

"It's warm," he said. "Very, very warm." Holding the obelisk like an actress might carry an Oscar statuette, he lowered it carefully to the marble counter.

In the meantime, Ryan searched drawers until he found a box of plastic bags and a container of margarita salt.

"Magical nullification," Ryan said. With a flick of the small knife he pulled from his belt, he flipped the plastic lid from the salt and upended it into a zip-top bag. He held the bag open, glanced at Ethan. "Put her in."

Ethan looked dubious but complied, carefully placing the obelisk in its bed of salt. Orange and blue sparks lit where alabaster and salt met. After a few seconds, the sparks dissipated, and the alabaster's dull glow faded. A breeze flowed through the room, and the air seemed to thin, as if the obelisk's glamour had thickened it, weighed it down.

"Damn," I murmured. "That was heavy magic."

Ryan carefully closed the bag, rolled the extra plastic around it, and stuffed it into a thin nylon bag he'd pulled from his utility belt. He stuffed the wrapped object into one of the zipped pockets on his cargo pants.

There was a groan from the other room.

"Ryan!" Cord called out. "He's back."

We rushed back in. Darius was sitting straight up in his chair, his knuckles white around the arms, his eyes open and blinking, and no longer dilated.

He looked up at us, blinked, his expression equally haughty and confused. "Sullivan? What the hell's going on?"

"That will be a rather long and involved story." Ethan went to him, offered a hand to help him out of the chair. "Suffice it to say, we think you've been glamoured or charmed in order to get money from the GP coffers, and we need to get you up and out of here."

Darius looked at Ethan for a moment, eyes searching for truth. "You mean it."

"All of it. And we need to get out of here. *Now.*"

"No 'sire' from you anymore, Sullivan?" Darius asked, but he let Ethan pull him to his feet.

"Since the GP has deemed us enemies, not a chance in hell."

The elevator chose that moment to *ding* its arrival.

The sound of footsteps echoed in the marble hallway outside the suite.

"Cover him," Ethan said to Cord, then unsheathed his sword and dragged Darius, still unsteady on his feet, back into the corner.

I'd have preferred they switch places, but I couldn't exactly call him out in the middle of an op.

"Shit," Ryan said, putting a hand on his ear. His instinct was the same as mine—that someone on the first floor had gone down; that was the only way they could have made it up the elevator.

"Luc here."

"Lindsey here."

Their responses echoed through our earpieces, but they were the only ones. Max didn't respond.

"Goddamn it," Ryan said, accent even stronger with his fury.

We unsheathed our swords and faced the three men who stepped into the doorway. Two were men we'd seen earlier tonight—the big man and his smaller friend. The third was new. That was five men, altogether, assigned the task of keeping Darius under wraps. Someone had pull . . . and plenty of cash.

The big one bore a long and mean-looking dagger, and the short one held a small handgun, pointed at all of us.

I was getting sick of being on the receiving end of handguns this week.

"If you're looking for your friend," the big one said, his voice gravelly and harsh, "he's in the elevator with a very big headache. He was trespassing, and it looks like you are, too."

"This is Darius's room," Ryan said, arms extended, the gun in a two-handed grip. With Cord and Ethan watching Darius, I stepped forward, joined the front line, relished the hot rush of adrenaline that silvered my eyes. "So you're trespassing. Who hired you?"

"Our employer. And speaking of whom, you've walked into something that's none of your business. I suggest you take your girlfriend and walk right out again."

"I don't suppose there's any point in simply offering you more money to make you walk away right now?"

The man laughed, the sound like rain over rusted metal. "Now, that's a good one. I enjoyed that. But what kind of businessman would I be if I ditched one deal for another? Not a very loyal one, I'd say."

"Loyalty doesn't strike me as one of your better qualities."

"Maybe not. But I've others." The blade was already in the air before I registered the flick of his hand. Ryan pivoted to dodge the attack, but the dagger's gleaming edge caught his upper arm, painting a stripe of red across his sleeve.

The fight was on.

"I'll take him," I said to Ryan, and let him move toward the little guy.

I launched forward and sliced sideways, but the man was sprier than he looked. He jumped out of the way, stuck out a foot to trip me as I moved forward. I anticipated, jumped, and landed closer to the elevator.

"You're a pretty little thing," he said.

"I'm not little," I promised, swinging a half circle with the sword extended, hoping to throw him off balance if I couldn't bring him down. He stumbled backward out of the way, barely missing the edge of a console table that would have put him on his ass.

My bad luck there.

He pulled another gleaming dagger from the interior of his jacket, switched it from hand to hand.

"Tell me why a girl with your looks, your fine ass, is playing with a sword?"

He meant to piss me off, and it worked. My eyes silvered, but I'd been in battle before, knew better than to let this dirtbag throw me off.

I ignored the pop of bullets behind me, a groan I thought came from Ethan, tried to slow panic and keep my focus.

I lowered my sword arm, put my other hand on my hip, and grinned at him. "I don't need to *play* with a sword. I know how to use one."

His smile was lascivious, and aimed at my chest. So he didn't see me kick up the bottom of my katana, launch it into a spin. But he saw the blade catch light, glinting once, then twice, as it spun like a baton. His hand moved, the dagger piercing forward, but I was already gone.

I snapped the handle out of the air, edged to his right, the katana trailing me, and shifted my hands forward against his bulk. The blade caught, slicing him across the chest. He screamed out a curse, stumbled forward, hit the opposite wall with braced arms.

As I finished the rotation, he roared with anger, turned back with his dagger gleaming, his other arm pressed against the bleeding stripe across his chest. He lunged clumsily, but he still had plenty of strength. I whipped aside to dodge the dagger, but it caught the bottom edge of my jacket before digging into the wall, pinning me against it like a scientific specimen.

He'd lost his weapon, but he still had two ham-sized fists. I jerked free with a tear of leather, but the delay took precious seconds. His fist connected with my stomach, sending a wave of nausea through my belly even as the blow pushed the air from my lungs.

I hit the stone floor on my knees, the queasiness matched only by the fury that lashed through me.

I huffed quick breaths through clenched teeth, trying not to hurl, pushed myself to my feet again, and leveled him with the fiercest stare I could manage. "You. *Punched*. Me." Every word took effort.

He smiled. "And I'll do it again, bitch, if you don't step aside."

He'd punched me . . . and called me a bitch.

Blood roared through my ears, and everything else faded—the sounds of his labored breathing, the fight in the other room. My vision seemed to dim to the cone where he stood in front of me, grinning maniacally and scenting the air with my fury.

I imagined myself a sword-bearing dervish—I apparently got creative while fighting in a pain-induced frenzy—lifted my sword, and dove into battle.

I moved in with a slice from right to left, and he used the dagger to block it, then rotated his arm, using the momentum against me to push me back. But I didn't stop. I came in again, sliced upward from the left. He dodged, then kicked out with his right leg, making contact with my knee. The impact made my body shudder, pain radiating like forks of lightning, but I stayed on my feet. He wasn't the only one who could fight dirty.

I feinted to the left, reaching for my knee like he'd done serious damage. His ugly smile bloomed; he thought he'd won. But I kicked upward with my good leg, made direct contact with his crotch, and sent him moaning to the floor on his knees.

"Bitch," he muttered again, spittle flying, but he wasn't down, and he wasn't done. He flipped his dagger and held it backward, the blade aligned with his forearm, then flipped it out with a mo-

tion that just nicked the edge of my thigh as I jumped backward
to avoid it. I bumped that damned console table, sent a lamp to
the floor with a crash of ceramic and glass.

He pulled his bulk to his feet again, lumbered forward, murder in his eyes.

"*Bitch*," he said one more time, the word thick in his mouth, as
if it was an incantation, a gleam in his eyes as if saying the word
gave him power.

My power wasn't his to take.

He swiped left, then right. I moved backward, putting space
between us, his body between me and the rest of the building. I
bumped up against the elevator wall, bluffed surprise, let my katana clank to the ground.

"You aren't going anywhere," he said.

He was right. I wasn't.

He roared, lunged, his body set for a frontal attack, so focused that he didn't see me kick up the katana and thrust it in
front of me.

But he was already moving, and skin and flesh were hardly a
barrier to honed steel. He was skewered, the handle of the katana
protruding just below his breastbone.

Eyes wide with shock, he looked down, took in the handle
sticking out of his gut, then stumbled backward, wrenching the
handle—now slippery with blood—from my grip.

"You weren't playing," he murmured, before his eyes went
dull. He fell backward, hitting the floor with a thud.

I took a shuddering breath, wiping sweat from my eyes. I'd
killed before, and would again. But it didn't get easier, no matter
that the death saved lives, including my own.

A *crash* from the living room pulled me from my shock. I
moved forward, pulling out my katana, cleaned it of gore. There

were many things required of a vampire warrior; some of them were more disturbing than others.

"Ethan?" I called out.

"I'm good."

I said a silent prayer of thanks, then glanced around, checked the others. The little guy was on the floor in the foyer. Ryan lay on the floor in front of the kitchenette.

I ran forward. He lay on his back, a nasty wound across his left arm, another across his left leg, and a lot of blood. The scent of it interested my vampire sensibilities, but I ignored the surge of interest and leaned down.

"Ryan." I tapped his cheeks. "Ryan."

His eyes fluttered open, focused. "I'm okay." But he winced with the pain.

Ethan walked toward us, wiping the blood from his sword. There was blood on his right thigh.

"You're hit?" I asked.

"Glanced me."

I nodded. "Ryan's injured. You got the little guy?"

"And his friend. Cord's got Darius. You got the big guy?"

"I did. Had some unflattering things to say."

Ethan adjusted his earpiece. "Lucas, we're done here, and it's gonna be dirty."

"Exit's prepared, van is ready to go. Cleanup crew en route."

I hadn't even thought about a cleanup crew, about the necessity of having someone take care of the mess we'd left. I was glad he had.

"Fine," he said, glanced at Ryan. "Let's get the hell out of here."

I rose to grab a blanket from the back of a nearby love seat, preparing to drape it across Ryan's body. I wasn't sure if vampires could go into shock, but I didn't feel like it was time to find out.

I saw the instant widening of his eyes, the flare of his irises.

"Behind you," Ryan cried out, and I snapped my head to look.

The shorter man, blood streaming across his face and his abdomen, had lifted his arm . . . and his gun was pointed at Ethan.

Light and smoke emerged from the barrel.

I didn't stop to think or plan or evaluate risk. *I moved.*

I dove in front of Ethan, covering his body with mine as the explosion of sound filled the air. There was only pain, bright and searing, until I hit the ground.

The world spun . . . and went dark.

◆━━◆◈◆━━◆

CHAPTER TEN

THE RULES OF VAMPIRELAND

I blinked once, then again, before the world cleared. I stared up at a pale ceiling with intricate molding around the edges. I was home.

"She's awake," said a woman's voice beside me.

Fingers clasped my wrist, felt for the pulse I knew was strong. I could feel it throbbing in my head like I was sitting inside a bass drum.

I glanced beside me, recognized the décor of our apartments. I lay on the bed. A woman crouched beside me, her dark skin set off by brilliant fuchsia scrubs. She was Delia, the House's doctor.

"What happened?" I asked.

"You took one in the line of duty, Sentinel. Shot in the shoulder."

Mortification replaced confusion. "I didn't pass out, did I?"

Delia smiled. "No. But your head took a good bounce on the floor when you went down."

"We've actually found something harder than our Sentinel's head. You've been out since last night."

I glanced at my side, found Ethan behind Delia, his expression pinched with concern. Luc stood behind them, watching cautiously.

"Last night? I missed an entire day? What time is it?"

"A day and part of an evening again," Ethan said. "It's midnight."

I began to sit up, but Delia put a hand on my arm. "Slowly," she said. "Give it a moment. Concussion, and you might be dizzy for a bit, but you'll be right as rain soon enough."

Slowly, I sat up, got my bearings. The room stopped spinning after a moment, and the dull buzz began to fade away.

Delia checked my heartbeat and my temperature. She pushed back the sleeve of my shirt, checked the dressing there, and, with a smile, stripped it away.

"And you're healed. The benefits of vampire genetics," she said with a smile. "But you do have a very small scar."

I bent my shoulder forward to see, found a pale, star-shaped mark no bigger than a dime.

"It was a hollow-point bullet. The shard popped right out as you were healing, but they do tend to leave scars on vampires."

I'd be in good company there. Ethan still bore the small pucker of skin above his heart where he'd taken an aspen stake for me. And since he stood healthy beside me, I said, "I can deal with a scar. I kinda like it, actually."

"We're glad you're all right, Sentinel," Luc said. "That was a damn brave thing you did."

"Thanks," I said, pressing gingerly at the back of my head, feeling the lump that had blossomed there. Hopefully vampire genetics would take care of that, too.

"And sorry about the damage. You missed a rule," Luc said, and I nodded, already anticipating the joke.

"I forgot to double-tap the little guy," I said.

"You forgot to double-tap the little guy," he agreed.

Delia glanced at her watch, rose. "I need to jet. I've got a shift in twenty. Merit should stay off her feet for a little while."

"Noted, Delia. Thank you for taking a look."

"Happy to help, as always, Liege." She walked to the apartment doors, opened them, announced to the vampires who apparently stood there, waiting for news: "She's awake. You can all go about your business now."

There were hoots and catcalls that warmed my cheeks, but I didn't mind the attention. I'd thrown my body in front of Ethan to protect him. I was proud of myself—not because I'd been brave, but because I hadn't let fear stop me from moving.

Ethan sat down on the bed beside me.

"Is Ryan okay? Darius?"

Ethan stroked a hand along my calf, which soothed as if by magical osmosis. "Both are fine. Ryan and Cord returned to New York." His face fell. "I'm sorry to say that Max didn't make it. He was staked."

I had the sudden, sharp memory of Ethan disappearing in front of my eyes. The sight of Malik, eyes swollen, grieving, carrying a bundle of amaranth at Ethan's memorial service. His death had been erased by magic, but the memories still bore a terrible weight.

He reached out, squeezed my hand. "I'm here, Sentinel."

I nodded.

"Max's memorial will be tomorrow night at Cabot House. We've made a donation to the House's charitable fund. And we did the same for Brett Jacobs—Arthur opened a scholarship fund at Columbia College and we made a generous donation."

I exhaled. "Good. That's good. Thank you, Ethan."

"Of course."

"And Darius?" I asked.

"Lakshmi arrived just before dawn to help him back to London. They left right after dusk."

"Does she have any idea who planned this?"

Ethan's gaze darkened. "She does not. She didn't believe any current members of the GP were capable of it, but I think she's still trying to accept what actually happened."

"Several guards, seven million dollars, and a magical appliance, as you called it, capable of controlling a Master vampire. Who else has those kinds of resources?"

"And who else is brave enough to use them against the head of the GP?" I blew out a breath. "It doesn't pay to be a member of the GP these days," I said. I'd killed Celina. Ethan had killed Harold. Michael Donovan had nearly taken out Darius and Lakshmi, as had the unidentified vampire who had planted the obelisk and used it to control him. This wasn't exactly the situation I wanted to drop Ethan into.

"No, it doesn't."

"The money's the key. We need to figure out who stood to gain by the transfers. Did you bring the obelisk home?"

"Safe and secure," Luc put in. "It's downstairs in the vault."

"I called Catcher and Mallory," Ethan added, "told them you were all right and that you'd take the obelisk to them."

"What about my grandfather and Brett Jacobs's murder?"

He shook his head. "He called earlier to check on you, but we didn't chat about the murder. You'll need to call him as soon as you can."

"I will."

Lindsey walked in, a bottle of blood in hand. "I saw Delia in the hallway," she said, offering me the bottle. "She said you were awake. How do you feel?"

"Like a River troll stepped on my head." I opened the bottle and drained it in seconds.

"Jesus, Ethan. Don't you feed her?" Lindsey asked, taking the empty bottle again.

"Not as often as I need to, apparently."

"You scared the shit out of me," she said. "Glad to see you're up and about."

I nodded, wincing as the move turned the pain in my head to a pounding throb. "I'm fine, except for the headache."

"It will dissipate soon enough," Ethan said.

"Showering her with gifts would probably help her heal faster," Lindsey suggested with a grin, rocking back on her heels.

"She doesn't need gifts," Ethan said. "Although a dose of common sense would help."

Luc clucked his tongue, smiled at me. "You save his life and get no credit. What kind of Master is that?"

"The kind that prefers his Sentinel alive," Ethan said, reaching forward and brushing a lock of hair behind my ear.

Silence descended. Lindsey took Luc's hand and began pulling him toward the door. "Why don't we just let Ethan check her over?"

"We could stay and watch that," Luc said, grinning back at us. "You know, for science."

"'For science' will get you punched out by your Master," Lindsey said.

"Party pooper," Luc said with a grin.

When they left the room, I glanced back at Ethan, found his expression grim.

"What?"

His eyes clouded, and he put a hand on my face. "I worry for you, Sentinel."

I put my hand over his, laced our fingers together. "I'm not fragile."

"All evidence to the contrary."

"I'm awake and alive. Immortality has its advantages . . . primarily immortality."

"I know, Sentinel. And you grow stronger every day. But you are still mine to protect. And you have a concussion."

I gave him the arched eyebrow he preferred to give me. "I've been stabbed, kidnapped, imprisoned, and worse. A concussion is what worries you?"

I meant to make him laugh, but his expression didn't change.

"This is exactly what I feared would happen. That you'd end up hurt because of me, because of Darius. I have known fear," he quietly said. "I've soldiered, seen men die, walked toward death's door and gone through it. But I have never known fear like the sight of you unconscious."

"Because I was brave enough to take a shot for you?" I asked it with a smile, hoping to clear the gloom from his eyes. But to no avail.

"Because I challenged Darius. Because of the risk you'll be injured due to my actions."

"I got shot because someone is greedy," I reminded him. "And I'm also the reason we found out what was going on." Along with Jonah, Matthew, and Horace. I'd need to give them a call of thanks. And probably send a gift basket. How did you thank a group of rabble-rousing vampires for spilling the good secrets? Maybe wine.

Focus, I told myself. "This isn't exactly a new situation. I've been in danger since before I became a vampire."

"And each time our House is called upon, the danger increases. I believe in you," he said. "Don't think I don't. But I love you. And I want you safe."

"I got hurt because I did a stupendously brave thing. Let me have my moment."

He smiled slyly. "I suppose you are what I made you."

"The best Sentinel the GP has ever seen?"

"The sassiest, certainly."

"Did Darius mention anything about the challenge before he left?"

"He did not." He picked up my hand, brushed his lips softly over my fingers. "Officially, my challenge is still outstanding. I won't revoke it; I owe more to the House than that. And more to you."

"Well, I did save your life."

"Are you going to be pulling that one out for a while?"

I gave him a flat look. "And you never mention taking an aspen stake for me?"

He nodded in acknowledgment. "That's fair, I suppose. And you got me off track. When Darius has the GP in hand again, we'll see where he stands. He'll have to respond to the challenge one way or the other."

Ethan's phone rang. He pulled it out, smiled at the screen, then handed it to me. "It's your grandfather."

I took the phone from him, answered it. "Hi, Grandpa."

I'd spent a lot of my childhood with my grandfather. My parents, wealthy and a little pretentious, hadn't understood me; I hadn't been what they'd expected. My grandparents, on the other hand, had welcomed me with open arms. Even now, years later, my grandfather still sounded relieved to hear my voice.

"Baby girl. I didn't expect to hear your voice, but I'm certainly relieved. Not thrilled to hear you'd been injured."

"Part of the job," I said. "But I'm fine now. Just a little sore. Sorry to make you worry."

"Don't even think a thing about it. I'd rather know the uncomfortable facts than be left in the dark, although I'd much rather have you behind a desk."

"There are nights I couldn't agree more."

"That's actually why I'm calling. There's been another murder. We think it might be connected to the Jacobs death."

"What makes you think it's related?"

"There was a blue cross on Jacobs's hand."

"I remember."

"There's one on this victim's hand, as well, and we hadn't revealed that particular detail to the press." He paused. "I almost didn't call you, given your last twenty-four hours, but we'd appreciate your thoughts. I wouldn't ask if I didn't think it might help Brett and Arthur."

I could hear the worry in his voice, but it was unnecessary. He'd taken care of me too many times for me to turn down the request.

"It's not a problem. I'll come take a look. I've been down for way too long, anyway. Where is she?"

"Montrose Beach. South end."

"I need to get dressed, and I'll be on my way." I hung up the phone, handed it back to Ethan. "Another body's been found, likely connected to the Jacobs murder. Same mark on the body, and it wasn't a public detail."

Ethan's mouth stayed in the same firm line. "You can't go."

"I have to. I said I'd help him, and I'm not going back on my word." Slowly, I stood up, then closed my eyes and breathed through my nose, trying to stay on my feet without falling over as the room spun around me.

"Your grandfather can do this without you."

I knew fear put the irritability in his voice, but his irritability triggered mine. "It's something I have to do," I said, and glanced back at him. "Isn't that what you said to me about the note?"

His jaw tightened. "This is different."

"I don't think it is."

"You can barely stand up."

"And your safety's at risk." I put my hands over my eyes, rubbed. "I don't want to argue about that goddamned note anymore. I don't know how to talk to you about it—not when there's something you won't tell me about."

"*Can't* tell you about."

I dropped my hands, looked back at him. "Because?"

Ethan looked at me silently for a very long time. "It's to do with the threat." He sighed, walked to the bathroom. "There's a woman. She has information. About me. About my past."

"You're being blackmailed? Why? Why would . . ."

The pieces fell into place even as I said the words. The driver had wanted Ethan to bow out of the GP race. He hadn't, and the communications kept coming.

"You know who she is—who sent the driver. Or you knew her, and she wants you to withdraw your challenge, or she'll share the details of your past."

I followed him into the bathroom, watched him splash water on his face. He dried his face with a towel before dropping it to the counter again.

He nodded, incrementally.

"She's no longer trying to do this anonymously—not just by sending a messenger."

"So it seems."

"Who is she, and what does she know?"

"Your jealousy is showing, Sentinel."

The response baffled me. "I'm not jealous. I'm scared shitless because this clearly bothers you, and you won't tell me about it."

He braced his hands on the counter, met my gaze in the mirror. "She is a woman I knew once upon a time."

Seconds passed, and he didn't elaborate, which only made the gears in my mind turn faster. Was it someone he'd loved? Someone he'd lost?

"And?"

"And, because she knew me, she knows my regrets."

Regrets. What a word—so full of frightening possibilities. I knew of one in particular . . .

"Is this about Balthasar?" Ethan had imagined himself a monster due to Balthasar's tutelage. Was "she" from that part of his past?

"The 'what' doesn't matter. There's no point in talking about it. I'm not going to talk about it."

"Not even to someone you want to spend the rest of eternity with?"

His eyes flashed hot tendrils of green fire. "To anyone. The past is the past, and it's going to stay that way."

"You have to tell Luc. If the House is at risk, if the driver comes back—"

"He won't come back," Ethan said. "Not now."

"Are you going to revoke your challenge?"

"I don't know what I'm going to do."

I opened my mouth to object, but he shook his head.

"Let it go, Merit. Just give me some space."

Words stuck in my throat, but I managed to keep them down.

We were both adults, and he had a right to space. I could give that to him. But I turned around so he wouldn't see the tears welling in my eyes. I would not cry in front of him. Not for this.

"Fine. I'll give you space, and I'll give you time." I looked back at him, silver eyed and furious. "But you will *not* shut me out. Because I love you too much to let you act like an idiot."

By the time I dressed, he was gone. He'd get his space, one way or another.

For now, I needed mine. I needed to help those who'd actually asked me to help, including my grandfather. I pulled out my phone, sent my apparent partner in this investigation a message: I'M ALIVE, BUT THERE'S BEEN ANOTHER MURDER—RELATED TO BRETT JACOBS. TIME TO INVESTIGATE?

His answer was nearly immediate: COLOR ME RELIEVED—ABOUT YOU, NOT VIC. WHEN AND WHERE?

I gave him the instructions, tucked the phone away again. At least he wasn't pushing me away.

Since I had a job to do as vampire courier, I walked downstairs to the basement. The Ops Room hummed busily as it often did. Vampires sat at the computers along the wall. Lindsey was gone, probably outside on patrol around the grounds. Luc was at the computer station, eating popcorn from a giant blue Garrett's canister. If I'd had any appetite, I'd have snagged some of it.

"Merit," Luc said, sitting up when I walked in. "What the hell are you doing up?"

"There's been another murder," I said, and gave them the information my grandfather had offered me.

Luc's brows lifted. "And you're going now? In your condition?"

"I'm fine. And murder waits for no man. Or vampire. Catcher

and Jeff are occupied, and the body apparently was marked, so my grandfather needs a consult."

"And everyone's eager to close Brett Jacobs's case and let his family mourn him."

I nodded. "Precisely. Jonah's going to meet me, primarily because Ethan has a very large stick up his ass."

Luc looked amused. "Oh? Not happy you took a bullet?"

I debated how much I could tell him, decided I couldn't divulge the blackmail, not that I knew much to divulge. But if Ethan knew the driver's identity—or at least who sent him—Luc had to know that. "He has suspicions about who sent the driver. But he won't tell me who it is. He doesn't think they're a threat to the House."

That was true enough, but Luc saw through it, knew that wasn't all of it.

"And what aren't you telling me?"

I shook my head. "He asked me for space. I think, being an adult, I'm supposed to give that to him. And you can't ask him about it directly. He'll deny it, deflect it. This goes back a long way for him, and he thinks he wants to handle it on his own."

There was a glimmer in Luc's eyes. "And you disagree?"

"He has the rest of us for a reason. Do what you can—but do it carefully." I rose. "I'm going to give the obelisk to my grandfather, or track down Catcher afterward."

Luc nodded and rose, and I followed him down the hallway to the vault built into the wall. He pulled a set of keys from his pocket, plugged the square key into the vault's door, and it flipped open.

The obelisk lay on its side, looking admittedly pitiful in the plastic bag on its bed of margarita salt. Luc pulled out the bag with two fingers, handed it over.

"I don't think the magic can get on you," I assured him with a smile, tucking it under my arm like a football. "It's not a virus."

"No sense in taking a chance with our health, Sentinel." He closed the door again, looked at me. "Check in with us tonight, will you?"

I gave him the stink eye. "Are you asking as my boss, or because Ethan told you to keep an eye on me?"

He snorted. "I'm not going to tell you every conversation I have with your Master and mine. House business is House business."

"And I thought we had a solid, trusting relationship."

"Guilt doesn't work on me, Sentinel!" he called out as I walked toward the basement door. "At least not as much as physical threats from a certain Master vampire."

Every man had a price.

The best way to take a drive that led only to murder and loss? A sleek silver roadster purchased from a pack of shape-shifters and outfitted with a state-of-the-art engine.

I nestled the obelisk in the passenger seat behind my katana, strapped in, and turned over the engine, goose bumps lifting on my arms at the smooth and rhythmic purr of her engine.

I pulled out of the garage and into a clear spring night. The sky overhead was dark, but there was too much light in the city to see more than a few stars in the dark blanket of sky.

Because Chicago curved around the edge of Lake Michigan, there were dozens of beaches in the city. Montrose was on the north side of the city in Lakeview.

I pulled into the small parking lot across the street from the beach, but it was clear that something had happened. Police cruisers were parked along the side of the street, their lights flashing.

Jonah walked toward me, his car parked a few slots away.

"Good evening," he said, looking dapper in jeans, a button-up, and a brown sport coat. "You all right? How's your head?"

"Concussed, but I'll manage."

"I'm glad you're conscious again."

"I'm glad to be conscious again." We walked to the edge of the lot, waited for traffic to clear before jogging across the street to the sidewalk that led toward the beach. My pulse pounded in my head with the effort, and I hoped I could make it through the rest of the night without a fight or a 5K.

"Did you get enough of the rescue story from Ethan?"

Jonah nodded. "He gave me the basic rundown. Nice job."

"We couldn't have done it without Matthew's information. Still, not entirely a success. Cabot House lost a man."

"So I heard. Scott sent his condolences to the House."

"Yeah, Ethan, too."

"Did Darius mention the challenge?"

"He did not. We got him back to the House just before dawn, and he left with Lakshmi just after sunset. Have you heard anything?"

"Only her outrage that someone dared attack Darius."

Speaking of Lakshmi, she'd known Ethan for a long time and, considering her position, probably knew some of his history. Could Lakshmi be the "she" attempting to blackmail Ethan?

As we walked down the sidewalk toward the southeast end of the beach, I rejected that idea. She'd wanted me to encourage Ethan to challenge Darius. Why bother doing that, only to then threaten Ethan not to run? And more, she was on the GP. If she'd wanted to reject Ethan's challenge, she could have done it directly.

The beach curved north, the southernmost chunk of it reserved as a sanctuary for birds, sand giving way to scrubby grass.

That was where they'd gathered—a gaggle of reporters barely contained by police tape, trying to snap photographs of the latest victim. They saw us approaching, began shouting out questions.

"Have vampires murdered someone else?"

"Why are you here, Merit? Did you know the victim?"

"Are you involved in her murder?"

"Are supernaturals killing humans?"

That one drew an irritated look—and nearly a verbal barrage—from Jonah, but I took his arm, squeezed. "Keep it in," I murmured. "And let it go."

"All right, all right," my grandfather said, moving forward and guiding us through the tape and ignoring the questions they peppered at him. "That's enough for now."

"When Shakespeare said kill all the lawyers," Jonah said, "he hadn't met the paparazzi."

"True enough," my grandfather said, escorting us to the area where cops and investigators had gathered.

Detective Jacobs stood with several uniformed officers. Jacobs was tall and lean, with dark skin and a short crop of graying hair. Dark freckles were sprinkled across his nose. Tonight he wore a dark suit, overcoat, and matching fedora, always the gentleman, even when grief settled lines across his face.

"I'm surprised he's here tonight," I whispered.

My grandfather nodded. "Normally, he wouldn't be allowed—he's too close to the crime. But he's a good man and a good detective, so the lieutenant cut him some slack. He wanted to work. It was important to him that he contribute to the process. It might be therapeutic, I think."

"And where are Catcher and Jeff?"

"Ah," my grandfather said. "That's right. You haven't gotten that story. They're actually assisting the nymphs tonight."

I opened my mouth, closed it again. "Color me intrigued, and give me the quick version." Nymph drama was invariably entertaining.

"A New York artist created a giant floating hot dog. It's supposed to represent anticonsumerism and remind folks to donate to food banks, that type of thing. The tourism folks think the project would be a great boon to the city. The nymphs were less enthused. They didn't want a plastic hot dog in their waterway. Consider it a mockery of the river's historic significance to the city and their jobs."

Considering what I'd seen of the nymphs—including screaming and hair pulling—I presumed "were less enthused" was a euphemism for "went crazy."

"We brokered a deal. The nymphs agreed to let the hot dog sit in the river for three days. In exchange, I have to agree to attend one of their dinner parties."

I blinked. "You're going to a nymph dinner party?"

He sighed, nodded. "They've been requesting I attend." He looked over the scene in front of him. "For better or worse, tonight's the night."

"And Catcher and Jeff?" I asked.

"Catcher let them borrow the gym for the space, and they're helping get things set up."

Catcher owned a spare gym in the River North neighborhood. That was where he'd trained me to use my sword, although I hadn't been there in months. Considering how much time he'd spent with my grandfather, I hadn't assumed he'd been there, either.

I squinted, trying to imagine what a nymph dinner party might involve. Giggles, maybe. Pink champagne. Soundtrack by Kylie Minogue.

"How would one go about getting an invitation to a nymph dinner party?"

My grandfather smiled. "Do you want to go?"

"Not in the sense that I want to spend an evening with nymphs, or hear an evening with nymphs, so much as I want to *see* an evening with nymphs. Oh, actually, I do need to see Catcher. I have the obelisk that was used to control Darius. I'm hoping he and Mallory can give us some thoughts about who made the magic."

He nodded. "I'm sure they'll be happy to see you—and the nymphs, too." He waved at Detective Jacobs, who walked over and extended a hand.

"Detective," I said, squeezing his hand. "We're so sorry for your loss."

"Thank you, Merit. Jonah," he said, and they shook, as well. "Thank you for coming to assist."

"We're happy to do whatever we can," Jonah said.

Jacobs nodded, looked at me. "I understand you took a hit in the line of duty last night."

It seemed insensitive to mention immortality or vampire healing to a man who'd lost his son, so I kept my answer short. "I did. I'm working through it."

My grandfather patted my back supportively.

"Shall we?" he asked, then gestured to the woman who lay on the sand. We walked closer.

She wore a simple sheath dress in deep red, the type a businesswoman might pair with a blazer. Her arms were at her sides. Her feet were bare, and her hair long, blond, and wavy. It spread like a halo beneath her.

There were no swords, but there was no mistaking the insult she'd suffered. Her neck was swollen, and there was a purple line of bruising across it. The blue cross my grandfather had mentioned marked her right hand, and added to the insult were the marks across her chest: three red pentagrams.

"You're thinking a serial killer?" I asked, dread settling low and heavy in my belly. I looked up at my grandfather. "Two killings within a week."

He looked, first and foremost, sad. Sad, perhaps, that someone in Chicago had turned to murder, or that Chicago would have to face the fear and horror of it.

"We don't release the cross," Jacobs said. "The victims are our priorities; finding justice for them. If we say 'serial killer,' the press and city will go wild."

I nodded, and Jonah, who'd walked around, peering at the woman's face, quietly swore, looked up at me, grief in his eyes. "I know her," he said on a sigh.

Jacobs looked up. "You do?"

"Her name is Samantha Ingram. She's a potential Initiate."

"An Initiate?"

"That means she applied to join Grey House," I said.

Jacobs frowned. "She's a vampire?"

"She wanted to be one," Jonah explained. "Some applicants are already vampires, but most are human. They seek immortality and House membership." He looked down at Samantha. "She wasn't scheduled to be interviewed until next week, but she's on the short list. Good application. Had a history degree from Northwestern."

"I see." Jacobs looked back at Samantha, considering the new information.

"Did you publicize that she had applied to join the House?" my grandfather asked.

Jonah shook his head. "Applicants submit their materials; we review them in House, ask some in for interviews. If she's selected, we tell her and the North American Vampire Registry. They'll eventually identify the chosen Initiates, but no one's gotten that far yet."

I'd been one of those Initiates. My Initiate status had been listed in the *Tribune* by the NAVR, which kept me from going back to grad school. I hadn't been thrilled, and I'd stormed into Ethan's office for the first time to protest it. We hadn't had an opportunity to select Initiates this year; there'd been too much drama.

"So it's unlikely her selection was an attempt to pin this on vampires."

"Considering the pentagrams," my grandfather said, "it appears they're trying to blame sorcerers."

"Considering the reporters' questions," I said, "it's working."

My grandfather nodded. "I sent Catcher a photograph. He confirmed they're magical symbols but said they weren't used much by 'legitimate' sorcerers—his word. Since the last murder had vampire connotations—the swords—we wanted to get your take on it, too."

Jonah nodded. "They're magical. Ancient in nature, related to King Solomon's key. But I'm not aware of any symbolic use by vampires. Vampires don't have much in common historically with sorcerers. We have rituals of our own, but they're based in feudalism, not sorcery."

"Oath swearing, calling our Masters 'Liege,' that kind of thing," I explained.

"What about the placement of the pentagrams on the body?" Jacobs asked.

"They're roughly over the heart, which obviously has an important connotation for blood-drinking vampires. But other than that, not that I can think of." He looked at me. "Anything in Cadogan House?"

I shook my head. "Not that I'm aware of."

"She was strangled?" Jonah quietly asked.

"That's our initial conclusion," Jacobs said. "We'll confirm when we see Lin's report. Could we get a copy of her Initiate application?"

"I'll have to ask Scott," Jonah said. "We want to protect her privacy, but I guess that's moot now."

"Do we know if Samantha knew Brett or Mitzy Burrows?" I asked.

"We don't," Jacobs said. "But that will be one of the first things we'll look into. The presence of the connection—the crosses—suggests some relationship between them, but we'll have to ferret that out."

"Any sign of Mitzy since the raid?" Jonah asked.

Jacobs shook his head. "None. No sightings, no credit card activity, and she hasn't gone back to the house; we've been watching it."

"Smart enough to lay low," Jonah said.

Jacobs nodded. "Some are. Chicago is a big city, and there are many places to hide." He looked back at Samantha Ingram, who'd only just missed her chance at immortality, and possibly thought of his son, who could have used it.

The thought was unbearably sad, and I touched Jonah's arm in sympathy.

"No murder is perfect," Jacobs quietly added. "We'll find her."

"You can go home if you want," I told Jonah, as we avoided the press and took the long way to the parking lot. "I can handle Catcher and Mallory. I've got to deliver the obelisk and the bobblehead, anyway." I was, admittedly, a little afraid of the nymphs, but as long as Jeff was there, I'd be fine.

Jonah snorted. "Do you honestly think there's a chance in hell I don't want to see a nymph dinner party?"

"You're a pervert."

"I'm a healthy American vampire," he said, stretching his arms like he was preparing for battle.

Considering the nymphs' personalities, not a bad analogy.

CHAPTER ELEVEN

┄ ═◈═ ┄

AIN'T NO PARTY LIKE A NYMPH PARTY

Because they were nymphs—giggly and busty and short-skirted women—I'd assumed a dinner party would be pretty much the same.

I was wrong. Truly and utterly—and pretty judgmentally—wrong.

They'd turned Catcher's River North gym into a Moroccan festival. The equipment and mats had been removed, and the entire space had been draped in colorful printed fabrics gathered together in the middle of the ceiling like a tent. Metal lanterns with intricate shades hung from the ceiling, and a dozen low, round tables were placed at intervals around the outside of the room, with low cushions for seating. The floor was covered in threadbare rugs in glorious colors and patterns, and an enormous buffet was stocked with tagines of meat and rice. Music played softly in the background.

"I have seriously not been giving the nymphs enough credit."

When three of them emerged from a back room with petite bodies, braided hair, and flowing jewel-toned gowns dotted with silver coins—the fabric nearly transparent—Jonah's smile turned dreamy. "Neither have I."

I elbowed him, caught his following "Urck," and walked forward.

Each nymph had control of a segment of the river and a signature color. I recognized two of the three who approached us. Cassie was raven haired and controlled the river's North Branch. Melaina was platinum blond and controlled the West Fork. Cassie had also recently been the victim of a magical attack by a woman intent on creating a menagerie of supernaturals.

The nymphs were notoriously temperamental—going from giggles to tears to catfights in seconds flat—so I stayed perfectly still, kept my eyes on them as they moved forward, ready to dart if they arched their wolverine nails.

But Cassie, apparently realizing who I was, bobbed toward me, hands clasped together. "You saved me!" she said delightedly. "You should feast with us."

"Oh, that's okay. We don't need anything. We actually just came to talk to Catcher and Mallory."

Her lower lip quivered as the other nymphs joined her. "You won't feast with us?"

Crap, I thought. I didn't have time to babysit nymphs tonight. I needed to get this job done and get back to the House for the supernatural delights that undoubtedly awaited me there.

Jonah took a step forward. "We would be delighted to feast with you, but we don't want to interrupt your party or take the attention away from you and your invited guests. Maybe we could enjoy just a small taste of what you have to offer if Mallory and Catcher also could join us? It would help them have energy for the rest of their work this evening."

The nymphs, who hadn't so much as glanced at Jonah, now

regarded him with interest. They'd made a deal with my grandfather and Catcher to hold this event. Maybe that was the secret to their affection: much like vampires, they liked to negotiate.

Melaina stepped forward, playing teasingly with the bottom of her braid. "You are tall," she said to the auburn-haired guard captain. He blushed to the roots, grinned like an idiot.

"I have many outstanding qualities."

Melaina giggled, wrapped herself around one of Jonah's arms. "I think we should invite them!"

"You aren't in charge," Cassie said, her pout still in place, and a storm of magic and trouble brewing.

"You are clearly a thoughtful and dedicated leader of women," I said. "And your hair looks *awesome*."

Her eyes widened with delight. "I applied a very thorough mask last night. The trolls recommended it."

Of course they had. "If it would be okay with you, could we talk to Mallory and Catcher? Or maybe Jeff?"

"I suppose," she said. "But you can't sit by Jeff."

A woman had to have her boundaries.

Jonah and I had already sat on the low pillows when the Ombuddies emerged from the back room, arms laden with décor: flowers, hanging lamps, extra pillows. They placed them as directed by the nymphs—who promptly adjusted them because two sorcerers and a shifter apparently were unable to arrange throw pillows according to the nymphs' exacting specifications.

"Save me," Mallory murmured, as she placed an orchid on the table the nymphs had designated for us. She wore an orange tunic over jeans tonight, her blue hair divided into two braids that had been twisted into knots on the back of her head.

Catcher joined us, and I was shocked to see that he'd traded his usual sarcastic T-shirt for a button-down shirt, the sleeves rolled nearly to his elbows.

"You look very handsome," I said, as he arranged his long legs with obvious discomfort.

"I look like a banker."

I wasn't sure a banker would combine a button-down, jeans, and angry-looking black boots, but I thought it wise not to mention that.

"For all your faults, I'm glad to see you up and about. Heard you took a good fall."

"It wasn't my best night, but I'm okay now."

When she'd finished with the flowers, Mallory put her hands on my arms. "You sure?"

I nodded. "Concussion, bullet through the shoulder. A little dizzy and headachy earlier, but I'm fine other than that."

"And to think you were once a total English lit dork. Ethan must have had a fit."

"He was worried," I agreed. "Bad part about dating the vampire you trained to be a warrior? You worry every time you send her into battle."

"It's a job hazard," Catcher acknowledged.

"Well," Mallory said, sitting down beside us, "she did single-handedly rescue Darius West from the clutches of an evildoer."

"It wasn't exactly like that, but close enough."

"What happens next with Darius?" Catcher asked.

"We're still waiting for that part."

Jeff came out bearing a glazed terra-cotta tagine that smelled absolutely heavenly. He normally paired a button-down with khakis, and he'd kept the same look today.

"That smells amazing," I told Cassie, whose eyes had gone large and glassy at the sight of Jeff. Nymphs absolutely adored the lanky shifter. I liked Jeff, but their interest in him went far beyond "like" and was somewhere closer to "bewitched."

Cassie pointed Jeff to a chevron cushion across the table, and he smiled at me and shrugged.

"I think they're afraid I'll hit on you," I whispered to Jeff when Cassie had moved away. "Do they know about Fallon?"

"They haven't asked, and I haven't told. Besides, they all have boyfriends." That had actually been the topic of discussion the first time I'd met the nymphs. Cassie and Melaina had been fighting over a boy who, based on the argument, hadn't seemed worthy of either of them.

"Wise man," Catcher said.

Melaina moved back to the table, the fabric shushing around her as she moved. "Please enjoy your meal," she said, placing a giant ceramic platter in the middle of the table. It held mounds of dark meat—lamb, I guessed—inside a halo of couscous. "But eat quickly. The rest of the party will be here soon."

She walked away again.

"I guess this is the staff table?" I asked.

"They like to feed people," Catcher said. "That doesn't mean they don't divide them into castes."

With the mound of food in the middle of the table, all eyes turned to me.

"Oh, come *on*," I said.

"We've all eaten with you before," Catcher said. "And we prefer to keep our fingers."

"How do I begin?" I asked, sheepish at the question, but there was no silverware to be found, and I'd never eaten Moroccan food before, more's the pity.

"Use the *khobz*," Catcher said, pointing to round loaves of flatbread that looked something like Indian naan. "It's Moroccan bread. Pull off a small piece, use it to pick up the meat and cous-cous. And try to keep your fingers out of our food."

I did as directed, tore off a piece of bread, picked up meat and couscous, and tasted.

It was absolutely delicious. Spicy and savory chunks of lamb, with hints of clove and cinnamon and the sweetness of raisins and dates.

"I assume you came by for a reason," Catcher said, scooping up his dinner.

"A couple, actually." I wiped my hands on my napkin, picked up the box I'd tucked beside me, and smiled at Jeff. "We were at SpringCon, and I saw this and thought you had to have it."

I passed it over, watched the smile blossom and brighten on his face. "Dude," he said, grinning over at me with such puppy adoration I thought my heart would melt right onto the floor. "You got me a Roland."

"Yeah, I saw it and I just thought—"

Before I could finish the sentence he leaped to his feet and had rounded the table and wrapped his arms around my shoulders from behind.

"That is so freaking thoughtful!"

I felt the heat rise in my cheeks and must have been blushing furiously. "You're very welcome," I said, patting his arms. "Don't do anything Fallon would kill me for."

"And sit your ass down before Melaina comes back over here and gives you the stink eye," Catcher barked. "I'm not doing this again if she cancels it in tears."

"I'm sitting, I'm sitting," Jeff said, tucking back onto his pil-low with the box in his lap. He looked up at me, beamed. "Seri-ously, awesome."

"I think you made the right choice," Jonah quietly whispered.

"Yeah," I said, tearing off a bit of *khobz*. "I feel pretty good about my choice."

Catcher's phone beeped and he pulled it out, checked it, smiled. "Your grandfather," he said with a smile, putting it away again. "He wanted to make sure you got here all right."

I pointed to my stuffed mouth.

"Yeah, I told him you were fine. He said you went by the scene."

I nodded, chewed, swallowed. "We did. He said you didn't think the pentagrams pointed to a 'legitimate' sorcerer? His words, not mine," I added at Mallory's lifted brows.

"A pentagram isn't a magical object per se," Catcher said, stirring a hunk of bread in sauce. "It's a symbol, typically used for a minor charm or incantation."

"So legitimate sorcerers *could* use them?" Jonah asked with a smile.

"They could. But they typically don't. They're useful as, let's say, training wheels. Magical shorthand. A spell crib sheet—"

"I think they get the idea, hon," Mallory gently prompted.

"It's like the swords," Catcher said. "They're vampirish, but not vampirish enough. These are magical, but not quite magical enough."

"So the killer understands the broad strokes," Jonah said, "but not the nuance."

"I'd agree with that," Catcher said.

"What about vampires?" Jonah asked. "I told them I didn't know of any historic use by vampires."

Catcher shook his head. "Me, either."

"What about the three pentagrams together?" I asked, trying

unsuccessfully to pick up more food. After years of using a fork, eating with fingers was a weirdly difficult process. "Does that maybe reference any particular charm or spell?"

Mallory held up a hand. "Wait. The first murder involved swords, and the second involved pentagrams?"

"Yeah," I said. "Why?"

Malloy looked at Catcher. "And you seriously don't know what's going on here?"

Catcher and I looked at each other, then Mallory. "No?" he said.

Her eyes went absolutely flat, and very unimpressed with us. "Are you freaking kidding me?"

"Maybe?" I asked, glancing around for help, but Jonah and Jeff just shrugged.

She made a dramatic sound of frustration, wiped her hands, and maneuvered her way to her feet again. Then she scurried off, leaving all of us peeking around the walls of the tent, trying to find our sorceress.

She dug through a purple leather tote spread open on the floor, then pulled out a smaller, dark blue bag. She practically skipped back to the table.

"Give me some room," she said, settling herself on her pillow as we moved plates out of the way, clearing a spot on the red, purple, and gold scarves that colored the tabletop.

"This isn't random," she said. "And it's not about vampires. It's probably not even about sorcerers."

She opened the bag and pulled out a large stack of rectangular cards with die-cut notches on the corners.

"The first murder didn't involve two swords," she said. "It involved the Two *of* Swords." She flipped through the deck, pulled out a card, and placed it on the table with a *snap*.

A dark-haired man in a blue tunic and pants stood in a grassy field, seven bloodred poppies punctuating the grass. His arms were outstretched, just like Brett Jacobs's in the church courtyard. Two broadswords floated in front of him, crossing just above his abdomen.

"The Two of Swords," she said, then pulled out and flipped over another card. This one showed a woman in a burgundy off-the-shoulder dress with trumpet sleeves standing in the middle of a brilliantly white and snowy tundra. Three golden pentagrams floated in the air above her. The only green in the image was from the flowering vine that wound through her hair and across her shoulders.

"And the Three of Pentacles," Mallory said.

"Holy shit," Catcher said. "The killer's using the suits of the tarot."

"Not just the suits," I said, putting the cards beside each other. "The *cards*." I pointed to the Two of Swords. "The Jacobs murder—his body was in the same position, on the grass in the courtyard, and the swords were basically in the same position, at least two-dimensionally." Three-dimensionally, they'd skewered him.

"And the Three of Pentacles?" Mallory asked.

I had to think back, focus shifting between the card and my mental image of Ingram's murder scene.

"Samantha Ingram wore a red dress," I said, then pointed to the flowering vine. "She was strangled, and the pentagrams are obvious."

"There was no snow," Catcher pointed out, and I nodded.

"True. But there was sand. It's spring; maybe that's the best he could do. The semblance isn't perfect—chalk it up to artistic license—but the major elements are the same."

"Jesus," Catcher muttered. "How did I not see that?"

"Because you're not me," Mallory jauntily said, and proceeded to place the cards in a vertical line of four. "Let's correct the terminology—pentacles, not pentagrams. Also called coins. And they aren't suits. They're the major arcana, minor arcana. The numbered cards are the latter. Swords. Pentacles. Cups. Wands."

"We aren't looking for someone obsessed with vampires," Catcher said. "We're looking for someone obsessed with tarot. Or at least someone who's interested enough to choose them as his particular vehicle of death." He looked at Mallory. "That's damned impressive."

"Thank you, sir."

"Mitzy Burrows is the CPD's current suspect," I said. "Does this fit with her background?"

"I don't know that much about her," Catcher admitted. "She's human, so the CPD's handling that part of the investigation. She worked at the Magic Shoppe, so she'd obviously be familiar with tarot cards. Right?" he asked Mallory.

"MS has the best selection of tarot cards in the metro area, at least until you get to Racine. There's a little store near one of the kringle shops. Really nice cards, including replicas of some of the old French and Italian sets—"

"So the Magic Shoppe?" Catcher prompted, heading off a derailment.

"Yeah. They have them—I've seen a set there before. But these aren't run-of-the-mill cards." She held one out to me. "Touch."

I did, felt the nubbiness of the paper. "It's got texture."

"It's die-cut watercolor paper," she said. "The Fletcher deck is hand-watercolored. There are hundreds of different kinds of tarot decks. Each one has its own symbolism. The suits, the numbers—they're all the same. So Two of Swords could be from any deck,

Three of Pentacles from any deck. But these particular images are specific to the Fletcher deck. The artist is from Chicago, actually."

I looked at Catcher, who nodded, noting the coincidence. The artist who created the deck—the deck being used as a model for human murder scenes—lived in the city.

"And who is Fletcher?" he asked.

"June Fletcher, I think," Mallory said. "Or maybe Jane. But she's gone—she died five or six years ago."

I actually felt myself deflate. "So she's not our suspect."

"Maybe not," Catcher said, "but she's another lead. Chuck will be very happy about that." He looked at Mallory. "What's the connection to the Magic Shoppe?"

"Her husband was also getting on in years, didn't want the cards stuck in some box in the house, so he took them to the store. They bought the remaining sets."

"That's a nice link," Catcher said.

"Will I get in trouble for noticing that of all the kinds of tarot cards out there, you just happen to have the same deck the killer's using?" Jonah asked, his gaze flipping from the cards to her face.

She looked down at them. "I've had these for years, actually. The Magic Shoppe is in Wicker Park. It's my hometown store, so to speak."

"Wait," I said, memories trickling in. "Is that the place where Venom worked?"

"Venom?" Catcher asked, sarcasm dripping.

"Former beau," she said. "During one of my Goth phases."

"The second one, I think. You were Rayven."

"Oh, I was." She clapped her hands together delightedly. With the classically pretty features, blue eyes, and sparking blue hair, it was hard to imagine Mallory in kohl and black lace.

"Those were good times."

I looked at Catcher. "So the cards were likely purchased at the same place where the swords were purchased, and where Mitzy Burrows was employed. I doubt that's a coincidence."

"It seems unlikely," he agreed. "But the CPD ran the store and other employees. They were clean, at least on the surface."

"So why tarot cards?" Jonah asked.

"Maybe it's just a game to her," Jeff said. "Tarot cards have number cards, suits, just like a regular deck of playing cards."

"If it's a game," I said, "it's a bloody one. Whoever's doing this doesn't care who he or she hurts, or how, or when."

"Or maybe the killer cares too much," Jeff said. "You don't have to be coldhearted to kill. You can be as passionate as anyone else—more passionate. We just have to figure out what he or she was passionate about."

Catcher pulled out his phone, rose, and walked away from the table to make the call. "I'm going to advise Chuck of our little breakthrough. Good job, Mallocake."

We all looked at Mallory. "Did he just call you Mallocake?"

She blushed to the roots of her blue hair, shrugged one shoulder. "It's a nickname."

It was also my all-time favorite snack food—a log-shaped chocolate cake with a marshmallow cream center. They were absolutely delectable. And that was kind of adorable, especially for someone like Catcher, who made Eeyore seem like an optimist.

"Young love," Jeff sang, pouring water into a ruby-colored glass. "So adorable."

I looked at him. "Haven't you and Fallon only been an official item for a few weeks?"

"We're old souls," he said matter-of-factly, as if the issue had already been decided.

"And there is an advantage to being single," Jonah said, giving me a wink as he took another bite of food.

Mallory, not yet done with her tarot reading, flipped out more cards to create a symmetrical cross.

That rang another bell. "This—the cross. Why did you put them that way?"

She looked at me, then back down at the cards. "Because that's how you do it. It's the cross form. Pretty common."

And it was another connection between the murders. "Both victims had small crosses painted on their hands."

"So the killer doesn't just know the cards," Jonah said. "She knows how to use them."

Mallory placed a final card above the cross—the Priestess, a womanly figure covered by a black hooded cape. Her outstretched hands, palms up, were the only visible portions of her body.

"Interesting," Mallory said.

"That I'm going to be made a priestess?"

"That there's conflict in your future."

Catcher came back to the table, tucking his phone away. "Chuck's going to tell Jacobs. They'll do another run on Mitzy, see what they can find."

But Mallory shook her head. "That's the wrong approach." She leaned forward, pointed at the cards. "Someone is working their way through the tarot. You don't check files or databases for this. You go to the source."

"Which is?" Catcher asked.

She rolled her eyes. "All four of you are basically paid investigators."

"But you're the occult expert," I said, remembering the old days, when we hunkered in the town house on a Friday night,

Mallory with episodes of *Buffy* and me with my favorite book of fairy tales. And look where we ended up. At a Moroccan feast organized by River nymphs in a gym owned by a sorcerer. Life was crazy that way.

"I usually work for free," she said. "I mean, I'm an honorary Ombuddy, and I've got the SWOB deal going on, but I wouldn't mind taking home a paycheck."

"I'm sorry," I said, holding up a hand. "SWOB?"

"Sorcerers Without Borders," she said. "Remember I talked about doing some community service? It's my initiative, I guess. We help folks newly identified with magic in states where the Order doesn't have an official presence."

"Like Illinois," I said, and she nodded.

"We explain the whole deal, get them mentors and training, make sure someone watches over them." She blushed a little. "You know, so as not to repeat the whole Army of Darkness in Chicago scenario."

"That's awesome," I said. "Really, really awesome."

She shrugged. "Anywho, I'd just like to bring some money into the household, you know? Make my contribution. Other than with my sweet, sweet sexual prowess."

I winced. Like most people at the table, I presumed, I neither needed nor wanted a play-by-play of Mallory and Catcher's romantic life.

"Back to the work you don't get paid for," Catcher prompted. Mallory nodded, and I tried not to think of how he'd issued "payment" for the work she did get paid for.

"You mentioned something about going to a source?" Jonah said.

"The Magic Shoppe," she said, tapping the cards.

Catcher rolled his eyes. "We took a damn long trip to get back to the Magic Shoppe."

I held in a snicker, glanced at Jonah. "Did you already go by the store?"

He shook his head. "I didn't, actually. The CPD settled on Mitzy Burrows before I could get over there. Looked like a cool place online, though. It used to be a very old-school pharmacy back in the day. Wooden floors, old-fashioned soda counter, big wall of herbal ingredients."

"We'll go tomorrow," Mallory said with a nod, the issue decided. "When the sun goes down again and there's no risk of you turning into vampire jerky on the sidewalk. Verky?" she absently considered, but rejected the word with a toss of her head. "Not the point. The point is, tomorrow."

I nodded. "Give me a call. I'll see what I can do." Seeing as how my boyfriend and I were fighting and he'd still challenged the king of vampires, my schedule could get tight.

Catcher looked at Mallory. "Don't get squirrelly and go without one of us—wait until I can go with you, or Merit can get away. Until we're sure the store's not directly connected, I want you to be careful."

"I will be," she said, and I wondered whether my voice had had the same petulant tone when I told Ethan I'd be careful. "Especially since this probably isn't over."

Catcher turned to her sharply. "What do you mean?"

Mallory put the cards she'd pulled out in numerical order again. "The killer's modeled murders on the Two of Swords and the Three of Pentacles." She pulled out the Four of Cups and Four of Wands, placed the cards on the table.

On the Four of Wands, a naked woman with a blond braid that

fell strategically across her breasts rode sidesaddle on a black destrier. She carried two long wands in each hand, and she and the horse were headed toward a castle festooned with pennants.

On the Four of Cups, a generously breasted woman in a white robe sat on the edge of a fountain and dipped her hand into the water. Four golden chalices sat on the fountain's edge around her, and a crescent moon dotted the blue sky.

"The question is—who's going to be number four?"

Cassie came back and tapped a delicate gold watch. "Time's up. Back to work."

"Easy on the eyes," Jonah said as she walked away again, "but hard on the heart."

"Trust me," Jeff said, standing and lifting the ceramic platter, which had been stripped bare of food by supernaturals. "You have no idea."

Once again, he left us speechless.

╾━┅═╍╾

CHAPTER TWELVE

PRIVATE DANCER

Jonah and I had been served by Ombuddies, which made it only fair we help bus the table in preparation for the meal to come—the one with the honored guests. We carted dirty dishes back to the gym's kitchen, exchanged used linens for clean ones.

I grabbed the obelisk from my car—thinking it safer to keep it behind steel, all things considered—and, when Catcher emerged first from the back room, handed it over.

Catcher's immediate expression was bland. He was clearly not impressed with our magical technique. "A plastic bag and salt? That's the best you could do?"

When Jonah snickered, I elbowed him. "We were trespassing in a penthouse at the time," I said. "We didn't really have time to pore through an ancient tome and figure out how to turn down the magic on an alabaster obelisk. Because, you know, assassins."

I wouldn't have admitted it to anyone, but I was really getting the hang of arguing with Catcher. And enjoying the hell out of it. A little verbal sparring put me in a good mood.

"Did you have time to pull out your phone? There's an app."

"There's no app."

Catcher gave me a flat look, pulled out his phone, thumbed the screen, and turned it to face me. A graphic of a rotary phone dial filled the screen below the words "Dial-A-Spell."

"Why do I even argue with people about this stuff anymore?"

"Because you're a vampire. It's what you do."

Mallory and Jeff walked out, eyes on the bag. "That's your charm?" she asked.

"It's something."

Mallory tapped a finger on her chin, brow furrowed as she stared through the plastic. "The salt actually neutralized it?"

"Darius came back to his senses, if that's what you mean."

"Instantly, or over time?"

"Pretty much instantly. It was like the air cleared."

Mallory nodded matter-of-factly. "Okay, okay. That helps. Some sorcerers have a style," she explained, hands moving as she talked. "You break the magic down into its component parts and actions, maybe you can figure that out. Digging through it might take a little time."

"I'd appreciate any help you can give us."

"We all would," Jonah added. "Whoever spelled that thing used it to coerce a very powerful vampire and steal a whole lot of coin. Take whatever time you need."

She looked back at the obelisk, sighed heavily. "I can deal with the salt. But seriously, a plastic bag?"

"It wasn't my idea. The other vampire did it."

"If I had a nickel . . . ," Catcher muttered.

He'd probably have been a very wealthy man.

————

By the time I returned to the House, it was a couple of hours before dawn.

On the one hand, I needed to check in with Ethan, update him about the murder, and find out whether we'd heard anything from Darius.

On the other hand, I didn't want to check in with Ethan. Didn't want to talk to him, didn't want to not talk to him about things that were obviously important, didn't want to deal with his pissy way of turning fear into anger and irritability.

But I was a grown-up, which meant eating the proverbial broccoli before dessert. So I walked to his office, promised myself a Mallocake later for doing the right thing.

When I found him staring out his office window, shoulders tight and buzzing magic in the air, I gave myself permission to have two.

I waited until he acknowledged me. When he finally glanced around, his eyes were cold marble. "Long night, Sentinel?"

I put my sword on the conference table, walked to the bar, grabbed a bottle of water. "Well, I was unconscious for most of it, due to saving your life and the resulting concussion. Most recently, I had dinner with Jonah and the Ombuddies."

I enjoyed too much that his eyes flashed at Jonah's name. If he wasn't going to be civil, I wouldn't be, either.

"I didn't realize your schedule was so . . . pliable."

I uncapped the bottle, took a drink. "It wasn't. I investigated a murder, provided an update to Mallory, Catcher, and Jeff, who were assisting my grandfather with a nymph truce, was served dinner by nymphs—an offer I didn't have the luxury of refusing—and got one step closer to a killer. In other words, I was doing my job."

His eyes changed, just a little. "One step closer?"

"The woman found tonight was Samantha Ingram. A potential Initiate at Grey House."

"That's a miserable thing to discover."

"It was. And a miserable Jonah to have to tell Scott. She had the same mark as Brett Jacobs—a small blue cross painted on her hand. That's how the CPD figured out they were connected. And Mallory realized their deaths are related to the tarot."

"How so?"

"Brett's murder involved two swords. Samantha's involved three pentagrams."

"The Two of Swords and Three of Pentacles," he said, with a nod.

"Yep. So the CPD will move forward there, look for connections between Samantha, Brett, Mitzy. Did you hear from Darius tonight?"

"Only that he's landed. He hasn't made any pronouncements, if there are any to make."

I was home safe and he'd had no contact from Darius, but his shoulders were still as stiff as granite. Something else was going on. *Damn the space he thinks he needs*, I thought, and asked the question. "And your blackmailer? Has she contacted you again?"

The tightness in his eyes was answer enough.

"She did."

He wet his lips, turned away again.

"What are you going to do?"

"I don't know."

Short and brittle answers were beginning to piss me off. "Do you think I'm going to walk away because you're being snarky? Or let you walk away from me because of something you think you did? Some wrong you committed centuries ago?"

He turned back, his eyes green fire, as if angry that I'd guessed his darkest secret, the cancer on his psyche.

"You don't know who or what I was." There was danger in his voice and in his eyes, as if he meant to remind me he was Master of his goddamned House.

"Then tell me."

He shook his head.

"You know what? I think that's bullshit. I think it's a cop-out."

"I don't care if you think it's a cop-out. I'll do whatever I think is best—whether or not that includes you."

I stiffened, leveling him with a glance that should have stripped the hide off a lesser man. There was a time I'd have been afraid to challenge him. But we'd come well past that time.

"While you're doing that thinking, I hope you manage to pull that stick out of your ass."

He stared at me, shock in his eyes.

Good, I thought. It was about time. Maybe a little anger would allow him to work through the fear.

"Don't test me, Sentinel."

"I'm not testing you. I'm promising you. If you think for one moment that I'd do anything less than give my life to protect you—*again, since I've already done it once this week*—regardless who you were back then, then you can just kiss my ass. And after all we've been through, that you don't trust me enough to tell me." I shook my head, fury burning in my eyes. "That's beneath you, Ethan. It's beneath both of us."

I walked out of the office and slammed the door, hard enough to hear pictures fall and break behind me.

That made me feel a little better.

———

It wasn't often that I needed to train to let off physical steam. There was usually trouble enough brewing in and around the House that regular workouts took care of any excess energy.

Ethan was afraid, and shutting me out, and I was hurt and angry and frustrated.

But instead of my training ensemble, I opted for old friends. A black leotard, tights that reached midcalf, and a cropped wrap sweater in pale pink that I hadn't worn in at least a year. It had been too long since I'd worn toe shoes. I guessed I'd be able to make the transition, but I didn't have the time or materials to break in a new pair of toe shoes, so I opted for ballet slippers.

Shoes in hand, I closed the apartment doors as I shrugged into the wrap sweater, then went downstairs to the basement training room. I cracked open the door, found the room empty. I walked inside, closed and locked it, and leaned back against it with a smile.

This was my time, and it had been much too long.

I rolled back the tatami mats that covered the center of the floor, then turned on the audio system. Music was one of Luc's favorite ways to ensure we fought with appropriate rhythm, which he was convinced was crucial to defending an attack. Tonight, it was crucial to maintaining my sanity.

Music—a diva singing over a heavy bass line—filled the air. *Perfect*, I thought, adjusting the volume so Luc, in the Ops Room next door, wouldn't think the building was under attack.

I walked to the middle of the room, racked with a sudden bout of self-consciousness. I hadn't done this in a really long time. I closed my eyes, rolled my shoulders, and began to stretch out. Arms, back, calves, hamstrings. I imagined one of my former ballet teachers' favorite cadences: *Plié! Relevé! Plié! Relevé!* Over and over again.

When my body was warm, I pulled off the shrug, tossed it near the door. I closed my eyes, dropped my head, and let my body feel the thud of the bass.

It started like ballet, with long lines, arabesques, and pirouettes. Then *grand battement* and *grand jeté*, the stretch and flex of muscles and tendons glorious. Sword fighting was an art, certainly. But dance was something altogether different.

The song turned mournful, and I slowed, spinning with arms above me, arms around me, arms out. A kick, an arabesque, then hands on the ground, legs flipping over one at a time until I was on my feet again.

Arm work. Fast moves—in, out, arms above my head, hips moving in time. Footwork—shuffled steps, a spin with bent knees, then straight up again. Backward flip into a spin. I hit the floor on my knees, draped my torso over my legs, let my hands fall to the floor.

Applause lit through the room.

Shocked, I looked up, mopped my bangs from my face, and found two dozen vampires on the balcony, including a green-eyed devil—presently silver eyed—who stared down at me.

I hadn't thought to lock the balcony door, and I'd been so completely involved in the stretch and flex of muscle that I hadn't realized I wasn't alone. Which, I guess, was exactly the point.

I had no idea what he was thinking or feeling—not just because he hadn't talked to me about it, but because the look in his eyes was unfathomable. Pain, confusion, fear, love, pride, or maybe all of them. I don't know how long we stood there. Master and ballerina staring each other down, Ethan's past between us again. This wasn't the first time we'd locked horns over it, and I doubted it would be the last. Ethan had four hundred years of experience and memories packed into his brain, and all the issues that came with them. He was an enigma—probably the most frustrating enigma I'd ever met.

He blinked first, dropping his gaze, turning, and disappearing through the balcony door, still a mystery to me.

Dawn was approaching. Since I'd wrung out my anger, it was time to get some work done.

I pulled on the wrap sweater, thanked the vampires who made their way down to the floor to thank me, and put the training room back in order.

I stepped outside, found vampires filing back into the Ops Room or upstairs; Ethan was already gone.

"Good workout, Sentinel?" Luc was already at the conference table, ankles kicked up. There was a shit-eating grin on his face. "If we'd known you could dance like that, we'd have made you social chair. Oh, wait. Did that."

I gave him a look.

"Have you and Ethan made up yet?"

"You'd have to ask him," I said, accepting with a smile the bottle of water that Brody handed me. "Thank you."

"You're very welcome. You earned it after that little display. You had quite an audience in the gallery."

I wiped my face, wrapped the towel around my neck. "So I saw."

"The murder?" Luc asked.

"Samantha Ingram, one of Grey House's Initiate applicants."

"Jesus, add that to the swords, and it's a horrible coincidence."

"Actually, it looks like they were trying to peg sorcerers here. The body was marked with pentagrams. But we think we found the connection. What do you know about the tarot?"

"The cards?" Luc asked, sitting back and linking his hands

behind his head in what I'd come to learn was his classic "thinking" pose.

"The cards," I confirmed. "The murders actually match up pretty well with the artwork in an exclusive tarot deck made by a Chicago artist."

His brows shot up. "That's something."

"It would have been, except she's deceased. The murders we've seen so far? Two of Swords and Three of Pentacles."

"That fit with their suspect? Missy? That she'd use tarot?"

"Mitzy. And we don't know yet. The CPD's going to look into it, but Mallory thinks the real deal is the Magic Shoppe—it's where the swords were purchased, and it's apparently the only place to get this particular deck."

"That's a lead," Luc agreed with a nod. "You following it up?"

"With Mallory, hopefully tomorrow." I leaned forward. "Did you talk to Ethan about his"—I noted the interested expressions in a few of the temps at computer stations around the room and lowered my voice—"his troubles?"

Luc's expression flattened. "Ethan didn't talk to you about them?"

"No. He's decided shutting me out is a good strategy."

Luc whistled. "All due respect to my Liege and Master, I seriously hope you blistered his hide."

"I'm not sure really sure what that means, but I did give him a very pointed piece of my mind."

"Good for you."

"What happened, exactly?"

Luc frowned, clearly torn by his loyalty to his Master—and his likely promise to keep his Master's word. "All I know is, he got a phone call. And he wasn't thrilled about it."

That would be "her." "He didn't say who called?"

Luc shook his head. "A few fierce and quietly spoken words."

"That's no good," I said.

"Maybe. But it got you in a leotard again," Luc said, winging up his brows suggestively. "He'll come around."

I hoped Luc was right. I hoped Ethan would come around, share with me whatever he was afraid to share.

And I hoped, when he did, it was something I could handle.

When I returned to the apartments, I found a small tray of snacks and a short vase of creamy white peonies. They put a heady floral scent in the air. Margot's doing, undoubtedly.

Ethan stood in front of his bureau, placing watch and accoutrements into a leather valet. He watched me come in but didn't speak. I took a quick shower, exchanged workout clothes for a tank and pajama bottoms. Brushed my teeth. Generally took my time.

When I emerged, Ethan stood beside the bed in shirtsleeves. He looked at me, eyes almost painfully green. But he didn't move forward. He let the bed stand between us, a physical symbol of his unspecified "regrets."

"I saw you dance."

I sat down on the bed. "I wasn't dancing for you."

"No," he said. "I suppose you weren't. I expect you were dancing in opposition to me."

"That sounds closer."

His frustration was nearly palpable, his magic irritable. "I do what I do to protect you. That I trained you to fight, to bear a sword, to act with honor, doesn't negate the fact that I would give my life for you, Merit."

My heart softened, and I ached for him. My chest hurt with it;

my stomach was raw with it. "Not telling me about your past doesn't protect me. It doesn't shield me from anything but the truth of who you are."

Silence. "Perhaps you're right," he said, his voice growing thicker, his words slower. "But the past is immutable. Only the future can be written."

The shutters closed over the windows, and the sun rose again, as it always did. And we fell into slumber beside each other with nothing else resolved.

CHAPTER THIRTEEN

EAT YOUR HEART OUT

Ethan was gone when I rose, the remains of breakfast on the tray Margot usually left by the door at sunset. An empty bottle of blood, crumbs from a croissant. He'd left me a second bottle and pastry, and a trio of lusciously red strawberries that made me glad spring was on its way.

I sat down at the small desk in the sitting area, glanced at the folded *Tribune* that sat beside the tray. Samantha Ingram's murder was the main story, and the headline was telling: WOULD-BE VAMP KILLED—SUPERNATURALS AT FAULT?

On the other hand, reading through the story, it looked like the reporter hadn't yet made the connection between the sword and pentacle murders. Not that several cops, an Ombudsman, two vamps, a sorcerer, and a shifter had made the connection, either. It took a sorceress with a love of all things weird and witchy.

When I felt prepared to face the night, I checked my phone, found messages waiting.

Mallory had worked her particular magic. YOU'RE LUCKY, she'd said. THE MAGIC SHOPPE HAS OVERNIGHT INVENTORY TONIGHT; THEY'LL BE EXPECTING US.

I arranged to meet her in an hour, traffic depending, at her Wicker Park home.

My grandfather had also sent a message: There was, unfortunately, still no sign of Mitzy Burrows. But they had confirmed—and quickly this time—that Samantha Ingram had been given Rohypnol, just like Brett.

Both victims had been drugged, killed, laid out in very public spaces, their bodies arranged like scenes in a very particular type of tarot card. Both had been marked with small blue crosses. Those were particular, unusual, and supernatural elements. But why? Because the killer loved magic? Or hated it? Or did the killer not care either way, but wanted to take out a handful of people, and found the city's supernaturals very convenient scapegoats?

Unfortunately, I didn't have the answers. I did have a sword and a fast car, and no specific interest in talking to Ethan yet tonight. So I sent him and Luc a message, advised them of my travel plans, and grabbed my jacket and sword.

I headed north toward Wicker Park. Mallory and Catcher lived in the town house I'd once shared with her, a home she'd inherited when her only living relative, an aunt, had passed away. It still held her aunt's flowery and comfy furniture, although Catcher had upgraded the audio equipment, and Catcher had transformed the musty and spider-laden basement into a spell-crafting room worthy of Martha Stewart.

I took the opportunity to call Jonah and check in.

"Hey," he slowly said. "Thanks for calling me, Grandma. Hold on just a minute."

I blinked at the non sequitur—and the muffled words I couldn't make out in the interim—but kept my eyes on the road. "I'm holding and assume you'll explain what this is momentarily."

"Absolutely, Grandma."

More muffled words, followed by the squeak of furniture and shuffling. The reason for the pretense belatedly occurred to me.

"You're on a date!"

"I am sorry I missed your birthday, Grandma, and I'm glad you called so we could talk it over."

"Is she cute? Ooh, is she human? River nymph?" It was immature, but flustering him was fun. It also helped our relationship from becoming too awkward, since he'd once expressed feelings for me.

"Uncool, Merit."

I grinned. "You called me your grandmother. Which I take to mean you're dating a human, since I'm not aware you have any living relatives."

"First date," he admitted. "I found it didn't work so well when I told girls I was a vampire right off the bat."

"*Twilight* effect?"

"*Twilight* effect," he agreed. "They get bummed when I show up without brown hair, pale skin, a moody expression, and sparkles."

"And how's it going?"

"It's going. And since it's going, what can I do for you?"

"Sorry, small update: They found Rohypnol in Samantha Ingram's system, too."

"Another connection between the murders."

"Yeah. I'm heading to the Magic Shoppe right now to take a look-see with Mallory."

"Excellent. You get on that, and give me an update when you can. Go team. And I'm hanging up now, because my date is beginning to look at me suspiciously."

"Just wait until she sees your fangs, sunshine."

Wicker Park was technically part of the West Town neighborhood and had a main street full of quirky shops, restaurants, and bars. The streets were quiet tonight, although humans still stood outside bars, cigarettes in hand, and music still pumped from the open doorways of clubs.

Parking in Wicker Park, like in most Chicago neighborhoods, was tricky. Mallory was one of the lucky few to have a garage behind her town house, but the small drive was filled by her and Catcher's vehicles.

I cruised for a few minutes, just in case rock-star-quality parking was available outside her town house, but gave up and parked Moneypenny a block away. The spot wasn't ideal; I'd wedged her in between a truck and an SUV whose drivers I hoped were good at squeaking their way out of parallel spots without bumping the cars around them. But at least the piles of snow were nearly gone, and I didn't have to climb a gray wall of ice and gravel in order to make it to the sidewalk.

I walked to the house, climbed the front steps, and knocked on the door. Catcher answered it a moment later, a frilly apron tied around his waist.

I opened my mouth, closed it again. Settled on, "There are hardly words."

"Oh, good. Vampire humor. You should really think about doing stand-up."

I spiraled a finger in the air, pointing at the apron. It featured cats knitting, although I wasn't sure how they managed to hold knitting needles in their little paws. "The apron," I said. "Let's discuss."

"I'm making cookies. I didn't want to ruin my shirt. It was in a drawer."

I bypassed the apron to focus on the more important part. "You bake?"

"Very well. Would you like a madeleine?"

"When wouldn't I want a madeleine?"

"Fair point," he said, turning toward the kitchen.

I followed him through the house's dining room and into the quaint kitchen, the smells of butter and lemon wafting through the air.

"They smell amazing."

"They are." Catcher wasn't one for modesty. He donned a quilted mitt and pulled a narrow aluminum tray of shell-shaped cakes from the oven. They were beautifully puffed and golden and made my stomach rumble immediately. It didn't care that I'd had breakfast; it recognized sugar and fat.

"These need to rest," he said, putting the pan carefully on a wire rack to cool. "But there's more over there." He slid another tray into the oven, then pulled off the mitt, gestured to a plastic container half-full of the small cakes.

I grabbed one, bit in, and had a new kind of respect for Catcher. He took care of my grandfather, seemed to make Mallory happy, and had taught me how to wield a sword. And he could bake.

"Amazing," I said, leaning against the counter as I savored the small cake—buttery and sweet with the tang of fresh lemon— bite by tiny bite. "What's the occasion?"

The oven timer beeped, and he donned the mitt again, pulled

out another tray, and made room on the cooling rack for a new batch of madeleines.

"I don't need an occasion to bake, any more than you need an occasion to eat."

"I'll chalk that down as 'I enjoy it.' Where's your intrepid blue-haired girlfriend? We're supposed to go to the magic store."

"Downstairs. She's just finishing something up with the obelisk. Looking for source. Color of magic or some such. Frankly, it's a bit more chemistry than I'm usually into."

Since he'd just made madeleines—with carefully measured ingredients, if the digital scale on the counter was any indication—I found that ironic.

"I'll see myself downstairs," I said, and grabbed two more madeleines for good measure, tossing them between my fingers to keep from boiling myself.

I took the stairs to the basement and the meticulously organized workshop that had supplanted the cobweb-infested basement. The walls had been finished, the floors redone, the ingredients for charms or hexes or whatever she worked up down here in neat jars and baskets along shelved walls.

Mallory sat cross-legged on a white stool in front of the large white table that tonight held a stack of books and an array of ingredients in white ceramic pots, the obelisk in front of them.

Her hair was pulled into two side buns that made her look like Princess Leia had been dunked in Kool-Aid. She held a yogurt container in one hand and a spoon in the other, and she'd paired jeans with a T-shirt with HONORARY OMBUDDY across the front in block letters.

"Where did you get that?" I asked as she dug around the container for the remnants of vanilla with blueberries.

"The official Ombudsman gift shop, all rights reserved."

I offered a (single) madeleine, which she happily accepted in exchange for the empty yogurt cup, which I tossed away. "Nobody told me about a gift shop. Or brought me a T-shirt. I want to be an honorary Ombuddy."

"I think you probably are because, you know, genetics. Your grandfather hasn't given you one yet?"

"No," I said, jealousy prickling. "But the last time I saw him he did have other things on his mind."

"Murder and whatnot?" she asked.

"In fairness, yeah. Mostly the murder. Little bit of the whatnot. You working on the obelisk?"

"I am," she said with a frown, nibbling the cookie and using a hand to push off the tabletop, rotate on her stool. "And I am getting nowhere. Except that it's a polyglot."

"I'm sorry—the obelisk is a polyglot?"

She rotated again. "It speaks several languages."

"I understand the word; I don't understand the application."

She grabbed the table's edge with her fingertips, pulled herself to a stop. "So, when you magick something—as this bit of alabaster has been charmed—there are different ways you apply the magic. You can do it with words; you can do it with stuff; you can do it with feeling."

"That will of the universe stuff?" That was how Catcher had first explained his and Mallory's magic to me—that they were able to exert their wills on the universe. I'd learned later that was one of many approaches to the magical world, which were as varied and sundry as human religions.

Mallory nodded. "Precisely. And within each one of those ways, there are sub-ways. If you're working up a spell, you can add the ingredients in a different order, say the words differently, mix it under a full moon, what have you. Those are basically languages."

"And you can tell what language was used?"

"To some degree, yeah. Each step leaves a kind of"—she searched for a word—"fingerprint in the magic. You work a little reverse magic, you can try to read all those fingerprints."

"That's really awesome. It's like magic forensics."

"It is magic forensics," Mallory said. "Just don't tell Catcher that you said so. Too 'newfangled' for him. Although I am super good at it."

"You could add it to your résumé. Along with SWOB."

"SWOB!" she playfully chanted, throwing a fist in the air.

"So what are the fingerprints here?"

"Little bit of *Speilwerk*—that's magic with Pennsylvania Dutch origins. Little bit of British herbalism. But the primary language is American, including the main ingredient." She reached out, grabbed a bowl, and held it out to me. "Smell."

I lifted a brow, looked down into the bowl, which held a fine gray-green powder. "Will it turn me into a newt?"

"Yes," she flatly said. "Smell it anyway."

I leaned toward the bowl, sniffed delicately. "It smells . . . green. Pungent. Herby. What is it?"

Mallory smiled, put the bowl back on the table. "Exactly. It's filé powder—the ground leaves of the sassafras tree. It's primarily used in gumbo or, in certain locations in the South, in certain herbal remedies and charms. Such as this little gal here." She picked up the obelisk, put it down again.

"What does that tell you about the person who magicked it?"

"That's what I'm still trying to figure out. First impression?

Someone who's versed in different schools of magic, but not just academically. There's a certain creativity here—a willingness to mix the different styles. Like jazz. This was, kind of, a magical riff."

"Is this the work of a sorcerer?" There was concern behind the question, and from her expression, she realized it. A rogue sorcerer was bad enough; a rogue sorcerer helping unknown parties control vampires was much, much worse.

"It could be," she said. "This improvisational magic—you have to have a certain level of experience and knowledge to do that. Otherwise every third grader with a plastic recorder would be a Coltrane. But you don't have to be a sorcerer—the way we define it—to make magic. Spells, charms, herbalism. Those are approaches to magic that we can use, but we aren't the only ones."

"So we have the what, but not really the who?"

She smiled sadly. "I'm sorry. It's possible I'll get something else out of it, but there's not a guidebook I can use for this. I kind of have to make it up as I go along." She pointed at me. "Now, if you can get me something from a suspect, I could see if the magicks match."

"You'll be the first to know."

"I will say this: To get involved in that kind of vampire drama—that level of vampire drama?—they'd demand a price. Money, power . . . I don't know. But it would be steep."

I nodded, thinking of the GP—its current members all based in Europe. They seemed the most likely to have the connections, resources, and opportunity to hijack Darius's brain.

I realized I hadn't yet heard from my dad about the Swiss account to which the U.S. money had been transferred, and sent him a follow-up message. I felt a little guilty asking him for help when I hadn't seen him in weeks. On the other hand, he'd tried to bribe Ethan to make me a vampire, and he was still working off that particular debt.

"Does the Order have any contact with their European counterparts?" The Order was the American union of sorcerers.

"Once upon a time," Mallory said, leaning forward and linking her hands on the table, "there was this little thing called the American Revolution."

"I'm vaguely familiar."

She stuck out her tongue. "The answer is no. They don't communicate. Postrevolutionary bitterness."

"One if by land, grouchy if by sea."

"Exactly." She glanced at the clock on the wall. "We should get going. I told them we'd be there around ten." She uncrossed her legs and hopped off the stool. I followed her upstairs to the living room, where she grabbed a jacket from the back of the love seat. "We're leaving," she told Catcher.

He looked up from his spot on the other couch, already tucked in with a bottle of 312 beer and a magazine. "Did you take out the trash?"

"What? Oh, sorry, can't hear you . . ." she mumbled, grabbing her keys and purse and hustling me outside.

I guessed she wasn't taking out the trash.

"Sounds like things are back to normal with you and Catcher," I said as we walked down the stairs to the sidewalk.

"Things are domestic." At my look of concern, she waved me off.

"It's not a bad thing, just an adjustment. You've seen him mostly naked. He has the body of a god, Merit. Seriously—he has muscles I didn't even know existed. Very nommable hills and valleys. And he's going on about the trash."

Ethan and I hadn't really had the opportunity to argue about the trash—both because we usually had too much other drama to deal with and, frankly, because he hired staff to do that kind of thing. Helen, the House's den mother, managed the general up-keep of the centuries-old building, so Ethan and I hadn't once had to argue about the vacuuming or the dishes. Considering my preference for equality and his imperial nature, I bet those con-versations would have been frequent and unpleasant.

Score one for Helen.

"Car's right here," I said, gesturing, but she waved me on and kept walking toward Division.

"It's, like, six blocks away. We'll chat, get a little exercise." She hooked an arm through mine. "Now, give me all the dish at Cado-gan House."

There was, of course, a lot to tell, at least as far as my relation-ship was concerned. As we walked past the town houses of Wicker Park—tall, narrow, and brick, with cute stoops and tiny patches of green in front—I told her about Ethan and the mysterious woman in his past.

"So he's got a mysterious lady in his past, and she's making threats because she doesn't want him to lead the GP?" She kicked a rock, sent it skipping down the sidewalk. "Were they lovers?"

Mallory wasn't one to mince words, which was exactly why I'd told her. "I don't know. But it wouldn't matter to me if she was. I mean, I accept that he has a past. I wasn't a saint before we met."

She slid me a glance.

"I wasn't."

"You were a nerdy English lit student; you were as close as it gets without beatification. But keep going."

For the sake of my emotional well-being, I ignored my urge to fight the point, got us back on track. "I can live with Ethan's past, his ego, the fact that he's an alpha. But he's pushing me away about this, and I don't understand why."

"You really don't see it?" she asked, spritely dodging a suspicious brown pile in the middle of the sidewalk.

"See what?"

"His problem. To not put too fine a point on it, he's a control freak. I don't mean that in a bad way. He works hard to protect what's his, and now he's trying to extend that range of protection. He's trying to exert his sizable will on the GP, the Houses in Europe and the U.S.

"But he's got people from his past—including this crazy woman—coming out of the woodwork. He doesn't like to be reminded that he's vulnerable—or that you are—and she knows exactly what buttons to push. She knows how to get to Ethan. And that scares the shit out of him. Especially now, the very time he's trying to prove how strong and powerful and fearless he is. That's like a Darth Sullivan tornado of horrors."

Faux words aside, she made a lot of sense.

"Bottom line, he loves you. Powerfully. And he's trying to build a life with you. This heifer's getting in the way. Maybe he's a little embarrassed he can't control it; maybe he's a little afraid he'll lose you because of it."

"He's been pushing me away."

"Better to push you away than have you see him as less or different than you do now. I've seen you look at him, Merit. He's seen you look at him. There's a lot of things there—love, heat, amusement. But there's also admiration. A man like Ethan isn't going to risk that lightly."

I nodded, and we walked a few steps in companionable silence. I cleared my throat, told her the rest of it. "Before all this, he was hinting about a proposal."

She stopped short, jaw dropped. "You are shitting me."

"Not even a little."

Mallory looked at me for a moment, and then her smile dawned bright and excited. "Darth Sullivan is going to *propose*."

"Well, he *was* going to propose. Now who the hell knows?" I blew out a breath, rolled my shoulders in frustration. "What do I do about this, Mallory? It makes me want to scream and cry at the same time."

"You two have always run hot," she said. "Most people, I think they operate somewhere between four and seven."

"Four and seven?"

"On a scale of one to ten. One being totally disinterested, ten being crazy, can't-keep-our-hands-off-each-other love."

"Angelina and Billy Bob."

"Correct. You two operate in the seven to nine zone, and that's only the stuff I've actually been around to see. I'd guess you two run hot the rest of the time, too."

"He told me he just gave me the chance to blossom, to become the person I was meant to be."

Mallory put a hand on her chest, sighed. "For all his faults, which are legion, Darth Sullivan has a way with words. I assume he also has a way with what I'm assuming is an impressive endowment. Is sex an option? I find it fixes many things that ail the alpha type."

"That's not really a problematic area."

"Good. And not surprising. Vampire or not, he cleans up well." She bobbed her head as she considered. "In that case, I say you have to mix things up. Steal the ball. Run a new play. Jump higher than everyone else. Fake out the QB."

"You can stop with the mixed sports metaphors. I suppose I need to stage some kind of Ethan intervention."

She nodded emphatically. "Merit, sneaking around behind Darth Sullivan's back? I love it."

"If he kicks me out, I can sleep under your table in the crafts room, right?"

"No," she said, without hesitation. "But you can sleep on the floor of the Ombud's van."

But not with my own Ombuddy T-shirt, I glumly thought.

CHAPTER FOURTEEN

FILL IT 'TIL YOU SPILL IT

It was late, and most of the restaurants and shops on Division were locked up tight for the night. But lights shined brightly in the "all-nite" pizza joint and the bar next door, and the store that sat beside them in a small strip.

"The Magic Shoppe" was painted across the front glass in old-fashioned gold letters that looked like they'd been chiseled. Although the lights were on, the store looked empty. Mallory squinted as she peered through the glass, then tapped a fist against the door.

It took a few minutes—and another round of tapping—before a tall man, as lean as a whipcord—walked up one of the long aisles. He wore a snug plaid shirt and corduroys, and his brown hair was cut into a short Caesar. His face was long, his chin covered in a thick goatee, and there were bags under his eyes.

Late for him, I guessed.

He had a clipboard and large round key ring in hand, and he stuck the clipboard under his arm to unlock the door. He pulled it, the mechanism squealing in protest and a leather strap with a bell jangling.

"Hey, Mallory," he said. "Long time no see. Come on in."

"Hey, Curt. It's been a while," she agreed. I followed her inside. "Trying to work off my current stock. The store looks good," she said, glancing around.

It looked much like Jonah had described it. The store was long and narrow, the floor made of scarred wooden planks, the walls lined in wooden bead board. A long wooden counter filled the left side of the room, its backer mirrored and edged in fluted wooden columns that reached from the floor to the ceiling of the wall behind it. "Smithson Pharmacy" was etched in faded gold letters across the top of the mirror, and on glass apothecary jars of mysterious substances. The right-hand side of the store was lined with shelves, and the weapons FaireMaker Nan had mentioned hung high along the back wall. Katanas, *wakizashi*, daggers, sais. There was an array to choose from, and at least far away, they looked like quality instruments.

The place smelled witchy—the scents of dust and paper mixed with the bright fragrance of dried plants and herbs.

"Business is good," he agreed. "Although I'm tired tonight."

Mallory nodded sympathetically. "We appreciate your opening up the store."

"You said something about tarot cards?"

"Yeah. We actually think they're being used in a crime. I wanted to show Merit your stash, maybe get your thoughts?"

He scratched the back of his head, yawned hugely—and sourly—while he led us to a glass case in the back of the store. He pointed at it. "Cards are in there. I'm right in the middle of a count. Let me get someone to help you."

She put a hand on his arm. "Actually, before you go, a question— Mitzy Burrows. What do you think of her?"

His expression went guarded. "The CPD has already asked me about Mitzy. They asked all of us."

"And I'm sure they appreciate your cooperation. It's just—someone else was killed. We really need to find her."

"Someone else was . . ." He began to talk, but then shook his head. "Look, nobody was perfect. But she wouldn't kill anybody. She certainly wouldn't kill two people."

"You were friends?"

Something flashed in his eyes. "We were, and I'm not going to stand around gossiping about her. I'm sorry, but she doesn't work here anymore, so what she does isn't my business. And frankly, I don't see that it's any of yours."

Mallory waited until he was gone. "He's tense."

"Yeah," I agreed. "And maybe a little bitter. Did you see his eyes? There was something there when you asked if they were friends."

"You're thinking ex-friends?"

"Or ex–something else."

Mallory nodded, gestured to the glass case he'd pointed out, and we made our way toward it.

Boxes of cards were displayed in tidy rows, from oversized cards that could have doubled as door hangers to a deck of cards half as big as a credit card. The art varied from fantastic to art nouveau, and so did the price. The decks ranged from a few dollars to several hundred.

"The Rider-Waite," Mallory said, pointing to a yellow box. "Probably the classic American tarot card. Old-fashioned artwork, lots of delicious symbolism."

Most telling was the empty spot in the third row.

"Someone bought a box of tarot cards recently," Mallory said. "And they haven't restocked yet."

"Inventory," said a woman behind us.

We turned around, found a petite human with her dark hair

pulled into a topknot, the tips of her ears shaped into delicate elf-like points. She wasn't an elf—or magic at all, as far as I could tell—so the ears must have been an homage. She wore a black skirt over chevron tights, clunky boots with thick, flat soles, and a shirt with short, puffy sleeves. She also carried a clipboard, a yellow pencil tucked beneath the silver clip.

"I'm Skylar-Katherine Tyler," she said.

"Hi, Skylar. I'm Mallory, and this is Merit."

"Skylar-Katherine."

Mallory blinked. "I'm sorry?"

"My name is Skylar-Katherine. With a hyphen. Middle name Mary Francis. Last name Tyler. Skylar-Katherine Mary Francis Tyler."

That seemed like a lot of letters to lay on a kid. More power to her for remembering them in order. "I bet when you were little you could never find one of those little license plates with your name. I certainly couldn't."

Skylar-Katherine stared at me. "You're asking about the tarot cards. We had a Fletcher deck. Sold it a week ago."

Excitement built, and I saw the gleam of success in Mallory's eyes. It was the right deck and the right timing—a week before both of the murders.

"You haven't replaced it yet?" I wondered. "I understood you bought the back stock?"

Skylar-Katherine nodded. "We did." She gestured toward the stockroom. "Inventory. We're not bringing anything else out until we've counted everything."

"Could you tell us who bought the deck?" Mallory asked.

"Our customers like their privacy. Not everyone who shops here likes that fact announced to the public."

Mal's blue eyes flashed with irritation. "I'm one of your customers, and normally I'd agree with you. But we think the deck was used to commit a crime."

Skylar-Katherine looked us over, and she didn't seem impressed. "You're not cops."

"We're working with the CPD and the Ombudsman's office," Mallory said. "We thought your staff and customers would prefer a visit from us—people who know the ropes—instead of police in uniforms. I don't imagine that would be very good for business."

Skylar-Katherine looked irritated, but she must have recognized the logic. "Fine," she said. "Give me a minute."

"Damn," I said, as she disappeared through the door. "That was seriously impressive."

"I have mad skills. But, you know, if Mitzy really did this, she could have just taken the box. There may not be a receipt."

True, but I doubted Skylar-Katherine wanted to answer our questions about Mitzy. On the other hand . . . "If Mitzy—or any other employee—was going to take a deck, why take it from the display box? They'd know it was missing. They could have lifted it from the back room."

"True," she said.

I shrugged. "We'll want to see the receipt either way."

When Skylar-Katherine emerged a minute later with a slip of paper in her hand, I decided they should be paying Mallory a lot. At least until she spoke.

"The receipts from a week ago are already in storage. Inventory," she said again, this time her tone haggard. "This is the manager's name and address. You want the information, you'll have to talk to him."

"Will he be available later today?" Mallory asked.

"He might be. He might not."

"Let me guess," Mallory said, tucking the paper away. "Inventory."

Mallory chatted with Skylar-Katherine about a deal on phoenix feathers (or so I guessed) while I perused the store. It was an opportunity I couldn't exactly pass up.

Every time I thought I'd begun to get a handle on the world of the supernatural, something surprised me. In this particular case, it was the half dozen shelves of jars that apparently held ingredients for charms and spells.

Shakespeare had been right: "Eye of newt" was really a thing, as were toe of frog, wool of bat, and lizard's leg. I decided to believe the newt, bat, frog, and lizard had been thoroughly compensated for their contributions to the magical arts, because they didn't look especially content as their bits floated in yellowish liquid.

"I think we're all done," Mallory said when she joined me.

"Do you buy this stuff?"

She glanced at the shelves. "Sometimes. I really like to browse, but I try not to pay retail," she said, dropping her voice to a whisper. "You go through a lot of stuff, you need to keep an eye on the coin. I use Spellseller.com quite a bit. It's cheaper, free shipping, points with every purchase. Although . . . ," she said, trailing off as she picked up a white box with "Wolfsbane" printed in calligraphy on the end.

Mallory opened the box but then closed it and returned it to the shelf. "Hey, Skylar-Katherine!" she called out.

A pause, then "What?" echoed through the store.

"The wolfsbane. Do you have any more in stock?"

"Isn't that poisonous?" I asked, vaguely remembering a warning Catcher had given.

"Deadly to shifters in large quantities, but according to Berna,

pretty useful in smaller doses. And hella hard to find online."
Berna was a shifter, aunt to the Apex of the North American Central Pack, and a damn good cook.

Skylar-Katherine appeared at the end of the row. "Empty box?"

Mallory nodded as Skylar-Katherine checked her clipboard. I guess the inventory had been useful after all. "Not at the moment. Hey, Curt!"

"Yeah?"

"Wolfsbane?"

He appeared on the other end of the row, a stack of boxes in hand. "What about it?"

"You got any restock in the back? They need some."

Curt looked at Mallory appraisingly. "That's dangerous stuff. Could make someone sick."

"I'm all but licensed," she said. "And it won't be for humans, if you catch my drift."

"Okay. Just so you know. There's a shipment from our herbalist coming in day after tomorrow. It should be on that truck." He adjusted his boxes, scratched his cheek. "We can hold it for you."

"Might be after hours before I can get over here."

Skylar-Katherine tapped the clipboard, walked toward the back of the store. "We'll be here. Inventory."

"When was the last time you ate?" Mallory asked as the bell rang us out and Curt locked the door again.

"I had a bite of breakfast. And several madeleines. But I should probably get back to the House. I can grab something on the way." I needed to process what we'd learned, update Luc and Jonah, find out whether we'd heard anything else about Darius.

"You probably should get back to the House," she agreed as

we walked back down Division. "But right now you're with me, and I'm starving, and you have to eat anyway, and I'm jealous."

That stopped me in the middle of the sidewalk. "Jealous? Of what?"

"Of Ethan. Of Jonah." She cleared her throat self-consciously. "Of Lindsey. We're getting our shit back together—I'm getting *my* shit back together—and I miss you."

"You do recall that I had to move into Cadogan House in the first place because you invited Catcher in?"

"Young love," she blandly said. "It had been a really long time since I'd been with someone who got me the way that he gets me. I kind of dived headfirst into it."

"You did," I agreed. "And I don't fault you for that. But I didn't pick teams. I just needed a place to live. Furniture that Catcher hadn't been bare-ass naked on."

"He and Ethan were friends," Mallory pointed out. "There's no telling how bare that ass has been in Cadogan House."

"Don't want to think about it."

"I just—I miss you. And I'd like us to spend more time to-gether. Maybe I can't make up for that lost time, for choosing dicks over chicks, so to speak, but I'd like to see you more often."

She said it so shyly, so meekly, that I nearly got teary-eyed. But I'd had enough near-tear moments in the last few days, so I sucked it up.

"You're right—I have to eat, and you'll definitely be better company than Darth Sullivan. I can check in with the House while we eat. And speaking of"—I glanced around the darkened streets—"there's not much open around here."

"Oh, but there is," she said, turning around so she walked backward in front of me. "Do you remember what we've always talked about? Our dream restaurant?"

"The All You Can Eat Bacon Hut?"

"The other one."

I searched my memory, stopped still. "No."

Mallory stopped in front of me, grinned. "Yes."

"No freaking way."

She nodded briskly. "Uh-huh. Some restaurateurs are doing a 'beta test' or something, and it's only two blocks away."

This time, I tucked my arm in hers. "In that case, let's eat."

It was the concept of our dreams, born after one too many nights at restaurants that offered rice bowls of the Choose Your Own Adventure variety.

But what if the bowl wasn't just rice? What if it wasn't just faux Chinese or Tex-Mex?

What if the bowl could hold *anything*?

We'd spent one warm spring night on her stingy back porch with cheap blush wine and her current incarnation of a boyfriend, and we'd set out a plan: a restaurant in which you could assemble the bowl of your dreams. The bowl of your deepest longings. From shepherd's pie to a barbecue sundae, seven-layer dip or a trifle of cakes and berries if that floated your boat. There'd be cold stations, hot stations, and plenty of snacks.

We'd called it "Baller Bowl." And it was going to be legendary.

The restaurateurs called it "Layers," and they'd built it in a long, narrow space with exposed-brick walls and small tables in front of an equally long oak banquette.

A man with black disks in his earlobes and wearing a snug plaid shirt brought cups of water and two sturdy white bowls to our table.

"Welcome to Layers, ladies." He reached for silverware in the black apron around his neck. "Spoon, fork, or spork?"

Mallory and I looked at each other, eyes wide. "Sporks," we simultaneously said as our dreams came true.

The waiter put two silver sporks on the table. "Hot bars on the right, cold bars on the left. One trip per bowl, and each bowl's ten dollars. Fill it 'til you spill it," he added, pointing at the motto on the wall behind us, and left us to work our magic.

I walked Mallory back to the town house with a belly full of layers—heavy on the mashed potatoes, lardons, peas, and grilled chicken.

We reached the front porch, turned to face each other like teenagers at the end of an evening. "Now that you've fed me, I should get back to the House. Do me a favor? Don't tell anyone about the proposal thing. Especially not Catcher. I don't think I'm up for that kind of teasing."

"Like he would tease you about that."

I gave her a flat look, and she waved away her argument.

"You're right. He'd be unmerciful. We'll wait until Darth Sullivan pops the question and plants a two-carat"—she paused to let me argue with the prediction, but I just shrugged—"or four-carat or whatever ring on your finger, and let Catcher torture *him* instead. That seems safest."

"I appreciate it."

She flapped her hands. "Come here," she said. "Give me a hug before you leave."

She squeezed so hard I coughed, vampire healing or not. At the sound, she pulled back, looked at me.

"Sorry. It's just—we've been off our game for a really long time, because I was a crazy witch for a really long time. And yes, I said 'witch,'" she snarked, eyes narrowed. "And I saw that damn *Tribune* article. But we're getting back there, because you're giving me more chances than I deserve. And that means a lot to me."

"It means a lot to me, too, Mallory."

She went inside, and I heard the strain of the television and the *snap* and *jangle* of the door's several locks.

So much for taking out the trash.

Cadogan glowed quietly in the dark of Hyde Park as I drove back into the basement parking area. The Ops Room was closest, so I dropped by there first, found Luc at the conference table reviewing documents in a binder, Lindsey and the others at the computer stations.

Luc glanced up when I walked in, tapped an unsharpened pencil on the tabletop. "What's the good word, Sentinel?"

I took a seat. "The obelisk was magicked by someone with knowledge of magic, ability to improvise. Could be a sorcerer, could be not a sorcerer."

"Not very helpful," he said.

"No, it's not, at least without more. But we did confirm the Magic Shoppe sold a Fletcher tarot deck last week. They're going to look for the receipts, but they're already boxed up. The store's doing inventory. Mallory's got the manager's contact information. She'll give him a call, and hopefully that will lead somewhere."

"Good work."

"What about you?" I quietly asked, leaning forward. "Have you spoken with him?"

The sudden tightness in his eyes told me they'd talked, and Luc wasn't comfortable sharing the details.

"Just tell me—is he in danger?"

"I don't believe so. I don't," he added, when I gave him a look. "He didn't tell me all the details. Just hinted at the edge of it."

Somehow, that was more of a punch than his not talking to anyone at all. He'd talk to the head of his guard corps about his past, and what he was about to face, but not his Sentinel? Not his future fiancée? What the hell was going on? What was he trying to hide, or hoping I didn't find out about?

"This is really pissing me off," I said.

The phone in the middle of the conference table rang—two short chirps—and Luc picked it up, lifted it to his ear.

"We'll be right up," he said, put the receiver down again, looked up at me. "It's time. Darius is about to make an announcement."

We were on the stairs when the message went out, when Helen announced over the rarely used Cadogan House intercom that Darius was making a statement, and vampires were welcome to watch in the televisions in the front parlors and ballroom.

By the time we got to the first floor, vampires were already gathering in the front parlors, where televisions had been turned on and tuned in.

History would be made today, one way or another.

It was the tenor we weren't sure about.

My phone signaled, and I pulled it out, found a message from Jonah.

YOU TUNED IN?

ON MY WAY TO ETHAN'S OFFICE, I answered. GREY HOUSE WATCHING?

WITH BATED BREATH. HOPING SOMEONE MAKES A RATIONAL DECISION FOR ONCE.

IT WOULD MAKE A NICE CHANGE, I agreed. SORRY I INTERRUPTED YOUR DATE. GOOD ONE?

MORE FISH IN THE SEA was his response. I guess she'd learned he didn't sparkle.

We walked to Ethan's office, found the door cracked open, Malik, Helen, and Margot already in the sitting area, eyes on the television mounted above the bookshelves. The screen showed a pale green background, "Greenwich Presidium" written across it in neat black script.

Ethan stood slightly apart from the rest of them, hands on his hips, his hair tied back, the ends curling just below the back of his starched collar. His shoulders were rigid, bearing once again, I knew, the mantle of authority that so often weighed on him. But it was a mantle he wore willingly. It was a weight he honored and would wear for the American and European Houses if the GP would allow it.

And tonight, I supposed, we'd see about that.

I blew out a breath, prepared myself for whatever might come, and walked inside behind Luc and Lindsey.

Margot was closest to the door. She reached out and took my hand as I walked in, squeezing in solidarity. Say what you would about the asses in the GP, the vampires of Cadogan House were a solid bunch.

Helen looked up, nodded before turning back to the television. I let Luc and Lindsey take the remaining chairs, and I stood beside Ethan.

He turned and glanced at me, his eyes swirling silver with emotion. With bated hope, fear, readiness for the fight. For taking up arms and facing down enemies, instead of politicking, threatening, backbiting. God knew Ethan could politick with the best of them, had been politicking for much of his four hundred years, and with extra intensity the last few weeks. But he was still an alpha. Words had their place, but alphas preferred to get to the goddamned fight.

I saw that in his eyes now, that relief that things might move forward, even if going forward might be exponentially more dangerous.

Unfortunately, there was something else there: need. There was only a foot of actual distance between us, but the emotional wall might have been a thousand miles high. It was built of bricks of his past, mortared together with his pride, his fear.

I needed, as Mallory had suggested, a surprise play. Something to shake him out of his rhythm, and the very crappy coping mechanism he was using right now. I hadn't yet figured out what that might be.

Maybe, for right now, kindness would be enough. I reached out across the distance, above the wall, and took his hand, squeezed, kept my eyes level on his. I was still angry; he was still angry. But we were still *us*.

"Here we go," Luc said, and we looked back at the television. The green faded and Darius filled the screen.

His blue eyes looked sharp again, bright and clear. He wore a starched, striped shirt, and a little of the cockiness was back in his gaze.

He sat in a chair behind a large, pale desk dotted with antiques. A tapestry hung on the wall behind him.

"His office," Ethan quietly said.

He adjusted the microphone at his lapel, linked his hands on the desk, and looked into the camera.

"Good evening, vampires. I hope this message finds you with peace, with prosperity, and with growth and renewal as spring spreads across our lands.

"I have, in the many years of my reign, done what I believed was necessary to keep the vampires within my authority safe and secure. Those decisions were sanctified by some, questioned by others. Some decisions had unintended consequences. But never doubt that they were meant to secure the safety of all vampires. Individual humans, individual vampires"—he paused but kept his gaze steady—"individual Houses, were not my concern. Our kind was and ever is my concern.

"You will by now have heard that I was recently in the United States, and not entirely of my own accord. Our investigation is ongoing but suffice it to say that when it is done, the perpetrators will be held fully accountable for their crimes. And they will give their immortality in payment."

Goose bumps lifted on my arms at the deadly calm in his eyes. I'd seen Darius at his worst; at his best, there was no question of his power and authority.

"The vampires that found me—that relieved me of the magic that kept me prisoner—represented Cabot House and Cadogan House. One vampire lost his life in the effort to save me. Others faced danger unflinchingly in order to see me home again. For their acts of bravery, I commend the Houses and their Masters.

"In particular, that the vampires of Cadogan House searched me out when they had no obligation to me or us, when they are no longer members of our union, is noteworthy. Their behavior was exemplary, and they deserve our thanks—and mine."

I realized our hands were still linked when Ethan squeezed my hand. Magic—pleased, relieved, and utterly *validated*—spilled across the room. After a long war, after standing as the enemy for so many for so long, we were no longer anathema.

"But the past is past," Darius said. "We must, as we have done for eons, move forward." He looked down at the desktop for a moment, a breach in his composure, and then lifted his eyes to the screen again, his sadness obvious.

"Life, immortal or otherwise, is seldom what we expect it will be. But that is no matter. The leader of this union of vampires must show him- or herself as strong, capable, fearless, and above reproach. I am saddened to admit that I have not fulfilled those roles.

"As such, I intend to step down as leader of the Greenwich Presidium. As you may be aware, challenges to my rule have already been issued."

"Challenges?" I quietly murmured. "Plural?"

"So it seems," Ethan said, gaze on the screen, eyes narrowed with concentration.

"As I am stepping down, I have no need of a formal response to those challenges. Rather, those who have challenged me will be deemed candidates for this position. Testing will begin immediately—psychological and physical. The vampires with the top three scores will be placed on the ballot to all our Houses. The winner will take my place. Lakshmi Rao, acting Council Prelect, will oversee the process."

"It's a bloodless coup," Luc said, awe in his voice. "No duels or anything else—and moving right into a traditional testing process."

Not entirely, I thought. No blood had been spilled today, but plenty had been spilled in the recent past.

"In Europe," Darius continued, "standing for nomination will be Danica Cummings, Teresa Perez, and Albert Christian." Danica was one of the current GP members. The other names weren't familiar to me.

"And in the United States, standing for nomination will be Ethan Sullivan . . . and Nicole Heart."

Nicole Heart was a vampire I had heard the name of before. She was the head of Atlanta's Heart House, another American Master, and apparently the only other American challenging Darius for the throne.

It should have been a magical moment. It should have been a time of excitement, of preparation, of plans for what would come.

But instead, there was only fury—an angry, biting ball of magic that rose with such fervor the floor vibrated with it. The entire House shook on its foundations, as if Chicago had become suddenly situated above a fault line. A vase hit the floor. Photographs toppled.

The center of the magic, the eye of the storm, stood beside me.

All eyes turned to Ethan . . . and the green fire raging in his eyes.

CHAPTER FIFTEEN

LONG LIVE THE KING

He dropped my hand. His entire body had gone rigid, shoulders back and head dipped as if waiting for a counterstrike.

I looked at Malik, found his gaze on Ethan, his expression as pinched with concern as Ethan's had been with anger.

"Goddamn her," Ethan said through clenched teeth.

Her, was all I thought.

"For simplicity's sake," Darius continued, "and in appreciation of Cadogan House's recent service to the GP, the American candidates will subject themselves to testing in Chicago. The European candidates will be tested in London."

That was handy for us; it meant Ethan would be tested on his home turf. It also meant Nicole would be traveling to Chicago.

"The psychological test will be administered tonight, two hours before dawn. The physical test will be administered at midnight tomorrow."

"Jesus," Luc said, head whipping back to look at Ethan.

"There's hardly any time." He glanced at the clock on the wall. "We hardly have time to prepare."

When Darius said his thanks and the screen faded to green again, Ethan dragged his gaze to Luc. "That's the point. To keep us off balance, to see how we react in crisis. Focus on the House; ensure she is secure."

Then he looked at Malik. "Find out when she's coming and where she's staying. I want eyes on her at all times." With that, he threw open the door and stalked out of the room, leaving us in stunned silence.

"What the hell just happened?" Lindsey asked.

"Not what," I said. "Who."

They suggested I stay, that I wait patiently—as if that was even possible—for Ethan to come back into the House. That I wait for him to give a sign that he was ready to talk.

But that wasn't our relationship, and it wasn't me. Not to stand by while he was hurt or angry, and certainly not while the object of his roiling emotions was a woman from his past.

The front parlors were empty, as was the cafeteria. But I glanced outside the windows, saw his rigid form on the back lawn. I stepped outside onto the back patio, closed the door behind me.

The wind was picking up, and I zipped up my leather jacket. Ethan sat on a bench beneath a wooden pergola still under construction in the backyard. When the weather was warm enough, he'd plant climbing roses to grow up and over it.

He didn't acknowledge my approach but undoubtedly heard me sloshing through the spring-wet grass. When I reached him, he kept his eyes on the fence that protected the property and the lights of the city beyond, visible because the plantings were still winter bare. His body was rigid, his shoulders straight.

"Are you all right?"

"I'm fine."

Since my question was met with an apparent unwillingness to elaborate, I elaborated for him, putting the pieces together.

"Nicole Heart is the woman who threatened you."

He paused before answering. "Yes."

"And?" I prompted.

He shifted his body but didn't look at me. "And she's my problem."

He was baffling and utterly infuriating. I kept my voice low and steady, barely masking my rage.

"She's coming here tonight, this woman who's blackmailing you. She's blackmailing you because she wants you to back down from seeking the GP spot, which you obviously haven't done."

"And?"

"*And?* And, what if she reveals the information she has on you?"

He was quiet for a moment. "She won't. Not now."

"Because?"

"Because, for better or worse, Darius just sanctioned the House and my challenge. She can't make a play now, not with blackmail. Not when she knows I could just as easily reveal her ploy—her very dishonorable ploy—to Lakshmi and the other Houses. She may try other things," he added, sounding very tired, "but it won't be blackmail."

"It doesn't have to be blackmail to be torturous," I pointed out.

Ethan lifted a shoulder, resigned.

Being a Master, I realized, was like playing an eternal and worldwide game of chess. I took a cautious step forward. "Let me help you with this. Let me take some of the burden." Let me help *us*.

"I talked to Luc."

I opted for honesty . . . and the vulnerability it brought with it.

"I know. And I'm glad you talked to somebody, but honestly, Ethan, it's a punch that you won't talk to me."

"It's not a punch. It has nothing to do with you. And it's better that way."

Two excuses, both of them crap. "Better for me, or for you?"

I waited for an answer but got none. Just the stiff set of his shoulders and the obvious weight on his heart and soul. "This conversation is done."

I walked closer to him. "You may think you're protecting me. But keeping me in the dark doesn't protect me. It hides the monsters, and it sets us back."

It sets me back, I thought.

But Ethan just looked at the skyline again. "Get to the Ops Room and help Luc get ready."

"*Liege,*" I bit out, then turned on my heel and stalked back into the House, muttering very unflattering things about its Master.

I found Luc and Lindsey in the foyer, heading for the basement stairs.

"Luc."

He stopped and turned back, sent Lindsey on her way while he waited for me to catch up.

"We should talk about Nicole. I've already put most of it together," I quietly said, recognizing the discomfort in his expression.

Luc looked around, drew me into an alcove behind the staircase. "I don't know all the history. Just that they knew each other when Ethan became a vampire."

"With Balthasar?"

He nodded.

"Were they lovers?"

"I don't know."

"Nicole's the one who's been threatening the House—and doing it because she wants to lead the GP. And now she's coming here to face him outright. He doesn't think she'll go through with her . . . original . . . plan." I skipped the word "blackmail" since I still wasn't sure how much Luc knew. "But we know she's conniving, so she may try something else. Will she hurt him? Or the House?"

"If she's willing to blackmail Ethan to win a spot on the GP, I imagine her ethics are flexible."

I guessed Ethan had told him the truth. "Tell me what you know about her."

"I'm going to pretend you didn't just give me an order because you're under some stress."

"Sorry," I murmured, since he had a point.

He nodded, acknowledging the apology. "Nicole's smart, competent. Extra-strong strat. She was assimilated for a very long time before Heart House was founded. Went to college, law school, business school. Excelled at all three. Was married to another vampire for a while, but it didn't last. Her doing, I understand. Staring down eternity made her less than thrilled about 'settling.' That type. Heart's a fairly insular House. Good reputation, solid financial standing, but they don't mix it up with the other Houses very often."

"Is she supportive of the GP?"

"Very much so." He crossed his arms. "Frankly, I'm a little surprised to learn she issued a challenge."

So had Nicole bided her time—obeyed the rules—and waited for an opportunity to take over the throne? Had she been angry that Ethan had beaten her to the punch? That would explain why she wanted him out of the race, and why she was willing to resort to blackmail to do that.

"How much are you going to tell the others about her?"

Luc frowned, scratched an ear. "That she sent the driver. I can't let her catch the guards—the House—unawares. But I don't see any need to get into the specifics with Ethan. If he hasn't told you . . ."

"Then he wouldn't want the guards to know," I finished for him.

"He'll come around," Luc quietly said, sympathy etched on his face.

He would or wouldn't. Either way, she'd threatened me and mine, and we were going to have a chat about that. "I want five minutes alone with Nicole."

He watched me for a moment. "Do you think that's a good idea?"

I let him see the pent-up anger, fear, frustration, in my eyes. "Not at all. Which makes me want to do it even more."

Luc smiled, probably against his better judgment, and nodded. "What my Sentinel wants, my Sentinel gets." He put a hand on his chest. "Just remember—keeping him safe is my life's work. Let's get downstairs and get ready for this thing."

The atmosphere in the Ops Room was intense. Luc kept two temps on the security cameras, gathered the rest of us around the conference table while he took the chair at the end.

"Brody," Luc prompted.

Brody tapped a tablet on the table in front of him. The projector screen on the opposite wall brightened and filled with a tidy black-and-white chart.

"This is the schedule Darius's people just sent over," he said.

"Lakshmi is presently en route. Darius apparently got the message to her early."

"How thoughtful," Lindsey dryly said.

"No shit," Luc muttered, then gestured to Brody to continue. "Continue, newbie."

Brody nodded, aimed at the schedule with a laser pointer. "Lakshmi will be here first. Her plane lands in about two hours. Nicole will be here about three. Lakshmi will meet with both of them, and the psych test will take place at five o'clock. The physical test will take place tomorrow at midnight, and the scores from both tests will be tabulated. The top three contenders make it onto the slate, and then the Houses vote."

I leaned forward, linked my hands on the table. "How bad are the tests going to be? They have to run an obstacle course, or what?"

"The Prelect sets the challenges," Luc said. "That's Lakshmi, at least temporarily, so that could help us. The psych test is . . . intrusive. He'll face a strong psych who'll access his mind, his memories, his love, his fears. Poke around in there with a stick and see what gets stirred up."

Vampires weren't universally strong. Their abilities varied, and they were rated internationally by three measures: strength, psychic skill, strategic ability. Amit Patel, a friend of Ethan's, was currently the strongest vampire in the world. It took strength, skill, and resolve to become a Master, but that didn't mean I wanted Ethan subjected to psychological battery.

"Will it hurt him?" I asked.

"It won't be a skip through the park with Mary Poppins. There's at least one report on record of a Master being incapacitated by the testing. They broke his mind."

"Oh good," I weakly said, and sat back in the chair.

"In fairness, that particular vampire was notoriously weak—got the job as Master because of some well-placed bribes."

So Ethan's innate, infuriating stubbornness would actually help him here. That was something, anyway. "And the physical test?"

"The obstacle-course analogy isn't totally off," Luc said. "He'll be presented with a physical challenge, and he'll be scored on his success."

"His strength?" I asked.

"His survival."

My blood ran cold. "Jesus, Luc."

"That's the deal, Sentinel. He knew what he was getting into, and you know he's stubborn enough to go forward with it."

I nodded, but I wasn't sure that made me feel better.

"Now," Luc said. "As we all know, in addition to the rigorous and dangerous testing practices, there is one more small wrinkle. Brody," he prompted, and Brody replaced the schedule with a photograph of Nicole Heart.

"We have information which does not leave this room," Luc said, "that Nicole Heart is responsible for the shooting at the Cadogan Dash."

There were murmurs around the room.

"And now she's coming to our House, to stand against our Master. She's an official challenger, so she has a right to be here. But I do not trust her, any of her entourage, and you shouldn't, either. Her primary goal is to win the GP, at any cost. She apparently believes that Ethan is a real contender for that throne, and she's willing to do what it takes to keep him out of it."

"You're thinking she could fix the tests?" Lindsey asked. "Or sabotage them?"

"Lakshmi's proctoring," Luc said, "so we've got an ally there. I don't think she'd let Nicole get away with any obvious hanky-panky. The problem is, we don't know what she'll try, so we can't plan ahead for the specifics. Thus, we go in on high alert, and we treat her like an enemy combatant. If you see or hear anything suspicious, you report it. She's already demonstrated a willingness to be violent. She will not be violent in this House. Is that understood?"

There was a peppering of "sirs" around the room.

"Good. In that case, you know what you have to do." He looked at me. "Merit, why don't you take a stroll around the grounds, get a good look-see? No point in taking any chances, and you haven't had the joy of a patrol walk recently."

I rose from my chair as guards and temps returned to their stations. But I had one more trick up my sleeve, so I walked to the other end of the table, took the chair beside Luc.

"Sentinel?" he asked.

Mallory had suggested I make a secret play to break through Ethan's stalemate. She was right. And talk of Balthasar and Nicole made me think of the men and women he'd met in his centuries as a vampire.

Maybe some allies were better in situations like this than others. Maybe some were more powerful.

"I have an idea. Something I think might be the jolt Ethan needs. The timing's tight, but it might at least help him before the phys test tomorrow."

Luc cocked his head. "I'm listening."

"We need to support him, to support the House, and to show Nicole Heart that we don't stand for nonsense. I think we do that with sheer vampire power." I smiled fiercely.

"I think we call Amit Patel. And I think we invite him to Chicago."

The night air was cool, but compared to the claustrophobic energy inside the House, it was a welcome relief.

The guards at the gate nodded as I passed by them and turned to head around the block. Cadogan House was situated in the middle of a large tract of land, surrounded by green space on all sides, the border marked by a privacy hedge and a tall, black, iron gate. That was where I traveled tonight, walking the perimeter to ensure there'd been no breach, no enemy plot, just like a sentry might have done two hundred years ago at the perimeter of his castle, sword at the ready.

It wasn't unusual for paparazzi to be parked outside the House; their presence waxed and waned with the public's interest and their desire to find dirt. Tonight, with murders on Chicago's mind, there were half a dozen in their designated spot near the corner. Mostly men, mostly in their thirties, mostly with large black cameras or small digital recorders.

"Merit, what are you doing out tonight?"

"Merit, any comment on Samantha Ingram's murder?"

"Did vampires kill Brett Jacobs? Samantha Ingram?"

That one stopped me in my tracks. A hand on the pommel of my sword for emphasis, I walked back to the man who'd asked it, kept my eyes flat, and decided to give them something to print.

"We are Chicagoans," I said. "We love this city, have lived in this city for many, many years. We're from this city. Of this city. And there is nothing we like less than those who hurt it, who tear at its heart, who kill its citizens. Vampires didn't kill Brett Jacobs or Samantha Ingram. But we'll do all we can to help them find justice."

Cut and print, I thought, and turned the corner into darkness.

As I walked, I thought about the GP, the testing, and the trail that was currently going cold—the manipulation of Darius West.

Someone—still unknown and at large—had used Darius to take a sizable sum of money from the American Houses, sock it away in a European bank. That he or she was stealing money from the American Houses, sending it back to Europe, suggested a European perpetrator. Maybe the European perp didn't want to steal from his own—the European Houses.

I'd already suspected a GP member; they were the most likely to have the access and funds to get the scheme under way. Danica wanted Darius's position, so she had the ambition to do it. But why bother with a complicated theft when you'd already issued a challenge to take Darius's position—and control the funds yourself? If Diego and Lakshmi were clear as allies, that left Edmund and Dierks as the most likely GP suspects. Both were from European countries, so that didn't really narrow the list.

I still hadn't received a response from my father about the bank accounts' origins. I had asked him to dig out information no one was supposed to be able to access. That was, after all, the point of a Swiss bank account—total anonymity. Maybe he was still looking. And he was undoubtedly busy with his new building project. But ignoring me was still unusual.

Family. Couldn't live with them, couldn't run a stake through them.

Cadogan House, I thought, as I glanced up at the stories of stone and glass that glowed above the fence line, was a kind of family. A big, dysfunctional, hyperfashionable family of neurotic vampires who, for the most part, wanted to make something better of the world.

And at the center of it, Ethan. The House, its Novitiates—we were who he'd made us. Vampires with consciences. Regardless his past or what happened tonight and tomorrow, he would still be a Master of vampires to us.

I should tell Ethan that, I thought. Remind him of that before the testing.

When my double circuit of the grounds was done, I walked in the front door, found vampires milling about, waiting for something to happen. The entire House was tense, as if the building floated in a cloud of anxious magic. Testing was upon our Master, and we were nervous about it.

Ethan's office door was shut, and equally tense magic seeped from inside. I didn't want to interrupt him, not if he was trying to focus, to prepare himself. But the words still needed to be said.

I settled on a text message: I LOVE YOU, REGARDLESS. REMEMBER THAT TONIGHT.

And remember it, I thought, *before you drift so far away that you can't find your way back to me.*

I'd tucked away my phone, was preparing to go back to the Ops Room, when a familiar face stepped into the foyer.

Lakshmi Rao unbuttoned the short camel trench she wore over a knee-length black sheath, her straight black hair pulled into a low pony that settled on one shoulder. She scanned the foyer, settled her gaze on me.

I stepped toward them. "Lakshmi."

"Merit," she said. "Has the Heart House entourage arrived yet?" Her accent was British, and as refined as her clothes.

"Not yet," I said, taking her coat and hanging it on a rack just inside the door. She was no longer my GP superior, but that didn't negate a little common courtesy. "She has a couple of hours yet."

"He is ready?" Lakshmi asked.

The question made something squeeze tight in my chest, and

so did the fact that I couldn't answer it with any certainty. He was resigned to it, was the most I could say.

But where truth was hard to find, bluffing would suffice.

"Yes," I said simply, chin lifted confidently. "He is." I hoped I was right.

I silently told Ethan she'd arrived. A door opened down the hall, and he and Malik stepped into the foyer a moment later.

"Lakshmi," Ethan said, walking directly to her—and not making eye contact with me.

"Ethan. Malik."

While they stepped toward each other to make their greetings, I stood a few steps away, secondary to the meeting of the Masters.

"We've set up the ballroom for your introductory comments. There's also blood, coffee."

Lakshmi nodded. "I'd love some coffee. Perhaps we could go upstairs, discuss the rules before Nicole arrives?"

Light sparkled in Ethan's eyes, and I felt my chest loosen just a bit. We might have been far apart, but we had a proctor who was paying attention.

"Of course," he said, gesturing her toward the staircase.

I watched them ascend the stairs, Malik in front, then Lakshmi and Ethan at the rear. They reviewed preparations as they walked and had nearly reached the second floor when Ethan looked back, a hand on the banister, and gazed at me.

His eyes were dark, the color of deep forests. He didn't speak, or blink, or make any gesture. He just looked at me, as if words were perched on the end of his tongue, but he was powerless to release them.

Tears threatened, but I pushed them back, kept my gaze solid and steady. I had needs and wasn't ashamed of them. But tonight, here in the House with the edge of fear and magic, when the balance of power rested on a knife-edge, his needs were paramount.

I looked back at him and nodded. Just once, just barely, but enough to acknowledge his feelings, his fear, his pain, and the war that waged within him. The war that had consumed both of us.

It seemed to be enough. His posture didn't change, but something softened in his eyes. Would that something be enough? Enough to get him—and us—through these trials?

I'd offer him more if I knew what to offer. If I understood what solace I could provide that would make him feel better about his past, about Nicole, about us, I'd provide it. In a heartbeat.

◂—▸ ▰◆▰ ◂—▸

CHAPTER SIXTEEN

GOOD IS THE ENEMY OF BEST

As time ticked down to Nicole's arrival, House security ticked up. Vampires trickled into the ballroom, waiting for a glimpse of the contender, or perhaps just wanting to surround Ethan with support.

The room on the House's second floor was lovely on its own— a large space with wooden floors, gleaming chandeliers, and gilded mirrors on the walls. The ballroom glowed with light and smelled like hazelnut coffee and warm chocolate. A table draped in crisp white linens stood on one side of the room, beverage dispensers and baskets of pastries set atop it.

Ethan and Malik stood apart from the rest of the black-clad vampires who mingled in the room, the magic nervous and leaving a tingling edge in the air. We were riding on nerves, on possibilities our lives—and our House—would change substantially in a matter of days.

No—not the possibility of change. Change was inevitable. But the nature of that change. Whether involving ourselves with the GP again would be good or would bring more pain and drama.

Figures appeared in the ballroom doorway. Helen, a man and two women behind her. Nicole Heart and her retinue.

She was striking, with dark hair and skin and a lean, curvy figure. Her hair reached her shoulders and was curled into soft waves that reminded me of Marilyn Monroe. She wore a long-sleeved ivory top and long, straight pants in silk that flowed around her body like water. Her eyes were tipped with dark lashes, her mouth generous and accented with shimmery peach gloss, her cheeks two rosy apples.

The effect was impressive. She had a movie star's bearing and a princess's grace.

The next question—was she a contender?—was more of a mystery. She looked physically fit, with strong shoulders and a trim figure. And there was little doubt about the intelligent gleam in her eyes. (There was also calculation and assessment in her eyes, but that just made her a vampire.)

I suppose having the wherewithal to frighten Ethan into holding things back from me was telling enough. Emotionally or otherwise, she wouldn't be easy to best.

Behind her stood a man and a woman—the man was shorter, with dark skin, short hair, and a black suit. The woman was about my height, with a sleek bob of angled blond hair against vampirically pale skin. She wore an ensemble of black leather, and a cross-body holster for the katana sheath strapped to her back. She was me, but blond.

Weird.

"Bennett and Sarah," Nicole said, gesturing to the man and woman behind her. "My Second and Sentinel."

Another Sentinel—the first I'd met. Ethan had resurrected the position by Commending me into it. I guess he'd started a trend.

Sarah looked at me, lips pursed haughtily. I wasn't interested in playing Dueling Sentinels—not with so many things on my mind—but she looked entirely up for the challenge.

All right, I was a *little* interested in it. But this wasn't the time or place. Unfortunately. I gazed back at her beneath my lashes and long bangs, a hint of a smile across my face, just enough attitude to let her know I was a player.

She gave me the same sly smile back, tapped a thumb against the end of her katana's pommel, as if daring and impatience battled for control.

The Sentinel Games? A definite possibility.

"Malik," Ethan said, "my Second. Luc, captain of my guards. Merit, my Sentinel."

Nicole glanced at each of us, nodding quickly and dismissively. She was a Master, and we, quite simply, weren't.

"And, of course, you know Lakshmi," Ethan said.

Nicole bowed her head deferentially. "Madam."

"Your travel was pleasant?" Lakshmi asked.

"It was. Thank you for asking. And yours?"

"Fine, thank you."

Vampire drama had apparently ruined me for pleasant small talk, as I had to work not to roll my eyes irritably at the exchange. Or maybe it was just jealousy. We never had pleasant chitchat with the GP.

"Perhaps we should get the business out of the way," Lakshmi said. "Then I'll review the premises and you can talk, if you'd like."

Nicole and Ethan nodded.

"The psych testing will take place at five o'clock in the training room. I will proctor the exam."

"The testers?" Bennett asked.

"I won't reveal their Houses, so as not to provide an unfair advantage." Or an opportunity for the Heart and Cadogan minions to research the hell out of them before the test.

"They were selected by a random lottery and agreed to participate. Both are very strong psychs. Both are quite well equipped. I will monitor psychically and physically. No areas of inquiry are off-limits. That will complete the test. The physical test will be held tomorrow at midnight at a location to be announced by me. Each test will be scored, and the scores will be gathered."

"And then the Houses will vote?"

Lakshmi nodded at Ethan, smiling as if pleased he'd gotten the right answer. "I will return to London with the scores, and I'll receive the scores from the European candidates. The top three candidates will be placed on the slate, and the Houses will vote. Well," she added, a footnote, "the Houses without candidates will vote.

"The tests will not be easy," Lakshmi said, glancing between them. "They are not intended to be. They are intended to test your strength, your focus, your ability to lead vampires through challenges. The immortality of the GP's vampires lies in the hands of the man or woman chosen to lead them. It is no little responsibility, and they will be no little trials."

That didn't make me feel any better about what would be happening here today—or the fact that Ethan and I weren't on the same ground.

"Any questions?"

Nicole and Ethan shook their heads.

"In that case, perhaps you should relax for a few moments while I review the preparations with your Seconds."

"Nicole and I will wait in the anteroom," Ethan said, gesturing to a door at the side of the ballroom.

Lakshmi nodded. "Training room at five o'clock." Wordlessly, Malik guided Lakshmi back to the door, Bennett behind them.

Ethan and Nicole looked at each other. Whatever emotions they'd been hiding for the sake of their vampires, or for Lakshmi's sake, bubbled to the surface. Their eyes darkened, and for a moment they both looked like the vampires they truly were—and the darkness that lived inside both of them.

The anteroom was small but pleasantly furnished. There were a couple of oversized white couches, and along one wall a series of mirrors with bare bulbs overhead where—once upon a time—I'd waited as an Initiate to be Commended into Cadogan House.

Nicole walked around the room before settling on a couch. She sat down on one end, crossed her legs, linked her hands on the arm.

Ethan took a seat across from her. Sarah and I stayed on our feet.

"Your House is lovely," Nicole said. "The photographs don't do it justice."

"If that's your opening salvo, Nicole, it's not impressive."

"You think we're rivals, Ethan, but we aren't."

Ethan looked only mildly interested. "Aren't we?"

"We are vampires who want to improve the lot of our own kind. Make them full and integrated members of the society into which they've been flung. I'd say that makes us allies."

Ethan didn't seem impressed by the argument. "So you say, but I didn't send a man to attack you. To shoot at your vampires."

There was silence for a moment, and when Nicole did speak,

she was unapologetic. "As I've said, it wasn't an attempt to kill you—otherwise, it would have been a very sloppy attempt." She slid her gaze to me. "I thought, perhaps, that those closest to you would persuade you to step back."

"Those closest to me understand me and my drive. And they understand that Cadogan vampires do not stand back merely because we are afraid."

That angered her, undoubtedly. Her expression didn't show it, but magic lit through the room with such force I instinctively reached for my katana. Sarah did the same, and the surprise in her eyes matched mine. I shifted my weight, prepared to move in case Nicole or Sarah did, watched Sarah do the same. We both were poised on tenterhooks, in case the physical testing began early.

By her blackmail, Nicole had raised their mutual past as a weapon to be wielded. But Ethan wasn't afraid to battle back, with fear, anger, irritation, pent up and festering for several days. This was what he'd been holding on to. Anger at her betrayals: the threats, the blackmail, the challenge. From what I could gather, they'd both been the victims, the prey, of a monster. Maybe that was the root of his real anger and irritation—not just that she'd threatened to expose his past, but that *she* was the one making the threats.

They'd been cohorts, companions, vampires who'd survived trauma. He'd believed they were on the same side. Not friends, perhaps, but certainly not enemies. And then, in order to support her claim to the GP, she'd tried by violent means to dissuade him from taking up the gauntlet. She'd betrayed him doubly.

But if that was all there was to it, why not tell me? Why not explain his feelings to me? There was nothing about that I could possibly object to.

"A woman comes to understand things across the centuries of her existence," Nicole said. "She gains perspective. Balthasar, yes, was a monster. But he gave me immortality for a purpose. I intend to make the most of it."

"By threatening me? By challenging me?"

"By taking what is mine, and what you have no right to claim." Her eyes narrowed to slits, and she leaned forward, the bubble of magic moving with her like needle pricks on skin.

"I have bided my time, Ethan. Worked to build my own kingdom. I have dealt with monsters—vampire and human alike—and humans who treated me as if I were a dog because I had the unfortunate luck to be born with skin a shade darker than theirs. I stood Second, waited for my turn. *I* followed the rules."

Ethan's brows lifted. "And I haven't?"

"You quit the GP. Your House has killed two members of the GP. Darius was fine until his fateful trip to Chicago, where you let a mass murderer run him to ground. And then you have the temerity to challenge him? To demand that he give up his position for you?"

She'd missed several details—the fact that those GP members were killed in self-defense, that they'd put the House in receivership, that Darius had come to Chicago to close us down and strip us bare of assets, and that we'd left the GP because of their bad acts. She left out the facts that we saved Darius from Michael Donovan, that we'd just uncovered a plot to control him and steal money from the GP.

But when you lined up the bare facts against us—as the vampires who didn't know, or didn't want to know, the context were likely to do—it was hard to argue her point.

"As you're well aware, your story is incomplete," Ethan pointed out. "It also reeks of your own cowardice. Where were you when Darius was being manipulated? What attention were you paying?"

"I was minding the business of me and my House."

"Precisely," Ethan said. "And that's the kind of myopic attitude that has put us in the very situation we're in now." He tilted his head at her, donned his analytical expression, considered her. "All that aside, I'm curious, Nicole. What, precisely, would you have me do?"

Her eyes glowed with purpose. "Resign your candidacy. If we run against each other, we'll split the American vote. That weakens our chances of an American regent. Yes, there are three Houses in Chicago. But there are more Houses outside it—Houses that do not appreciate the chaos of this city, of your politics."

He was quiet for a long moment. "And if I don't resign?"

They kept their eyes on each other, one predator scoping out the other.

"I am a practical woman," Nicole finally said. "And I know very well how to adapt to shifting currents. I'm not interested in letting your, shall we say, past dalliances reflect negatively on me. But I am a player, Ethan. I am a contender. I will play this game as Darius wishes us to play it. And I will win."

Ethan had been right; she wouldn't go through with the blackmail, at least not now. But she felt free to torture him with the vaguely referenced "dalliances." And since she'd so carefully hinted at it, I wondered if she meant to torture me, as well.

Regardless, Ethan's response was clear and unequivocal, as was the grin that crossed his face. "There's not a chance in hell that I will step down from my challenge."

"Because your ego demands it?"

"Because my *honor* demands it. The GP, in large part, consists of monsters and bullies, and it is time for a change. You play the game, Nicole, and you always have. You play it skillfully. But it is time to dismantle the game, to rewrite the rules."

"Careful, Ethan. You sound like a rebel."

"We've already rejected the GP," he pointed out. "We are rebels."

Nicole rolled her eyes, rose from the couch. "You're naive. The system is in place for a reason, Ethan, and has been for centuries. You don't just pretend it doesn't exist."

He didn't comment, perhaps because it was as obvious to him as it was to me that talking wasn't going to change her mind. Whatever their relationship in the past—and regardless their history—Nicole Heart intended to challenge Ethan and win the throne from him if she could.

"Then I wish you the best of luck," Ethan said, rising as well. "And should you claim the victory, I hope you rule the GP with wisdom and honor."

But Nicole smiled, and it wasn't the smile of a good-natured contender.

It was the smile of a shark.

"This isn't over," she said, then cast a glance to me. "Until the testing is complete, until the next king or queen is sworn in, we are challengers, and enemies. I will not allow you to stand in my way."

Ethan nodded graciously, and without a further word, Nicole and Sarah strode defiantly from the room.

A heavy silence descended. Ethan looked back at me, still behind the couch, and I kept my expression carefully neutral. I had no idea what to say or do, no idea what might trigger some instinctive response in him, prickle him into anger.

"She's not going to stop," I finally said.

"I know."

I nodded. "It's worse when someone you know betrays you. Someone you trusted."

He looked surprised.

"Mallory," I explained. "I've been there."

"Ah," he said.

More silence.

"Well, you should probably get ready for testing."

Ethan sighed heavily, looked back at me again. "I know that you love me, appreciate that you love me regardless this misery. Am awed by it. Unfortunately, love doesn't change who I am, or who she is. That's what I have to come to terms with right now. I'll see you downstairs."

He walked out of the room without another word.

Without a single touch, he'd pushed me away again.

Lakshmi confirmed that the training room was the best place for the testing, and we offered her the anteroom to catch up on her own business. Nicole and her entourage set up camp in the front parlor, a security camera carefully trained on their activities. Ethan, Malik, Luc, Lindsey, and I camped in Ethan's office, waiting for the clock to strike five.

It was ten minutes 'til when Lindsey rose from a chair in the sitting area of Ethan's office, moved to him on the couch. Magic followed in her wake, waves of nervousness and fear.

"Do you know how to compartmentalize?" she asked him, searching his eyes, clearly nervous for her Master. She was a very strong psych, had the ability to ferret out others' emotions. And from the look in her eyes, I guessed Ethan's were concerning her.

"Compartmentalize?" I asked.

Lindsey kept her eyes on him. "It's a way of 'double thinking.'"

I frowned, and Ethan glanced at me. "You already do it, Sentinel. When you unlock your senses, you maintain the ability to think rationally."

"Double think," Lindsey agreed.

"Oh," I brightly said, feeling better about my vampiric capabilities. I hadn't come by them smoothly—trauma in the first instance and biological separation in the second—so it was comforting to know I was doing it right, at least by vampire standards.

"I can do it," Ethan agreed. "At least somewhat."

Lindsey nodded. "They'll test your strength, your resolve, your emotional stability. Try to compartmentalize it—let it happen, but keep part of yourself reserved just for yourself, just for you." She put a hand over his heart. "Keep part of yourself there, and she won't be able to touch you."

She meant to comfort him, and he seemed grateful, but the offer of help, the nature of it, made me increasingly nervous.

The clock's minute hand moved forward again, the click ominously loud in the silence of the room, and Malik rose. "Liege, we should go downstairs so you can change."

Ethan blew out a breath, nodded.

At five o'clock, Luc and I walked into the training room.

Four wooden chairs had been placed in the middle of the room—two rows of two chairs, the rows facing each other, each chair about four feet away from the others.

Lakshmi stood beside them, her hands linked behind her, an air of absolute certainty and authority in her posture. Malik and Bennett stood at her sides.

Ethan and Nicole walked in, both wearing gis. They acknowledged Lakshmi, walked to the chairs, and sat down like rigid dolls. Both of them looked nervous.

Two more vampires walked in, a blond woman and a man with graying hair. They took the chairs opposite Nicole and Ethan.

It looked so harmless, so simple—four vampires sitting in a small cluster as if they meant to talk, to share. I'd have much preferred if that was the agenda for the evening.

Lakshmi looked at the group of us. "You're satisfied?"

"We are," Malik said.

Bennett nodded. "We are."

They walked to the far end of the room, sat down in two more chairs, their postures as rigid and uncomfortable as those of the rest of them. Nerves fluttered in my chest like nervous birds, and I stared at Ethan, afraid to activate our telepathic connection but willing him to look at me, to make eye contact, to reassure me or tell me to be still, as was his way.

But his eyes were trained on the woman across from him, just as Nicole's were trained on the man in front of her. The game had begun, and their focus was sharp.

"One hour," Lakshmi said, and Malik checked his watch. "Clear the room."

We filed out. At the door, I looked back, cast one last glance at Ethan. This time, I found him looking back at me, and I saw something I'd seen only rarely in Ethan Sullivan's eyes.

Fear.

It had my belly going cold.

The doors closed with an ominous sound, leaving us bathed in silence.

CHAPTER SEVENTEEN

For a moment I simply stared at the closed door, at the wood grain, as if my staring at it would endow him with whatever strength he'd need to safely make it through this.

"Sentinel?"

I looked back, found Luc in the doorway.

"They won't start for a few more minutes," he said. "They'll discuss ground rules, and the psychics will need to calibrate their thoughts to Ethan's and Nicole's. In the meantime, I need you to do something."

I nodded, glad for anything that might take my mind off what would happen in that room. I walked toward the Ops Room, but when he gestured me back toward the stairs, I stopped, shook my head.

"I'm not leaving him."

He walked back to me. "I just need you to go upstairs."

I shook my head again. "What if something happens and I'm not here? What if something happens? What if he needs me?"

"I'll be here, Merit, right next door, where I have to be. Where

I have to be," he repeated, "which means I can't take care of Lindsey."

And the fear was in his eyes, too.

We walked silently to the third-floor room they shared, and Luc opened the door.

Lindsey sat on the small bed in the wildly colored room they shared. Novitiate quarters—like the ones I'd first had in Cadogan House—were much smaller than ours. A single room with attached bath and closet. Bed, bookshelf, bureau, nightstand. One or two windows, depending on the location.

She wore long pajamas and had wrapped herself in a fringed fleece Yankees blanket. There was no accounting for taste, I supposed.

"What's going on?" I asked, looking between them. Because something was definitely going on; I could tell by the nervous magic.

"They'll be testing Ethan and Nicole," Luc said. "But they'll use magic and their psychic connection to do it. It will bleed over."

Lindsey was psychic; Luc meant the trauma they put Ethan through would bleed over to her. It hadn't even occurred to me that would happen. I looked at Lindsey. She wasn't one to look worried, but she definitely looked worried now.

"How much will bleed over?" I asked.

"I don't know," Lindsey said. "It could be bad." She also wasn't one for showing fear, but it was clear in the set of her jaw and the pale cast to her skin. "We're connected since he's my Master, and I'm the most sensitive person in the House."

It could be bad, and she'd be getting only the *overflow* of

Ethan's emotions—not the raw bulk of them. That increased my worry exponentially.

"We put her up here," Luc said, "hoping the physical distance from Ethan would help. It's as high as you can get in the building, other than the widow's walk."

And you didn't want to be in the middle of a psychic crisis while perched on the edge of Cadogan's roof.

I took a seat beside her on the bed, brushed her hair over her shoulder. "What can I do?"

"Just be here," he said. "Malik's in the room with Ethan. I'll be right next door. He'll come through this." He eyed Lindsey, the love between them obvious. They'd danced at the edges of love for a very long time. But something had happened to solidify their connection—something neither had shared with me, but which I suspected involved a visit to the House from one of Lindsey's living human relatives. They'd gone away for a few days and come back practically inseparable.

"I'll be here," I promised him, and when he left us alone, I unbelted my katana and propped it up against the bed, then unzipped my boots and let them drop.

"Geez," Lindsey said, leaning back against the wall. "Make yourself at home, Merit."

"If you're going to lose it, and I'm going to deal with it, I'm doing it in comfort." Worried, I looked at her. "Are you going to barf? Because I am really not good with barf."

"I don't know."

She didn't sound confident, so I glanced around the room, spied a small New York Yankees trash can in one corner. I hopped off the bed, grabbed it, and put it on the nightstand beside her.

The look she gave me was unpleasant. But as a lifelong Cubs fan, I knew I was in the right.

"Really."

"Absolutely," I said with a grin, and pulled her toward me. "Come here. We might as well get comfortable."

She lay down, put her head in my lap. I stroked her blond hair and made sure the blanket covered her shoulders.

"You'll be fine," I said. "You'll be fine, and he'll be fine, and in an hour, this will all be over."

I hoped to God I was right.

It was obvious when the test began. Magic flowed, arced, rushed through the House with the force of a tsunami. The House shook with it, a low rumble that felt like someone was jackhammering in the core of the building. And with it, a cacophonous bubble of tension, malaise, and anger that settled over the House like a low-grade fever.

Those were, I assumed, the emotions that the psychics dredged up at Lakshmi's command. It made a horrible kind of sense. There was little point in testing the effects of joy on a vampire. It was the ability to fight through fear, sadness, anger, that mattered.

I was suddenly freezing, my hands shaking with cold. I pulled another blanket over us.

Lindsey screamed—the sound high and mewing—and clamped her hands over her ears as if the magic was something she could block out like sound. Tears pricked my eyes at her pain . . . a pain that mirrored what Ethan was feeling.

I shook with chills as hot tears slipped down my cheeks. *Keep him safe*, I silently said, and as the storm of emotions battered the House, as Lindsey sobbed in my lap, I cocooned her in my arms and repeated the mantra again and again.

Keep him safe.
Keep him safe.
Keep him safe.

It was undoubtedly hard on him. He was, after all, the man who endured it. But I hadn't known how hard it would be on the rest of us.

For an hour we fought it, battered by waves of emotions that pushed the air from our lungs, that plunged us into sadness, that tested us with pain. It was an irritating tingle to me but obviously painful to Lindsey, as she absorbed the heady emotions and magic that flashed through the House.

However skilled the psychics might have been, they weren't especially good at keeping their efforts geographically confined. *Maybe they should have been tested,* I grouchily thought.

An hour passed. And then, like a wave sweeping back out to sea, it was over. The sky cleared, the magic lifted, and the House was free again.

I closed my eyes, released an hour of pent-up tension. Lindsey, hair damp and eyes swollen and bruised from crying, sat slowly up.

"Careful," I said as her body shook with exhaustion. "You all right?"

"I'll be okay." She closed her eyes and leaned back against the wall. I hopped off the bed and went into the small bathroom, dampening a washcloth and filling a cup of water.

I came back, handed her the cup, watched her sip greedily. When she emptied it, I set it aside, handed her the washcloth.

"Thank you," she said, and pressed it to her face. A sob escaped her. I put the cup back in the bathroom, stalled to give her a few moments of privacy. I stared back at my own visage in the mirror, the dark circles under my eyes. I looked tired. Drained by drama and murder and tests. Drained because Ethan and I weren't connected right now, and that both scared and frustrated me.

When the room quieted again, I walked back in, sat down next to her.

"It was bad," I said, and she lowered the cloth again, nodded.

"It was pretty bad."

I hesitated to ask for details, thinking she wouldn't want to relive it. But I'd have to face Ethan and needed to know what I'd be walking into.

"What can you tell me?" I asked her.

She fisted the washcloth in her hands, squeezing it rhythmically. "I don't know details. Just general feelings—fear. Loss. They want to see if he can work through it. How he deals with it. If he can be manipulated by it—if someone can use his love against him." Her eyes widened as if she'd just remembered something, and when she looked at me, her gaze skittered down to my belly.

"You're going to—you and he are—"

"Not yet," I said. "Sometime in the future. Not yet. Not now."

She just blinked, head shaking as she tried to process the possibilities. "Sometime is soon enough. Jesus, Merit. That's huge. Do you know how big that is? What an historic achievement that is?"

"My getting laid isn't an historic achievement." I knew that was not what she'd meant, but I'd meant to put a smile on her face, and I incrementally relaxed when her lip curled, just a bit.

"I didn't mean *that*. But a child . . . My God. How did you find out?"

"Gabriel had a prophecy, a vision. But that's all it is—it's not a guarantee, so please don't mention it to anyone else. No one else knows. You can't even tell Luc."

She nodded. "Okay, okay."

Then she closed her eyes again, shuddered.

"What's wrong?"

"Nothing. Nothing." She opened her eyes, smiled. "He passed." Her smile blossomed. "I can feel his relief."

Fear loosened its hold on my heart, just a bit. "Thank God."

She chuckled. "You're not showing a lot of confidence in your Master and lover."

"I was worried. Not because I didn't think he could handle it, but because we aren't exactly in a good place right now," I confessed. "I didn't want us—where we are—to make it harder for him."

Lindsey smiled softly. "He didn't make it in spite of you, Merit. He passed it *because* of you. Because that's who you are to him. You may not feel it—not right now—but he's changed. He is happy because of you."

Tears blossomed. "Not always."

"Of course not always. I'm sure you're a righteous pain in the ass at times. But most times, he's happy. Ethan is a man of a type: strong, powerful, honorable. But he has always held himself back from the rest of his vampires. Partly because he's a Master, sure, but partly because he didn't quite fit. With you, he fits. He's no longer alone. He's part of a pair, and that's a really good thing."

I knuckled away the escaping tear. "Thanks for that."

"Of course. You were going to clean up my barf. We've had a whole new level of bonding tonight."

I grinned, pulled on my boots. "I'm going to go downstairs. You'll be all right?"

She nodded. "I'll be fine. Want a shower. A skin-blistering

shower and maybe three liters of blood. Send Luc up when you can?"

I picked up my katana, headed for the door. "Of course."

"Merit," she said, and I glanced back. "Thank you for staying with me. For being here for me."

"You're welcome. But it would have been more fun if you'd barfed on the Yankees."

The House was still quiet but seemed to be coming back to life. Doors were opening, vampires peeking out into the hallway.

"They're done," I told them. "He passed."

Their relief was palpable.

I jogged down the stairs but found the training room door still shut. Luc emerged from the Ops Room, put up a hand.

"Give him a minute, Sentinel. He'll need to get his bearings first."

I didn't want to wait but knew he was right.

"Lindsey?"

"She's okay. It was rough, but she made it through. No barfing. She's waiting on you, when you're ready."

I looked back at the closed door, then Luc. "What should I do?"

"Why don't you go back upstairs? Maybe grab him some blood, some food, a shot or two of the oldest Scotch you can find?"

Now, that was a plan I could execute.

I found Margot at a prep station rhythmically chopping celery— and at a speed considerably slower than I'd seen from her before.

"It looks like you made it through," I said.

She turned tired eyes on me. "Strong psych. I'm exhausted, and the rest of the team's pretty wiped out, too. I sent them to their rooms during. No one needed knives in hand while that emotional tornado was swirling." She gestured toward a giant stockpot. "I hope you like chicken soup."

"That seems like just the thing."

"Have you seen him yet? Is he okay?"

"I haven't seen him yet. He's—well, emotionally debriefing, I guess." I glanced around. "I thought I'd take him a tray."

"A good idea. We always have things. And speaking of—don't you owe him a dinner?"

She was right; I hadn't had a chance to make good on our race bet. "Unfortunately. And it will probably be French. And fancy. And require a knife."

"He does like French," she agreed, pulling a silver tray with handles from a tall wire shelf. "But because he likes classic preparations, not because he likes fancy. You know, I tried modernist cuisine on him once. Chicago's a hotbed of it, and I spent a little time with a certain very popular chef . . ." She wiggled her eyebrows, waiting for me to guess. Unfortunately, my knowledge of the Chicago food scene ran to deep-dish and Italian beef, not fancy.

"Oh, no kidding? Did a little tutoring, did he?"

"Lots of tutoring," she said, opening a glass-doored refrigerator and pulling out two bottles of Blood4You. She lined them up on the tray along with a glass and a napkin, then put a small basket of croissants beside it.

"Anyway, I gave Ethan a really nice petite filet with some foams—parsnip and beet, I think. He was not impressed. Kept asking why I'd served him bubble bath for dinner."

It was nice to know there were limits to even Ethan's pretentions.

"Comfort food, comfort food," Margot said, tapping her chin as she returned to the refrigerator. "Ah," she said, diving inside. She pulled out two ramekins. "Crème brûlée. I presume your objection to French doesn't include custard."

"I have no basis to object to custard," I confirmed, my stomach rumbling in agreement.

"Nor should you. I mean, unless it's fish custard." I couldn't hold back a grimace, but she waved it off. "It was more of my unfortunate molecular gastronomy phase. But it's over now. Back to simple, delicious foods. And speaking of, we could probably use something with more substance."

She walked back to the stove, pulled the lid off a pan, and scooped pasta and cheese into small, square bowls.

"Macaroni and cheese with prosciutto," she said, sprinkling bread crumbs over the top and using a white towel to clean the edges of the bowls. When she was satisfied, she put them on the tray, and we looked down at the meal she'd assembled, heads cocked.

"Lot of beige there," she said.

"Lot of beige," I agreed. Custard, macaroni and cheese, and croissants.

"Normally, I'd trade carbs and cheese for some green vegetables, maybe a little spice, or something with a little vinegar. But I think tonight he's going to want the cheesy and familiar. I'd throw on a grilled cheese and some butterscotch ice cream if we hadn't already loaded him up with dairy. Here," she said, crossing the room to the prep area, where she worked with something for a moment before carrying it carefully back.

She revealed two plump red strawberries, sliced into fans, and placed one atop each ramekin of custard. "Voilà."

"I think that will do it," I agreed with a smile, picking up the tray. "My compliments to the chef."

Margot snorted. "It's traditional to eat the food first before thanking the chef."

"I know you and your cooking," I said, making my way to the door. "Consider it payment in advance."

I had food, but I was still lacking a crucial ingredient on Luc's Chicken Soup for the Vampire's Soul list. I made my way into Ethan's office, set the tray on his desk, and headed to his bar. He had a full stash of bourbons, whiskeys, Scotches, so I pulled the oldest open bottle I could find—eighteen-year-old Glenmorangie—and added the bottle and a clean glass to the tray.

My stomach knotted with fear and anticipation, I made my way to the stairs.

◂—◂ ▦◆▦ ▸—▸

CHAPTER EIGHTEEN

INTERVIEW WITH THE VAMPIRE

The shower was roaring when I walked into the apartments, steam billowing from the open bathroom door. I put the tray on the table, picked up the gi Ethan had discarded along the way to the bathroom, and placed it across the end of the bed.

It wasn't the only trail in the room. Magic had been spilled, and it had followed him into the apartments like smoke behind a fire. It left a greasy feeling in the air, which explained the billowing steam. He'd have wanted to be clean. I couldn't blame him.

I stood by impatiently, gnawing on my thumb and pacing the room as I waited for him to emerge.

Finally, the water slowed to a trickle, nearly twenty minutes after I'd come into the room. There were footsteps, then the sound of fabric on skin.

He emerged a minute later, a towel wrapped around his waist, and scrubbing another through his hair. He might have been immortal, but he looked tired. Gaunt, as if the hour with the psychics had literally pulled away parts of him.

He spared me a glance, a line of worry between his eyes. "Is there a problem?"

I shook my head. "Just checking on you. I brought you something to eat in case you were hungry."

He nodded and wrapped the second towel around his neck, holding the ends with his hands. We stood there silently for a moment.

"That felt like hell. The House shook with it."

Ethan's gaze searched mine. "You're all right? Everyone's all right?"

"We're all fine. Worried about you."

"I survived," he said, and walked to his closet, a dark, script tattoo across the back of his calf.

I debated whether to follow him or give him space, had no idea of the appropriate behavior for a boyfriend who'd just been put through an emotional ringer. I doubted *Cosmo* had addressed it; my nerves in overdrive, I nearly laughed aloud at the thought of seeing *Sup Cosmo* on a supermarket shelf. Just consider the articles: "Woo Your Wolf with White Lingerie." "Sexy Scabbards Your Vamp Won't Forget." "Kicking Him to the Curb: Fifty Ways to Leave Your Vampire Lover."

I knew Ethan didn't need to be pushed—Luc had reminded me of that well enough—but at least I could try to tend to him the way he tended to me.

I picked up the bottle of Blood4You, uncapped the top, and carried it to the closet, offering him sustenance instead of peppering him with my burning questions.

He stood in front of the chest that sat in the middle of the closet, which was large enough to be a room in its own right. A drawer was open, and he pulled out a dark, folded T-shirt, placed it on the top of the bureau. His hair was wet and slicked back, and he'd already pulled on dark silk pajama bottoms that rode low on his hips. His toes peeked from the bottom hem, his abdomen bare above the waistband.

When I offered the bottle, he reached out and drained it in seconds, throat moving as he drank. Still silent, he placed the empty bottle atop the bureau and looked back at me, eyes silvered.

Lust bolted through me. Not the lust of seduction, but survival. He'd gone through something—something we'd experienced vicariously—and come through the other end. I wanted to be near him, close to him.

I missed him.

But there was still something between us, so I didn't step forward.

That didn't stop Ethan. He moved to me, sunk his lips into mine with enough force to draw blood. I felt his banked strength, even as his muscles trembled with exhaustion.

I had strength to offer. I tilted my head, offered myself to him—blood, body, and soul—shivered as he traced his lips across my jaw, to the nape of my neck, to the crux of my shoulder. Just to feel him touch me was a miracle.

But he stopped. He slid fingers along the line of my shoulder and cheek, cupped my face in his hand. When I lifted my eyes to him, I found his wracked with pain and fear.

"Do you want to know what I saw? When she was in my mind, when she was battling me, do you want to know what I saw?"

His agony was so obvious I was terrified to nod, but I was more terrified to decline. I nodded, and Ethan caressed my lips.

"I saw you. You and me. And you were taken from me. Ripped away. That's how they test you, Merit. Not with anger or pain, but with loss. With the loss of all that you love, all that you want, all that you don't even have the courage to hope for."

He stepped away, and I nearly gasped at the absence, the sudden chill against my skin, the loss of his comforting scent and the caress of his magic.

"I won," he said, and it took me a moment to catch up with him. "I beat Nicole." Lakshmi must have finished tallying the official scores.

"Good," I said. "That's good.

He nodded. "Tomorrow, the physical test."

I thought of the pain he'd obviously been through. I asked the difficult question. "Do you want to continue?"

He didn't answer for a very long time. "Yes."

I chose my words carefully. "She'll be angry that she lost to you. Afraid that she'll keep losing. She may escalate because of it. She may try harder to hit you." I paused. "And she may target your past again."

"She very probably will. But that doesn't change my mind." He smiled, just a little. "I've tried to teach you to fight beyond fear, Merit. I can't very well play the coward."

"Okay, then."

He looked back at me. "Okay?"

"Okay. I agreed to support you in this a long time ago. I'm not going to change my mind because it's hard." *And I won't change my mind about you either,* I thought. *But I still want to punch you a little.*

"This hasn't exactly been easy for us," he said.

"No, it hasn't. It's been downright miserable, and it's been hard on the House. But it's what I agreed to."

Many emotions crossed his face—awe, surprise, love. And maybe a bit of regret that I wasn't giving him an excuse to quit, to walk away when it would be so much easier to do so. But he hadn't trained me that way; quite the contrary. He pulled on the T-shirt, the damp ends of his hair just touching the collar. Then he leaned back against the bureau and slid down to the floor, knees raised.

I sat down on the facing wall, gave him silence.

"This is usually the part where you ask me to talk," he said.

"I've already asked. You declined."

He made a rough sound of agreement, pushed his hands through his hair.

And there on the floor, in a T-shirt and pajama bottoms, Ethan Sullivan began to talk.

"As you know, I was a soldier. As a human, I mean. We were in Nördlingen, in southern Germany. We were outnumbered and, frankly, outcommanded. But one did what one had to do."

My chest tightened. I'd seen him die as a vampire and didn't much want to imagine him dying as a human in the middle of a battlefield, dark and alone.

Ethan rubbed his shoulder, the place where an arrow had felled him, taken his life. "Night came, and so did Balthasar."

"He made you, and you traveled with him."

He nodded. "For a decade. We traveled. Pillaged, and worse."

"And Nicole was with you."

A pause, then another nod. "She'd been born in Martinique, traveled to Europe with the humans who believed they owned her. Balthasar made her a vampire."

"Effectively freeing her."

"Yes. She took to it immediately—biologically, strategically. He was crazed—unstable, difficult to predict. But she learned to work through that. He considered me a soldier; he considered her a prize. Their relationship was considerably different, although even she wouldn't argue he had little regard for life, human or otherwise. His immortality had, ironically, made him callous toward it. If anyone could have immortality by exchanging a bit of blood, then life was cheap.

"Life was cheap . . . as was love. Balthasar trained us to be monsters. To take what we wanted, discard the rest. To take who we wanted."

Fear curled low in my belly at the disquiet in his eyes. Then his gaze slipped away again and back into the past.

"There were women, Merit." He raked fingers through his hair. "For years on end. For decades on end, there were women. I hadn't yet learned to take blood without taking pleasure. It was part of who I was, who I'd learned to be. Been trained to be."

He looked at me again. "Who I'd been trained by Balthasar to be."

My voice sounded so quiet. "That's what you didn't want to tell me. Because you'd had affairs?"

He nodded. "There was no faithfulness. There was no fidelity. There was only . . . decadence." He paused. "Nicole was one of those lovers. Only for a brief time. But as, it seems, I'm being honest . . ."

He didn't finish the thought, but gave me, I knew, a moment to reflect, to gather my own.

None of it should have been a surprise. Not given how I'd come to know Ethan. Before we'd fallen in love, only days after we'd actually met, Ethan had asked me to be his Consort—the paid and titled vampire whose job was to see to his carnal satisfaction.

That was shortly before I'd seen him in flagrante delicto with Amber, the Consort I'd have replaced. That, strangely, had been the first time I'd seen him naked, the first time I'd seen him in the throes of lust. And Amber hadn't been the only of his lovers I'd faced down. Ethan was much desired.

But still . . . this was different in a way I couldn't yet name.

Amber hadn't meant anything to him. Hadn't affected him, and he hadn't hidden that relationship. He'd retired the position after learning of her treachery against the House, but he hadn't hidden it.

If he'd been afraid to tell me this—how much worse was it, at least in his own mind?

"That look in your eyes paralyzes me, Merit."

I shook my head. "I . . . just . . . I don't know what to say."

"I've lost you once tonight," he said, fear writing lines in his face, spilling magic into the room. "I saw you leave me, watched it happen. And I cannot see that happen again." His voice softened. "But if you'd leave me, then let it be for truth—because of who I am when you see the whole of me—and not because I was afraid to let you see it."

He swallowed hard. "There was a night in London. It was near the end, although not near enough in hindsight. We'd played at being ton, with titles bought and paid for." He paused. "There was a girl who fancied me. She was a wisp of a thing. Cream and roses complexion. Feminine in the most delicate sense."

Ethan smiled wistfully, his affection for the girl obvious in his expression, his tone. But there was sadness, too.

"I might have loved her. In time, in a fashion. In the way I'd been capable of then." Storm clouds crossed his face, darkened his eyes. "Balthasar watched us one night, saw me dance with her. Caught what was, to him, a hint of affection for someone other than himself. He was a narcissist; that was not allowed.

"She'd worn a white dress with small green flowers. White satin slippers. She lay on the floor of his den, blood everywhere.

She'd fought him; he made sure to tell me that. I came in—found them—just as he'd drained the life from her." His expression was vacant, as if he stared at a mental photograph of that moment.

"He'd been grinning. 'She fought me,' he'd said. 'You'd have been proud of her, for the fight in her.'" Ethan paused, tapped fingers against his knee. "He left me there with her, with her body limp on the ground.

"He'd wanted me to try to change her—or beg him to change her—to create another vampire he could manipulate. That was the way he operated, feeding on guilt and sadness and fear. She didn't deserve that, to be made one of us, to be dragged from her world into ours. So I didn't do it."

"She died."

He lifted dark eyes to mine. "Did she? Or did I kill her? Did I kill her and others, Merit?" He shook his head sharply, as if that might soothe his pain, clear the emotions from his face. "That's when I left him. And I didn't bite another human, didn't make another vampire, until I became Master of this House."

"Nicole knew about her?"

"She knew about all of it. About Balthasar. About the women. Nicole was there the night Persephone—that was her name: Persephone—died. And now, after biding her time for so many years, she's claiming what she believes is due to her—a crown."

We sat in heavy, impenetrable silence.

He needed, I knew, a decision from me. Unfair or not, there it was. Either I accepted who he was—good, bad, and ugly—or I walked away now. And that was the option he'd expected I'd choose.

I looked at him, found his gaze on me, fear in his eyes. "You were afraid I'd run from you if I knew who you'd been?"

After a moment, he nodded.

"You stopped so you wouldn't hurt anyone else."

He opened his mouth, closed it again. "Yes. Although at times like these, it hardly feels sufficient."

"That's because you care. Because Balthasar couldn't strip your humanity away. Not completely, even as much as you like to think otherwise."

And that was the sum of him. He might not ever truly forgive himself for the man—the boy—he'd been for so many years, for the things he'd been taught by a vampire bent on turning his pupils into the same monster he'd become. Ethan had tried in the ensuing centuries to make himself into something more than he'd been. He was still trying to make a better future for his vampires; that was why we were sitting on the floor of our closet as dawn crawled toward us.

I'd made my decision long ago. I leaned forward, met Ethan's gaze directly. "I have no blinders, Ethan. I see you exactly as you are."

The love in his eyes, the green fire of them, was nearly blinding. Relief and magic mixed and danced in the air.

"God, but I love you."

I smiled at him. "Once upon a time, I chose not to be your Consort. I did that because I deserved more, because we both deserved more than that. More than physical release. Because we both deserved love and understanding. And because we are more than the sum of our pasts. Far be it from me to snatch that back from you now."

He smiled at me. "Far be it from you, Sentinel."

Silence fell again, this time companionable. "You have to kick her ass in the phys testing."

Eyebrow arched, he slid me a glance. "I have to 'kick her ass'?"

"Between you and her, I'd much rather have you in charge."

"The devil you know?" he asked with a half smile.

"Pretty much."

We looked at each other for a long time. He still hadn't touched me, but he'd shared something. We weren't back on completely solid ground. But we were getting there. And I'd take progress over stagnation, over that barrier, any night of the week.

Ethan looked back, smiled softly. "Will things ever really be easy between us, Merit?"

Not easy, perhaps, but easier.

I reached forward, put a hand on his cheek. "She has no power over you anymore. Over us. Not with your past, not with your regrets."

I leaned forward and kissed him softly, then left him with his thoughts to change into my pajamas.

It wasn't yet dawn, but I was emotionally exhausted. I climbed into bed and closed my eyes, felt when he climbed into bed beside me.

We slept together, our arms and legs and bodies entwined, as if we might save each other.

And we forgot completely about the crème brûlée.

CHAPTER NINETEEN

HUNGER GAMES

I woke at dusk the next night with a hunger so fierce I wasn't capable of naming it. I sat up, found Ethan's side of the bed empty, but heard the shower running in the bathroom. I pushed back the covers, slid my feet onto the floor, clenched my hands into fists to stop them from shaking.

I rose to my feet, the dull ache at the back of my head a mere whisper compared to the lust for blood that colored my vision. I pushed open the bathroom door, took in Ethan's long and lean form in the shower, slicked with soap and water.

He must have sensed me, or the magic I was throwing off. His head snapped back, eyes widening. He turned off the spray, opened the door, stepped outside, body gleaming.

My breath hitched at the sight of him, at the sudden silvering of his eyes . . . and his sudden and obvious arousal.

"Merit," he said, the word a low and lusty growl. We were predators in a haze of bloodlust, facing each other like warriors prepared for another battle.

"Ethan," I managed, gripping the doorjamb to stay upright. "Blood."

He stalked forward, steam rising from his body, and took my face in his hands. His mouth crushed down onto mine, tongue and fangs and lips entwining. We sparred with our kiss, antagonizing and provoking. He was moved by lust, maybe love. I was moved by lust for body and blood. For all that he could offer, and all that I would take.

I pulled back, nipped his lip, caught the bright and sudden smell of blood.

A single drop of vermillion rose on his lip. I lunged forward, the taste of him filling my mouth as his guttural groan filled the air.

"Take me," he said, arching his neck to offer me access to all of him, to his life's blood, and the thing I wanted from him alone.

I kissed the smooth and golden skin . . . and then I bit. He cried out, the sound carried on a wave of magic that shook the room as it traveled.

I wrapped my arms around him, sunk my fingers into his hair. His hand moved between us, found his arousal, pulled rhythmically as I drank.

That lasted only a moment. He put an arm around me, pulled my body against the rigid length of his, ground his hips against mine as he breathed through bared teeth against the pleasure of the bite.

I ignored the wrench of lace and fabric as he ripped the nightgown down the middle, exposing my body.

Merit. As he spoke to me with his mind and his body, his hands found my breasts, fingers firm and insistent as I drank the life he offered. But it wasn't just hunger that wracked me. I felt his blood move through me, giving me strength and life, and carrying with it his love, his magic, his strength.

He found my core and pushed forward. He filled my body doubly now, the sensation so intense, so utterly fulfilling, that my body immediately convulsed with pleasure, a warm wash of it that spread through my body like liquid fire.

I gripped his hair tighter, pulling, and dug the nails of my other hand into his back. *Ethan. Jesus, Ethan.*

He groaned deliciously, cursed in Swedish, picked me up. I wrapped my legs around his waist, pulled his body closer to mine as we moved.

In the bedroom he went to his knees, braced hands and arms on the floor behind him, pushed his body upward into mine as I drank, took what he offered.

His movements quickened, and I drew away, licking the final drops away from the small dots where I'd drunk from him. I met his eyes, which swirled with silver, and pulled the long length of my hair away from my neck.

His eyes widened at the offer, one hand rising from the floor to trace a line down the center of my body, pausing at my breast. He cupped it, thumbing the nipple to delicious pain that made need rise, hot and covetous, all over again.

I traced a fingertip down the arch of my neck, across my collarbone. Ethan's eyes shined with pleasure. He bared his fangs, put a hand behind my head and pulled me forward, then sunk teeth into the soft skin at my neck.

His other hand found my hip, pulling our bodies together as he drank and moved ferociously beneath me, a sheen of sweat slicking between our bodies.

Pleasure swamped me, a river that threatened to sink me completely. I gripped his shoulders as my body shook with it, as it sent him over, too.

Fuck, he silently said, ripping his mouth away from my neck, his lips still stained crimson, eyes unseeing and head thrown back as shudders wracked him. God, but he was a sight—a warrior in the throes of passion, body rigid and sheened with sweat.

Mine, I thought.

We ended up in a pile on the floor, chests heaving.

"Dear God, Sentinel. You may be the death of both of us."

"That was . . . definitely something."

"'Supernatural' is the only word I can think to describe it."

I opened my eyes, pointed at the tattered fabric that lay across the bathroom floor. "That's why vampires can't have nice things."

Ethan laughed hoarsely. "I'm not certain I'll allow you to dress ever again. I may just keep you here and naked."

"You did enjoy my wild side."

"I enjoy all sides of you," Ethan said, reaching out and grabbing my hand, linking our hands together. "But your wild side is particularly enjoyable."

I am a vampire sex warrior, I thought, with much satisfaction.

I let Ethan shower and dress, and then I prepared for the evening, thinking leathers were more appropriate than jeans or a suit considering the night's agenda.

I pulled on leather pants and my jacket, a bright red tank beneath, and my Cadogan medal. I pulled my hair into a high ponytail, brushed my bangs until they gleamed, and accented my pale skin with a wash of blush on my cheekbones and red gloss that made my lips look bloodstained. The result was spooky but effec-

266 + CHLOE NEILL

tive. I picked boots with the highest heels in my closet, tucked my dagger inside, and belted on my katana.

I checked the mirror before I left, straightening my ponytail and the short, motorcycle-style lapels of my jacket. I looked fierce, and a little otherworldly. That was, I thought, the best I'd be able to do today.

Sleep had done wonders for the House. Instead of fear, the House buzzed with energy and excitement. If they'd treated the psych testing like emotional battery, they seemed to anticipate the phys testing like a Super Bowl. And for good reason. They'd seen Ethan fight—in battles at the House, around the city, in sparring sessions with me and others. He was a skilled and capable fighter, wily and well trained.

A phone message from Luc directed me to Ethan's office, so I made my way downstairs. The office door was cracked, and I found Luc, Lindsey, Malik, and Ethan filling plates from a wheeled cart.

"You're just in time for breakfast," Luc said, using tongs to pile bacon on a plate.

I moved inside, smiled at Ethan, who was pouring orange juice into a short glass. "Carb loading?"

"Fueling, anyway," he said, handing the glass to me. "Good evening, Sentinel."

I drank, studying him over the rim of the glass. He was in good spirits. Maybe he was also ready for the challenge.

I was hungry, so I loaded a plate with eggs, bacon, wheat toast, and took a seat.

"He's on his way," Luc whispered when I sat beside him. It had been a week of mysterious pronouns, but this mystery I could solve. "He" meant Amit, my secret ploy, my Hail Mary to win the game.

"These have been tense nights," Ethan said, taking a seat at the head of the table. "And tonight is not likely to be any different. But I was recently reminded that vampires would hardly be well served by a process that didn't help the strongest challengers rise to the top. Whatever happens tonight, I wish us all well." He raised his glass. "To Cadogan House."

"To Cadogan House," we repeated, but my stomach felt leaden as I realized what he was doing. He might have felt good about the physical challenge—his mood said that clearly enough—but he'd gathered us together, offered us thanks, in case he didn't return home tonight.

He was offering his good-byes.

I put down my cup again, glanced at Malik, wondering if he'd understood, if he'd prepared himself for the possibility he'd soon be in control of the House. I found his gaze on mine, sympathy and acceptance in his eyes. He knew, then, what Ethan was mentally prepared to do, accepted it as an inevitability, that he'd give his life in service of the House.

I'd have to talk to him, steal time away. If he believed there was a chance he wouldn't come back, I'd be damned if we separated without a proper good-bye.

"Malik will attend the testing with me; Bennett will attend with Sarah. They will be the official witnesses. I've not yet been apprised of the location. Luc will have the House while we're gone."

"Lakshmi has authorized Bennett and me to report back," Malik said. "We'll keep everyone apprised."

Brody's lanky form appeared in the doorway, knocked on the jamb. "Liege, I'm sorry to interrupt, but there's someone here to see you. They've asked to speak with you directly."

Brody's expression was completely neutral, which told me he was in on the plan.

Ethan frowned. "Human? Vampire?"

"Vampire," he said.

Frowning, Ethan rose. "I suppose I'll be right back. Lucas, would you like to join me?"

"Sure, Liege." Luc made a move to stand but waited until Ethan was at the door before sitting down and gesturing me toward the door. "This is your present, Merit. You might as well be there when he opens it."

I nodded and rose, following Ethan to the front of the House.

A man stood in the foyer, around six feet tall, trim. He wore a pair of gray trousers and a white dress shirt. His skin was honeyed, his hair coal black, his eyes a doleful brown. His face was perfectly sculpted, his mouth sensuous, his huge brown eyes tipped by long, dark lashes and framed by dark brows.

He stood casually, hands in his pockets, a position I'd seen Ethan take hundreds of times. But where the carriage of his body was unassuming, even casual, his power was evident. It pulsed from him in soft, thick waves, nearly tangible enough to touch. I had to clench my fingers into fists to keep from reaching out, from touching him. But I resisted, guessing that the act would be akin to moth touching flame.

Instead I stared, taking in every line of his lean form, of the perfect drape of clothing over muscle and honey-dark skin. He was Amit Patel—the most powerful vampire in the world—and he was here because I'd asked him to come.

"Amit," Ethan said, obviously stunned. "What are you doing here?"

They embraced with claps on the back and obvious delight in each other's company.

"You're undertaking a rather monumental feat," Amit said. His voice was softly accented, the sound melodic. "Being here to support you seemed the least that I could do."

"I am bewildered and flattered," Ethan said. "And I appreciate your support."

Amit grinned, their camaraderie obvious. "I'm not here to support you, old man. I thought you could use a warm-up."

Ethan snorted. "I hardly need training from the likes of you."

"You need training every moment of your very distinguished life." Amit slanted me a glance. "And speaking of need, you must be Merit."

Ethan glanced back, realized I stood a few feet away and held out his hand, gesturing me forward.

"Merit. Meet Amit Patel."

Amit smiled slyly. "Merit. It's lovely to finally meet you."

Beside me, Ethan snickered. "You've done the impossible, Amit—rendered her speechless."

"It's lovely to meet you. Sorry, I'm a little"—*completely in your thrall, which you probably aren't even doing on purpose*—"sleepy, I guess."

Amit smiled and took my hand, and my knees nearly buckled from the pleasure of it. I had to lock them to stay standing, and had to force air through my lungs.

"Merit," Ethan said, and I felt his hand at my waist as he looked at Amit again. "What did you do?"

Amit cocked his head at me. "I think she likes me."

I coughed out a laugh. "The magic likes you. I don't know you."

He smiled beneath impossibly long, half-lowered lashes. "It's lovely to meet your magic, then." He looked back at Ethan. "Since you've got phys today, I thought perhaps a warm-up might be just the thing." His dark eyes sparkled merrily. "Speed the heart, warm the blood."

Ethan's relief was palpable. "I think that would be just the thing. You've been traveling—would you like to clean up first? Perhaps have blood?"

"In that order," Amit said with a nod.

Helen appeared behind us in the foyer, hands linked officially in front of her. "Liege?" she said, apparently responding to Ethan's silent call.

"Arrangements for Amit?" Ethan asked.

"Already prepared." Helen offered Amit a smile so wide I thought her usually brittle expression might break with it. She never smiled at us like that. Actually, she never smiled like that at all.

"Amit," she said, walking toward him. She put her hands on his arms, and they exchanged affectionate cheek kisses.

Maybe he glamoured her, I thought sourly.

"Helen," he said. "You look absolutely lovely."

"I try," she said, and slipped her arm into his. "Your room is prepared."

"I appreciate it," he said, patting her hand. As they walked toward the stairs, Amit looked back at me. "And I look forward to our next encounter."

When they disappeared into the second-floor hallway, I looked back at Ethan, found his gaze on mine, awe in his eyes. "You brought him here."

"I suggested it. Luc actually made the call."

His brows lifted. "You went above my head, invited the most powerful vampire in the world to our House in the middle of a testing cycle."

"I did."

His smile dawned slowly. "That was rather . . . inspired."

Relief flooded me. I knew seeing Amit would make him feel better. But he was right—it was a pretty risky undertaking, even if I'd gotten Luc (and the rest of the staff) on board.

"Thank you. Considering the drama, I thought giving you another ally to commiserate with might be helpful."

He moved forward, tipped up my chin, looked into my eyes. His own were dark, like clouded malachite.

"Breakfast," I said. "That was a good-bye. Just in case."

His mouth tightened, as if he hadn't wanted to admit the risk to me. "Just in case," he quietly said, and wrapped his arms around me. I buried my face in his shirt, let his warmth and magic and scent embrace me. God, but it felt good to be there again.

"I'll take care, Sentinel."

You'd better, I thought, but I wasn't giving up on the possibility of monitoring the testing. I didn't want to cheat per se, and I certainly didn't want to jinx Ethan's chances at a win. But I'd be damned if he went into something this dangerous without a backup plan.

"Yes, Helen?"

I glanced back, found her standing at the bottom of the stairs, hands folded as she waited for Ethan's attention. I hadn't even heard her approach.

"Amit is settled, asked that you meet him in the training room in half an hour."

Ethan smiled slyly. "I will. Thank you for coordinating."

Helen nodded, disappeared efficiently down the hallway toward her office.

"Will you let him beat you since he came all this way?"

His laugh was strangled. "He's the most powerful vampire in the world for good reason. Although I know a few tricks here and there."

"I'd avoid the one where you kiss your opponent in order to throw him off balance."

His eyes shone like emeralds. "I'd never do that, Sentinel. That's a foolish boy's trick."

"Which you, being a mature, centuries-old vampire, certainly wouldn't employ?"

"Certainly not," he said, but kissed me again, nearly throwing me off balance.

I suppose even the most mature of men had the occasional ornery impulse.

T minus three hours until the testing, and the House still rang with excitement. Not just because of the challenge—a line of fear trickled through the magic at the risk he was undertaking. But Amit was the most powerful vampire in the world, and he was a friend of our Master's and here to help him prepare.

Cadogan's Novitiates weren't going to miss that show. Hell, most of the vampires in Chicago wouldn't have missed the show if they'd had the opportunity to watch. I belatedly realized I should have invited Catcher and Jonah. They'd have enjoyed the spectacle just as the vampires in the training room's balcony, which was nearly full, were prepared to do.

Lindsey and I edged past bent knees in the balcony's front row, squeezing into small gaps beside Malik and Luc.

"Does anyone else suddenly want popcorn?" she asked as she leaned forward over the balcony rail. Magic filled the air.

Popcorn would have been good. The balcony hummed with energy, like we were all settling in to watch a blockbuster movie on opening night.

The training room door opened, and Amit and Ethan walked inside. Both wore black gis. Both had bare feet. Ethan had pulled back his hair, and his Cadogan medal shone at the base of his neck.

They met in the center of the mat and bowed formally. Then Amit clapped Ethan on the back and they shared a few private words.

When they were done, Amit looked up at those of us in the balcony. "You love and respect your Master, of course. But he is one of the finest warriors I have ever known. And I have known many." Amit grinned slyly. "But that does not mean he is a better warrior than I am."

There were good-natured jeers from the audience, which Ethan tamped down with a raised hand. "If he believes he is so, shall we say, Masterful, then we should invite him to show us, don't you think?"

The vampires erupted with applause, of course. They both knew how to work a crowd. They were handsome and strong vampires in their prime, and I suspected they were equally arrogant. And there on the tatami mats preparing to battle each other, they looked as happy as anyone I'd seen in a long time.

Since they were so happy, I allowed myself to relax, to take a temporary respite from worry and anticipation and simply watch them play.

They began with *katas*, the building blocks of vampire fighting. They stood beside each other and worked through strikes and blocks, their motions remarkably similar and fluid.

When they glistened with sweat, they shared a few words and separated again. Ten feet away, facing each other across the tatami, they bowed again, then angled their bodies in preparation for a fight.

The crowd went wild again, and Ethan looked up at us and winked jauntily. Someone thought to turn on the radio, and AWOLNATION pumped through the speakers with driving bass and canny lyrics.

"Anytime, old man," Amit said, and beckoned him forward.

Ethan moved first, with a crescent kick that Amit batted away with a hand. He struck with a jab that would have connected with Ethan's liver, but he pulled his punch at the last moment. This was a warm-up, after all.

But that he didn't mean harm didn't also mean he wasn't going to challenge Ethan.

Ethan was good; there was no doubt. But Amit was . . . something else altogether. If there was a creature beyond vampire—a being with the strength and grace to make being a vampire look ungainly and awkward—Amit was it. The benefit of being the most powerful of vampires, I supposed. His moves were perfectly efficient, perfectly balanced. His power looked deceptively effortless, and I bet there were plenty in history who'd underestimated him, who'd mistaken grace for weakness.

Actually, Amit's style had a lot in common with ballet. One of the most amazing feats of skilled ballet dancers, male or female, was their ability to make incredibly challenging moves look effortless. Through years of practice, they honed muscle and tuned muscle memory to make leaping splits and pirouettes *en pointe* look as simple as walking. They had preeminent control, just like Amit Patel.

Ethan made an advance, a series of kicks and strikes that moved them halfway across the room, his motions nearly blurred with speed. Amit deflected them, but not as easily as he had the individual strikes. He had to work to battle Ethan back, which made my own blood race with excitement. Amit was a beauty to watch, certainly. But Ethan was execution and power—the modern dance to Amit's ballet.

He executed a side kick that reached high enough to nearly brush Amit's hair back from his head. Amit bent backward from the waist to avoid it, then completed the rotation, hands to the ground, flipping his feet over so he was standing again.

Amit's eyes went wide with pleasure. "You've been practicing."

"I have a very good sparring partner," he said, and I flushed with pride as the vampires around me chuckled collegially and patted me on the back.

"Way to be, Sentinel," Lindsey whispered.

I nodded but kept my eyes on the duo and their pas de deux on the mats. They made it very easy to watch.

CHAPTER TWENTY

CONFESSION IS GOOD FOR THE SOUL

When their workout was over, they cleaned up and returned to Ethan's office to reminisce. I gave them time to chat, checking my messages and returning to the Ops Room.

I found Luc and Lindsey at the conference table. "Where is she?"

I didn't need to specify. "Still at the hotel, waiting for details about the physical test. Kelley's got eyes on her, lots of room service being delivered."

"Stress eating," Lindsey suggested.

"That's what I'd do," I agreed, and thought of the carb loading I'd done at Layers. I was nervous enough now that I wasn't hungry for anything.

Luc put an arm around my shoulders. "This will all turn out fine," he said. "I know it's stressful now, but this is Ethan we're talking about. The man loves a challenge. He Commended you, after all."

My elbow connecting with his ribs felt nearly as good as his reassurances.

When another hour had passed, and we were but an hour away from the testing, I decided it was time to enact the other part of my Amit Patel plan.

My motivation in bringing him here had been primarily selfless—finding someone whose strength would inspire Ethan, remind him of his friends and allies and the support that he'd have regardless the outcome of the trials.

But it was secondarily completely selfish. Ethan and Amit had been friends for a very long time. When I'd asked him to come, I'd thought Amit might help me break down Ethan's walls. We'd made much progress last night—progress I was afraid we'd never make—and I'd made my choice. But there were still things to be said, worries in my heart about who Ethan was and what I still might learn.

I walked upstairs to find him. Ethan's door was open, the office empty, as was Malik's. I found Helen in her office a few doors down, writing in a large binder.

I tapped lightly on her door, caught the quick look of irritation when she lifted her head. "Yes, Merit?"

"Have you seen Amit, by chance?"

"I believe he wanted a look around the grounds. Said the quiet would do him good."

"Thank you," I said, and turned to go.

"Merit—wait."

I looked back at her, found her face screwed up with obvious discomfort. "You did a very thoughtful thing, bringing him here. Ethan is under considerable stress, as you know, and he seems to have lightened the load considerably."

"Thank you, Helen," I said, and left her to her note-taking.

I found Amit outside beside the fountain, finally bubbling

after a long, cold winter. His arms rested loosely on his bent knees.

He glanced up at the sound of my footsteps. "Good evening, Merit."

"Hi, Amit." I glanced at the fountain, the shifting of lights on water. I'd always loved that—lights on water at night. The sound of it, the hypnotic and changing sight of it.

I sat down cross-legged beside him. For a few minutes, we looked quietly at the water, watched the light reflect and bounce off its surface.

"It's lovely out here," he said.

"It is."

"You're worried about him," Amit said, breaking the silence.

"Not worried. Just . . . concerned." I glanced at him, took in the dark slope of nose, the dark hair, the preternaturally thoughtful eyes. "He's been thinking a lot about his past. It's been eating at him and, frankly, Nicole has only dredged it up. We talked last night. But he is still, in so many ways, a mystery to me."

A corner of his mouth lifted, and he looked back at the water. "He is a complicated man. Very strong. Very loyal. Very confident."

"*Ultra*confident," I agreed. "Probably too confident sometimes."

"He was not always so. He fought back his own demons, as we all must do. He closed the doors of his past, and I suspect does not want to open them again."

"Yeah. I'd agree with that."

Amit slid me a glance. "You think he does not trust you."

"I think he doesn't feel comfortable unburdening himself with me. He still feels I might run."

"And will you?"

"No," I said, and instinctively reached for the Cadogan medal at my throat, realized I hadn't put it on this evening, and fisted my hand, dropped it again.

Amit nodded at my answer.

"I made my choice many, many months ago. He gave his life for me, Amit. Everything else—every bit of drama in his past—pales in comparison. But what if he can't overcome his demons?"

"He has told you of the monster that lives in the centuries behind him?"

"Of Balthasar?" I quietly asked, as if saying his name loudly might give him power. "Yes."

"Balthasar was, for all intents and purposes, his god for many, many years. He made Ethan, in many respects, a vampire in his own image. He hasn't attempted to hide that from you—or the fact that it impacted him. So what difference will details make?"

I opened my mouth. Closed it again. Amit was polite, but blunt.

"It won't make me love him less. But if he doesn't trust me . . ."

"Consider, Merit, that this has nothing to do with trust." He glanced at me. "Have you told Ethan of every incident in your past? Every mistake? Every regret? And is your relationship worth less because of it? He is your lover, Merit, and he may very well be your partner for eternity. But he is not your father confessor, nor are you his."

"That puts me in my place," I admitted.

Amit patted my knee, that spark of magic jumping between us like the blue fire of static electricity.

"Each relationship is different," he said. "Every couple must decide what works for them. For some, it is unmitigated honesty. For others, it is discretion. I think Ethan does not wish to speak too much about who he was before, for fear his past—and the desires that ruled him then—will be given power over him again. He

fears those desires, that past, will destroy what you have built together."

"You're very wise."

Amit smiled again, and this time there was sadness in it. "Not
so wise. Just experienced. We've all made mistakes, Merit. I am
no exception." He looked at me, head tilted, as if puzzling me out.
"I think you have changed him, just as he has changed you."

"Yes, to both. For better and worse."

This time, Amit laughed from the belly, fully and with gusto.
"Truer words, Merit." When he was done laughing, he wiped at
his eyes. "Now that we've had our fun, I've a favor to ask you."

I nodded. An enormous and endearing smile dawned on his
face. "I am absolutely starving. Perhaps we could find something
to eat?"

Finally, something I was actually good at.

I led Amit to the kitchen, introduced him to Margot, and, when I
was assured they'd get along fine, headed back to the stairs to
grab my Cadogan medal from our apartments.

I stopped short ten feet away. The door was cracked open,
light streaming into the hallway.

I thought at first it was Ethan, that maybe he'd forgotten his
medal, too. But the vibration of unfamiliar magic told me it wasn't.
I flipped the thumb guard on my katana and crept to the crack in
the door, peered inside.

A man stood in front of the small desk where I'd had breakfast, rifling through an open drawer. He wore jeans, boots, and a
fitted gray T-shirt. He was picking out papers, replacing them
again, as he searched for something.

By the time he'd turned, I was through the door, the katana in
my hand, its deadly point aimed at his heart.

He smiled back at me, his face handsome and expressive, his body muscular beneath the V-neck and jeans. It was enough to make me remember him, even without the crescent tattoo.

"The driver," I said, remembering.

"And the Sentinel." His smile was disarmingly charming, dimples at both corners of his mouth.

He didn't look the least bit guilty at having been caught in our apartments.

And considering Nicole's warnings, his purpose was easy to guess.

"Looking for something?"

He didn't answer.

"Did losing the psych test make her feel a little desperate? Is she afraid she won't be able to win on her own, so she has to dig for whatever dirt she might be able to find? I have to tell you, that's not really engendering a lot of confidence in her leadership abilities."

He shrugged. "She's my Liege."

I wasn't sure if that meant he wouldn't speak ill of her, or he automatically excused her bad deeds because of her position. "And you're the one who does her dirty work. I can't say that I respect a Master who's afraid to get her hands dirty."

"She's not afraid," he casually said. "It's simply not her job to perform tasks like these. You should know—you stand Sentinel."

"Protector of the House. Not secret operative." Well, that wasn't entirely true, but mostly because of my RG membership, not my status as Sentinel. At any rate, I generally didn't break and enter—okay, also not true, but my behavior wasn't at issue here.

"Potato, *potato*. But regardless, here we are." He spread his hands wide. "What are we going to do about it?"

"You're awfully relaxed for someone in your position—I didn't get your name."

"Iain. And you're Merit."

"All night long," I agreed. And speaking of, the night was ticking away. I glanced at the clock behind him, watched the minute hand inch forward again. *Nicole's driver has broken into our apartments.*

Iain must have sensed the delay, and he made his move. He darted toward the opposite wall and pulled a *bokken* from its mount, then spun the *bokken* in one hand, ready to dance.

"Then I guess that's what we'll do about it," I said, and made my first strike.

He used the *bokken* to block my advance, then aimed it like a slugger staring down a fastball. I dropped and rolled, popping up again near the doorway that led to the bedroom.

"Not bad," he said with a grin.

I resituated my fingers on the handle of my katana, kept my expression flat, although it was hard in light of his infectious smile. "I get a lot of practice."

"I'll bet." This time he took the offensive, sweeping the *bokken* down to try to take me off my feet. I jumped and came down again with a slice from my left that had him skittering across the room.

He looked at me, then at the *bokken* in his hand, and flung it away so it clattered across the hardwood floor.

"Giving up?" I asked, grinning back at him.

"Not at all. Just in a bit of a hurry."

My sword extended, I moved closer as he walked across the room, examining the objects on the side table. He glanced at the door, and I moved my body between him and it, preventing his exit.

But he was a creative thinker. He picked up an onyx horse from the side table, pitched it at the window.

Glass exploded into the darkness outside. Without looking back, he jumped to the window ledge and disappeared into the night.

"Son of a bitch," I muttered, and added destruction of property to the list of Cadogan's grievances against Heart House.

I sheathed my katana, ran to the window, and grabbed the edges as I pulled myself up. I caught a shard of glass, winced as it tore open my palm. But I ignored the pain, stepped through the window, and took flight.

The fall was exhilarating, the sensation more like taking a really large step than like falling three stories to the ground below. I hit the ground in a crouch, one hand extended for balance, and saw Iain running toward the fence.

His goal was easy enough to guess: He'd disappear into the night, and Nicole would fake shock that anyone in her House would attempt such a childish stunt, *blah blah blah*.

Best solution? Save the evidence. Namely, him.

I lit out after him, hurdling the expensive lawn furniture he'd turned over in my path and unsheathing my katana again. He turned and ran toward the pergola, edging toward the gap of light in the fence that probably looked, to him, like freedom.

But the pergola shadowed the yard—and the construction materials that still littered the grass. Iain caught something with a foot, lost his balance, and flew forward.

He hit the ground on his belly, tried to skitter forward and crawl back to his feet.

He was absolutely not getting away from us this time. I leaped, launching myself forward, and landed with a foot on his back that audibly knocked the air from his lungs. I flipped him over and pointed the katana at his carotid, pressing just enough to prove my point, not enough to draw blood.

Back lawn, I told Ethan. *And you might want to hurry.*

Iain sat in a chair in the cafeteria, which Luc had cleared of vampires, swiping at the fresh grass stains on his jeans, as if his only crime had been the ruination of what looked to be very expensive denim.

Nicole, Ethan, and Lakshmi stood in a semicircle around him. I stood a few feet away, napkins pressed to the healing cut on my palm, drinking the bottle of blood Ethan had pressed into my hand. As much as he'd enjoyed our interlude at dusk, apparently he didn't want a midnight repeat.

"This is highly unusual," Lakshmi said, glancing at Nicole, whose expression was blank except for a tightness around her eyes. She was a Master, and skilled at hiding her emotions.

"I'm as surprised as you are," she said. "And very disappointed in my Novitiate."

I seriously doubted that, but I'd already told them what I'd seen and what Iain had said. The rest of it was up to them.

"The circumstances are suspect," Lakshmi said. "But without direct evidence that Iain was directed by Nicole to engage in his questionable behavior—"

"Felonious behavior," I clarified. "Assault, battery, breaking and entering, destruction of property, etcetera." And we hadn't even told her about the attack on the Cadogan Dash or the threats of blackmail.

"Felonious behavior," Lakshmi allowed, "we are at an impasse." She looked at Ethan, long hair falling over one shoulder as she moved. "This is your House, and a violation of your privacy."

She checked a delicate gold watch. "And it is nearly time to begin the physical testing. You have the right to demand an inquiry—and that she be disqualified."

Nicole stiffened.

She'd sent Iain to our apartments precisely to support her claim to the throne, and now she was faced with losing it altogether. She hadn't thought he'd be caught—and if I hadn't forgotten my medal, he wouldn't have been.

He invaded our privacy, Ethan said. *He's threatened you twice now. But if she is disqualified now, for this—*

You'll never be rid of her, I finished. *Even if you win, she'll still be out there, waiting for an opportunity, because she'll believe you robbed her of her chance.*

He looked relieved that I'd realized it, that I could recognize an unwinnable play. If he let the testing move forward, the results—whatever they were—would be her own doing, not because he'd taken something away from her. And, if she was smart, she'd remember what he'd done and learn something from it: Winning at any cost wasn't really a win.

"No," he said. "I will not press for her disqualification. We move forward."

Nicole blinked but recovered, nodded officiously. "That's the most appropriate course of action."

"Don't push it," Ethan murmured.

Lakshmi leveled Nicole with a look. "I presume we will not see any further mischief on the part of your House?"

"We will not."

"In that case, the physical testing will proceed as indicated. Nicole, how do you propose to secure your Novitiate?"

Nicole glanced at Iain, her irritation obvious. "There's a car outside, waiting to take him to the airport. He will go back to the House and remain until my return."

Iain bowed his head obediently. Just as, I bet, he'd obediently bowed his head when Nicole told him to ransack our rooms.

Iain rose, and vampires shifted, preparing to get back to the task of preparing for the night's testing.

But I had a bit of business first. It was time for me to have those five minutes I'd requested with Nicole, so I met Luc's gaze, reminding him of our agreement.

He nodded slightly. "Ethan, why don't we ensure Iain makes his way off the property?"

Lakshmi, who must have caught the look that passed between me and Luc and looked very satisfied by it, nodded.

"I'll help ensure he's settled and won't cause any additional trouble," she said. "Nicole, perhaps you'll speak briefly with Merit, discuss any necessary repairs or reparations that your House will need to arrange?"

Yes, Lakshmi was definitely an ally.

Nicole watched them go before turning back to me, her expression unfailingly polite. "You appear to have bested my Novitiate."

"Your Novitiate broke into my home, violated our privacy, and destroyed possessions."

She circled me, her glamour rising, flowing. I nearly smiled. She wasn't the first female Master to test me with glamour, and wouldn't be the last.

"You don't need to bother with the glamour. It doesn't work on me."

She didn't comment, kept her expression mild except for the flash of irritation in her eyes. "I am a Master of my House."

"And he is the Master of mine. You've threatened him, and

used your vampires to threaten him, but you don't have the honor to own up to it. You don't even have the gall to do the dirty work yourself. If this is how you propose to rule, I'm not impressed."

Her eyes lit with fire that made me smile wider than I probably should have, considering her obvious animus.

She leaned forward. "I am a *Master*."

I held up a hand. "Let me go ahead and stop you right there. I've known several Masters in my short tenure as a vampire, and very few of them have impressed me. I'm not going to genuflect just because someone gave you a title."

She glowered. "You may believe you have him wrapped around your precious little finger, but you are wrong. I doubt he's told you of his lovers. You think you've tamed him? You're a naive child. And I suspect he sees you the same way. He uses women, drinks their pleasure, and, when he's done, discards them. His past is littered with his seductions, their tears. You're only one of many. And if his history is any indication, you definitely won't be the last." Her eyes glimmered with excitement, with victory.

This was precisely what Ethan had been afraid of—that Nicole would confess this to me, tell me what he'd been and whom he'd been with, and I'd run screaming into the night. Perhaps she thought that if I ran, he'd be too distracted to carry on with the testing and he'd withdraw, giving her the victory. Or perhaps she was merely angry I'd ruined her plans tonight, and thought she'd get her revenge by ruining something of mine.

Her reasons didn't really matter.

I thought of Ethan and our talk the night before, our interlude this evening, his wild eyes and chest-heaving recovery. I thought of his promises, of the eternity he'd already promised me, and the ring he'd hinted would someday make it official.

She was right: I didn't want to know any more about his former lovers.

But Amit was also right: Ultimately, they didn't matter. None of it mattered but me and Ethan. Ethan had told me what he'd needed to, and that was enough for me.

Still . . . "That's really cruel of you to say."

Nicole shrugged. "I suppose all's fair in love and war."

I moved toward her, putting mere inches between us, and let a predatory smile curve my lips. "Then any acts of mine are equally justified. And let me tell you this right now, Nicole: If you come for him, you come for me."

Her nostrils flared as anger poured through her. "You wouldn't dare harm me."

I smiled, catlike. "I would dare many things, Nicole. I have faced down many kinds of monsters—human, vampire, demon, and much, much worse than you. If you make another move against him—if you do anything other than finish out this testing completely aboveboard—you'd better run, and you'd better run fast. Because there's no place in this world you can hide that I won't find you."

There was a flare of anger in her eyes, but I matched it with magic of my own. I wasn't afraid of her. There was nothing she could do to me, because I'd face death again before letting her harm him.

But she wasn't done yet.

"Consider the possibility, Merit, that you and your House and its Master are better off in your own small kingdom."

"Is that a threat?"

Something flashed in her eyes—deep and haunting and very, very old.

"You think winning is all he'll need to do, child? That holding the throne shields him? You saw what they did to Darius. He won't be invincible, or immune. He'll be targeted. Let that comfort you in your bed tonight."

We stared at each other until Ethan stepped back into the doorway, his cautious magic filling the room. "Ladies. Is there a problem?"

"No," Nicole said, stepping back and brushing a lock of hair behind her ear. "We were quite finished."

"Iain would like to speak with you before he leaves."

She nodded, walked to the door with the bearing of a queen. I'd be damned if I'd ever bow down to her.

"Sentinel?"

I looked back at Ethan, found his forehead pinched in concern, shook my head. "Just clearing the air. She is a piece of work."

He watched me for a moment, as if gauging what she might have told me, and my reaction to it.

I patted his chest. "We're fine," I assured him. "And I reiterate: Go kick her ass back to Georgia."

So I could start to worry about what would happen if he actually won . . .

Ethan went upstairs to dress, to don more comfortable clothes for the challenge. I was heading to the Ops Room for our final check-in when my phone rang.

"It's Catcher," he said. "Just FYI, we talked to the manager at the Magic Shoppe, asked for records about the Fletcher tarot deck sale. They're locked away, and he can't get to them until tomorrow. They use a big document-storage facility, so you have to wait until they're delivered."

"Thanks for the update. I assume you've filled in the CPD?"

"I filled in Chuck, and he filled in the CPD."

"Any sign of Mitzy Burrows?"

"Still nothing," Catcher said. "They're looking, and they've got eyes on the store. There are too many connections to ignore there. But they still don't have anything that ties to employees other than Mitzy."

"How's Arthur doing?"

"Coping, I think. They're going to release Brett's body tomorrow, so the family can start to get some closure."

"Good. That's good."

"Listen, I've heard through the grapevine that phys testing is today."

"It is. At midnight." I checked the hallway clock, found we were nearly there.

"How is he?"

"Managing. Amit's here, and they had a good warm-up session. He's as ready as he's going to get."

"You don't sound confident."

"I'm confident in him. I'm less than confident in the GP, or his competitor. She's as conniving as they come. Malik's the only witness we can have. Apparently the GP has very particular rules about the involvement of others during testing."

Catcher's chuckle sounded sneaky. "That tenet may apply to the House, but it doesn't apply to me. If you can find out the location, we could roll the van to a spot nearby like we did with Darius, just in case."

Relief swamped me, and I was damned glad Kowalcyzk had come to her senses and given them a van. "I love you guys."

"Don't get gushy. Just keep your head on straight. You and Ethan have friends and allies, Merit. And it's times like this when we rally."

That made me feel incrementally better. If I couldn't be there, at least having the Ombuddies nearby would help. I decided not to tell Luc, or anyone else, about the idea. In case Lakshmi caught wind of the plan, plausible deniability seemed the best course of action.

"Hey, before you go, has Mallory found out anything else about the obelisk?"

"No, shit, but that reminds me." I heard the sound of paper shuffling. "Chuck called, said you'd asked your father about some financial information."

"I did. I was looking for the accounts into which the stolen money was transferred. They're Swiss accounts, so I thought my dad could get there quicker, considering his connections. Why?"

"I guess your dad got an answer, asked your grandfather to pass it along."

That hit me harder than it should have. I'd readily admit I didn't take much time for my family, but my father couldn't even deign to call or text me back? He had to work through my grandfather?

Nothing to do about it now, I told myself. *Get the job done, and have a cathartic cry about family later.* "What did you get?"

"I guess he was able to find a name for one of the accounts? The smaller one, he said. The registered beneficiary is Ronald Weatherby."

We'd theorized the smaller account was for an accomplice, someone who got a piece of the larger seven-million-dollar take. But the name didn't ring any bells. I guess it would have been too much to ask for the account to have been registered to Edmund, Danica, or Dierks in their own names.

"Listen," Catcher said, "I've got to run. The nymphs are peddling Moroccan leftovers without a license, and I need to intervene there. Let me know about the phys testing."

I promised I would, put the phone away, and walked back to Ethan's office. He was back, this time in jeans and a smoky green T-shirt that intensified the color of his eyes. He sat with Amit and Malik in the conversation area, an open bottle of blood in his hands.

His eyes flashed with alarm when I walked in, but I settled him down with a hand. "It's about Darius. The smaller Swiss account is registered to Ronald Weatherby. Does that ring any bells for anyone?"

Ethan considered, shook his head. "Not for me. Amit? Malik?"

Both of them shook their heads.

"Perhaps one of the GP members' former names?" Amit asked.

I moved to Ethan's computer, typed in a search. Unfortunately, Ronald Weatherby wasn't an uncommon name. There was an actor, a pub owner, a man with a gardening show on a local television station, a member of Parliament, and two soccer players . . .

Wait. I stopped short, scrolled back through the results.

Mallory had said the obelisk had been magicked, in part, by someone who knew his or her way around flowers and herbs, including the sassafras powder.

The Ronald Weatherby with the gardening show lived in Henley-on-Thames. His photo showed a small, hobbitesque man with an impressive belly, crown of white curls, and four adorable Corgis. He owned and operated a small flower shop and traveled around the world to acquaint himself with plant varieties.

He also considered himself a top-notch herbalist.

Ethan walked toward me. "Have you got something, Sentinel?"

"Actually," I said, smile dawning, "I think I have." I swiveled the screen so he could see it. "Mallory did a forensic analysis of the obelisk, culled out all the spells and charms and whatnot that went into spelling it. There were herbs and magic in the mix from the US and the UK, but she couldn't tell us any more. Turns out, there's a Ronald Weatherby in England who's an herbalist and fancies himself a 'botanical traveler.'"

Ethan arched an eyebrow at the screen. "He doesn't appear the type to manipulate a Master vampire and arrange an international theft."

"No, he does not. But I'd bet he prepared that obelisk and got a nice little paycheck for his trouble. His name was on the smaller account."

"The payoff," Malik said.

"Exactly."

Ethan's eyes went hard. "Good work, Sentinel. Find Lakshmi. He's in the UK, so we'll set the GP's dogs on his trail—and his vampiric employer's."

I nodded, switched places with Ethan, and left the office. I expected Lakshmi would be upstairs in the ballroom planning out her obstacle course, but when I rounded the stairs, I heard my name.

I glanced behind me, found Lakshmi in jeans, a leather jacket, and black boots, which she wore like a model. There was something in her eyes I didn't like.

"Hey, Ethan's looking for you."

Her expression stayed flat. "We're preparing to begin the test. I presume by now you've heard only the Masters and their Seconds will attend the physical testing alone?"

Shit, I thought, my first reaction being that she knew about our plan to spy on the proceedings and keep an eye on Ethan. I bluffed. "Yes. Ethan told us."

"Well, that's not entirely accurate. We'd actually like your assistance, as well."

Before I could register relief, I felt a sudden sharp pain at my shoulder. For the second time in a matter of days, night came early.

＋―＝◆＝―＋

CHAPTER TWENTY-ONE

IRON MAN

My eyes opened again, and dark hair swam into focus. My head seemed to be spinning on my neck, or maybe that was just the room. "What did you do to me?"

"Apologies for the intrigue and nerve pinch," Lakshmi said, standing in front of me. "That seemed the best way to transport you without incident."

"Transport me? Where the hell am I?"

"The testing location. An unused warehouse complex on the south side of the city."

Lakshmi stepped aside, let me get a look at my surroundings. I was in a room with brick walls and a worn wooden floor. I faced an open doorway, the door heavy and metal and set on giant brass hinges. I was in a simple wooden chair, my arms tied behind me. I pulled, moved forward to break free, but their hold was tight. The sensation made me panicky, but it also woke me from my stupor.

"What the hell is going on? Why am I here?"

"We find most vampires expect the physical testing will pit them, solo, against some obstacle. We find that's not the best way to test a potential head of the GP. Their job, of course, is not to stand alone against enemies, but to lead their soldiers into battle. To strategize. To partner."

I struggled against my bonds again. "Where is he?"

"Nearly here," she said, without elaboration. "Your goal is to find him and escape before your time is up."

My heart began to thud louder. "What time? How much time do we have?"

She pulled a long box from an interior jacket pocket, slid it open, and held out a very long pink-tipped match.

I pulled against the ropes, the chair bouncing beneath me. "You have got to be fucking kidding me. The floors are wooden. This place will go up like a tinderbox."

She struck the match against the side of the box, and the flame bounced orange and blue at the tip. She watched it burn for a moment, then looked back at me.

"Becoming head of the Greenwich Presidium is the most important position a vampire can hold, Merit. He or she will control the fates of thousands of vampires. Must protect thousands of vampires, even at great personal cost. That is not a job to be undertaken lightly, or without a full understanding of the sacrifices. He has every opportunity to find you and get you out without danger. He must be strong, cunning, creative, all while fearing for your safety. That is no more than we ask of every GP leader every day."

The match still in hand, she stepped outside before settling her gaze on me. "I wish you and Ethan luck, Merit, and hope to see you soon."

It didn't matter to me that her justifications were logical. I was scared—for me and him—and I was pissed. "You're a psychopath!" I yelled out, pulling against the chair again. "The entire GP is made up of sadists!"

And since she'd been the one who'd asked me to convince Ethan to run for the position, I screamed out a few more choice phrases that ripped through every curse in my arsenal.

She only smiled politely, then pulled the door closed behind her. It was enormous and thick, overlaid with a metal plate and held in place by large brass bolts.

"She's going to set us on fire," I said, glancing around the room. How, exactly, was I supposed to get out of this?

I tried to reach Ethan telepathically, but he didn't respond. Too far away, I guessed. The telepathy didn't cover long distances.

I forced myself to breathe, to stay calm, to think. The only way I was going to ignore the panic attack was to focus on one small task at a time. The first step was to get the hell out of this chair, and out of this room.

The ropes that bound me were old-fashioned hemp, which chafed against my wrists. They were tied together, and to the chair, but the chair wasn't fastened to the floor.

"Then that's the first to go," I said, shifting my weight to rock gently back, then forth, then back, then forth again, until I leaned forward enough to get my feet solidly on the ground, and the back of the chair in the air.

That put me half standing, bent over, with a chair tied to my back. I shuffled to the wall, stood perpendicular to it, and prepared to smash.

"I really hope this isn't aspen," I murmured, closed my eyes, rotated from my hips, and slammed the chair into the wall.

Wood shattered and splintered, and my elbow—which also made contact—sang with pain that radiated up my arm. But the chair had cracked, and I'd take the victory.

I cursed like a sailor against the pain but turned my face away and smashed one more time. I felt my bonds loosen as the chair broke into pieces. One end of the rope hung down, and I stepped on it, kept stepping on rope until I'd pulled the rest of the tangled mess to the floor.

My arms were chafed and my shoulders ached, but I'd survive. I rolled them out, tried to reach Ethan again.

Sentinel? Thank God. Where are you?

My racing heart slowed, just a little. He must have arrived at the building—and within telepathy range. *In a room. I was tied to a chair but got free. The door's bolted.*

I've got you beat, he said, and even his psychic voice sounded stressed. *I was tied to a table—Lakshmi didn't take my dagger, thankfully—and now I'm staring down a very burly River troll.*

The building shook, and I had to hope that wasn't the result of Ethan being thrown about by his nemesis. River trolls were burly men and women who made their homes beneath the bascule bridges that crossed the Chicago River, and helped the nymphs enforce their rulings.

And in case you didn't know, he grunted, *Lakshmi torched the building.*

Oh, I know. She lit the damn match in here. I'm going to punch her in that pretty little face if I survive this.

We will survive it, and we'll both punch her in her pretty little face.

I'd gotten out of the chair, linked to Ethan. The door was my next task. I tried the obvious first—wiggling the latch, bumping a shoulder against it to test its nudge-ability, trying to pry the bar out of the hinges with a piece of the splintered chair.

That was five minutes wasted, because I was not getting through the door.

I closed my eyes, forced myself to think.

I didn't have a better thought, but I did feel a breeze behind me. I looked back, spied a small and narrow window. I ran to it, looked outside. It was a long way down, which I could handle, but I was afraid that if I got out, I wouldn't be able to get back in. And that put Ethan even more at risk.

I was preparing to make another run at the door when a wave of hot air flew up from the cracks in the floor.

The cracks in the floor. Could that have been more obvious? If I couldn't get through the door, I'd go through the floor.

I grabbed the biggest remaining chunk of the chair, a hefty piece of the seat, and walked carefully around the room, looking for the bounciest boards. That award went to a spot near the middle of the room, where it looked like water had pooled and rotted the boards from the top down.

I lifted the wedge over my head, slammed it down with a giant crack that sent dust and particles of wood into the air.

One more crack, then two, and the seat burst through the boards, leaving a hole just wide enough to fit the edge of the seat. I wedged it into the hole, stood up, and pulled until boards cracked and split, then pulled up large splinters of wood until the hole was large enough for me to fit through.

I looked back, grabbed the rope, wound it around my arm just in case, then put my fingers on the edge of the hole, leaned forward until my torso was out. The room below was the same size and materials as mine, but the door was open.

Done, I thought, then levered the rest of my torso through the hole, flipping forward so I hung by my arms, and dropped to the floor.

I ran through the door, which led to an enormous room marked by white columns and stacks of dilapidated office furniture.

Ethan emerged from a room on the other end of the space, dirty and showing off an impressive shiner. He was also grinning like a maniac.

We jogged toward each other, met in the middle, embraced. He kissed me good and hard.

"It really wouldn't have been fair for you to sit this one out," he said, with sparkling eyes. He was in surprisingly good spirits. Maybe this really did appeal to his alpha-male mentality.

"Sure it would have, because I don't want to be in the GP. What do you think is next?"

I needn't have bothered to ask. Wood cracked on the other side of the room, and a giant timber split and dropped through the ceiling, crashing to the floor ten feet in front of us—and then crashing with enough force to rip through the floor. Smoke and sparks poured through the fissures above and below us.

"Let's get the hell out of here," Ethan said, grabbing my hand and moving toward a large bank of windows on the other side of the room.

But a shadow stepped into our path. He was large, six feet tall, with broad shoulders and an upturned nose. River troll number two.

I actually knew one troll, a man named George whom I'd met at one of the open houses my grandfather had held for the city's supernatural communities. Unfortunately, this wasn't George.

He walked toward us with heavy footsteps.

"Thoughts? Recommendations?" I asked, the question mooted when the troll struck out, tossing a hand that sent Ethan skittering across the ground.

My heart stopped until Ethan blinked, climbed to his feet, shook his head.

I looked back at the troll. "That was rude." I spun and executed a flying scissor kick that would have sent a vampire flying but landed dully on the River troll's abdomen. As I landed, he took a stiff step backward, regained his footing, then moved forward again.

This time the slap was for me. I turned my body to the side to reduce the impact, but pain still lit up my arm when he made contact, knocking me to the ground.

But he turned back toward Ethan, his apparent target.

The troll lurched forward, and this time Ethan dodged him, spinning to kick the troll in the butt and send him forward. Trolls were strong, but they weren't especially nimble. Ethan was both, and he used it to his advantage. The troll stumbled, hit the ground, whacked his head on the corner of an old desk, but after a moment, rose to his feet again.

He glanced back, rushed Ethan again, correctly guessed that Ethan's feint to the left had been just that. He aimed low, wrapped his arms around Ethan's knees, sending them both to the floor with a crash.

They rolled once, then twice, sending up smoke and sparks with each revolution. Ethan crawled free, kicked back when the troll tried to grab his feet again. Ethan grabbed an office chair, nailed the troll on the back, and sent him sprawling again. His chest still bobbed, but he didn't get up.

Ethan wiped blood from his forehead with the back of his hand, then glanced at me. "And I think, Sentinel, that will do for now."

He'd just taken a step when a trapdoor opened beneath him, swallowing him and sending smoke and sparks billowing into the room.

"Ethan!" I screamed, dropping to the ground at the edge of the door. "Ethan, you are not allowed to die again!"

I didn't breathe again until I felt his fingers, straining at the rim of the square gap the trapdoor had created.

He reached up and I grabbed his arm, planting my feet to try to pull him back. But his hand was slick with sweat and soot and he began to slip from my fingers. Fear lanced through me.

"Give me your other hand, Ethan. You're slipping!"

He cursed, shifted his weight, trying to swing his body up to give me his other hand . . . when he slipped forward another inch, and then he was moving and my hand was empty.

My mouth opened in a scream, but suddenly the troll was there, reaching out, grabbing Ethan by the shirt. With a grunt and shower of wood and smoke, the troll hauled him out, tossing him onto the floor of the room. Ethan lay on his back, face streaming with blackened sweat, coughed vigorously.

He climbed to his feet, looked at the troll, extended a hand. "I appreciate that."

The troll nodded. "You beat me fair and square. That's all she said I had to do."

Ethan coughed again. "Now that we've all fulfilled our bargains, perhaps we should leave?"

Together, the three of us carefully picked our way across the room, coughing and dodging showers of sparks that poured down from the ceiling above us, and fountains that burst through the floor every time the fire took another bite of it.

We reached the door in the room's far corner, the EXIT sign still glowing above it, and pushed.

Nothing happened. The door didn't budge, even an inch. Ethan rammed it with a shoulder, wincing, but tried again.

"She probably welded the damn doors shut," Ethan said, kicking it in frustration, and with enough force to fell a shape-shifter—but not to even rattle a very inappropriately labeled door.

"I will try," the troll said, stepping forward.

We moved aside, watching as he rammed his impressive bulk into the door once, then twice, then a third time. When blood began to speckle through his pale gray shirt, I put a hand on his arm. "Maybe let's try a different option."

"Window," Ethan said, and we followed him to the perpendicular wall, which was marked by a horizontal band of windows.

Ethan dug through debris, pulled out what looked like a pipe, and smashed through the glass to allow us egress.

I looked back at the troll. "If you jump, will you be okay?"

He walked to the window, peered down. "Long way down."

"It is."

"I can make it," he said, and, without hesitation, climbed onto the ledge and jumped. Ethan and I peered out, watched as he hit the ground with a thud that shook the entire building and left a crater in the ground that sent up a plume of smoke.

I stretched out the window, struggling to see anything in the darkness, and holding my breath until I saw him rise and walk away.

"He's clear," I said.

"Then let's move, Sentinel. Because I believe we're running out of time."

I climbed onto the ledge in stiletto boots, moved to the side so Ethan could climb out, too.

I made the mistake of looking down, and vertigo wracked me. It was only the iron grip of Ethan's fingers on my forearm that kept me from tilting forward into darkness. Vampires could jump, sure. But I didn't think falling face-first was the same thing.

"Three . . . two . . . one," Ethan said, and as the door burst open and flame rushed us, we took the step.

Time slowed as the ground moved slickly up to meet us, and

we landed with our hands still together. My knees wobbled from the impact, but I stood straight again and, as timbers crashed to the ground around us, hauled ass to get away from the fire raging behind us.

Malik, Bennett, and Lakshmi waited twenty yards away. Relieved magic enveloped us as Malik jumped forward to embrace us both.

"Where are Nicole and Sarah?" Ethan asked.

Lakshmi kept her gaze on the warehouse, which mooted the very venomous stare I offered her. "They aren't out yet."

Ethan's eyes widened, and he cast a glance at the building. The structure was enormous—eight stories of sheer brick walls, nearly as long as a football field. The roof over the end of the building where I'd been held was already falling in.

"The building won't be standing much longer," Ethan said.

"She'll want to finish it herself," Bennett insisted.

"She'll die and won't care if she finishes it. Besides, I've already won. She has nothing to lose."

Bennett looked nervously back at the building. To save his Master's life, or her pride? That was the question.

"If you go," Lakshmi said, "points will be deducted, as you'll have interfered with the test."

"Lakshmi, respectfully, you can fuck your test. If your GP believes a vampire is worth more because he leaves his colleagues to die, then it's even less reputable than I imagined." Ethan looked back at me. "I'm going back for her. Stay here."

Panic rose, hot and suffocating. "You're not going back in there. At least, not without me."

"I'm going," he said, in a voice that brooked no argument.

"This isn't the time to play Master of the House."

He looked back at me, his expression fierce. "This is my test, and I will finish what remains of it, whether they score it or not. You will not risk your life any further than it's already been risked tonight. If you step one foot toward that building, there'll be hell to pay. Malik, keep an eye on her."

"Liege."

Ethan turned to face me and pressed a hard kiss to my lips. "Stay here."

But I was as stubborn as him, and I tried to follow him until Malik's hand clamped around my arm. I threw my gaze to his. "You cannot be serious."

"This isn't about you. It's about him. It's his battle, and he needs to fight it."

"To the death? Over her? She tried to kill him."

"He is a better vampire than she is, but he isn't sure of it. Let him prove it to himself. You know that he needs that, Merit. To know that he is who he believes—and not the monster others would try to make of him."

I moistened my lips, looking at Malik, then the building into which Ethan and Bennett raced headlong. I didn't want him moving back into danger . . . but Malik was absolutely right. We knew who Ethan was. But Ethan needed to prove it to himself.

"He will survive this," Malik said. "Trust him."

"I do trust him." It was Nicole I didn't trust. "And you'd better hope he'll be okay," I said, training my gaze on Malik. "If anything happens to him, I will gut you like a trout and not feel bad about it."

He managed a small smile. "I'd look forward to the challenge, Sentinel."

And speaking of which, I had unfinished business. I walked to Lakshmi, planted myself in front of her, forcing her gaze to mine.

With obvious reluctance, she shifted her gaze from the building to me. "Yes?"

"You are responsible for him," I told her. "And I don't care about your excuses, or your justifications, or whether you think you're serving all vampires by sacrificing the few. I don't care who you are, or what position you're in. This is complete, unmitigated bullshit."

Her eyes flattened with insult, and she opened her mouth to respond. But I had no interest in whatever she might say. With fire in my eyes, I walked away before she could respond and before I made good on my promise to punch her. I was so angry, so afraid, that the risk I'd do it just to feel some other emotion was too high.

I walked back to Malik, whose eyes shined with curiosity.

"Everything all right?"

I fixed my gaze on the warehouse. "Just setting the record straight."

His fingers found mine, squeezed.

The windows on the first floor burst after two minutes had passed. I knew the time, because I counted each second in the cadence I'd learned as a child—*one one thousand, two one thousand, three one thousand, four one thousand*—waiting for him to appear again.

We ducked as glass flew, but I still felt the prick of shards that touched skin not covered by my leathers.

The second-floor windows burst at three minutes, flames shooting through the building's husk like they were reaching for us, trying to draw us back in.

"He has thirty seconds," I said, without bothering to look back at Malik. "He can have his pride, but I'm not going to let him kill himself."

Malik kept his eyes on the building, casting back and forth

across the facade as he searched for Ethan. "I was only going to give him fifteen."

Timbers creaked and lurched ominously, the same sounds I imagined passengers might hear on a ship before it split and disappeared beneath the water.

"Fuck it," I said, and started forward. More windows burst, and I covered my head with my arms as glass fell to the ground around me like snow.

Several figures emerged.

I'd seen Ethan walk through smoke and ash before, emerge through a cloud of magic and fire. We'd been lovers then, when I'd thought him dead. But we hadn't loved. Not like this. Not like we did now. I'd grieved when he was gone, but this would have killed me. Because now he was my eternity.

My smoky, sooty boyfriend had never looked so good.

He carried Sarah in his arms. Nicole limped along behind them with Bennett's help, holding one arm stiffly at her side.

We all flinched as an enormous *crack* lit the air, and the building's roof crumpled from the middle, falling inside and bringing down half the building with it. Smoke, dust, and debris poured around us. Supernaturals had destroyed yet another building. But everyone was alive.

Ethan was alive.

He placed Sarah carefully on the ground. "Smoke inhalation," he said, stepping away again so Bennett and Nicole could attend to her.

I strode to him, wrapped my arms around his neck, and kissed him fiercely.

"That was the dumbest and bravest and most amazing thing I've ever seen anyone do. And if you ever do anything like that again, I'll kill you myself."

Lakshmi moved toward us and didn't mince words. "Your score will be reduced for interfering. Hers will be reduced for failing to finish."

Ethan looked unconcerned by the pronouncement. "We all must act according to the dictates of our consciences. I have done so. You must do so as well."

Lakshmi walked away, pulled out her phone. When she was gone, Nicole walked closer, and there was no mistaking the befuddlement on her face.

"You helped me."

"I believed you could use a hand."

Her clothes were singed, her face sooty, her hair coated with ash. And she just kept staring at him, as if she was reevaluating hundreds of years of history.

"We're competitors."

"We are," Ethan agreed. "But we're also colleagues. And at one time, Nicola, we were friends. I won't take your immortality in order to prove a point."

My love for him—my respect for him—blossomed like a spring rose, filling my chest with love and utter pride that he was mine.

"So I see." Nicole swallowed hard but held out a hand.

He shook her hand, nodded, and when that was done, Nicole and Bennett helped Heart House's Sentinel into the waiting car.

I walked back to Lakshmi, called out her name.

"Yes?" she asked, when she glanced back.

"When you knocked me out and brought me here, you interrupted me. I had information for you: Some of the money stolen from the American Houses was transferred to a Swiss account registered to Ronald Weatherby. I believe you'll find he's a British herbalist who worked on the obelisk but probably wasn't told what it would be used for. Find him, interview him, ask him who paid him for his services. That will be the vampire who magicked and manipulated Darius. Now," I said, flicking a bit of ash from the sleeve of her jacket, then smiling at her again. "Figure that into your score."

Her mouth opened, closed. I gave her a jaunty salute, and walked back toward Ethan.

Once again, he showered while I searched for the right words to say. Tonight was no different, except that we'd showered together. I rubbed at the oily soot that stained my skin, while he washed my hair, a habit he'd apparently come to enjoy.

My fingers were wrinkled by the time we finally stepped from the shower, pulled on clothes. Ethan settled on his typical favorite—emerald green silk pajama bottoms that rode low on his hips. I'm fairly certain he wore them as a kind of dare, a challenge for me to resist him. But I had words to say, so I managed.

I opted for plaid shorts with a Cadogan "C" embroidered on the leg and a matching tank. If he expected me to ogle his abs, he might as well do a little ogling of my legs.

"You hungry?" he asked.

"Starving, actually. And you must be, too."

"My appetite is coming back." He picked up his phone. "I'll ask Margot to send something up, and Malik to hold down the fort. We can spend the rest of the evening here. I think we deserve a bit of quiet time together. And besides—you owe me a dinner, as I recall."

I managed not to make a comment about frighteningly fancy food. He was right; I did owe him. "I think that sounds magnificent." But as he checked his phone, his shoulders tensed.

"Ethan?" I prompted.

"We made the final ballot." He looked up at me, awe in his eyes. "Me, Nicole, Danica. Lakshmi didn't fail us after all. She gave us point deductions, but even with that we made the ballot. Granted, we're the bottom two on the ballot," he said with a chuckle, "but we're there. The other Houses will vote tonight. That means we'll know shortly after dusk tomorrow."

I walked to him, put my hands on his face. "Whatever happens, we are proud of you. So incredibly proud of you, for what you did and who you are."

He pulled me against his body, already hard and ready, and kissed me, tongue probing and my body going immediately hot, but I took a regrettable step backward and closed my eyes as I sought control. If he touched me, we'd both be lost.

"Wait," I said, opening my eyes again. "There are things we need to talk about. Or things I'd like to say."

He watched me carefully, took a step back, crossed his arms. That only seemed to accentuate his flat abs and hip muscles even more, but I dragged my gaze to his face.

"All right, Sentinel. Go ahead."

"Maybe let's sit down."

I felt the jarring spike of his magic, but moved to the sitting room, sat down on the couch, tucking one leg beneath me.

He looked decidedly skeptical but followed me over and took a seat, arching an arm over the back. "You have my attention."

"I was wild with fear tonight that I'd lose you again. But you came out alive. And not just alive—victorious. Regardless the points or the vote, or whatever happens here, you won. You had a choice: You could have left Nicole there. You could have taken the victory and walked away. But that's not who you are. You saved her. She *couldn't* make you an asshole, despite everything she tried to put you through."

I felt his shuddering sigh, and he put a hand on my cheek. "How did you suddenly become so wise?"

"I had a good teacher."

"Thank you, Merit."

"I actually meant Amit," I said with a grin. "But you were a really good teacher, too."

"Flattering Amit will get you nowhere with me, Sentinel."

There was a knock at the door. Ethan rose, checked the peephole, and when he was sure of our security, opened the door.

Margot wheeled in a cart topped with silver domes that smelled deliciously of meat. With much amusement, I watched her eyes drop and widen as she took in Ethan's scantily clad form. But she sucked it up, pulled off the silver domes.

"Liege, Merit. Dinner is served."

I braced myself for fish stuffed with more fish, or a mousse of meat. But the meal that stared back from gleaming white plates was perfectly normal. Bacon cheeseburgers with hand-cut fries and tumblers of chocolate milk shakes.

He smiled at me. "I decided for our award dinner we might have a meal that suited us both."

"I've never loved you more."

"Are you talking to me, Margot, or the burgers?"

"Yes," I said, and pulled up a chair as she flipped out the sides of the cart to make a round table.

When she crouched to stow the plate covers on the cart's bottom shelf, she looked back at me, mouth and eyes wide. She mouthed, *"Hubba-hubba,"* and gave me a very bawdy wink before disappearing out the door again.

"Never let it be said I'm not willing to sacrifice for my Sentinel."

"Nobody doubted it," I said, and ate a fry to prove just that.

I had to give him props. The dinner was absolutely delicious. Margot had even thought to bring dessert—chocolate cheesecake neatly sliced on two small plates, accompanied by a drizzle of raspberry sauce and a fresh sprig of mint.

"I believe there's something you'll need, Sentinel."

Ethan slid from his chair, dropped to one knee on the carpet.

My mind had to race to keep up, but my heart pounded madly.

Ethan looked up at me, grinned. "That thing, of course, is this." He held up a small dessert fork. "You dropped your fork, Sentinel."

My blood pounded in my ears. I stood up, swatted his arms with slaps. "You are a jerk."

He roared with laughter. "Ah, Sentinel. The look on your face." He doubled over with laughter. "Such terror."

I kept swatting. "At the thought of marrying you, you pretentious ass."

He roared again, then picked me up and carried me to the bed. "My pretentions are well earned, Sentinel."

"You have got to stop doing that."

"I can't. It's hilarious."

Only a man would think fake proposals were so funny. "It's nothing near hilarious. It's several thousand light-years from hilarious."

He dropped me onto the duvet, covered his body with mine, nipped at my lip, then trailed kisses to his favorite spot on my neck. "Let's see, my Sentinel, just how hilarious I can be."

I'd been right.

There was nothing hilarious about it.

·◦·→◄·◆·►→·◦·

CHAPTER TWENTY-TWO

THE LIONS, THE WITCH, THE WARDROBE

Someone screamed shrilly in my ear, over and over and over again.

"Phone," Ethan murmured, elbowing me. "Your phone."

I snapped awake, sat up, reached out for the phone that threatened to vibrate its way across the nightstand. My grandfather's name flashed on the screen, which made my heart jump uncomfortably.

"Hello?"

"I'm sorry for the rude awakening," he said.

"It's okay. I'm awake. Is everything all right?"

"With us, yes. With Mitzy Burrows, no. We've found her body."

"Damn it," I muttered, then apologized for cursing, which would have earned me a stern look. "Where?"

"The south garden at the Art Institute." That was downtown, in the middle of Chicago's business sector and the area known as the Loop.

"All right. I'll meet you there. Forty minutes or so, depending on traffic."

"We'll see you," my grandfather said, and the line went dead.

"Could I have one night without calamity?" I asked, putting the phone back on the nightstand and pulling a pillow over my face.

The bed shifted, and Ethan lifted the pillow away. "Not for a Sentinel sworn to uphold justice."

"I don't think I swore to that. Although I did swear to protect the House against all creatures living or dead. What's up with that?"

Ethan rose, pushed his hair back. "Ghosts, poltergeists, your greater and lesser banshees."

"Those things don't exist."

His look was flat. "You know better, Sentinel. Another tarot death?"

"Mitzy Burrows."

Ethan grimaced. "Wasn't she your prime suspect?"

"She was. And if the killer's still using the tarot, she'd be the Four of Wands or Four of Cups. She's at the Art Institute—with my grandfather."

"I'll go with you."

I glanced up at him. "Don't you want to stay here, wait to hear about the vote?"

He stretched his arms over his head, bent slightly at the waist as if loosening up for another run. "The message will come to me. If it's bad news, I'd just as soon hear about it outside the House. I need to go. I need a distraction, and I haven't been much help in this investigation so far."

"Okay," I said. "But I'm driving."

Ethan drove.

Apparently, a man who'd been through two nights of rigorous

psychological and physical testing deserved a night behind the wheel of his Ferrari.

I could hardly argue with that, mostly because it would have made me look bad. So I sucked it up.

Ethan gave Luc our itinerary, and I sent Jonah a message advising him of the murder, promising to stay in touch. He wished Ethan luck and asked me to give him an update if the GP got in touch. I guessed that request was equally motivated by personal curiosity, House curiosity, and RG curiosity. If Ethan won, there seemed little doubt the RG would have more questions, especially about my loyalty.

The Art Institute of Chicago took up a prime spot on Michigan Avenue. We parked a few blocks away, then locked the car and set out for the park on foot.

The building was one of the city's most famous landmarks, the classical architecture marked by columns and two giant stone lions that guarded the door. When I was younger, I'd stare at the lions, totally transfixed, wishing they'd come to life like twin Aslans.

I'd also spent plenty of time inside the building, staring at paintings and sculpture, obsessing over the museum's collection of miniature rooms, and imagining myself a tiny denizen.

None of the tales I'd spun featured vampires, sparkling or otherwise. But there might have been pirates.

We walked past the lions, heads nobly pointed toward the sky. Ethan reached up and rubbed a hand along one's leg, as if for good luck—or to ward off bad juju.

The sculpture garden was on the north side of the building, and half the park was boxed by lumber and clear plastic. That something had happened was obvious. Cops were parked on the street, their lights flashing. My grandfather stood on the sidewalk with Catcher, who nodded as we approached.

"Construction?" I wondered, gesturing toward what looked like temporary cover.

"Closed for a couple of weeks while they replace the concrete. They don't want people initialing it in the meantime." He gestured with his cane to a make-do door in the construction wrapping, and we walked inside.

Once again, temporary lights had been set up inside the barrier. The light bouncing off the plastic gave the garden an ethereal glow.

Cops and forensic folks were sprinkled around the park, looking for evidence, measuring, taking photographs. Detective Jacobs, looking drawn, and Detective Stowe talked to a construction worker who held his hard hat with white-knuckled fingers. His face looked equally bloodless. Perhaps he'd discovered the body.

We followed my grandfather to the park's water feature, a long rectangular pool of water topped by a circular fountain. An enormous pedestal emerged from it, topped by five bronze figures. The lowest figure reached out, her eyes closed, toward the body that lay at her feet.

That body wasn't sculpture, but very human.

Mitzy Burrows was propped beside the fountain, legs curled beneath her, one arm in her lap, the hand holding a golden cup marked by a blue cross. She wore a white dress; her feet were bare but, like the rest of her body, swollen with decay.

Her other arm lay across the edge of the fountain, and her head rested on it, as if she gazed longingly into the water. Both of her wrists had been cut, and blood stained the concrete around her and the water that pooled in the fountain. The scent of death was lifted by the breeze, and I used every bit of control to block it out.

"This isn't the Four of Cups." I looked at my grandfather. "I've seen that card, and this isn't it. So this death doesn't match the pattern. Two of Swords. Three of Pentacles. Four of Cups."

"It's not the Four of Cups," my grandfather agreed. "But she wasn't killed today. She was killed a week ago."

I looked back at the body, the single cup. She may have been our best lead, but she'd never been our killer. "She was killed first, and she started it all. The Ace of Cups?"

Catcher swiped at his phone, scanned, then passed it over. The card he'd pulled up was remarkably identical—a woman in a white toga-style gown beside a circular fountain, cup in hand, fingers trailing in the water.

"How did no one find her?" Ethan asked.

"Dumb luck," my grandfather said. "The concrete's been curing, and the workers haven't been on the site in a few days. No one saw her until tonight." He gestured toward Detective Jacobs and the others. "The construction manager got word vandals were cutting through the plastic, so he came out to have a look."

As the forensic team moved closer, we stepped back to give them room.

"So someone killed Mitzy Burrows," I said, when we'd moved a few feet away. "Then her ex-boyfriend, then Samantha Ingram. And the killer is going in order: Ace of Cups, Two of Swords, Three of Pentacles."

"Four of Wands would be next," Catcher said. "Naked woman on a horse in front of a castle."

"Lady Godiva?" Ethan suggested.

Catcher nodded. "Quite similar." He looked at my grandfather. "What ties the victims together? Or to the killer?"

"The Magic Shoppe," I said. "Mitzy used to work there, and she bought the swords there. There's a good chance the tarot cards were purchased there, too, based on the limited supply. Have you heard anything from the manager?"

Catcher shook his head. "The records were supposed to be released today. We're just waiting for him to take a look. Might be worth a drop-in later if we still haven't heard."

My grandfather nodded. "Follow up with them again, and drop by the store if you can't reach them."

"Not to be the bearer of bad news," Ethan said, "but three deaths within a single week means the killer's moving quickly."

"And the media's caught on to the tarot angle," my grandfather said. "There was a story in the paper this morning: 'City under Siege as Tarot Killer Strikes Chicago.'"

"Thank God they didn't exaggerate," Catcher said blandly. "If this was the killer's first body, maybe he was sloppy. We could get lucky in the forensics."

"That would be my hope. Detective Jacobs will run the investigation on the ground, follow up again with Brett's, Mitzy's, and Samantha's neighbors, try to find the connection between them. I wouldn't be surprised if he'll want to visit the store, as well."

"Anything we can do?" I asked.

"Not at the moment. But we'd appreciate it if you'd stay available. We've got folks dabbling in magic, purposefully or not, and we'd appreciate your take. That's what got us to the Magic Shoppe in the first place."

I had to give credit where credit was due. "That was Jonah's doing, actually. And we'll circle around with him, just in case."

"Appreciate it." My grandfather glanced back at Mitzy, grief darkening his eyes. Decades as a cop hadn't carved the emotion out of him.

"We'll be in touch," he said, a hand on Catcher's back as they moved back.

I sighed, rubbed my eyes. "I, for one, am sick of murder."

Ethan rubbed my neck. "You and me both, Sentinel. You and me both."

We walked back to Ethan's car, climbed inside. Ethan pulled out his phone to check it before we pulled into traffic.

My heart jumped immediately. "News?"

"Yes, but not of the variety we were expecting. The GP located Ronald Weatherby. And the GP is now down another vampire."

I half turned in the seat. "Down another vampire—as in dead? They found out who did it?"

"It was Dierks; at least, it was Dierks in the end, God rest his soul. Ronald Weatherby actually named Harold Monmouth as the instigator. He made the plan to steal the money from the GP, and when he was gone"—by Ethan's hand, notably—"Dierks continued the tradition."

"Weatherby prepped the obelisk?"

Ethan paused, scrolling through the GP's message. "He did. Said he had no idea what the vampires planned to use it for. 'Bit of hypnosis,' he told them."

I sat back again. "Damn. And what did Dierks say?"

"He offered Darius a full confession, which might be the first honorable thing he's done. Ironically, he said the GP was falling apart, and he wanted out. He decided continuing Monmouth's plan was the easiest way to do that."

"How did they kill Dierks?" I quietly asked.

"Decapitation. A relatively easy out for a vampire who committed treason and larceny, all things considered, but they'd have given him consideration since he's a GP member."

"What will happen to Ronald?"

More scrolling. The GP apparently prepared very thorough reports. "Lakshmi is communicating with the European version of the Order to ensure Ronald uses more care in the future."

"That's a familiar story," I said, thinking of Mallory and her former tutor, Simon.

"Perhaps," Ethan said with a smile. But when he looked down at his phone again, the smile faded. A pulse of despondent magic filled the car.

I put a hand on his arm but stayed quiet. From the look on his face, I didn't need to ask what news he'd received.

"I didn't win," Ethan said. "I lost the vote." He looked sad, shocked, befuddled, all at once.

I waited for him, gave him time to say the rest of it aloud.

"She won—Nicole. She'll be the next head of the GP." He put the phone down, put both hands on the steering wheel, stared into the night.

"I'm so sorry," I quietly said. "So very sorry. I know how much you wanted it—how much good you would have done."

He nodded but kept his eyes on the street.

"Will you want to address the House?"

Silence, then: "No, Merit. I just want quiet. Peace and quiet. We'll broadcast the coronation in the ballroom, and I'll address the House then. I'll thank them for their service, for putting up with the intrigue and the testing, for all of it. But for now, let's just have peace."

"Then that's what we'll do. Can I ply you with food? That's really my go-to response."

Before he could answer, my phone rang again. "Damn, but we're popular," I murmured, switching it to speaker mode.

"Merit and Ethan."

"It's Catcher. Just heard from the manager of the Magic Shoppe."

"That was fast."

"Yeah. Apparently he saw the story in the paper, actually got to work. He confirmed Samantha Ingram was a customer. Bought some vampire memorabilia a couple of days ago."

"Probably excited about being a potential Initiate," I said.

"Yeah, possible. He also finally checked the box, and the cards were actually purchased by a store employee—Curt Wachman. Jacobs is going to the store as soon as the scene is processed."

"Curt? Curt bought the tarot cards?"

"You know him?"

"He was at the store when Mallory and I went. We asked him about Mitzy. He didn't say anything unusual . . ." Something horrible occurred to me, because Mitzy wasn't the only thing we'd talked to him about.

Ace of Cups. Two of Swords. Three of Pentacles . . . and Four of Wands, something a practitioner of magic might use.

"Catcher," I said, forcing my voice to not shake. "Where's Mallory?"

"At home, I assume. Why?"

My heart began to pound. "She talked to Curt about going back to the store. She wants some wolfsbane, and he said they had some on the way." I calculated the timing. "She was going to pick it up. He tried to warn her off buying it, but she said she knew what she was doing. Didn't say she was a sorceress outright, but nudged around it. And it's her favorite shop—he knew her, had sold things to her before."

I heard only the sound of breathing. "I'm going to call her right now."

"I'll call her," I said. "We're already in the car and driving." I gestured to Ethan to start the car, pull out into traffic. He didn't waste any time. "And we're on our way to the store."

"Maybe this is nothing," he said. "Maybe it's nothing at all."

"You're probably right," I said, but it didn't feel right in my gut. And just in case: "Talk to my grandfather. Get the CPD to Curt's house, too, just in case he's off today. Maybe this is all a coincidence."

"Find her, Merit."

As soon as the call was disconnected, I dialed her number. The phone rang three times, then four, and my chest tightened with fear. Until, on the fifth ring, she answered.

"Hey, Merit—"

"Mallory, thank God."

"Hey, I'm actually right in the middle of something right now. Can I call you back?"

Shit. "Mallory, are you in the Magic Shoppe?"

"Well, yeah, actually. How did you know?"

Blood roared in my ears, but I forced myself to stay calm, to think. "I need you to turn around and walk out of there, Mallory. Pretend that nothing's wrong, just turn around and walk out. And don't ask questions. Don't ask me why; just turn around and walk out. Right to the door, and then back to the town house. Pretend I called, and I need something. It's an emergency. Okay?"

I had to give her credit. She didn't argue or ask questions. I must have sounded like a crazy person, but she didn't panic.

"Oh, hey, Curt," I heard her say. "Sorry, but Merit's got something she needs to talk about right away. Some kind of boy nonsense. Could you hold that wolfsbane for me for a few minutes? I'm going to step outside and try to calm her down."

"She's good," Ethan quietly said, eyes on the road as he took a sharp turn, then squeezed between cars to get a better spot in a different lane.

"You're doing great, Mal," I quietly told her. "You're doing great."

But her tone changed. "Get your hand off me, Curt. I don't want to have to hurt you."

I could actually feel the charge of magic through the phone, as if the cell tower had sent an echo of it along with her words.

"Just walk out, Mallory. Just turn and run."

I don't know whether she heard me or not. The phone crack-led and sizzled with magic and the sound of breaking glass.

"Get your hands off me, you psychopath!" And then the magic deflated, like it had been sucked back through the phone with a vacuum.

"Oh. Shit," she woozily said. "It's Curt . . . isn't it?"

The call went dead.

I called my grandfather back, hand shaking around the phone, and told him what we'd heard. Ethan drove like the proverbial bat out of hell, my grandfather, Catcher, and the rest of the CPD zooming along behind us.

Ethan squealed to a halt outside the Magic Shoppe, and I had my katana unsheathed before I reached the door. The lights were on, and the door was unlocked. There was a trail of magical de-struction behind the counter—a line of broken jars and a light-ning strike of broken glass across the mirror.

I gestured Ethan to the right, and I took the left, creeping down the row, checking the cross aisles for signs of life. When we met in the back of the store, he shook his head. I gestured to the door, counted quietly down. "Three . . . two . . . one."

We went in, katanas in hand, blades pointed and ready for action but ultimately unnecessary. Skylar-Katherine lay on the floor in front of us.

"Shit," I said, falling to my knees in front of her. I checked her breathing, which was slow but regular. A bruise was rising on her temple. He'd knocked her out.

I patted her cheeks. "Skylar-Katherine. Skylar-Katherine, wake up.

"There's probably a bathroom," I said, gesturing Ethan to the back of the store. "Damp towels?"

"On it," he said, and rose to a quick jog.

After several seconds, her eyes fluttered, opened. She looked around, then focused on me. "What's going on?"

"Somebody knocked you out?"

"Somebody . . . Curt. It was Curt. I think Curt knocked me out."

"I think so, too. Can you sit up?"

She nodded, but I put a hand behind her shoulders, helped her move into a sitting position. "My head," she said, touching her temple gingerly with the heel of her hand.

"I know the feeling," I said. "Do you know where Curt is?"

"No. There was—someone came to the door. It was your blue-haired friend. He said he had business, and he needed to attend to it. And then he hit me." Tears rushed to her eyes. "Why would he hit me? We're friends."

There wasn't going to be an easy way to say this, so I didn't bother sugarcoating it. "You heard about the tarot murders?"

All the color drained from her face. "Sure. Why?"

"We think Curt is the killer."

It was obvious she wanted to argue; I could see it in her face. The assault had made her enough of a believer. "Is that why he hit me?"

"We think so." Ethan came back with wet towels, and I

pressed them against the bump on her head. She hissed with pain.

"I don't know him," she said, leveling him with a suspicious glance. She was clearly coming around.

"He's Ethan. My boyfriend. Skylar-Katherine," I said, snapping my fingers until she looked at me again. "Why would Curt hurt Mitzy? Or Brett?"

"Mitzy? Oh, because he loved her. And she didn't love him back."

I frowned, very confused. That didn't match what the CPD had learned. "Wait. I thought Mitzy was dating Brett."

"She went on a date with Brett. She'd been dating Curt, but they broke up. It was nasty, too. He really had a thing for her. She quit the store a couple of weeks after that."

"Do you know where Curt was going?"

"I don't—I don't know. This is so confusing."

"Stay with her," I told Ethan. "And call Catcher, let him know."

I rose and ran to the back corner of the store, looked at the tarot card case. I'd expected the spot for the Fletcher deck to still be empty, but there was a new deck where the old one had been.

I pulled up the glass lid, but it didn't budge. There wasn't time for keys, so I grabbed the closest thing I could find—a candleholder made of antler—and stabbed it into the top of the case. Glass shattered and dropped into the case.

"What the hell do you think you're doing?"

I glanced back, saw Skylar-Katherine behind me, limping forward with Ethan's support.

"Catcher will be here in a couple of minutes," he said. "CPD's nearly at Curt's house."

"I asked what you were doing to our case!"

"I'm finding out where your crazy coworker took my best

friend." I brushed glass aside with the edge of my sleeve and plucked out the box of Fletcher tarot cards.

I ripped away cellophane and paper, destroying the box to get to the cards, flipping through them until I found the card I was looking for.

"Four of Wands," I said, pulling it out and holding it up so they could see the Lady Godiva-esque feature, her horse, her *castle*.

I turned the card so they could look at it, too. "He's been literal so far with the symbolism. If he keeps that here, he needs a castle."

"The Water Tower?" Ethan suggested. "It looks medieval."

It was the type of place he'd like—a public space with lots of attention. But he had an eye for detail. The Water Tower was much too small to look like the enormous battlement on the card.

"Too small," I said. "What about that castle in River North?"

"It's a club now," Skylar-Katherine said. "Good scene."

"But surrounded by concrete," Ethan said, tapping the card. "And he won't want that much attention, not at first. He's too particular, and he'll want time to arrange things. He can't do that privately downtown."

"Oh, I know something!" Skylar-Katherine walked to the back of the store, grabbing shelves for balance as she moved. The shuffling of paper and moving drawers echoed through the store.

"This," Skylar-Katherine said, emerging from the back room only seconds later, one hand on the doorjamb as she made the turn into the store again, feet practically skidding on the carpet as she moved. A newspaper, folded open, was in her hand.

"This," she said again, thrusting it at us. "The Bellwether Castle—it used to be a private school, but they rent it out now for weddings or whatever. They're having a spring open house."

Ethan took the paper, and we looked at the black-and-white photograph of a building that, yeah, looked very much like a castle. Large, square, and tall, with a turret on each corner. The stones were roughly hewed, and the giant front door consisted of large planks of wood butted together with golden bolts. The building was set back on the lot, with plenty of green space behind it.

Ethan held the picture beside the card, whistled. "That's pretty damn close."

"We don't have time for 'pretty damn close,'" I said.

"There's a stable behind the building," Skylar-Katherine said. "I don't know if they still have horses, but there's a stable."

"*That's* pretty damn close," I said, and took a picture of the newspaper to send to Jeff just as tires squealed outside the front of the building.

"Where the fuck is she?" demanded the voice that rushed inside over the clang of the bells on the door.

Catcher had arrived. His magic—sharp and dangerous—was telling enough. He emerged around the row in a T-shirt that read, fittingly enough, YOU'RE MY PROBLEM.

He and Mallory might have had their problems, and their relationship might have been endangered during her Nebraska period, but there was no doubting the ferocity in his eyes or the cloud of magic behind him. His woman had been threatened, and he'd damn well take care of it.

Jeff and my grandfather rounded the corner behind him. Not just Catcher taking care of it, but Mallory's entire magical family.

"We think she's here," Ethan said, extending the paper to Catcher. He grabbed it, took a look, lifted his gaze again before handing it off to Jeff.

"Why?" my grandfather asked.

"There's a castle on the Four of Wands." Ethan handed him the card.

Catcher reviewed, nodded. "Jeff?"

"On it," he said, handing the paper down the line to my grandfather as he pulled out a thin tablet that looked like little more than a thin sheet of glass. He swiped fingers across it.

"Bellwether Castle," he read. "Formerly Bellwether Beaux Arts Academy, built 1891." He looked up. "It's in Logan Square. Near the park."

"That's only a couple of miles from here," I said.

Catcher turned and started for the door, but my grandfather adjusted to block him.

"Chuck," Catcher warned, his eyes wild with fear and fury. "He's probably drugged her, and he'll kill her if we don't get there."

But my grandfather stayed calm. "If we don't go in there with a plan, we risk her getting hurt in the process. And we don't want that. We'll get to her first," my grandfather said, keeping his gaze on Catcher.

"Curt is careful," my grandfather continued. "The arrangement, the positioning. Think of the trouble he goes to. We do this right, and she'll be fine. But we have to do this right."

Catcher nodded, stepped aside.

"There are a couple of other places," I said. "Water Tower, the castle. Low chance he's there, because they don't quite match, but . . ."

My grandfather pulled out his phone. "I'll tell Arthur. Have him send squads to both places just in case. They'll need to go in quietly. No sirens. We don't want to startle or scare him."

He looked at me. "You said you talked to Curt?"

I nodded. "Day before yesterday, when we came to ask about

the purchase of the tarot deck. I was with Mallory when she ordered the stuff."

"So he'll recognize you. I'll talk to Jacobs, but you might be the best candidate to go in. How do you feel about that?"

I expected Ethan to protest, but he was silent. I glanced at him, saw concern on his face. But by his silence, he offered me trust, faith. He squeezed my hand supportively.

"Fine," I said. "I'm fine with it. I'll go in. I can talk to him about what he did, why he did it. Try to build a bond?"

My grandfather nodded. "The card. What weapon would he use?"

I offered it to him, but it wasn't clear from the simple artwork. Castle. Horse. Wands. Pennants.

"The wands?" Ethan asked. "That's a possibility."

"Or the braid," I suggested. "Strangulation?"

"Each murder has been different," Catcher grimly said. "He won't repeat something he's done before. He's strangled, stabbed, slit wrists. This would be something else."

"That will have to wait until we get there." My grandfather held up his phone, stepped away. "Two minutes," he said to Catcher, "to work the details. And then we'll get your girl. Because she's our girl, too."

—•—✖✚✖—•—

CHAPTER TWENTY-THREE

KING OF THE CASTLE

L ike many places in Chicago, Logan Square was the name of a neighborhood and a park within it. And as in other Chicago neighborhoods, the economics of Logan Square varied from block to block. Well-manicured lawns could quickly give way to empty, trash-strewn lots where violence was all too common.

We met in a long strip of parking lot on the street between Logan Square Park and Bellwether Castle. Detective Jacobs was there already, along with a black van, out of which poured some of the city's best warriors in their black SWAT uniforms.

Jacobs had spread maps on the trunk of his cruiser, and everyone was gathered around.

My grandfather gestured us over, and the warriors smiled and made space in the circle for me. I was nervous but ridiculously humbled by their encouragement.

"Merit will make the approach," Detective Jacobs said. "And to bring you up to speed, Merit, we've got uniforms at Curt's house right now. They found, I suppose we'll call it a shrine, to Mitzy Burrows."

I nodded. "So he's obsessed with her, and their breakup is probably what got the ball rolling."

"Probably had the animosity in him for a long time," said a woman in a suit on the other side of the trunk. I put her in her late thirties, with wavy blond hair and a pretty face. She extended a hand. "Rainey Valentine. Staff psychologist."

"Nice to meet you," I said, as we shook. "You think he's got innate violent tendencies."

"In my experience, this is more a case of a recent trauma lowering his inhibitions. He may not have been engaged in this level of violence in the recent past, but it's possible he wanted to and suppressed the urge."

"Whatever the reason," Ethan said, "he's violent now."

"Indeed." Jacobs nodded. "And we want to keep Merit and Ms. Carmichael as safe as we can." He looked at Catcher. "We've got quiet eyes on the building. He's there with her, and making arrangements. If anything happens before we can move in, they'll move in first."

At Catcher's nod, Jacobs pointed to the map, to a spot in the front of the building where the turret rose. "They're here, just in front of the turret. Merit, you'll approach him directly, across the lawn." He traced a finger from the street to the spot where Curt had Mallory. "We want him to be able to see you, to watch you move forward. No swords, no weapons. You'll walk nice and slow, and you'll keep your hands in the air. You just want to talk to him."

"Am I negotiating?"

"Excellent question," Rainey said. "And kind of. You'll ask him about himself. Find out his needs. You're there to help him. These elaborate presentations show a kind of pridefulness, a flair for the dramatic. Appeal to that, to his ego. We want a safe resolution of this problem for everyone, and you're there to facilitate it."

I nodded. "And if he doesn't go for it?"

"I suspect he'll want to talk to you," Rainey said. "To talk through Mitzy's betrayal, to talk about his creations."

"In the meantime," Jacobs said, "we'll surround the building. We'll come in from the back, while you approach from the front."

I generally saw Jacobs as a kind of grandfatherly figure: smart, dedicated, and gentlemanly, much like my own. But there was nothing gentlemanly about the look in his eyes. It was cold, and it was all cop.

"You keep him occupied until we can bust the little shit."

I had no objection to that.

We proceeded on foot in teams. The SWAT members and Jacobs to the back of the building, the Ombuddies, me, and Ethan to the front. My grandfather was the connection between them, a headset in place so he could communicate with the other half of the team.

The photograph had been true to the building. It was square and squat and looked like a castle. I could easily imagine a bride and groom posing for photographs, the castle behind them, surrounded by their wedding party.

But tonight, the scene was much more grim.

A floodlight in the landscaping shone on the turret, highlighting notches in the masonry and tile roof . . . and the woman who lay on the sloping ground in front of it. Her arms and legs were spread and tied, and she was naked, her hair awkwardly braided to fall across one breast. Her eyes were closed—and I didn't mind if she was unconscious for this part—but her chest rose and fell slowly. She was alive. Not that that helped Catcher's rage.

Magic burst from him as he took in the sight of her. "I'll kill him. I will rip each of his arms from his body and shove them up his"—but Ethan pulled him back.

"Stick to the plan. You rush in there, he'll act rashly. You know that."

When he was certain Catcher wouldn't move, he turned to me, put his hands on my shoulders, rubbed. "Fix this for me, Merit. Fix this, and be careful. We'll be here, waiting."

I blew out a breath, nerves beginning to fire, fear beginning to settle in. I was about to walk across the lawn to the spot where a serial killer prepared to summarily execute my best friend.

I glanced at Ethan. "What if I can't stop him?"

His responding gaze was unequivocal, his tone matter-of-fact. "Nonsense. You are Sentinel of my House. You have a job, and you'll do it with gusto, as you always have." He moved in and, despite the crowd around us, pressed his lips to mine.

Now stand Sentinel for Mallory, he silently said.

He was excellent at motivation. I looked at my grandfather and, at his nod, walked across the lawn.

Curt knelt beside Mallory, a set of small pennants in his hands, which were marked with blue crosses. He stuck them in the ground around her body, presumably to mirror the castle pennants on the card. Her arms and legs, I could see now, were tied to small wooden stakes in the ground. I didn't see any weapon, but I could feel the tingle of them.

He raised his head like a startled deer, jumped to his feet, and pulled a handgun from the waistband of his pants. He pointed it at Mallory with an unwavering arm. "If you take one step closer, I will kill her."

I stopped, held up my hands. "Okay. You're in charge. I'll do whatever you want."

He looked at me suspiciously. "You can't stop me. Not now." He gestured toward the scene he'd prepared. "I'm nearly done."

"So I see. And with the Four of Wands of the Fletcher deck."

His eyes shined with pride. "Fucking A."

"That was tricky—using the tarot. It took us some time to figure it out."

"That's because I'm smarter than most of the assholes that come into the store. They waste money on herbs, on spells, on nonsense."

"You don't believe in magic?"

"Of course not. It's a waste of time and money. But it's a job, you know? Pays my fucking bills." His smile was cold. "I get to make money off their ignorance, and that's fine with me."

If Curt could see Mallory in her prime, fiery eyes and flames shooting from her fingertips, he'd have a very different view of what was and was not bullshit.

But the comeuppance would have to wait. My job was to keep him talking.

"Was Mitzy one of the ignorant ones?"

Like a switch had been flipped, his entire expression changed, softened. "Mitzy was part of me. We were connected. I got her a job at the Magic Shoppe—did you know that? Got her a job, helped her get her apartment. Tried to teach her how to respect me—how to respect the man she was dating." His eyes filled with tears, and he wiped them away with his hand, which smeared blue paint across his face.

"You loved Mitzy," I said.

"I *love* her," he corrected. "We have a real connection. An honest connection."

"But she was unfaithful to you?"

She hadn't been, actually. Skylar-Katherine said they'd already broken up when Mitzy went on the date with Brett. But if Curt had built a shrine to Mitzy in his house, I doubt he appreciated the distinction.

His jaw trembled as he tried to stem his rising anger. "She was confused. I got her the job," he said again. "And she didn't give me a single word of thanks. And then she left me—" His voice wavered, but he shook his head, tried to control himself. "She just needed to learn. She needed to learn what was real, and what wasn't."

"And you tried to teach her?"

"She needed to be taught," he said, voice low and sinister. Angry Curt was back again. "She went out with that asshole, like she had the right. He's a big fucking deal because his dad's a cop."

He grinned, but there was no happiness in his eyes. "Cop or not, I took care of him. He came into the store once looking for her while I was there. Said he got a kick out of the 'magic stuff.' But I was the one who worked at the store, wasn't I? Me, not him. Asshole. He likes magic so much, he can die with it."

"And Mitzy? Did you take care of her?"

Curt jerked his hand around his head, as if waving off a nest of hornets. "I took care of her, too. And made it magical." He rubbed the backs of his hands over his face, smearing more blue across it, his white teeth a maniacal contrast.

"Fucking tarot. It's a pack of cards with pretty pictures. She wants to believe in that nonsense? Fine. I'll help her believe in it."

As if remembering what he was doing here, he kicked the stake that held Mallory's left arm, jarring it. Her eyes were still closed, but she made a low groan.

"What about Samantha Ingram?" I asked, shifting so he'd look at me again, trying to keep his focus off her—and the SWAT team members who were inevitably moving toward us from the back of the property.

He looked irritated by the question. "Who?"

"The Three of Pentacles. The girl on the beach."

He waved off the question. Samantha Ingram meant nothing more to him than Brett Jacobs, maybe less. "Some dumbass who came into the store, went on and on about vampires."

I wanted to show him. Oh God, how I wanted to bare my fangs and silver my eyes, rush forward and scare the living shit out of him just for the effect, just so he could understand that there were far worse monsters in the world than he, that he wasn't nearly as innovative as he imagined himself to be.

I knew how the adrenaline would feel, how satisfying it would be to hear his heart pound and his blood race in fear.

Focus, I demanded before my eyes could silver. *Focus*.

"The blue crosses," I slowly said, fighting for my own control. "That was a nice touch. It's one of the tarot formations, right?"

He looked pleased I'd gotten it. "My signature, is what it is. Everybody who does something like this—who takes the time to plan it, to be careful about it—has to have a signature."

He seemed oblivious to the fact that the signature was precisely the thing that had helped the CPD connect the crimes—and put the blame on him. And it would be the thing that put him away for a very, very long time.

I screwed up my face with worry. "Listen, that gun's kind of freaking me out. Do you think you could put it away for right now?"

"Why? So you can try to take it from me?"

I offered my most guileless smile. "Do I look like someone who could take a gun from someone like you? I don't even own a gun. You, on the other hand, look like you actually know what you're doing."

"Fucking A," he said. Slowly but surely, he lowered his weapon.

That was his mistake. A twig snapped in the dark on his left. He turned and pointed the gun with both hands at the coming threat, but it had been a feint. The SWAT team came in from the right, sweeping around him.

Curt made a high sound of fear and turned in a half circle to face them.

But I'd come out here and done my part. It was time to claim my small victory. I held the SWAT team off with a hand, ran forward and kicked, connecting with his forearm and sending the gun into the air. It fell a few feet away as he screamed keenly at the pain.

"Yeah, that does look broken," I said, and gave him a very satisfying and much-deserved knee to the balls.

He groaned, spittle at the corners of his mouth as he hit the ground on his knees. "You. Fucking. Bitch."

"Music to my ears," I said. "Would you like to try again?"

His face was crimson with rage. He climbed to his feet again, rushed me like a linebacker. I ducked his grasping arms, spun around to face him again, then kicked him so he stumbled forward into the grass.

The obscenities grew even more creative when the SWAT team surrounded him, guns pointed in his face.

As Catcher and Ethan ran across the lawn, I pulled off my jacket, laid it across Mallory's body as Catcher tugged the stakes from the ground. She opened her eyes, glanced at me groggily.

"You told me to get out of the store. I tried."

"I know. You did really good."

"It was Curt. He drugged me, I think."

"I know. You did exactly what I told you to do. He was only a little bit faster."

"I think I'm naked right now."

I patted the jacket in around her, tucked it around her bare skin. "You are, but you look amazing, as always." I brushed her hair back from her face.

"It's sorcerer monkey sex. Does amazing things for the abs." She swallowed thickly. "Holy shit, Merit. I was scared. So scared."

"I know, Mal. We were scared, too. Catcher just about lost his shit. For all his faults—and they are numerous—he really, really loves you."

She nodded. "He's a good egg. And I'm really, really cold."

"He's almost done, Mal. In just a minute, we'll get you warm clothes and all the Chunky Monkey you can eat."

Catcher threw away the last of the stakes, moved up, and lifted Mallory's body from the ground. She winced in pain but looked up at him with doe-like and still-groggy eyes.

"Hey, Catcher Bell. Did you come to rescue me?"

"I did. There's a whole team of us out there. All this for a little wolfsbane, huh?"

"Was going to make something for Connor Keene. He'll be teething soon, you know. And that will hurt."

Her composure cracked, and she turned her face into his chest, silently wept. He wrapped his arms around her, held her on the wet grass.

I leaned forward and pressed a kiss to the back of her head. "I'm going to give you guys a few minutes. I'm assuming *all* the Ben and Jerry's is required."

"All of it," Catcher agreed.

I rose, found Ethan waiting with Jeff a few yards away. Ethan gathered me into his arms. "Well done, Sentinel."

I nodded. "She's still a little drugged. Might have an ugly time with it when she's fully aware."

"And you'll be there for her, probably with ice cream."

"I already promised it," I said, and slipped my arms around him. "Let's go load up the car with it and take care of our girl."

"Absofuckinglutely," he said, and we walked arm in arm back to the car.

Mallory had been injured, so she got to pick the evening's entertainment. She opted for a Bruce Campbell marathon, so the four of us snuggled into the couches in her living room, *The Evil Dead* and *Army of Darkness* on-screen, ice cream pints, spoons, and whipped cream in a can scattered across the coffee table.

"I love you guys," Mallory randomly said at intervals. Catcher and I took turns at responding until Ethan beat us to the punch.

"We love you, too, Mallory."

She went still, slowly turned her gaze on him, her eyes filling with tears again. Without a word, he untangled himself from me, rose to her, and pressed a kiss to her forehead. And as tears filled my eyes, too, he whispered something in her ear.

Tears still spilled down her cheeks, but she looked like he'd swept away all the weight on her shoulders.

Later, when we lay boneless in a bubble-filled tub, I asked Ethan what he'd said to her.

"Just something she needed to hear. Something a very wise woman once said to me. That she was more than the sum of her past."

I wasn't sure it was possible to love him more.

✦ ⫸◆⫷ ✦

CHAPTER TWENTY-FOUR

DON'T CRY FOR ME, ARGENTINA

The night of Nicole's coronation bloomed beautiful and warm, if not especially cheerfully, considering it was Nicole's coronation.

When we could delay the inevitable no longer, we gathered together in the ballroom, the festivities on a giant screen hung from one end. A long table bore gold and black party hats, noise-makers, and yellow bottles of champagne, which Helen poured into tall, elegant flutes.

Our man hadn't become king, but the coronation of a queen was still a big deal, even if she wasn't actually our queen. Even vampires—*especially* vampires—liked pomp and circumstance.

Novitiates mingled nervously, excited about the drama and guilty about their excitement. They stole glances at Ethan, checking his mood and temperament, and at Amit, who'd decided to stay in Chicago for a few more nights.

I decided the best course of action was to keep things light, so I swept two flutes of champagne from the table and handed one to him.

"I think we both need a drink," I said. "No—deserve a drink. Or all of them."

"Or all of them," he agreed, and took a sip.

The ballroom filled and the lights dimmed, and the screen lit up with color. The video showed a large room, empty and made of stone, floor to ceiling. Seven heavy wooden armchairs stood in a semicircle, the back of the middle chair two feet taller than the rest.

Darius, Nicole, and the few remaining members of the GP sat in their chairs, each formally attired. The men wore deep gray tuxedos with long tails. Lakshmi wore a sari in a deep buttercup yellow accented with ruby red jewels. Her hair flowed straight down her back, her eyes darkly outlined.

I may not have been a fan, but Nicole looked radiant in a pale peach bias-cut sheath, with long sleeves and a sharp cut at the neck that revealed a glittering heart-shaped pendant. The dress swept the floor, and her hair was curled into a shiny bob.

"I don't like her," Lindsey said, sidling beside me. "But that dress is a ten."

"Reluctantly agreed," I said, clinking my glass lightly against hers.

"How will this play out?" I asked Ethan.

He sipped from his glass. "First will be the 'May' speech," he said. "Then the crowning and oath swearing by the GP members. And then she'll have an opportunity to speak to her subjects."

Envy tinged his voice. He wanted the job, the opportunity to lead, the chance to improve supernaturals' lives.

I linked an arm through his. "And then she gets the unenviable task of making something good of the GP."

On my other side, Amit chuckled. "You are right, Merit. That is no enviable task."

Another man in a tuxedo walked to Darius's chair, offered a crimson velvet pillow, on which was placed a silver crown laden with glimmering diamonds and rubies, and a long fluted scepter topped by a ruby the size of a golf ball.

"Spare no expense," I murmured, as Darius picked up the crown jewels and dismissed the servant.

He stood, and Nicole did the same, walking toward him so they stood in the middle of the semicircle.

"Place a hand on your heart," he said. "The source of life."

She did.

"You've been voted regent of the vampires ruled by the Greenwich Presidium. Do you promise to protect them, to serve them, and to place them above all others?"

"I do."

To my surprise, that was apparently the extent of the oath. It didn't escape my notice that Novitiates and Masters said longer and more involved oaths than the leader of vampires.

"May you rule with wisdom and justice. May your rule be eternal. May you provide abundant treasures for your vampires. May you protect them wholly from all creatures living and dead."

That, I presumed, was the "May" speech.

Nicole nodded, accepted the scepter Darius handed her, and leaned forward so Darius could place the crown on her head.

When she bore the jewels, he stepped back, leaving Nicole in the spotlight. And the deed was done. For a moment, Nicole stood silently, staring down at the scepter in her hand, her thumb tracing the smooth curve of the ruby.

Then she lifted dark eyes to the camera. "I thank those who challenged me for their dedication to this office. I thank the Houses who voted for me for their loyalty and belief in my rule. I thank the Masters of the Houses for their service to their vampires and this organization for two centuries. And I thank those who came before me on the Greenwich Presidium.

"For my first act as head of the GP . . ." She paused, took a breath, and exhaled through pursed lips. And we all leaned forward a little bit.

". . . I hereby abolish it."

The remaining GP members burst into argument. The crowd in the ballroom erupted with shock, filling the room with sound.

Ethan's eyes widened, mostly with curiosity.

"What in God's name . . . ," Malik murmured, gaze fixed on the screen.

"Well, well, well," Amit said with a Cheshire smile.

"I will have *order*," Nicole said, with enough push behind the word that even I stood a little straighter.

It was effective. The crowd in the ballroom quieted immediately.

"The GP is antiquated," Nicole said. "American and European vampires lack the connection they once had—culturally, politically, economically. It is time for a change.

"This is our Declaration of Independence," she said. "The GP is no more. European vampires can decide how to rule themselves, as should be, and I leave to them how they would control their affairs. I give up any authority to rule the European houses. They should decide their ruler for themselves."

More outbursts until she spoke again. "As for America," she began again, and silence fell, "we need no queen and no king. Our existence was announced to the world more than a year ago, and not once have we convened to discuss it. That's what we need: frank discussion. The opportunity to plan, to discuss. We need to take control of our new destiny . . . and we can do that most effectively together. Effective today, I call into creation the Assembly of American Masters, consisting of the Master of each American House—including Cadogan House."

Every pair of eyes in the room flew to Ethan, to the widening of his eyes, the parting of his lips, the shock in his expression.

"Each House will have an equal vote, and each Master will share the responsibility of shaping our mutual future. If there are any American Masters who decline to serve their vampires, their Houses, their country, they should speak now."

"This will never work." The camera panned to Edmund's face. "If you segregate us now, you create only more division among vampires. The world is getting smaller, and you're ignoring it."

"No," Nicole calmly said, as if utterly unperturbed. "I'm respecting the boundaries that exist, not those that existed two hundred years ago. The world is changing. Humans know about us, technology continues to march along, and we cannot afford to pretend that all is the same.

"I've spoken my piece," Nicole said. "I was duly tested and elected, and these are my decisions. We will provide sufficient time to address the legal and financial formalities of our division." She glanced around at her colleagues. "But as for Europe, I shall leave you to govern yourselves."

Having gotten in the last words, Nicole turned, peach silk sweeping at her feet, and walked to the edge of the room and out the door again, her bodyguards behind her.

For a moment, the throne room went silent. The other members of the GP stared at one another, evaluating, strategizing, anticipating. The things vampires did best.

With slow deliberation and the bearing of a queen, Lakshmi

took a seat, her fingers curving over the arms of the chair. Chin tilted, she slid glances to the rest of the GP.

"If we are to rule ourselves, the American Houses can have no interest in it." She looked directly at the camera, and the screen went dark.

The dramatics of the Greenwich Presidium were no longer our concern.

Silence fell in the ballroom, and we all turned to look at Ethan, whose gaze was still on the darkened screen. There was pride in his eyes, excitement. But also no little suspicion.

Yes, Nicole had just given him power, but by doing so she'd made a new set of allies—every American Master. Every colleague in her new Assembly. And she'd need their support: Not all vampires would take kindly to her plan to so neatly divide the world and wealth.

He looked at me, squeezed my hand. I nodded back.

Footsteps rang out as Malik walked to the other end of the room, stepped onto the dais, looked over the gathering in the ballroom.

"This is an unexpected development," Malik said, voice loud and ringing across the ballroom. "A historically unprecedented development. But it is for reasons like this—for the turning pages of history—that we have come together as a House, that we make promises to each other."

Malik looked earnestly at Ethan, gestured him forward. Anticipation built as Ethan crossed the room, mounted the dais.

"Ethan Sullivan," Malik began, "Master of Cadogan House, you have apparently been named a member of the new Assembly of American Masters. At times like these, it is important to remember the bonds that bind us together, and the promise we have made to each other."

Ethan smiled at him.

"In the presence of your brothers and sisters," Malik continued, "do you pledge that you still shall show fealty and allegiance to Cadogan House, to its honor? Do you pledge to be true and faithful to Cadogan House and to its members to the exclusion of all others, without deception? Do you pledge to uphold the liberty of your brothers and sisters?"

He was repeating the oath that Cadogan Initiates took at Commendation, when we became full and official members of the House. But Malik had adjusted it, creating a new oath, and a new promise for Ethan. A reminder of his loyalties.

"Do you pledge to serve the House without hesitation, and to never, by word or deed, seek to harm the House or its members? Will you help to hold and defend her against any creature, living or dead, and make this promise, gladly and without dread, and keep it for as long as you shall live?"

A thousand emotions crossed Ethan's face, but mostly there was pride and love and earnestness. He wanted to do right, to do better, for his vampires. "I do," he called out.

"In that case," Malik said with a smile, stepping forward and going down on one knee, "in the presence of my brothers and sisters, I pledge fealty and allegiance to the Assembly of American Vampires, and to you, our Master . . . and our *sire*." He glanced at the other vampires in the room. "If you will join me, show your fealty."

To a one, with the *shush* of fabric and the *squeak* of shoes on the wooden floors, every vampire in the room, including myself, dropped to one knee, reiterating our loyalty to Ethan.

Magic lifted and draped the room, loving and proud and hopeful. It was the magic of a Master who'd been called to serve, and those who'd agreed to serve him still.

My eyes filled with tears, and I heard muted sniffles around me.

Ethan stared around the room, taking in the sight before him, the vampires who'd prostrated themselves to his service. His eyes were wide, his surprise at the turn of events still obvious.

"Rise, please," Ethan said, and the vampires stood again, patting him on the back and calling for him to make a speech.

"You humble me," Ethan said. "To be frank, I assumed I would leave this room tonight feeling envious and bitter. Instead, I leave it humbled. Proud. And honestly, a little relieved."

There were light chuckles in the crowd. Ethan knew how to work an audience.

"I did not expect this—either for us, or from Nicole." He moistened his lips. "Tonight, she showed she is willing to give the American Houses the voice they've long been denied."

That was a very diplomatic way of putting it. There was no point—right now—in detailing exactly how untrustworthy Nicole Heart really was.

"We are fortunate enough to stand in the crossroads of history. For the first time, we will know independence for the American Houses. But let us not forget the challenges that we face, and the uncertainties of the future. Our path is new, untrodden, but I will do my best to serve you, the House, and the Assembly."

"Hear, hear," Luc shouted, and a hundred other vampires followed suit.

"I think, all things considered, that a celebration is in order." He found Helen in the crowd, nodded at her. "Keep the champagne flowing."

"And snacks!" Margot yelled out, which earned a whistle from me.

"In that case, let's celebrate!" Ethan said, and a rousing ver-

sion of Journey's "Don't Stop Believin'" filled the air when someone turned on the audio system.

Grinning from ear to ear, Ethan stepped down from the dais,
began to shake the hands of the vampires who moved forward to
congratulate him.

I felt my phone vibrate but resisted the urge to check the
screen. I already knew who would be calling.

Ethan was now one of twelve.

The RG would have plenty to say about that.

When the festivities were over, we returned to Ethan's office,
chatting with the vampires who stopped by to congratulate him
and wish him well. He opened the Glenmorangie, which had
made its way back into the liquor cabinet, and still seemed to be
in shock at the turn of events. But it was the best kind of shock.

Eventually, the well-wishers cleared away and we returned to
our apartments.

"So," I said, when the door was closed behind us and we had
privacy and quiet again. "I guess congratulations are in order."

"Of a type," he agreed. "But let's not think too kindly about
her motives."

"Oh, I don't. She's conniving. And I think we can safely assume this move wasn't because she really believes in honor and
valor, but because she gained eleven new allies by appointing
them all to her brand-new council."

"It was a cunning move," he agreed. "Come here, Sentinel,"
he said, crooking his finger at me. I walked into his arms, pressed
my mouth to his, kissed him until my muscles went lax and he
wound his fingers through my hair.

He pulled back, kissed me more softly, then released me.

I pulled off my jacket, then the boots and leather pants. Still wearing my tank, I pulled the band from my hair, shaking it until it fell around my shoulders in a dark waterfall, and sat down on the edge of the bed.

"You paint quite a picture," Ethan said.

I smiled back at him, stretched my arms behind me. If I was going to play seductress, I might as well get into the part. "There's more canvas to be revealed," I said with a wink.

A finger touched a sharp edge, and I glanced behind me. A small white card and envelope was propped on a blue velvet pillow on the bed. Grinning, I snatched it up and slid the card from the envelope, expecting to read words of love or seduction.

But it was neither. The card was handwritten, the ink a deep scarlet, the script small, neat, and slanted.

> *I have missed you, mon ami. So many centuries and continents between us. I look forward to our reunion.*
> *—B*

My hand shook, and breath escaped me. I didn't know I'd dropped the card, or that Ethan had moved closer, until he'd bent to pick it up from the floor.

I looked up at him, hoping against hope that my fear was baseless, that the "B" who'd signed the note wasn't the monster who'd made him, who'd put such fear into his heart, who'd come between us once even after centuries in the ground.

But Balthasar was dead.

I couldn't form words to speak, but I begged him in silence to say we'd been pranked, to rail against the vampire who'd made a very poor joke at the end of a very long night.

But all the color had drained from Ethan's face. My heart pounded in sympathy—and fear.

Ethan? I silently managed.

Wordlessly, he crumpled the note in his hand, walked to the fireplace, and tossed it in.

"We can't pretend we didn't see that," I quietly said. "If he's alive . . ."

"We aren't going to pretend," he said, looking back at me with eyes of quicksilver. "And he isn't alive. Someone is playing a very dangerous game, and we're going to win it."

Chloe Neill was born and raised in the South, but now makes her home in the Midwest – just close enough to Cadogan House and St. Sophia's to keep an eye on things. When not transcribing Merit's and Lily's adventures, she bakes, works, and scours the Internet for good recipes and great graphic design. Chloe also maintains her sanity by spending time with her boys – her favorite landscape photographer (her husband) and their dogs, Baxter and Scout (both she and the photographer understand the dogs are in charge).

Visit her on the web at:

www.chloeneill.com
www.facebook.com/authorchloeneill
www.twitter.com/chloeneill

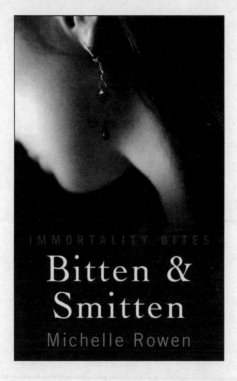